WET
WORK

WET WORK

DONNA MEREDITH

Wild Women Writers
An independent publishing company

WET WORK

This book is a work of fiction. Names, characters, places and incidents are either the product of the author's imagination or are used fictitiously. Any resemblance to actual persons, living or dead, or real events is entirely coincidental.

ISBN: 978-0-9829015-9-5

Published by Wild Women Writers, Tallahassee, FL
January 2014

Logo design by E'Layne Koenigsberg of 3 Hip Chics, Tallahassee, FL
www.3HipChics.com

Printed in the United States of America

For John

ALSO BY DONNA MEREDITH

The Glass Madonna (2010)
> First Place, Women's Fiction (unpublished), Royal Palm Literary
> Awards, Florida Writers Association, 2009
> Runner-Up Gulf Coast Novel Contest

The Color of Lies (2011)
> First Place, Women's Fiction (unpublished), Royal Palm Literary
> Awards, Florida Writers Association, 2010
> Gold Medal, Adult Fiction, Florida Publishers Association, 2012

**Magic in the Mountains: Kelsey Murphy, Robert Bomkamp, and
the West Virginia Cameo Glass Revolution** (2012)
> Silver Medal, Adult Nonfiction, Florida Publishers Association,
> 2013

Wet Work (2014)
> Second Place, Thriller/Suspense (unpublished), Royal Palm
> Literary Awards, Florida Writers Association, 2013

Available through amazon.com, barnesandnoble.com, and independent bookstores.

A woman is like a tea bag - you can't tell how strong she is until you put her in hot water.
    -Eleanor Roosevelt

If there is magic on this planet, it is contained in water.
    -Loren Eiseley

ONE

Tuesday

THE CRY THAT AROSE FROM THE SWAMP SQUEALED three octaves higher than an eighteen-wheeler's air brakes. Paulo Alvarez's torso jerked, his cigarette sailed into the scrubby vegetation, and "Ehhhh" pitched out of his mouth before he managed to swallow the sound.

A bird the color of dirt crashed from the brush. It lumbered awkwardly into the air, feet dangling during the beginning of its ascent. Once airborne, its legs trailed behind in vee-formation, the right and left wings creating lift and balance, a perfect piece of engineering.

Just another creepy bird in the saw palmettos, but man, for a second there, it scared the bejeezus out of him. Paulo scanned the area but found no witness to his less than virile reaction. No one else would be foolish enough to linger out here in the middle of nowhere. And certainly no other man would smoke outside of his own truck because his wife frowned if he sullied their vehicles or her furniture. Crazy, yet here he stood, trying to please her even though he hadn't seen her for two long years.

Paulo stooped to retrieve his cigarette and two-fingered it into his mouth. He inhaled, savored the nicotine rush, and blew smoke into air that clung like a damp sock to his forearms. The sun slid below the horizon, though it was still light. Barely.

Nature Boys at his job site raved about the beautiful rivers and fine fishing, but they could keep their stinky swamps. Place smelled of sulfur, like rotten eggs.

The door creaked as he climbed back inside his truck, safe from the disgusting creatures that inhabited the north central Florida countryside. Snakes as fat as a TV wrestler's arms. Gators hidden in every puddle of water. Paulo wouldn't be surprised if any one of those creatures bit his butt one morning when he sat down to take a crap. You can bet he checked the commode first. He was a city boy and proud of it.

He clasped the steering wheel to quiet the trembling of his fingers. Ordered himself to stop acting like a silly *chica*. Yet he had cause for the jitters. Way more than a dumbass bird.

If the transaction went well, he would leave this dirt road with a one-way plane ticket back to Mexico. Not home to Tijuana. Too dangerous. He'd had a good engineering job there, one he should have appreciated more. Administrative, shuffling papers on well inspections.

It had been two years since Paulo fled in the night. He sent his wife and mama every penny he wrung from his wages. But it wasn't the same as being there for Paulito, the boy he'd never seen except in photos.

Paulo's eyes closed and he imagined his hands sliding over Bella's soft flesh. Soon. The fat payoff tonight would buy a fine house for his family somewhere south of all the trouble. Querétaro. His auntie lived in the capital there.

How was he going to explain this sudden infusion of cash? He felt his mama's eyes burn through him from a thousand miles away, heard her voice saying, "I raised you better than that." But Mama, he imagined telling her, these guys deserve a smack-down, and besides, how else would I ever get enough money to come home and start over? *Home*—the word made his ribs contract until he thought his chest might implode.

He shouldn't have let his cousin Tito talk him into playing in the little band on weekends, though it had been plenty fun at first. Fun, until Tito took $1,500 from Juan, a minor drug lord, to write a ballad praising his deeds.

Poor foolish Tito! A rival cartel member swaggered into the bar one night while his cousin was singing of Juan's virtues. Paulo only prayed—oh God, how he prayed!—that his cousin had died before the cartel's enforcer, The Cook, stuffed Tito into the barrel of acid.

As the last light faded from the sky, Paulo shifted his weight to his left haunch and rested his forearm along the open window. Didn't it figure they would be late? One more attempt to intimidate a Border Rat—yes, he had overheard their insults.

His mobile vibrated in his pants pocket. They better not renege on their deal. But no, the number belonged to Mrs. Montera, his land-lady. "*Hola, chachorrito.*" He loved to tease her about how tiny she was.

"Why you not home, Paulo?"

"I explained this morning I had business to take care of. I'll be home soon. You go ahead and eat dinner."

"Who worried about dinner? Worried about you. Something tell me this bad business."

Giving her the documents for safe-keeping had frightened her, but he had no one else he trusted in this country. "No, *chachorrito*, this is good business."

Once you were in the States illegally, they had you by the short hairs. Well, no more. This Mexican's luck was about to change.

He bent his neck forward, kneading it with his left hand. Mother of God—the muck he'd uncovered. If investors got a whiff of the company's financial troubles, it would torpedo their stock. Paulo had more than a whiff. He had proof.

In the distance an engine hummed like an insect. He grew rigid and nearly dropped the phone. Mrs. Montera chattered away but he no longer processed her words over the growing insistence of the rumble. At last, the glow of headlights rounded the final curve. Show time.

He spoke into the phone. "I have to go."

"Something wrong, Paulo. I feel it in bones." Her voice was full of tears.

He pushed the truck door open, his landlady still scolding in his ear. The small sedan edged closer, its tires crunching against the hard-packed dirt road. It stopped three feet away, blinding him in the headlights. A dark shape slid out.

"I'll be home soon, *chachorrito.*" Paulo shielded his eyes and spoke to the one approaching. "Hey, how about cutting those lights?"

The silhouetted form moved closer. Why didn't the fool answer him? His throat tightened, but he finally made out who it was. He exhaled. "You were about the last person I expected to see."

He swiveled his torso toward the truck. "Gotta go," he told his landlady, snapping his phone shut and tossing it through the open window onto the seat. He turned back into the headlight's glare and addressed the liaison. "Let's get this over with."

An arm raised toward him and stopped parallel to the ground.

His eyebrows knit together. "Hey, what the—"

A sharp crack exploded in his ears, and the worst pain he'd ever experienced stabbed his gut. Heat rocketed through his right shoulder blade.

He pressed his palms to his abdomen. He pulled his hands away and turned them over. Damp. Red. Couldn't be. Couldn't be his blood. Not now. It wasn't fair. Not when he was so close to returning to Bella. Her lips parted in front of his. The image wavered, fading into the photograph he carried in his wallet—the innocence of Paulito's fat cheeks framed by dark bangs. Not fair—he'd never held his son. Why would God let this happen?

A third crack spun him around. His mother's face spread through his mind like sunshine. "Mama!" he called out, though he wasn't sure if he'd voiced her name or only thought it.

Paulo's legs folded like the accordion he played in Tito's band, but instead of music, he heard the thunderous flap of many wings.

TWO

Wednesday

SUMMER CASSIDY CLICKED HER TONGUE against her teeth as she entered the latest measurements into her laptop's database. Elevated carcinogens in Isaac Harewood's wells, just like the spectrometry tests run before—not what anyone wanted to hear. She had tested two different samples to be sure she hadn't made a mistake.

Usually hydrogeology was a hoot, like playing that old game "Clue" with the Earth's surface as her board. Her task: to unlock the mystery of how water moved. She traced the path of the rain that fell on lawns, roofs, parking lots and highways. She figured out how it seeped into the vast storage chambers of the Floridan aquifer and what pollutants it took along for the ride. Couldn't get much more fun than that.

No joy this time. Her test results were certain to aggravate her lead professor. Small amounts of arsenic always showed up in water, but not three hundred parts per billion. Not after a year of cycling water in and out of an underground well. And uranium levels were out of whack too.

The metallic thunk of the lab door and light chatter intruded on her concentration. She always arrived by eight to get at least an hour of work in before the distractions started.

She printed her results, the words *Harewood Energy Corporation* glaring from the cover sheet and on the header of each page. HEC provided the university with half a million in grant funds for this study and it gave millions more to other departments.

Even the master's degree Summer was so close to earning was funded by a Harewood Foundation scholarship. She felt a degree of loyalty, of gratitude, toward the firm, but she couldn't make the data

lie. Chemicals were leaching out of those underground rock forma-
tions at unusual rates.

She made a few changes in the wording of her thesis conclusion,
recommending against further use of Harewood's Aquifer Storage and
Recovery (ASR) wells located near Tampa. If the water wasn't potable
by now, it wasn't going to improve for years.

She printed her latest results and hurried down the hall to share
them with Dr. Dunham, chair of the Geology Department. With
graduation looming two months away, Summer didn't want to disap-
point Claire Dunham. She could open—or slam—doors on Summer's future as a hydrogeologist. Summer thought her professor would
support her findings, but so much money was at stake.

She threaded her way through the corridor, dodging students who
almost universally were texting or phone-chatting. Summer wondered
how many even knew what an Aquifer Storage and Recovery well was.
Millions of Americans drank water from them, but most people never
stopped to wonder where their tapwater came from. During the rainy
season in over-populated areas like South Florida, municipal facilities
pumped excess water from lakes and canals into microscopic pores
in the rocks deep underground. During droughts they pumped water back up.

One episode of forcing water underground and pumping it back
to the surface again was called a cycle. Typically, there might be four
cycles in a year, but there might be more.

Harewood's ASR wells were the first owned by a private citizen,
or the first Summer knew of anyway. An environmental group called
Water Warriors had sampled the toxic brew Harewood was peddling
to a bottling company and cried foul. The university's tests were supposed to prove Harewood's water was pristine—only it wasn't.

The door to Dr. Dunham's cubicle at the end of the hall stood halfway open. As Summer neared the office, she saw the professor hunched
over her desk, attacking paper with pen. Dr. Dunham's handwriting
was as notoriously messy as her desk was neat. One of the woman's
many contradictions. She could be as wickedly funny as Jon Stewart
or as gravely serious as a president declaring war.

Summer secretly thought of her professor as Claire, though she
never dared call her that to her face. Claire Dunham possessed a re-

serve that kept students, even her favorites, at a distance.

Ever since Summer's sophomore year, the professor had taken a special interest in her. For three years, they had played handball most Tuesdays. While Summer's long limbs and lean body lent her the speed of a race horse, Claire had the muscular build and endurance of a mule.

Many evenings after handball and a quick shower, Summer had watched one of Claire's various men whisk her away to dinner.

Last year, a man Summer recognized as a history professor became a permanent fixture in Claire's life, but they must have had a falling out. Soon after he stopped picking Claire up at the gym, she took her anger out by attacking her prematurely gray hair with a comb. Two teeth broke off, partly because Claire's hair resembled a steel wool scrub pad, but also, Summer speculated, because her professor was in a bitchin-bad mood. The comb went airborne and clunked off the side of the locker room trash can.

"Two points," Summer had said, pulling her still-damp hair into a ponytail.

Claire jammed her workout clothes into a gym bag. "Don't marry young. If ever. Someone's career has to come first, and it's always his while yours collapses faster than a sinkhole. You have too much potential, Summer, to sacrifice yourself on the altar of a little dick."

Summer remembered her response: "No worries. I'm shooting for a doctorate." She was serious about her studies in geology and environmental science. Young women who attended the Florida Institute of Science and Technology set more challenging goals than finding a guy to marry. Summer had no intentions of traipsing down the same aisle as her mother, who earned her degree but never pursued a career.

Florida Sci-Tech was solidly credentialed, sure, but Summer would have gone elsewhere had her mother agreed. Instead, she insisted Summer stay in Loblolly Lake—the most boring town in the developed world. The university was the town's only claim to fame. Summer had been lucky to wheedle a compromise from her mother, allowing her to live in an apartment rather than at home.

"You take too many risks," her mother said. "Someone needs to keep an eye on you." As if her mother ever bothered.

A few steps ahead in the hallway a man with dark curly hair loped along at a pace so slow Summer was tempted to step on his heels. Dirt smudged the left sleeve of his billowy white shirt. The knees of his jeans sagged, suggesting they'd been worn many days. She restrained herself from jetting around him. In a few seconds she'd be in Claire's office without being rude.

When Mr. Saggy Jeans entered Claire's door first, she wished she'd followed her instinct and passed him. She groaned. Another delay before receiving final approval of her thesis. He better not tie up Dr. Dunham long. This grant report needed to zip through cyberspace to Harewood Energy Corporation today.

As she waited in the hall, she couldn't help overhearing bits of conversation. The timbre of Claire's voice was deeper than most females, somewhat gravelly; her enunciation, precise.

"It was inexcusably inappropriate for you to come here. This is my professional life. Look, this whole affair has been a colossal mistake. Please let the door smack you on your ass on the way out."

Summer choked off the laugh that threatened to escape, and stifled a second wave as she recalled a campus legend. Supposedly, when Claire had been the only female undergrad in a lab course, a male student made a crack about her being a distraction. Claire lifted her tee-shirt—no bra, of course—and said, "These are tits. No great mystery. Get over it." Then, legend had it, she reached for her zipper. Stunned silence erupted into a riot of male laughter. The guy who'd caused it all told her he'd seen enough. Claimed she had bigger balls than any guy in class. Summer could absolutely picture it happening.

To call attention to her presence at the door, she rattled her papers. As the man brushed past, Summer glimpsed a glowering face and tousled dark hair. Guess he'd come looking for nookie and gotten a Dunham slap-down instead.

Impulsively, Summer adopted a light tone with her professor. "I demand the right to confiscate any guns, knives, rocket launchers, or nukes before I enter. I have a personal stake in protecting the messenger."

Claire Dunham scowled over the top of her reading glasses with a look capable of draining Lake Okeechobee. "This is hardly a joke."

"Sorry, Dr. Dunham." Summer swallowed, her eyes lowered. What had she been thinking? She'd never been able to do humor. The rare occasions when she tried exposed her true self: the alien, the outsider, the antithesis of the charming Southern belle.

Claire's expression softened as she leaned back in her chair. "That bad, huh?"

"This isn't what Isaac Harewood hoped to buy with his money."

The concept of private companies appropriating a basic resource like water troubled her. How could you put a price on clean, safe drinking water, when every creature needed it to survive? And ASR wells weren't cheap. At least three mil a piece. Isaac Harewood would be less than thrilled to discover he'd thrown his money down a dozen useless holes.

"His money is irrelevant," Dr. Dunham said. "Only the science matters."

Thank God. Summer should never have doubted where Claire Dunham would stand. By the time Summer opened the door to leave, the bugs jumping around in her stomach were squashed.

Immediately, a young man jerked his tee-shirt-clad back away from the wall near Dunham's office. "About time," he said.

She eyed his boot camp haircut and the hint of beard and mustache. If he was so concerned with time, why did he waste it on that meticulously unshaven look? It was annoyingly Hollywood.

"About time for what?" she asked.

"I had an appointment with Dr. Dunham." Boot Camp glanced at his watch. "Ten minutes ago," he added. Summer suspected he'd checked it every thirty seconds while he waited.

He crossed the hall toward her with a slightly uneven gait. Barely noticeable, but she did notice and blinked. His features grew even more rigid.

"Ditch the scowl," she suggested. "The last guy wearing that expression in her office didn't get what he wanted."

THREE

Thursday

I

A HEAVY SCENT LIKE FURNITURE WAX hit Summer in the face as the exterior door to Harewood Energy Corporation Headquarters swooshed closed behind her. She checked her watch. Ten minutes early. Amazing, considering how impromptu the appointment was. Self-consciously, she touched her still-damp ponytail.

An hour ago, Julia Lambert from Harewood Energy Corporation had called and wanted to interview Summer. She jumped in the shower, threw on her only pair of black dress slacks, and drove across town. Lambert tagged the meeting as a final step to approve continuation of Summer's scholarship. If the folks with the money wanted to meet her in person, well then, she would skip her afternoon class, do handstands, throw Frisbees, sing the national anthem. Whatever it took.

A young woman in a tailored gray suit emerged from an interior suite of offices to greet her. "Have a seat and someone will be with you shortly, Miss Cassidy." The lady disappeared behind the double doors. In the vast waiting room Summer wallowed in the cushions of the smallest overstuffed chair.

She had visited several of Harewood's ASR well sites while she worked on her thesis but never the corporate offices. She knew where headquarters was—everyone in Loblolly Lake knew. These folks had a whole compound—a gated community you couldn't miss on the outskirts of town.

Driving by the fences differed from sitting in the plush reception area, surrounded by what she suspected were genuine antiques rather than replicas.

A refrigerator-sized photograph of nacreous anthracite riveted

Summer's attention. The rock's surface rippled with waves of iridescent blues, blacks, and purples. Beside it, hung a smaller photo, signed by David Moynahan. Its haunting blend of light and shadow captured limestone cliffs towering over a river. Had to be the Suwannee—she had kayaked by that exact spot.

Mirrored glass etched with egrets stretched from ceiling to floor to form one interior wall. Hairs on her neck prickled, and she had the eerie feeling someone was spying on her through the mirrors. Fear-induced piloerection, which was ridiculous, of course. Why would anyone watch her? She massaged her collarbone.

At last, a grandmotherly woman in a navy suit emerged from the double doors.

"I'm Julia Lambert, honey. Mr. Harewood and I will be inter-viewing you."

The Great Man himself? The Harewood Foundation was set up as a trust independent from HEC and the scholarships awarded by a board of directors. But Summer did not suffer from any delusion that the Foundation's independence was absolute. Isaac Harewood's opinion would hold tremendous sway.

Summer had met him once—sort of. On the stage of her high school's auditorium, Isaac Harewood had handed her a certificate with his left and shook hands with his right. All the award recipients had practiced with the guidance counselor to make sure they mastered the required maneuver. There would be no rehearsal this time to insure she didn't make a fool of herself.

They went behind the double doors and rode an elevator to a top-floor conference room. Twenty well-padded brown leather chairs lined a table crafted from an exotic striped wood Summer couldn't identify. Mr. Harewood rose from the head of the table, and Summer shook the hand of Loblolly Lake's most famous citizen for the second time. His bald head appeared to be oiled, reflecting light from the chande-lier, which drew Summer's eyes upward in amazement. Sculpted art glass swirled from the ceiling in a rainbow of pastel shades. Had to be one-of-a-kind.

After they were seated, Mr. Harewood and the grandmother-type studied folders of papers. Summer assumed they were reviewing her application, but seconds elongated into minutes of ignoring her while papers rustled. Summer forced herself not to squirm or clear her throat or blurt out inane proclamations about the weather.

Finally, Julia Lambert set her papers in order and clasped her hands on top of them, her eyes twinkling. "I see you've been accepted into several prestigious graduate programs. These schools must be expensive, particularly doctoral level courses."

Now they were getting somewhere. Summer leaned forward, resting her arms on the table. "Yes, ma'am."

"What will you study?"

"Environmental studies and geology." Summer felt a little silly. The woman already knew that from the application. If Summer wanted to impress, she'd better offer more. "When I was thirteen, I had an opportunity to watch Lake Jackson drain into Porter Hole Sink."

A neighbor had told her he was taking his son with him to catch stranded fish. Summer begged her mother to let her tag along. Summer returned four days in a row. If she closed her eyes, she could still smell the rotting fish; feel the tug of muck against her rubber boots; hear the swift rush of water spiraling down, down into the limestone caves that lay beneath the red clay.

Summer motioned with her hands, trying to convey her passion. "Watching four thousand acres of water disappear—it was magical. I wanted to understand where it all went. I've been studying water flow and aquifers ever since."

"My, that sounds interesting." Julia Lambert tilted her neatly coifed gray head to the left as she smiled. "I'm sure it would be helpful if the Harewood Foundation continued funding your education."

Summer wanted to say, Well, duh. "Yes, very helpful, Mrs. Lambert."

Isaac Harewood's chin jerked up from the papers for the first time. "Then I'm sure you see the necessity of keeping the corporation standing behind the Harewood Foundation profitable."

The moisture evaporated from Summer's mouth. She felt like she'd sucked on an unripe persimmon. She pulled her arms off the table. "Of course you have to be profitable."

"She knows that, Mr. Harewood," Julia agreed, her voice silvery as bells. "This one's smart as a whip. Look at that transcript."

Harewood steepled his fingers and held them to his lips as though deep in contemplation. After a pause, he offered this insight: "University research has far-reaching impacts on the employment security of thousands of people."

Summer steadied her voice—at least she hoped she did. "It impacts lives in other ways, too, important ways."

Mrs. Lambert handed her a copy of the preliminary grant report. She and Mr. Harewood opened their folders to their copies. Summer and Dr. Dunham had submitted the preliminary yesterday. HEC didn't lose any time, did they?

"It's all about jobs, young lady," Harewood lectured. "If you are unemployed, not much else is important. I'm sure you're aware that reports like yours are more than classroom exercises. They have real world consequences. Effects on the monetary policies and stability of corporations."

"The most important effects are on families," Julia Lambert said. "Harewood Corporation provides food on the table and good health insurance for over 50,000 families nationwide."

"The impact on communities reaches far beyond those families." While he spoke, Mr. Harewood was fidgeting with a small object in his left fist, his thumb massaging it rhythmically until, at last, he released a polished brown stone onto the table. What a strange habit! Summer's attention returned to his words. "Think of the wages spent on cars, houses, the trickle-down effect the company has on every business in the towns where we're located."

"She's a good girl, Mr. Harewood. She doesn't want to see anyone lose their jobs because of her report."

Summer shook her head. "No, but a scientific report must be based on data, on facts. I based the conclusions on observable measurements."

Julia's laugh wiggled into the corners of the room. "Oh, those are just statistics, and my daddy always said there are lies, darn lies, and statistics."

Summer would bet money Julia's daddy hadn't said *darn*.

Julia plunged on. "We at Harewood want to keep our employees on the job so they can feed their families. And we take great pride in helping students like you get a good education. Can't you see any way you might be able to help us in return?"

Like lie? Summer felt nauseated. "I'm not sure what you mean."

Harewood flipped through several pages. "For example, on page ten, look at the wording. "*Will not* is too strong. What about changing it to *may not?*"

The meeting lasted forty-five minutes. Harewood pointed out paragraphs in the report, questioned the phrasing, and suggested changes. The grandmother smiled and cajoled. Summer made noncommittal noises periodically and took notes on her copy, her stomach flopping around like a fish dying on a mud bank.

Harewood stood. "Give Mrs. Lambert the revised report tomorrow at the public hearing."

"I'm not sure how much I'll be able to change," Summer said, "but I'll look over these notes tonight."

Mrs. Lambert glossed over Summer's uncertainty. "Only smart and sensible people earn as many A's as you have on your transcript. I'm sure you'll do fine. We'll talk tomorrow, honey."

Harewood's pinched face told the truth: If she didn't change the report, she'd never see another dime of Harewood money.

2

THOUGH THE PETITE WOMAN SPOKE BROKEN ENGLISH, Detective George Theofanis was doing his best to understand her problem.

Isadora Montera made her points mostly by waving her hands in the air. She wore old jeans and a loose cotton blouse, gray hair pulled back into a bun. "He never miss come home before."

"You're not related to Mr. Alvarez?"

"No. He renter. Paulo always come home from work. Six-thirty."

Theofanis glanced up from his notes. "Let me see if I've got this straight. Mr. Alvarez went to work yesterday and hasn't come back to the room he rents from you since then. Technically he hasn't been gone forty-eight hours yet—is that right?"

"Yes, gone two days."

"But you wouldn't have seen him again until after work on Wednesday. Until tonight at 6:30, he hasn't been gone forty-eight hours and I can't file a missing persons report. You say he's a young man. He probably found a girlfriend."

"No, he married. Love his wife and son. All he talk about. I call at his job this morning and he not there."

"I bet he missed his wife so much he headed back home."

"No, he wouldn't not pay rent he owes. He would say goodbye."

Lots of folks who seemed nice skipped out on rent. Theofanis's skepticism must have shown on his face because Mrs. Montera's mouth twisted until she looked like a snarling dog.

"He good boy. Like a son. Like my son. Write that in report." She stabbed her finger repeatedly against Theofanis's notepad. Nervy woman—police officers intimidated most folks, especially immigrants. Theofanis ignored the coughs of his colleague, Burns, who sat outside his office hanging on every word.

Theofanis walked her out of his office, past the disorganized clot of desks belonging to Loblolly Lake's finest, to the front of the station. "Stay calm, Mrs. Montera. We're going to do our best to find Mr. Alvarez. I'll do a little checking around. Meanwhile, you call me if he turns up."

Her eyes narrowed. "You not look like police. Your face look like little boy."

She turned and sailed out the glass doors into the midday sun.

Theofanis holstered his phone and followed her, the "little boy" hoots and taunts trailing in his wake. He had no intention of sticking around for more attempts at humor. Since Theofanis had little else he particularly wanted to do right then, he would try to track down a wayward Mexican.

Besides, the immigrant community didn't usually invite the police to poke around in their business. Fear and worry surrounded the tiny woman like a dark cloud. What was it she hadn't shared with him?

3

CLAIRE DUNHAM SQUIRRELED AWAY a few more papers in her briefcase, ready to head home. She almost didn't answer her cell and was sorry after she did. John Hu, dean of the College of Arts and Science, wanted her in his office. Right away.

As if this week hadn't been crazy enough already, what with the former boyfriend materializing at her office. Though she wouldn't really call him that, more like a two-night stand. Then the leader of that environmental group, Water Warriors, got a tad overzealous. He demanded that the university denounce Harewood's wells. Claire wished she'd never heard of Harewood and his frigging wells.

She tromped down the hall to Hu's expensively furnished office, which was twice the size of hers. It even had a window, albeit a small one, and a huge tank full of expensive fish.

Hu leaned across his solid oak desk. Hers was cheap veneer over chipboard. Why did she latch onto these picayune details every blessed time she entered his office? Such petty resentment, but it galled her that she had raised boatloads of money for the department over the years, and she had published in major scientific journals. Hu's reputation and current position stemmed from one well-publicized publication early in his career. One! Breakthrough work, but now he coasted. Claire despised slackers. Besides, he wore more cologne than a Middle Eastern harem.

Hu's thickly accented English sounded suitably earnest as he sat erect at his desk. "You have brought honor and respect to the geology department. Your research on the Florida karst system and ASR wells continues to add so much depth and breadth to our knowledge base."

Claire struggled to keep her disgust from showing. He could at least be less obvious that he wanted something from her. His hair was slicked back with so much grease not a strand budged as he shuffled through the pages of her grant report as though he were skimming them for the first time. A joke. He knew what the pages contained or she wouldn't be here in his office.

"We appreciate the effort you've put into securing grants, especially the Harewood funding," he said.

Claire Dunham strove to control her expression. She hated grants with a bloody passion even though she plowed hours into writing them. Science should be pure. If only she could concentrate on work in her field without interference.

Dr. Hu rolled an expensive pen between his fingers. "I don't have to tell you the importance of Harewood's support to this university."

No, he didn't, but Claire knew he was going to.

"He's made major contributions to the alumni association and our science scholarship funds. Not to mention the endowed chair, which may soon be yours."

Ah, dangle the carrot, a reward for doing what the dean wanted. She wished he'd get to the point: soften the report on the feasibility of Harewood's Aquifer Storage and Recovery wells.

Hu smiled his diplomatic best. After twice mentioning how the university president himself was following the course of the Harewood grant, Hu posed the question she'd been expecting. Time to employ Rule Number One when refusing to give an authority figure what he wanted: Massage the ego. Catering to the self-important personalities of academia was a vital tactic in navigating university life. Outsiders listening to this little conference would think it was a mutual admiration society instead of a battle of wills.

"We are so fortunate to have you as dean of this department, John. It's a pleasure to deal with a scientist of your magnitude, because you understand that facts are facts. I can't change them."

"Claire, no one would ever ask you to alter your data." Hu sounded suitably appalled at this suggestion. "Your ethical standards are beyond question. Highest caliber. We all use students to assist in our research. All I'm suggesting is perhaps one of them erred."

"Summer Cassidy ran the latest tests. You know how competent she is. Best student I've had in years." The kid was damn near a genius, with the closest approximation to a photographic memory Claire had ever encountered. Summer had finished her undergrad and her Master's in four years. Most kids these days took five just for the B.S. and another two for the Master's. At least. Besides, Claire had obtained fresh samples a month ago and run tests herself. She wasn't an idiot.

"The conclusion, though, is overstated, wouldn't you agree?" Hu asked.

"No, John, I wouldn't. Most ASR wells are safe after four to eight cycles. Summer's conclusion nails the central issue with Harewood's wells: adequate attenuation is never going to occur. It's time to stop wasting both Harewood's and the taxpayer dollars that are subsidizing this venture. Time to admit these particular wells have failed."

The dean frowned. "My understanding is HEC funded this venture by itself."

"Mostly. The wells are one of those public/private partnership deals, meaning the public helps pay for infrastructure. Or the state gives away public land and the corporation takes all the profits. Everyone says it's all good because it creates jobs."

Hu clicked his pen open and closed four times and, possibly because he managed to annoy even himself, he tossed the offending object onto his desk. "I think this report is, perhaps, harsher than it needs to be. A few changes in wording would make the conclusions more palatable. Anyone can spin material to make it less offensive to readers." He paused. "Or to donors."

Claire braced her fists against his desk, careful not to knock over either the photo of Hu's wife or the magnetic tray holding assorted paperclips. "I don't know how to put a softer spin on it. Harewood's water still registers arsenic far above the ten parts per billion the EPA allows. Should I suggest that only a small percentage of people who drink the water would develop bladder cancer because of increased carcinogenic exposure? We can write them off. And even fewer would get prostate or lung cancer, a reasonable price to pay so golfers can spend their Saturdays on perfect greens."

Dr. Hu sighed as if he were dealing with a recalcitrant child. "Your analysis of other sites suggests the amount of arsenic leaching into the groundwater is likely to decrease the longer the wells operate."

Claire felt the heat climb her neck again. The man gave her a rash. Why was he being so damn stubborn? "Let me repeat myself. Not if twelve cycles haven't already caused the levels to decrease. Other wells are safe. These aren't."

"There is that old expression: 'Accentuate the positive.' Technology will catch up to well construction. Enterprising scientists like you will develop methodologies to cheaply remove all toxins. I must emphasize the importance of making sure the research continues. This report will scare off other private investors. It may even slow down or stop construction of the government-funded Everglades wells. ASR wells are such a vital component in supplying water for agriculture and industry." Almost as an afterthought, he added, "As well as potable drinking water."

Now, perhaps without realizing it, Hu had plumbed deep enough to reach the truth. Big Business, Big Sugar, and Big Developers wanted more water. They'd found a way to get taxpayers to fund these massive water works projects by disguising them as a Save-the-Everglades plan. She was all for saving the Glades, but the Comprehensive Everglades Recovery Plan was only half about funding solid environmental improvements. The rest of the money was a well-disguised giveaway to businesses that benefited from attracting more people to South Florida.

The ethics of Harewood's venture troubled Claire deeply. A resource as basic to existence as water shouldn't be controlled by private companies. The bottled water industry already pumped out millions of gallons of the same water consumers could get for a few cents from their taps and sold it to them for dollars instead. Not to mention the amount of petroleum products and energy used to manufacture bottles that later glutted landfills or created islands of trash in the Pacific.

The ridiculously expensive Waterford pen lying on Hu's even more expensive desk suddenly pissed her off beyond all reason.

Claire stood. "You have my report."

As Hu swiveled his chair away from the desk, a crazy impulse made her palm the pen and pocket it. Wasn't that she wanted the damn thing, but she sensed how frantic he would be when he discovered the pen was missing. If only she could be there to watch him shuffle papers and get down on his knees and crawl around the floor searching for it.

She had pulled off a fine, audacious exit, hadn't she? Would she feel so brave if she lost her position?

This job defined her. She'd sacrificed everything for her career, jettisoned opportunities she regretted. She should have been more flexible, agreed to move to Boston with Joe Barrineau. Eventually, she would have found a position. Well, she had made her choice. She stayed. Joe went. Her career came first, and she would die alone one day.

No matter what she'd sacrificed for her career, she couldn't twist the data. Not if she held on to a shred of self respect. Besides, somebody needed to scream about Harewood's wells. People could die—actually die—from upending a water bottle or turning on their taps if he was allowed to sell his toxic brew. An unforgivable breach of public trust. She didn't think the folks over at the Department of Environmental Protection were going to recommend giving Harewood a green light any more than she would. The tests coming back from labs they contracted with had to be churning out the same results. Yet with the anti-regulation, pro-business stir in the capital these days, she knew DEP was experiencing the same pressure Hu was laying on her.

As she strode down the hall to her office, she slipped her hand into her pants pocket and fondled the Waterford pen. In a week or two she would drop it back onto Hu's desk. She chuckled as she imagined Hu raking his fingers through his hair trying to figure out how the pen had magically reappeared. Really, a scientist should have higher priorities.

4

IN A NEW FILE CALLED "CONCLUSIONS REVISED," Summer backspaced over "arsenic levels will not likely attenuate" and changed her report to read "arsenic levels may attenuate given enough time." Not exactly a lie. It was possible. She altered a dozen more phrases, as suggested by the Great Man himself, before slamming into the impenetrable wall of data. She couldn't change the numbers. Wouldn't.

But if she didn't, that Ph.D. dream could drift off into the sky like a helium balloon—way out of reach of her impoverished fingers. Sure, she would apply for other scholarships, but it was late to go looking for money for the fall term, especially since the recession had drained the pool of funds.

In the end, she made most of the changes Harewood wanted— not the numbers—printed the new document and laid it on top of her original report. She closed her laptop and rested her forehead on the hard plastic lid, her eyes shut. When her eyes opened, the photographic skin she'd applied to her laptop lid confronted her. An image of a wood stork reflected on the eerie green waters of Wakulla Springs. Beautiful liquid light.

Her rib cage squeezed inward and the fish in her stomach started squirming around again. The Floridan Aquifer was one of the most productive in the world. It extended over 100,000 square miles beneath the entire state of Florida and into parts of neighboring states. When the water pressure became great enough, groundwater broke out on the surface in the form of springs. Wakulla Springs averaged between 200-300 million gallons of water output a day.

All through her teens, one of Summer's greatest joys had been exploring the rivers and springs in North and Central Florida. Could she issue a report that might harm Florida's water system?

She pushed away from her desk. Screw this stupid pity party. So what if she compromised. Businesses did it. Politicians did it. She was an adult. Welcome to the real world.

She pulled on jeans and a clean blouse and hiked half a mile to the Foos and Booze. She slid into the booth across from Dayita Patel, letting her eyes adjust to the dim lighting. Tiffany-style lamps with beer advertisements hung over each table.

Dayita nursed her mojito as if she feared what a few extra calories might do to her body. Tall and model-thin, Dayita had exotic dark eyes and waist-long hair. She was obsessively neat, her cottons ironed to crispness, pants legs hemmed to the perfect length. Unlike Summer, whose jeans had shrunk enough to show her ankles.

The bartender brought Summer a Yuengling. He cut his eyes to a blue-jeaned young man standing by the foosball table. "That one looks like an easy hustle."

"Thanks, Tom."

Dayita toyed with the thick black braid that trailed over her shoulder. "How'd the scholarship meeting go?"

Summer grimaced. "It didn't. Harewood hauled me in there to talk about my water tests. The company's gung-ho on getting exemptions on chemicals that have leached out of the rocks. They made it clear they expect me to help them, which would mean changing my thesis conclusions."

"What makes these wells different from other water wells?"

Everything. "Think of rocks as having tiny pores like skin. During the rainy season, these well operations force water under pressure into the pores of rocks that are miles underground. When there's less available water, they pump it back up. It usually works fine."

Dayita frowned. "So what's the problem with Harewood's water?"

Summer shredded the edge of her cocktail napkin. "Water near the earth's surface contains a lot of dissolved oxygen. Injecting water with higher oxygen levels than the water in the aquifer causes the arsenic to dissolve out of the rocks. Usually when you move the water in and out of an ASR well in slow cycles—say four or six times a year—the leaching stops."

"Why didn't it stop this time?"

"I don't know. Maybe they over-pumped, trying to get a quicker profit from the water they were selling to that bottling plant."

Dayita nodded slowly. "Don't let them bully you, Summer."

The image of the revisions lying beside her laptop flashed in her mind. Enough of that. She smiled at the sweet-faced boy hanging around the nearest foosball table. Tom was right; this would be easy.

Dayita touched the end of her braid to her lips, and stared at the rim of her mojito glass. "I've never told you about my family."

Summer looked at her sharply. "Don't be silly. I've known your mother for—"

"Not my mother. Her family in Bangladesh. My uncle died of kidney cancer. My grandmother of bladder cancer. My cousins have skin sores."

"A genetic defect?"

"No. Well-intentioned western engineers drilled tube wells for the villagers so they wouldn't have to carry water long distances from the river. Those wells leached arsenic into the groundwater. Over 80 million people, all sick. The largest mass poisoning in history and no one has even heard of it. Don't let it happen here."

A bitter, metallic taste filled Summer's mouth. She had read about the poisonings in Bangladesh in the course of her research, but hadn't connected them to real human beings. A gulp of beer expunged the bad taste in her mouth. The alcohol cooled, and then warmed its way down her esophagus.

"I'll do what I can."

Dayita flashed her impossibly white teeth. "You have a good heart."

So not true. When Summer had read about the well poisonings, she hadn't thought to ask Dayita if she knew any of the victims. This was a flaw, a weakness stemming from her over-stimulated memory. She read. She remembered. She spouted statistics. Her classmates all through school were right. She was weird.

And now there was the revised report. If she earned her Ph.D., she would be empowered with the knowledge and clout to improve people's lives. Would that atone for the weakened conclusions?

A good heart. No, Joseph Conrad had it right: most hearts were dark and selfish. Without responding to Dayita's assessment, Summer strode over to the foosball table and hooked the cutie pie. "What's your name?"

"Adam."

She shifted most of her weight to her left heel and rotated the ball of her right foot back and forth, mirroring the motion with her shoulders. The little girl ploy disarmed even the toughest guys, and

Adam didn't look the least bit tough. "Well, Adam, I can whip the pants off you."

He smiled a Richie Cunningham smile. "Like to see you try."

Summer loved Richie Cunningham. She and her sister Chrissie used to watch *Happy Days* reruns when they were little. Richie was innocent. Like Chrissie.

Three games later—and an equal number of Yuenglings Adam had to buy for her when he lost—Summer took him over to meet Dayita. Summer ignored the unspoken scold of Dayita's jiggling foot. Why did Dayita bother to go out with her? A mystery. Dayita didn't play foosball. She nursed a drink so slowly waitresses gave her the evil eye for occupying tip-earning table space. She refused to flirt with the boys Summer sent over to the booth to chat her up.

Summer felt sorry for the latest one trying to impress Dayita. He was a friend of Summer's foosball buddy. Roddy, she thought his name was. Seemed nice enough. Poor guy stuttered trying to thaw Dayita's chill.

"No really—where'd you'd learn to play foosball like that?" Richie—no that wasn't his name—Alan, wasn't it?—asked.

Summer laughed and it came out louder than she'd expected. "Told you—studied how to play online and taught myself."

He threw back his head and howled. "No way."

"Way." Summer leaned into him and inhaled the clean scent of his neck.

Dayita's disapproving foot vibrated the whole booth. Summer knew without looking that her friend's sandal was flopping on and off. If the room had been quiet, everyone would have heard the angry tinkle of her little gold ankle bracelet.

Enough. Summer couldn't take any more disapproval today, Dayita's or her own. Summer bumped her hip against the sweet-faced boy.

"You ready to leave?" she asked. "Go somewhere else?"

Hope and disbelief lit his eyes in equal measure. "My apartment's two blocks away."

"Perfect."

His friend tried his charm on Dayita. "Would you like to—"

Dayita dismissed the boys with a haughty glance from those dark eyes. "Excuse us a minute." She grasped Summer's forearm and tugged her toward the ladies' room.

As soon as the swinging door closed, Dayita started the same old spiel. "Just stop. This stuff you do is really stupid. You'll contract a terrible disease—or worse. One of these guys is going to turn out to be a real creep."

Oh, gaaah—another lecture from the world's most determined virgin. "I'm careful. No condom, no sex. And I only choose nice guys."

"After three beers, Ted Bundy would seem nice."

"That's why I stop at two." Summer's eyes dropped away from Dayita's. As a distraction from her blatant dishonesty, she pulled the band off her ponytail and reset it with a hard twist. She caught a glimpse of herself in the mirror. Her blouse had a small stain right over her left boob. That and the mention of Bundy turned a good mood sour. Serial killers with All-American faces dwelled in the house next door. On the Florida State campus about an hour northwest of Loblolly Lake, Bundy had murdered one Chi Omega girl, raped and murdered another, and bludgeoned two more. All told, Bundy killed at least thirty women, possibly as many as a hundred. Might have happened decades ago, but the 1978 killing spree was part of Florida legend. And south of Loblolly Lake, Danny Rolling, the Gainesville Ripper, murdered five students in a rampage that terrorized the University of Florida campus in 1990. What brought all the freaks to Florida?

Surely if Summer talked to a real douche bag, she would sense it. A storm would flash across his eyes. His mouth would twitch or curl like a snake. Words would ring false. Besides, she was a young woman with normal desires. Why shouldn't she satisfy them, just as men had always done? As long as she never let a guy get between her and her Ph.D. She didn't do relationships.

"You need to get laid, Dayita. Or at least spend an entire day without working on a computer project."

"Not all of us can absorb information by touching a book's cover like you. We actually have to take notes and study."

It always came down to that, didn't it? Every kid in every class Summer had ever been in resented her amazing memory. As if she could help it. Early on, she'd learned never to volunteer an answer, and never, ever to correct teachers, no matter how wrong they were.

"Yeah? Well, I plan to memorize the curve of Alan's thighs to-night. I'll take notes for you in case you ever decide to drop the Ice Queen act."

Summer hipped the bathroom door open. Why had she said that? Even if it was true. Would she never learn to bite back mean words before regret bit her back?

Minutes later she stood beside the cash register and let the young man pay for her last beer. The gap-tooth smile on his driver's license photo beamed at her. She peered more closely. Adam. Not Alan. Adam Tidwell. Not that it mattered.

Four

Friday

I

SUMMER POSITIONED HERSELF IN THE HALLWAY to watch the door to the meeting room, both versions of her report inside the folder she clasped against her chest. She was reluctant to go inside. Mrs. Lambert and a man Summer assumed was a colleague strode by with the kind of confidence Summer wished she possessed. Unlike her, they had already chosen sides. Several people who looked like ordinary citizens—jeans, khakis, polo shirts—passed by next. She pegged them for environmental activists.

At first, she barely noticed the little girl who sat in a wing chair a few feet away, coloring book in her lap. As the minutes passed, the child's presence seemed odd. She was four or five, and Summer kept expecting someone to claim her. The girl chose a sky blue crayon and began filling in the outlined forms in the coloring book. She swung her feet, back and forth, back and forth, her legs so short those hot pink tennis shoes touched only air.

A memory floated up of Summer's sister Chrissie, swinging her feet under a chair the same way, except Chrissie's toes were painted with blue polish and peeped out of flip flops with a yellow plastic daisy fastened to the center. This kid was humming a tune Summer half-recognized from a kiddy TV show. A ditty about a funky jelly monster.

Though the coloring and the humming were perfectly normal activities, something about the girl didn't seem quite right. Her hair, for instance. Washed and brushed out, it would be two shades lighter. Ketchup stains marred her shorts. The child's socks didn't match, one a bit shorter than the other with differing widths between the elastic bands. What mother dressed a child so carelessly? Something else felt off about the child, though Summer couldn't quite pinpoint what. Developmentally disabled, most likely, like Chrissie, which was why Summer was associating them.

She moved into the chair beside the child and leaned in close. "What're you drawing?"

The child's hands and legs and song stilled all at once, but she didn't answer. After a brief pause, she continued coloring as if Summer wasn't there.

"Are you waiting for someone?" Summer asked.

The crayon's movement persisted.

Summer tried again. "May I see your picture?"

This time, the child hesitated, then rotated the coloring book toward her.

"Amazing. You stayed in the lines real good." The child had crayoned the father's face solid white and Princess Jasmine's arms sky blue. She subdivided the clothes into smaller geometric shapes, each triangle and parallelogram colored in bright primary shades.

"You must be waiting for someone."

"My brother." The voice, tiny enough to fit in a dolly's teacup.

"What's your brother's name? I could help you find him." Now that Summer was closer, she noticed a dirt ring on the girl's neck. She smelled not only of milk, but faintly like dirty underwear. How long had she been sitting by herself untended? The kid's expression remained unchanged and she didn't offer her brother's name.

"My name's Summer. What's yours?"

The child ignored her. She asked again.

"Grace." *Gwace* was the way it came out. Too cute.

"The Amazing Grace!" Summer said with false cheer. She brushed the child's soft arm with the back of her knuckles.

The child pulled away and grew rigid—as if Summer had slapped her. Had anyone been watching? She glanced around but no one was paying attention to them. Okay—one more try—hands-free. She sure wasn't going to touch the kid again. "Someone must have loved you very much to give you such a pretty name."

"Mommy."

"I could call your mommy. What's your phone number?"

Grace sucked in her bottom lip.

The meeting room was filling up. Through the doorway, Summer could see Mrs. Lambert and her colleague talking with a redhead who reeked of power, She carried herself like a tea service on a sterling silver tray. As he passed by, Summer recognized the senator from newspaper photos. Felipe Vargas. Supposed to be a friend of the Green Movement. Shaking hands as he worked his way to the front of the room, he made straight for the redhead. Who was that woman?

And where was this kid's brother? Summer had left her sister alone—only for a few minutes. That was all it had taken to change the world, to change "we" into "me."

Their mother named them Summer and Christmas. *I am so very, very lucky because I get to celebrate my two favorite seasons every day because I have you, Summer and Chrissie Cassidy,* their mother told them. At night she tucked them in, butterfly-kissing each girl on the forehead, kisses full of magic that would keep them safe until morning.

Christmas, the younger twin by several minutes, was born with hypoplastic left heart syndrome. Despite numerous surgeries, Chrissie's lack of stamina forced her to limit physical activities. She lagged behind Summer in every regard. Usually, Summer didn't mind. Usually, she did what her mother told them to do. Stick together. Look after each other. Which meant Summer looking after Chrissie. Especially after reduced oxygen during the last surgery made Chrissie what the family called "special" and others called "slow" or "retarded."

They were nine the day Summer violated her mother's most important rule and left Chrissie alone. That's when the accident happened. That much she could admit.

Once, when Summer was thirteen, her mother had taken her to St. Petersburg for one of her fund-raising events. Afterward, they stopped in the Dali museum. Summer's favorite was a print made from a woodcut of a fallen angel. The creature's wing was blotched, bones stuck out of its leg, and its torso consisted of a chest of drawers. The angel was pulling out those drawers and examining the contents. One compartment had a keyhole, suggesting secrets locked away.

Summer had looked deep into the painting and seen herself. The truth of that hot September day when Chrissie died was safe inside Summer's locked drawer, one she never opened. One she never shared with anyone. Not her mother. Not even her best friend.

Summer recognized The Scowler instantly even though his expression was no longer gloomy. The very same grouch who had been waiting outside Dr. Dunham's office. She remembered his dark eyes and the Hollywood facial hair. He addressed "Gwace" as Sugarpop.

"You shouldn't leave this child by herself," Summer said and hurried into the meeting room before he could reply.

She took a seat in the empty back row. The Scowler deposited Sugarpop at the other end of the row and walked away with the slightly uneven gait Summer had noticed before. He sat down near the front.

As The Scowler spoke to an elderly man in the next chair, Mrs. Lambert's companion nudged her with his elbow. His eyes narrowed and his jaw hardened. His fingers clenched the papers he held. Had they been flesh, they'd have bruised. His face reassembled itself into a professional demeanor so quickly Summer wondered if she'd imagined his reaction.

Alice Leymon, the head of the Department of Environmental Protection, introduced Senator Felipe Vargas and set the parameters for the public hearing. Speakers would have five minutes each to present their views, she said. "If you want to speak, put your name on the sign-up sheet, please."

Summer hadn't come to speak. Not this time. Today she wanted to scope out the major players, to understand the way these hearings worked so she wouldn't make a fool of herself when she helped Dr. Dunham make a formal presentation at the final hearing next week. And, of course, today she had to turn over her report to Mrs. Lambert. She picked at her folder with her thumbnail, defacing the edge with a row of tiny indentations.

The senator said a few words about balancing the need to create jobs with protection of natural resources. He also affirmed the importance of the public weighing in on this vital issue. After he resumed his seat, his aide, a slim, virile fellow in his thirties, leaned forward and whispered in the senator's ear.

Mrs. Lambert's companion, introducing himself as Niles Morrell, began his presentation. Despite short stature, his thick silver hair lent him an aura of wisdom. As Harewood's Chief Financial Officer, he enumerated the jobs created by Harewood's planned expansion of ASR wells across the state. "Harewood Corporation has already begun acquiring easements for pipelines to deliver water to thirsty citizens during dry seasons, which have been more frequent and of longer duration in recent years. Municipal governments can no longer afford to build and maintain the infrastructure needed to deliver water to citizens. Besides the pipelines, we are still hopeful that we can come to an agreement on construction of our own bottling facility in the future. We are committed to providing a quality product and to being good corporate citizens."

While he spoke, Mrs. Lambert distributed a slick handout with color charts and graphs. Many of the facts Summer already knew. The United Nations expected world demand for water to outstrip supply by more than thirty percent by 2040. An Alaskan company was already siphoning three billion gallons of water a year from Blue Lake in Sitka and selling it to a bottling plant near Mumbai. Private water utilities owned by foreign investors were now common in China where the water table had fallen so low that wells had to reach two thirds of a mile or more deep to hit fresh water. Shortages were a global problem, and Harewood Energy Corporation wanted to be part of the solution.

Summer opened her folder and looked at the revised report without seeing it. She assured herself the original still lay beneath it. Morrell made HEC sound like Boy Scouts—but the truth was more complicated. They could be corporate bullies, too. She tucked their handout underneath her reports. Which version would she submit?

A half dozen Chamber of Commerce representatives and local businessmen spoke about the need to diversify. Too many education and healthcare jobs. Too little manufacturing.

Environmentalists went next. As Summer had surmised, they were ordinary citizens concerned about water quality. They raised pertinent questions and were frothing mad over Morrell's suggestion of piping water from northern parts of the state to the over-populated southern areas. "This idea is even worse than the thieves who are bottling our spring water and trucking it out of Florida," one of them said.

Finally The Scowler stepped to the podium, and Summer learned his name: Ty Franceschi, son of the founder of Water Warriors, a group with a growing online following. Broad shouldered, Ty would stand out in any room. He wore black jeans and a short sleeve black cotton shirt. His baritone, while not overly loud, commanded attention. Like his body and his eyes, Franceschi's voice gave the impression of potential energy that might transform into action any moment.

"My organization works to prevent large scale water extraction, monitor local water districts, and enact legislative protections for our water," he said. "All across this country, corporations are appropriating this public resource that belongs to all of us. And it belongs to the deer, the bears—all the plants and animals that depend on water for life."

Anger and sorrow seemed to fuel his words, especially as he spoke about industrial pollutants and lax regulation. What was his story? When he finished, the environmentalists stood and clapped, making him the only speaker to earn such a response. She rose with them.

Summer stole a glance to see if his sister was impressed. Apparently not. She was still coloring.

The next speaker was the redhead. Summer had nearly forgotten about her. Her presence filled the room too, in a different way from Ty Franceschi. She introduced herself as Bailey Douglass of Douglass and Associates. Small wonder she had confidence—the beautiful woman owned her own firm, which represented Harewood Energy Corporation. The lights dimmed. She presented a professional video with patriotic music and testimonials from Harewood workers proud of keeping America moving toward energy independence. The final shot reiterated their slogan: "Making responsible investments in America's resources."

As the video closed, the pro-business contingent rose to their feet to applaud Ms. Douglass. The redhead exuded power, sexual energy, and competence. She wore a tasteful, expensive suit too, which prompted Summer to lift her folder to her chest to hide her clearance-rack tee-shirt. It was irrational to align herself against all these movers and shakers. How could she speak in front of all these influential people?

The final speaker was head of DEP. Alice Leymon made clear she favored maintaining the federal regulations as they were written. "The state opens itself to a long court battle if it attempts to override federal policy. The proposed legislation is almost certainly unconstitutional. The majority of citizens oppose the bottling of our water to sell elsewhere and are equally opposed to removal of our most important natural resource through pipelines. It would be a huge mistake for the legislature to consider this bill." She adjourned the meeting.

The room began to empty. The man from Harewood Corporation was practically snarling at the head of DEP. Alice Leymon took two steps backward and straightened the jacket of her suit.

"I'm not going to be intimidated by you, Mr. Morrell," she said. "I am charged by the state of Florida to oversee environmental regulations and that's what I intend to do."

Niles Morrell's face hardened again as he saw Ty Franceschi speaking with the Chamber of Commerce president.

Morrell broke into their conversation. "You just won't quit, will you Franceschi? I would have thought your arrest for that little demonstration you organized in West Virginia might have slowed you down. You should be smart enough to figure out HEC isn't about to let a save-the-earth hippie stand in our way. Your vendetta against Harewood Energy has become obsessive. I am going to recommend that our lawyers file stalking charges against you."

Stalking? For daring to speak in favor of clean water?

Summer glanced again at Grace Franceschi, those hot pink tennis shoes still swinging back and forth. A vision of Chrissie's daisy-topped flip flops filled her mind so completely she thought she heard her mother speaking: What do you want to be when you grow up? Chrissie answered in a chirrupy voice: I want to be a mad scientist, or else I want to be a bird.

Everyone in the room always laughed. Summer had set out to be the scientist her sister could never have become, even if she had lived.

Summer recalled Dr. Dunham's mantra: facts are facts. And Dayita's judgment: You have a good heart.

Time to prove it. She charged across the room to Mrs. Lambert before self-interest trumped a good heart.

2

ISAAC HAREWOOD SCRAPED HIS FINGERS over his bald scalp. "Julia, get in here, and bring that girl's paperwork."

She arrived with the materials so fast she must have been reading his mind. He snatched Summer Cassidy's folder from her hands and fed the scholarship application into the crosscut shredder, watching until the mechanical whir stopped. Next he seized the publicity photo taken when the girl received her first Harewood scholarship. A shot from the waist up. Isaac stood to her left, beaming, shaking her hand. That girl wasn't smiling for the camera the way most people would. Unnaturally serious. No doubt a spoiled idealist who didn't care if other people had jobs or retirement funds. She didn't understand what was at stake. Those academic types never lived in the real world. The shredder's knives sliced the girl's face into smithereens.

He accepted a cup of freshly brewed green tea with ginger from his secretary. Just the thought of that sickeningly sweet ice tea popular throughout the South gagged him. Give him the healthful effects of his imported green any day. "That little meeting we had with Ms. Cassidy didn't produce results, did it?"

"No, sir. She proved intractable."

Harewood set his cup down on the small mosaic-topped table, a custom design of a great blue heron, panther, and alligator against a background of cypress knees and swamp grasses. The cypress knees were formed from leopard skin jasper. His spiritual counselor claimed this spotted jasper had mystical abilities to bring you what you needed. If ever Isaac had needed good luck, it was now. Julia wore a matronly smile. The woman would look serene while Rome burnt to the ground around her.

"Plans B and C will be underway before the day is over," Julia said.

"What plans?"

"I won't trouble you with details, but our little world is headed back on track. I studied Ms. Cassidy's application and it's filled with fascinating information about her interests and hobbies. And further research uncovered some real vulnerabilities that we can use to our advantage. She once had a breakdown and didn't speak for two weeks. I'm afraid our college girl is going to experience a very rough week."

She wasn't the only one. Isaac checked his watch. He'd made a phone call. Alice Leymon had been placed on administrative leave at the Department of Environmental Protection while an auditor investigated her travel expenses. She would learn the hard way it didn't pay to thumb her nose at Isaac Harewood.

"Show time, Julia. Go downstairs to the auditorium. Tell everyone I'm on my way."

After she closed the door on his inner sanctum, Isaac looked out over the beautifully landscaped grounds of his empire. Three solid brick office buildings, an underground garage for his top people's vehicles, and various smaller facilities that warehoused equipment. He had worked so hard to obtain financial security, to build a successful business that provided thousands of jobs. He had done everything right. Joined the Rotary Club and tithed at church. Started a charitable foundation—money he couldn't touch. After so many good years, how had he been reduced to this?

He had made his first million from natural gas and coal. Acquired rights in West Virginia and Pennsylvania with an uncanny instinct for where the largest deposits would lie. God wanted him to succeed—of that he had no doubt. In the 1970s when everyone else was in a dither over the Arab oil embargo and resulting gasoline shortage, Isaac realized the next big resource wasn't going to be a fossil fuel at all. The next big shortage would be water. You didn't have to look far to discern the truth of his prediction. In Dubai they were desalinating the ocean. Florida, Georgia, and Alabama staged annual court battles over how much water could be diverted to Atlanta taps and golf courses without destroying the livelihoods of fishermen in the Gulf. Municipalities all over the country dictated citizens could only water lawns once a week during summer droughts. Suburbanites groused and groaned as they watched their lawns turn brown.

"Whiskey's for drinking and water's for fighting," Mark Twain once said. Isaac saw the war coming early. He quietly obtained water rights and well permits. Municipalities were drilling huge underground wells to store water during the rainy season and then sell it back to thirsty cities during droughts. Harewood aimed to be the first individual to operate privately owned ASR wells in Florida. Those wells would be his salvation.

Or his downfall.

He hardened his jaw. No way. Not going to happen.

Harewood took the executive elevator down to the auditorium where he only half listened to Niles Morrell introduce him. As if he needed an introduction to his own employees. He pulled his trademark confidence out of the mental closet and slipped it on like a second skin. He strode on stage to stand before his Board of Directors, the rank-and-file, and a top grade camcorder transmitting his message real time to employees in five states. When the applause died down, he motioned to the chart projected on the screen.

"As you can see, Harewood Energy Corporation expects to experience six percent growth this year and as much as ten percent the year after that. I can't talk publicly about this yet, but a couple of exciting developments convince me our stock values will explode over the next five years. This is our company—yours and mine. We all have a vested interest in seeing its continued growth and success. Our stock continues to offer a stable investment, even in this rocky economic climate. I am proud to stand before you and say that I believe in you. I have such confidence in your ability to bring about the progress our country needs, that I have doubled my own retirement investments in HEC. I hope you'll do the same."

A standing ovation followed. Isaac kept a smile pasted on while he shook the hand of Niles Morrell. Even managed to smile when he offered Julia his hand and she enveloped him in an unprofessional hug. He waved one more time for the camera and exited the rear door of the auditorium. The CFO and secretary hustled to stay beside him as he strode to the elevator.

As the door whooshed open, he swiveled around. "Niles, give me five minutes, then come on up. Julia, you stay down here and handle any questions. Make sure there's plenty of coffee."

In the privacy of his office, Harewood sank into his ergonomic leather chair and groaned. That performance had surely drained the marrow from his bones. How else to account for the exhaustion that emptied his mind and settled in his gut like a boulder. He had no time to be tired. From his desk, he picked up the file containing his stock portfolio, his throat tightening as he skimmed the summary his financial adviser had mailed to him. No wonder she hadn't delivered it in person. She should be ashamed—or afraid—to talk to him face-to-face. This recession was cannibalizing him. He had diversified, as she insisted, so that he wouldn't lose his shirt if one piece of the market dipped. Worked for a while—until every sector tanked, especially the speculative stocks and Florida real estate ventures she steered him into. He doubted he would live long enough to see a rebound on those.

Niles arrived with a sheaf of folders in his hand. He sat down across from Isaac and pulled a paper from the top file. He fussed through two other folders, retrieving documents.

Isaac ran his hand over his scalp. "Stop. No paperwork. Just tell me how bad it is."

Niles's mouth pinched. "Bad."

"How bad?"

"Worse than we thought. The price of natural gas keeps falling and it's killing our cash flow."

Who could have guessed the investments in hydraulic fracking would hurt HEC's bottom line? Natural gas should have been a gold mine—and would be, if HEC survived this downturn. But the glut of natural gas, just as world demand fell, drove down the market value. HEC's coal investments were under-performing as well. Prices would uptick as global economies rebounded and manufacturers required more energy. HEC didn't have time. Harewood stood, turned his back on the only other man who understood the company's true state. Except Alvarez, and that bastard didn't count any longer.

No one, not even Niles Morrell, knew about Isaac's personal financial situation. He stared out the wall of windows behind his desk. He didn't care who else got burned, he wasn't going under. He deserved better than that. He spun about on one heel.

"Damn that peckerhead Alvarez."

Niles winced. "Yes, he screwed up."

"Royally. Any idiot should have known better than to pump the wells completely dry."

"Absolutely. You can't accelerate the cycling process no matter how much pressure you're under to get results."

Was Niles trying to imply it was Harewood's fault for pushing Alvarez? Harewood glared until the CFO dropped his eyes and resumed shuffling through papers.

"*Ruin* is too strong a word, Niles. In time, the chemicals will fall into the normal range." What terrible luck when the EPA tightened the standards right after Isaac bought water rights all over the country. "If only that West Virginia yahoo hadn't stuck his nose in where it didn't belong."

"Franceschi spoke at the hearing this morning. Same old corporations-are-bad song and dance. The bastard really has it in for us. I still think it might be money well spent to pay him whatever it takes to go away."

"Except we don't have that kind of cash lying around." After all, Niles had already offered Franceschi half a million and he'd refused the settlement.

Niles sighed. "Guess not. I wish I knew how Alvarez figured out the company's financial statements were altered." He shook his head. "I've gone over the originals and photocopies with a magnifying glass and I can't tell any difference. I have taken care of matters, exactly as you suggested, in case anyone else noses into our finances. I Photo-Shopped in a new post office box for the bank. All communications will come directly to me. Any online queries to the bank concerning our account will be rerouted to a dummy site."

"Good. All we need is to buy a little more time until these wells pay off."

"It'll happen," Niles said.

Harewood paused. "One more item requires your attention. I've prayed over this, but I can't see any way around my dilemma. I require temporary liquidity. I want you to handle the sale of my HEC stock options. I know I can count on your utmost discretion."

"All of it?"

"In small chunks over several days to avoid notice. Keep it as quiet and anonymous as possible. I refuse to allow anything that might damage the company. I've worked way too hard to see HEC harmed now. And let's put a temporary freeze on employees so they can't cash in their options."

"For how long?"

Harewood flung one arm out. "As long as it takes. Until these ASR wells or our fracking operations in West Virginia come through."

He walked Niles through the door into the reception area.

At her desk, Julia Lambert blinked, as if she'd been caught misbehaving. Probably making personal phone calls or Internet shopping on company time or snooping into someone else's business. A sigh escaped his lips. He closed his office door, signaling he did not want to be disturbed. He switched off the microphone on his laptop and played back the tape of Niles confessing to bank and securities fraud. He erased part of the conversation. What remained after Nile's confession was Harewood's declaration of innocence: I refuse to allow anything that might damage the company. I've worked way too hard to see HEC harmed now.

Isaac couldn't buy a better safeguard to insulate himself. If anyone was going down, it wasn't going to be him. He could count on Niles to sell off his own shares of HEC stock as well, the self-serving worm. Isaac imagined the conversation with investigators, if it came to that: I was stunned and sickened when I learned about the stock sale and the shenanigans on financial statements. This was all done behind my back. I trusted my Chief Financial Officer completely. Obviously, that trust was misplaced, and as CEO, I have to accept the blame for that.

He stroked his jaw, the bristles prickly against his fingertips. He'd have his stylist stop by after lunch and give him a touch-up. He deserved to be pampered after such a dismal morning.

3

Even from a distance Summer recognized those hot pink tennis shoes. *Gwace.* About the last person Summer expected to see outside the Earth Sciences building, and she was alone again. Coloring and wiping a snotty nose on her forearm.

At Dr. Dunham's door, Summer barged right in and addressed Ty Franceschi. "Hey, did you forget and leave something important on the bench outside?"

Claire Dunham blinked over the top of her reading glasses.

Ty's scowl was back, the same one he'd worn the first day she'd seen him outside this office. "I was just leaving."

"Ought to report you to child services." Summer said it to his back, low enough she didn't think he'd hear, but geesh, someone should report him. How could someone who cared about the environment be so reckless with a child?

"What was that all about?" Claire asked.

"That guy's little sister is sitting outside the building all alone, and she's way too little to fend for herself." Summer shook her head. "I need to talk to you about this morning's meeting."

"That's what the young man was here for, as well."

"Yeah, he gave a pretty rousing speech. Good stuff. But I think I've gotten myself into a serious mess."

Claire's eyebrows arched. "That's not like you."

Summer explained the way Harewood had pressured her to change the conclusions of her study.

"And you didn't."

"No."

"I should hope not. I could never sign off on your thesis if you doctored your findings. So what mess?"

Whew—thank heavens Summer hadn't given in to Harewood's demands. She had been right all along about Claire's ethics. Yet the financial issues remained. "I've had a full ride through college on Harewood money."

Claire's eyes widened with understanding. "You were counting on them for the Ph.D."

"Yep."

"I can pull strings. Help you find other money."

"That would be great." This would all work out. Somehow. Summer hesitated, but another matter troubled her. "I've heard from every university I applied to except MIT."

"The one you want most of all."

"Yeah. I was wondering if you knew anyone . . . if you could find out why."

"Sure. Happy to do it. I'll call and give them hell."

Claire tapped a pen—it looked expensive—on her desk.

Summer took it as a signal to leave and stood. "There sure are a bunch of high-powered folks aligned against us on these wells."

"They've been putting the squeeze on me, too. I frigging hate corporate America. University's none too happy about these results. "

Summer's stomach flip-flopped again.

"Don't worry," Claire said. "Facts are facts. The truth always wins in the end."

By the time Summer pushed open the outside door of the Earth Sciences building, Claire had reassured her that even if the worst happened, there were other scholarships and other jobs to be had. Summer cringed, recalling her professor's words: *I frigging* hate *corporate America.* Summer didn't share that view. Sure, some companies operated without concern for the environment, but others were trying to make the world better. They developed new technology like ASR wells that made more water available for people. It was all about balance and good stewardship of resources. Not all companies were like HEC.

Sunlight warmed her face and her spirits. Gorgeous day. If only she had time to get out on the water. Paddle merrily down the stream away from stress. Realistically, though, any kayak adventure would have to wait for the weekend. She hoped the good weather held.

A few yards away, Ty Franceschi sprang off the concrete bench he shared with his sister.

"We need to talk," he said.

"We do?"

"You can't call child services."

Oh. He had heard her. "Why not? Someone should be taking better care of the kid."

Ty had a swimmer's broad shoulders and tapered body. Yet all his features were swallowed by the intensity of his eyes. They hung in his face, dog-dark and sad.

"I'm all she's got," Ty said.

The words twisted Summer's heart. Wrung it out like a soaked sponge. "But—"

"It's a long story."

She glanced at her watch. "I'm meeting a friend for frozen yogurt in ten minutes. Want to come along?"

He hesitated, his hand moving toward his pocket.

Did the gesture signal embarrassment—no money? "My treat. I want to hear your story."

His eyes darted to Grace.

"This place makes a great fresh fruit sundae. Very healthy. Grace will love it, and it's right across the street."

"I can pay for us."

He walked over to retrieve his sister, leaving Summer to admire the ripple of muscles in his shoulders. His leg was injured, though, no matter how hard he tried to disguise it.

Not that she had beaucoodles of spare cash, but close examination of his and the child's clothes told her he had even less. Ty held the door to the yogurt shop open and let Summer and Dayita pass first. This gave Summer the opportunity to present the cashier with her credit card and instructed her to put everyone on her tab. All he could do after that was gracefully accept.

Ty found a booster chair in the corner and set it on a bench for Grace. She pulled on the sleeve of his tee-shirt.

"Crayons?" *Cay-ons.*

"After you eat," he said.

"Crayons?" she repeated.

He shook his head. "After you eat."

Grace pouted, and he tugged her lower lip down even further. She froze at his touch, but he seemed oblivious to her reaction.

"Eat," he said. "Then you can color."

She stuck her spoon in her sundae gingerly, as if she were certain she wouldn't like it. By the second bite, she was shoveling the yogurt and fruit in with gusto, sometimes hitting her mouth, sometimes smearing the confection on her face. She was the first to finish. Ty dabbed a napkin in his water glass and cleaned the child's face and hands. She tolerated his ministrations but clearly didn't like them.

He took crayons and coloring book out of his backpack and laid them in front of her.

Summer suggested Dayita take Grace to the next table to color. "Ty and I need to talk."

He scooted his metal chair back on the concrete, producing a horrific scraping noise. "We can talk in front of Grace. Not much penetrates her shell these days. Not since our mother died. Not since I got back from Iraq."

So Grace did have developmental issues, and Iraq explained his leg, a war injury.

Ty rested his forearms on the round café table. "It would be good if she did listen to what I have to say."

Even though her brother was talking about her, the child ignored him. Dayita's brown eyes flashed concern at Summer. "Grace, could I color with you?" she asked.

The child carefully tore out a page from the coloring book. "I don't like tigers." *Like* came out as *wike.*

Dayita chose an orange crayon and began to stripe the body. Grace colored Aladdin's blousy shirt royal blue, lemon, and apricot, each color applied in connecting triangles. Kind of a stained glass effect. If she were twenty-four, dressed in all black, and lived in a New York loft, critics would proclaim her work a break-through; insist her triangles symbolized the fragmentation of modern life.

"Grace is what—four, five?" Summer asked.

"Four."

"What on earth were you thinking leaving her alone?"

"No choice."

"Everyone has choices." Once, Summer had made the wrong choice. "She could have wandered off and drowned in the campus pool or been"—she swallowed down the memory and choked out the rest— "hit by a car." Her voice reflected her anger again. "Or gone looking for you and gotten lost. Or been kidnapped." You never know what could happen, Summer's mother had always said. Look how right she'd been about that.

"Nothing's going to happen to her. She stays put and colors."

"It's not safe to leave her alone." Stick together, Summer's mother had always said. If only Summer had obeyed.

"I have to work."

And Summer had to have ice cream on that hot afternoon when she was nine, and she left her sister alone at the ice cream truck while she bicycled home for money.

"I'm a champion babysitter," Dayita said. "I can help out some-times. I like kids."

Summer supposed she could too, but surely there had to be a more permanent solution. "You're with that environment group, Water War-riors, right? Don't they pay you enough to hire a sitter?"

"Volunteer work. We're not highly capitalized."

"Isn't there someone who can watch her? A relative?"

"Here's the Cliff's Notes version. Our father died in a car accident rushing my mother to the emergency room. She had terminal cancer, but he died first. Head injuries. She passed three days later. I was in Iraq when it happened. Grace spent two weeks in foster care before I could get home and wade through all the paperwork to retrieve her."

The child looked up and Summer could smell milk and strawberries on her warm breath. "I want to go home."

"Can't, Sugarpop," Ty said.

None of the emotions Summer expected to see crossed the child's face. Weird. Grace just wiped her runny nose on her arm and resumed coloring. Summer offered her a napkin. "Use this to blow your nose."

"That's for hands."

"Works just fine for noses, too." Summer waved the napkin under the kid's nose, but Grace ignored her, trading a yellow crayon for peacock blue. Geesh. Finally Summer wiped Grace's nose herself. The child stiffened visibly but allowed Summer to use the napkin. What caused the kid's rejection of touch?

"She colors a lot," Summer said.

Ty shrugged. "Art's in our genes. I earned extra money in high school sketching people's faces. Turned family photos into charcoal drawings for Christmas gifts lickety split. Anyway, Dad had taken out a second mortgage on the house because Mom's health insurance wouldn't cover the treatments he thought would save her life. When the interest rate increased, he couldn't make the payments. The bank foreclosed a couple of months before they died. I flew home and found a bunch of guys trashing out our house. Whatever they didn't think they could sell was scattered all over the lawn."

Summer sucked in her breath. How could life rain down all this misfortune on one family? "Where did you go?" An apartment, an aunt, an old friend—many possibilities, surely.

"I traded my car for a van. We call it home."

Grace looked up again. "I want Mommy to come home. Ty says she can't."

Ty looked as if he'd been sucker-punched.

Dayita's dark eyes filled with tears. "We have to find a better place to raise her. My mother will have suggestions."

It was the word *home*. It penetrated the fog cloaking Grace's mind every time. For a moment, no one else moved or spoke.

The world shifted beneath Summer's skin, with a softening of her bones, liquid seeping into empty spaces. Time spurted back and forth as she relived her own losses. She was nine and losing her sister—and she might as well have lost her mother—she was never the same afterward. Then when Summer was eleven, she lost her father in the divorce.

Sunlight streamed through the plate glass window of the yogurt shop, uncommonly bright, ethereal and surreal. Dust motes floated in the rays. Summer discerned the atoms that composed the fine corn silk hairs on Grace's arms.

The smell of milk and strawberries intensified until she nearly swooned. Was the aroma real or imagined?

As if she were watching the scene from above, she saw herself place her hand on Grace's shoulder. "You can't raise a kid in a van. Move in with me. It's only a one bedroom apartment, but I have a sleeper sofa. We can work it out so she has a home."

Dayita reached across the table, grasped her arm and intoned her name.

Grace hopped up from her metal chair. With one little arm, she roped herself around Summer's right arm and the other around Ty's left, forming a bridge between them. "Let's go home and Summer can be my mommy."

Acid rocketed into Summer's esophagus and she plunged back to earth. The Ph.D.! She took a deep breath. "More like a big sister. Between all of us, we can make a schedule and supervise her 24/7."

Surely they could. She could do this one good deed and still earn her degree. The tension fell away like it did at the end of a good yoga session. For the first time since her sister's death, the hole inside Summer's chest shrunk a little.

Ty rose and pulled Grace to her feet. "Grace and I are fine on our own, but thanks for the yogurt."

Yeah, fine. Wasn't as if Summer needed more to worry about anyway. The Franceschis walked away toward campus and their van. She was glad to see them go. Glad she had dodged an ill-conceived commitment.

But the slope of Ty's shoulders, his fingers linked through his sister's, those tiny pink tennis shoes slapping the pavement—they were achingly, exquisitely beautiful, and all Summer could think about was how she had failed again. Not all the monsters in this world were made of funky jelly. Some taunted little girls like Grace who were different. Some hurt little girls and left them for dead.

Some were family members who looked away until it was too late.

4

"It's me again." The voice on the phone whispered as if what they were doing was mysterious.

Okay, the man known online as The Troubleshooter—no job too big or too dirty—would play along. "You have another assignment for me?"

"Yes. About that truck and its contents?"

"Yeah?"

"I need you to move it."

"I will require a larger fee."

"This should be less complicated."

"Anything involving that truck is complicated."

"How much?"

"Double.

A few beats of silence. "Fine." Then, "If you are willing to handle a few more complications, I'll triple it."

Triple. Talking serious money now. A year or three on a tropical island all expenses paid. Who could have guessed his online posting as a troubleshooter would pay off this way? "What exactly are we talking about?"

"The job involves timing. Very little risk."

He pushed his bangs away from his eyes. "I'm listening. How much risk?" Not that it mattered. For that kind of money, The Troubleshooter would do damn near anything. Hell, anyone would.

5

The Blues Revival Band started a new set with a lively guitar riff that shifted Summer's mood.

"Screw it all," she shouted over the music to Dayita. "Screw Harewood and his wells." And screw Ty Franceschi. If he wanted his sister to think life was all about sponge bathing in the sinks at Walmart, that was his business. Summer didn't need the complication of a kid in her life. As she drained her first beer, a young man slid into the booth beside her.

"Name's Justin," he said. "Bartender says you play a mean game of foosball. I just rolled into town a month ago and need a partner."

Summer shrugged. Why not? A girl named Ellen who frequently hung out in the bar partnered with this guy who looked like a Surfer Dude. Blond, tan, baggy shorts. Summer had never seen him before.

The game commenced with whacks and slams. Justin had wavy brown bangs he kept shoving out of his eyes. Not half bad at the game, though. He scored and everyone near the table erupted in cheers. Summer caught Dayita's eye and waved. She refocused on the game. Jammed her rod left and thwacked the soccer player into the ball. It shot past Ellen's players and Surfer Boy's goalie. Score! Cheers rose from all those clustered near the table. Justin whooped and picked Summer up off the floor.

"That makes five, baby," Justin said. "Pay up, dudes."

He collected six dollars and bought Summer another Yuengling. She never bet on her own games or anyone else's and rarely paid for her own drinks. She itched to play again, but her eyes trailed over to Dayita. Better not leave her alone in the booth any longer—too rude. She slid onto the opposite bench.

Justin sauntered over with his beer and joined them. He scooted in closer this time, his thigh warm against hers. He shoveled bangs away from his face and leaned in until his nose nearly touched her. His beer-scented breath whispered against her cheek. "You're one hell of a foosball player. Really hot."

"You're pretty hot yourself." She let one hand rest on Justin's thigh.

"What else do you do for fun?" he asked.

Dayita's body jiggled almost imperceptibly. "She reads textbooks."

Summer resisted sticking out her tongue. "I play on a Frisbee team, and I kayak most weekends."

Justin nudged her shoulder with his. "No kidding. I've wanted to go kayaking ever since I moved here. Never found anyone to go with."

A river expedition came close to violating Summer's rules of avoiding relationships—but she'd planned to go out on the water tomorrow anyway. "Guess I could be your guide."

"Let's paddle the Wacissa in the morning," Justin suggested.

"Ichetucknee would be a better choice." One fork off the Wacissa led into the Slave Canal, no place for beginners.

"Friend of mine from Cincinnati said he did the Wacissa and loved it. Said I should canoe it if I got the chance—how about it?"

Dayita kicked Summer's shin under the table. "Come with me to the little girls' room."

Not a chance. No more lectures on stranger danger. "Okay, Justin, the Wacissa it is. We can meet at Goose Pasture at seven. Don't be late. Gotta get an early start."

Dayita pressed her lips together and made a point of ignoring Summer.

Girl worried too much.

Surfer Dude strolled over and leered down at Summer, way too cocksure. "How about a game of darts? Let me earn back the money I lost in foosball."

The bartender, shaking a peach frozen concoction, winked at Summer.

"I don't know," she said.

"Come on. It's only fair."

"If you insist." Summer caught Dayita's eye—and even the Ice Queen smiled.

As Summer rose to accompany Surfer Dude, she heard Justin stage-whisper to Dayita, "If she throws darts like she plays foosball, I'm putting my money on her."

"She's even better at darts," Dayita said.

Not to brag—it was true. Even with a beer buzz she could whup his ass. But afterwards she was heading home without exacting another drink from the Surfer Boy. Buzzed was one thing. Shit-faced, another. Especially if she was headed out to the water tomorrow.

6

A SHOT OF DRAMBUIE IN HIS HAND, a smiling Isaac Harewood circulated through the sixty or so guests who filled the first floor of his 22,500 square foot lakefront home. A superbly tailored Italian suit disguised the slight increase in his waistline that accompanied middle age despite intense sessions with a personal trainer. Harewood made no attempt to hide his baldness. He embraced it by shaving and oiling his scalp.

Harewood was anxious to reach his high-powered, high-heeled lobbyist Bailey Douglass. The woman drew people to her with a feline attractiveness. With that auburn hair and impressive set of hooters, she looked more like a movie star than a lobbyist—a chief reason people

underestimated her. Her cleverness and connections proved dangerous weapons in the political games played in the state capital, Tallahassee. She befriended all the key players, accurately assessed their
strengths and weaknesses, and used any tactic to win. Isaac paid an
obscene retainer to keep her on his side. She served as one of his personal lawyers as well as his company's lobbyist. This reception at his
Loblolly Lake house was her idea. An opportunity to build good will.

The university president, Howard Grice, sauntered across Harewood's marble-tiled floor. He grasped Harewood's elbow with one
hand and shook with the other. Harewood found the move amusing,
one meant to convey intimacy.

"Isaac, always a pleasure to see you. Let's lunch together soon at
the University Clubroom."

Harewood brushed off Howard's shallow enthusiasm and meaningless invitation. These academic types feigned undying love because
of his generous donations, but never really cottoned to money men.

Grice nodded toward a small bronze bust of an African American boy. "I'm impressed by your art collection. Tell me, is that an
Augusta Savage?"

"You have a good eye."

The director of Loblolly Lake Memorial Hospital, the proprietor
of a local museum, and other guests queued for the art tour. Isaac
pointed out the Clyde Butcher photographs along one wall and a Robert Rauschenberg "combine" displayed above his white leather sofa.

Dressed in a god-awful get-up with an asymmetrical hem, the museum proprietor salivated over the Rauschenberg. "Gorgeous pieces.
You have impeccable taste, and so few people do, you know."

He did indeed. Her outfit proved her point.

"Any chance you'd consider loaning your collection to us for an
exhibition?" she said.

She gazed at him with a child-like reticence. Isaac supposed the
technique got her what she wanted most of the time or she'd have developed other skills. Producing his business card, Harewood suggested
contacting his office to arrange it.

"You're a wonderful man, Mr. Harewood."

"An asset to the community," President Grice agreed. "Never misses
a Rotary meeting, and you should hear his solos in the church choir.

Why, his voice is so moving it makes the ladies cry."

The admiration gratified Harewood. Money should buy beauty and approval, just as it bought access. Too bad his father hadn't lived long enough to see how far his son had come from their rundown two-bedroom house in Pennsylvania. He hoped his father from his prime location in hell could see how wrong he'd been about Isaac's potential.

Isaac escorted the small group down a hallway lined with original watercolors and oils by lesser known artists. After an appropriate pause to let his guests study each piece, he led them back to the living room where others congregated with drinks and hors d'oeuvres.

Across the room, his secretary directed the caterers to replenish the herb-baked Apalachicola Bay oysters. Julia Lambert often served as hostess at functions. Isaac wasn't married—and had no wish to make that mistake. Marriage had ruined so many people's lives, including his own miserable parents. For sex, he preferred variety rather than stability, and plenty of willing young women leaped at the chance to satisfy his needs. And if one wasn't readily available, there was always Julia.

Through the crowd, Isaac caught the eye of Senator Felipe Vargas and inclined his head in acknowledgment. The senator, who must have arrived during the art tour, dipped a piece of Maryland-style crab cake into mango salsa and forked it to his mouth, looking properly appreciative. Before he consumed a second morsel, Bailey Douglass closed in on him. The lobbyist backed the senator into a nook by the curio cabinet that held Isaac's extensive rock and gem collection.

The university president changed the subject from art to the football team's prospects. Isaac stared over Grice's shoulder at Bailey Douglass, making eye contact with Grice often enough to hide his lack of interest in bench strength and speed statistics. Football was for Neanderthals like his father. Isaac didn't waste time on games. All the while Grice jabbered, Harewood tried to lip read what Bailey Douglass might be saying to Senator Vargas. The senator chaired the Communications, Energy, and Public Utilities committee, a man whose influence could pump millions of badly needed cash into Isaac's bank accounts.

As much money as he'd donated to the university, he expected it to shine a green light on his wells and hurry up about it. Dr. Dunham could buttress HEC's position with Senator Vargas and the Department of Environmental Protection. Her support would go a long way in convincing them to grant an exemption on arsenic levels. Everyone knew the levels of contaminants would decrease significantly over time. They nearly always did. But HEC's cash flow required immediate relief.

Harewood interrupted the university president's speculation on who would start as quarterback in the fall. "Howard, about that grant I gave your geology department. I'd appreciate your nudging the director to complete the work. It's time to put the gold stamp of approval on this project."

The president's smile grew noticeably tighter. "I'll do what I can, of course, but you are aware, I'm sure, that the academic world is quite different from the one you're used to. Professors enjoy a certain amount of independence."

Harewood stroked the charcoal ribbon of stubble along his jawline. He kept the chin strap trimmed close and neat, a counterpoint to his baldness. "Surely you underestimate your influence."

Howard's eyes flicked away, a tacit admission that the president didn't have as much control over his employees as he would like. "I'll speak to the department chair."

"I'd appreciate it."

"The Everglades plan is such a fine project. All of us at the university admire the role you've assumed in supporting these efforts to restore Florida's water system. Public-private partnerships can accomplish more than either alone. "

"Just doing my part." Harewood inwardly laughed at Grice's naiveté. The purpose of his involvement with the Glades plan was to make more water available to South Florida agriculture and developers.

Once the university vetted his wells, he was confident Senator Vargas and government agencies would approve the plan to market water to cities. They could mix his water with other sources to bring down the levels of offending chemicals. Harewood had paid Bailey Douglass to ensure the latest water board appointees were friendly to corporate interests. His motto: leave nothing to chance. Instinctively, his hand slipped into his pocket to rub the small brown stone attached to his key ring for luck. He'd found the piece of jasper at the site of his first successful natural gas well.

He couldn't lip-read what Bailey was saying. Whatever it was, Senator Vargas blushed and looked as if he wanted to be anywhere else in the room except standing next to Bailey Douglass—his discomfort caused, no doubt, by proximity to Bailey's sumptuous rack. Isaac chuckled in sympathy. Those melons of hers intimidated. They jutted out and invaded the comfort zone people preferred to keep around their bodies. Bailey's crowding the senator into a corner was a deliberate act of aggression, a way of keeping Vargas off guard. Time to rescue the senator. Wouldn't hurt to incur his gratitude. Vargas was one of the last men capable of torpedoing Isaac's plans. After downing the Drambuie, Isaac excused himself from President Grice on the pretense of fetching a refill.

Instead, he deposited his glass on the wet bar and strode across the room. "Senator, so glad you made it."

Vargas skirted around Bailey Douglass and grasped Harewood's outstretched hand. The lobbyist looked like a cat as her tongue licked her plump red upper lip. With a flash of insight, Isaac Harewood understood why he didn't quite trust her. Everyone else kowtowed before money and power. She didn't. She accepted Harewood's greenbacks. Worked hard and competently for him. But he didn't control her. No one did. She kept files on everyone. What nuggets did her files contain on him?

7

BAILEY RAN HER TONGUE OVER HER LIPS, but the moisture barely brought a moment's relief. She needed a drink. Nonalcoholic. She'd been so dry lately, even her skin felt leathery. She was only forty-one, but she wondered if she might be experiencing early menopause.

Too bad Isaac pulled the senator away when she had nearly convinced him an exemption for Isaac's wells would be in everyone's best interests. Isaac had a peculiarly bad sense of timing for a businessman. Maybe that's why he was in such deep trouble now. Much deeper than most people in his company realized, except his chief financial officer. Isaac never admitted the extent of his problems to her, but she made a habit of investigating the financial health of all her clients. In his case, she demanded payment in advance. Sooner or later, he was going to bounce checks unless his fortunes miraculously reversed out of the freefall that began with the Great Recession.

While she sipped seltzer from a martini glass, Isaac schmoozed the senator. Vargas was an odd bird. His wife Ana, a brunette decked out in a cardinal red cocktail dress that flaunted her figure, seemed like the ideal politician's wife.

"You're a lucky man," Bailey had told the senator a few moments ago, "to have such a gorgeous wife." The senator had actually blushed and discomfort flickered in his eyes. Riding one of those weird hunches she sometimes got, Bailey added, "Senator, I suspect you're more at home in the company of men than women." The words could have been interpreted many ways. That he spent a lot of time legislating with his pals. That he was more at home hunting quail with the fellows than drinking tea at fundraisers. From the way he took a step backward, Bailey knew her comment meant something else to Vargas.

She eased his discomfort. "Like on a baseball field. Wasn't that a photograph of your handsome son on the pitcher's mound in Sunday's newspaper?"

The relief on Vargas's face was palpable. "Yes, Manny loves baseball."

They had discussed water regulations until Isaac drew the senator away, leaving Bailey to study Ana Vargas and wonder about the state of their marriage. Like Bailey, Ana turned heads.

When Bailey was a teenager, she got pissed off because boys stared, drooling, at her chest. In junior high, a clique of boys—and even two girls, the traitors!—had followed her from school, calling out every word they knew for tits and some she was sure they had made up. She'd run home crying to her grandmother.

Bailey still remembered the lecture: "You wipe those tears away and don't you dare cry over little piss-ants ever again, you hear me? Those girls are jealous and the boys would faint dead away if you so much as let them hold your hand. You're smarter than those kids. Know your assets, Bailey. Use them. Your real power is here." Her grandmother tapped her forehead. "Many will never see you for who you are. And if they don't, they deserve to lose."

At the time, Bailey only half understood what her grandmother was talking about. It became clear in high school. She joined the debate team and witnessed the shock in her opponents' eyes when a big-busted redhead trashed their arguments with cool logic. The same magic worked in law school and later in trials. But it was in her own lobbying firm, Douglass and Associates, that she truly mustered her assets to acquire power.

As Ana Vargas laid long red nails on the university president's jacket sleeve, Bailey intuited Ana liked power too, but the senator's wife chose to experience it vicariously through the men around her.

Bailey's mobile vibrated in her tiny clutch purse. She moved to the foyer and turned her back on the party guests to answer. Treela, one of her investigators, spoke breathlessly, as if she'd been running. "We've encountered a little problem concerning the engineer."

"Oh? Why don't we meet in an hour to discuss it?" She phrased it as a question but Treela would understand it wasn't debatable. "At the branch office in Loblolly Lake."

A hand clamped on Bailey's shoulder, and she closed the phone. She swiveled smoothly to face the owner of the hand—and remove it from her body at the same time. "Governor! I'm so glad to see you."

The most powerful man in Florida—at least, that's what Shane Armistead thought he was—brushed a kiss onto her forehead and laughed. "Is that right? What do you want from me now, Bailey?"

"What makes you think I want anything?"

"You always do. Let me guess. You want me to veto that bill decreasing Medicaid payments for disabled citizens. Or the law we're passing because it will help the little schoolchildren but you have decided it is evil? Who are you representing this time? Sit down and tell me all about it."

She let him lead her to the leather couch, his hand against the small of her back. Inwardly she was tickled over insider knowledge even the governor didn't have. She had successfully lobbied certain senators to strip the worst reductions out of that Medicaid bill. They'd vanished, thank heavens, in no small part thanks to the AARP's payments to Douglass and Associates. Some of her work benefitted society. Some didn't. She figured it balanced out, and if not, it balanced her checkbook.

"Governor, you're not known as a friend of regulations."

He chuckled. "True in general. What regulation are we talking about, little lady?"

Unbelievable, that people had elected the man. But Bailey smiled. If she seriously wanted something from Shane Armistead, she would tell him where to stuff the little lady crap. She had a file detailing illegal business practices that government regulators had suspected, but failed to find sufficient evidence to bring the man to trial. Or he kissed the right behind or greased the right palms. Didn't matter. Her investigators had solid proof of fraudulent billing involving government construction projects.

The governor's twenty-something son provided another convenient tool. In a burst of entrepreneurial spirit, he formed a partnership with Harewood's CFO Niles Morrell. Together they were funding grow factories throughout the state. Wanted to be the first to snag licenses when marijuana went legal in Florida as it had in other states. These tidbits Bailey had gleaned from a rival lobbyist. He was laying the groundwork for legalization with campaign contributions, including Governor Armistead's. Shane Armistead wouldn't want that bit of intel to go viral. Nor would the deputies paid to look the other way. So interesting, living in the Sunshine State.

For now she would tolerate the governor's eyes gawking at her chest. He was just another piss-ant, like Isaac Harewood.

"I'm concerned about those regulations in the Safe Drinking Water Act that inhibit business growth and food production," she said.

The governor laughed. "Who's paying you to worry about business, food, and water regulations?"

"You know the answer. Your campaign is familiar with my client's generosity."

He did a bit of play-acting and winced. "Ouch. How do you lobbyists sleep at night?"

"On the finest 700-thread-count Egyptian cotton sheets." Much better than politicians. She kept a penthouse apartment in downtown Tallahassee, but whenever possible she preferred to sleep in her lakefront retreat here in Loblolly Lake, an hour's remove from the capital.

Her home was nowhere near as large as Isaac Harewood's, but it was more than she needed and the title was free and clear, paid for in full by those who could afford the services of Douglass and Associates. She had her own opinions, her own values, but she had learned to set them aside where money was involved. She used her assets. Her grandmother would be proud.

She bid all the piss-ants goodbye and drove to her office. Treela

Timms was waiting.

A light brown stain that matched her skin streaked her investigator's white blouse. Uncharacteristic. Treela was usually the embodiment of cool perfection.

"Fill me in," Bailey said. "I gather you have bad news."

Treela crossed her arms, making a shelf under her ample bosom. "I tore the place apart and put it back together again. Didn't find the envelope or the photos."

Bailey frowned.

"It gets worse," Treela said. "I think the landlady spotted me leaving."

Bailey swore softly, then suppressed her anger. Long ago in law school she learned emotions got in the way of logic.

"She didn't see my face," Treela added.

Thank God for one piece of good news. They'd scoot by this one unscathed.

FIVE

Saturday

I

SUMMER LAID HER PADDLE across the rim of the cockpit so she could tighten the scrunchie holding her ponytail. She took a deep breath, resolving not to waste one more moment of the day wondering what happened to Justin. She'd driven all the way out here, waited half an hour, and where was he? Probably still asleep. Or maybe he'd been intimidated by the way she threw darts. Whatever. Abandonment was her reward for being nice and changing her plans to accommodate a guy she barely knew.

Nor would she worry about her thesis defense. The rest of her Saturday morning excursion would require intense exertion because without Justin, she was going to veer away from the beginner's course they would have taken together.

Morning light shimmered on the shallow green water, creating an illusion of serenity. Near the bank, a limpkin, long-legged and brown, stood perfectly still in the bulrushes. She whipped out her camera, focused, and captured the bird, water lapping gently in the foreground.

Directly across from the sign marking the entrance to the Slave Canal, a dead tree limb jutted over the Wacissa River. The wind rustled through a stand of wild rice to her left. Just ahead a swallow-tailed kite swooped down to snatch a fish from the water. Mullet. Summer had seen flotillas of them knifing by. Overhead the faint buzz of a small plane's engine intruded, a sound she welcomed because it made the silence that followed all the more profound. Though *silence* wasn't the right word. The river and marshes were awash in crackles and clicks and grunts and splashes if you listened for them.

Scraggly cypress and saw palmettos pressed closer to her kayak as the passage narrowed. She flinched as a gator on the bank to her left leapt into the water with a bone-chilling splash three feet ahead of her bow. She kept her paddle out of the water as the reptile swam beneath her kayak. Summer willed her shoulders to relax. The gator hadn't intended to charge her. It was just relocating to the water where it felt safer. It followed her a few yards before swimming toward the bank.

The air hung dense and thick with the smells of growth and decay, the continuous cycle that powered the factory of the swamp. Summer wasn't sure what compelled her to confront Old Florida. Florida the way the natives knew it, with bears, turtles, cottonmouths, and fist-sized skeeters. As she maneuvered her kayak down the channel, she thought about the slaves who dug limestone boulders out of the swamp to create the passageway between the Wacissa and Aucilla Rivers in the 1800s. Their ghosts played hide and seek among the cypress and sniggered at those who challenged the water. It had never been deep enough for commerce, so the slaves got the last laugh. After several hurricanes blew down trees, which now lay every-which-way across the passage, kayakers were forced into constant scrambles under and portages over logs when the water was low. The canal was a challenging passage—precisely why Summer liked it.

She rounded the first bend, her paddle slurping as it dragged the water. In front of her lay the trunks of two toppled trees, crossed like giant pick-up sticks. The gap between the wood and water near the left bank appeared to be about two and a half feet, just enough. If she misjudged the opening's depth, she would scrape her face. She leaned back flat against the deck, became one with her kayak, and glided beneath the trees, the bark inches above her nose. She held her breath. Her eyes darted sideways, watching for water moccasins curled in the branches, but she saw only the lacy fronds and dark spores of resurrection fern imbedded in the bark.

Paddling on, she could see every rock and pebble along the bottom, magnified by water just inches deep, the result of recent drought. Minnows and tadpoles darted about in search of meals in the moving shadows cast by Spanish moss draped overhead. A snake no bigger than her finger wriggled through the water.

Ahead, three trees crisscrossed the canal. Summer back-paddled to study the banks. An alligator lay half submerged in the muck on the far side of the trees, its eyes and cobbled tail visible. Gators were generally shy creatures as long as you left them alone. This one didn't move, but the six-footer sensed her presence. The creatures were capable of short bursts at thirty miles an hour on land. Capable of drowning large mammals like herself. The sensible choice would be to turn back. There was no one for miles around who could help if she slipped and broke a leg going over the trees. No one would know if the gator charged before she could climb into her kayak on the other side.

A deep-throated cackle rose from the scrub. A great white egret she had disturbed, but her imagination heard a slave spirit's challenge: *You scared? You should be.*

No way, she answered. *I've conquered this place dozens of times, dozens.*

Summer angled the kayak against the pile, its bow in the air, the stern in the water. She scrambled onto the top trunk. She could have thrown a rock at the gator, scared it off. She didn't. With both hands, she eased the kayak up until it teetered beside her for a few seconds. It splashed into the water on the far side. The current, though gentle, teased the kayak downstream. Welcoming the rush of blood to her brain, she leapt from the log to the side of the kayak away from the gator. She sloshed a few noisy steps and in seconds pulled herself into the cockpit.

She whooped. Listened to the echo. Whooped again and paddled on, her breath coming ever faster as she completed dozens of slide-unders and even more portages over the course of the next three hours. Frogs croaked from the saw palmettos, and the memory of a childhood song, "Froggie went a-courtin', and he did ride, uh-huh" brought a smile to her face. No swords or pistols by these froggies' sides, but they were horny little devils, singing their chorus and searching for mates.

The song reminded Summer of being stood up, and the river's spell was broken. Then the Harewood tests, which formed the basis for her master's thesis, shoved their way to the front of her head. She had to defend in a week. If Summer's test results caused the college to lose the grant, her other committee members might not look kindly on her thesis conclusions, despite Claire's support. The university was laying off professors, even tenured ones. Jettisoning whole departments. Claire's job or the whole geology department might be on the line.

Didn't matter. Claire had taught her only the science mattered. And the science said Harewood's water wasn't ever going to be drinkable unless it underwent expensive processing after withdrawal.

Without Harewood's money, Summer may have to flip burgers, but she would become Dr. Cassidy. Nothing would stand in her way.

Since she had a long paddle back, she turned around. The breeze was with her, allowing easier upstream paddling than usual, though the difficulty of the ins, the outs, the scrambles up, the jumps down increased with her exhaustion.

As she paddled the last curve before the exit from the canal, a shrill cry like a girl in distress rose above the cypress from deep within the marsh. For an instant, Summer froze. Her heart responded instinctively: *Chrissie, I'm coming!*

Summer waited, listening for seconds that stretched interminably in an aching journey through inner space. The only answer was a car whispering down the distant highway. The soft sound faded away. Summer gave her head a little shake. The cry belonged to a limpkin, of course. She knew that.

Goose Pasture and her truck came into sight. The sun lay low in the sky and her muscles were strained. By the time she secured her kayak on top of the truck, it was almost six. She was fully charged, revved up.

A breeze from the swamp delivered a whiff of rot that hadn't been present in the morning. A torn sack of garbage lay on the edge of puddled water. You had to be kidding. People who came here generally treated the area with respect. They came here because they loved the outdoors and attempted to leave behind only footprints. She dug an empty trash bag out of the back of her truck and scooped the contents in the new sack. But nothing in this mess caused the stench that overpowered all else.

Overhead to her left, a turkey vulture circled and then dove, its bald red head barely visible on its descent. Something dead decayed near the edge of the swamp. Vultures were the only birds with a sense of smell. Though many people hated vultures, she admired them. They were as necessary as garbage men. They kept the world clean, part of nature's fine balance.

The tall grasses appeared crushed as though a log or an animal had been dragged through them. The stench that had drawn the bird caused her to breathe only through her mouth. Her tennis shoes sank into the muck as she pushed past a clump of saw palmetto for a closer look. She expected to find a deer carcass.

A cry rose in her throat and one hand involuntarily flew to her mouth, the other to her abdomen to restrain its violent churning. She whirled around, whipped through the grass, leaped inside her truck and slammed the lock down. Her hands gripped the wheel so tight they hurt, yet on some level she was aware if she eased the pressure even a little, she would find that her fingers were shaking. A floating sensation took hold, as though she were watching herself in the scene from a distance. Eventually she became aware of the heaving of her chest and shoulders. *You're hyper-ventilating. That's why you're light headed. Slow it down.*

Deep, slow breaths brought her back in control. She analyzed what she had seen. The vulture, a speck of flesh already in its beak, had hissed, whooshed off to the limb of a longleaf pine. Waiting. A man's bloodless face stared unseeing at the sky. Summer had been so close she could see blow flies clustered on his eyes; two teetered on angular, thread-thin legs around his gaping mouth. Their presence meant he'd been dead for a couple of days.

Visualizing those flies convulsed her stomach. The man's face morphed into her sister's. Then back to the man. Then Chrissie. The images flashed in rapid succession. Again, she forced her breathing to slow. Blanked her mind. They weren't the same. They weren't. There hadn't been flies on her sister. Or vultures. She cocked her head to watch another bird descending. Her hands shook as she reached for her cell phone.

2

GEORGE THEOFANIS POKED A FORK into the chicken and cranberry salad and savored the tang of balsamic dressing for the briefest moment before he was interrupted by that jackass Burns.

"Oh, little boy, Granny wants to talk to you."

He flipped Burns a bird and took his time depressing the number two that would connect him to Mrs. Montera. He'd already told her he had no information on her boarder's whereabouts. A little perfunctory checking had produced zip.

Man was illegal, and those who might help them locate him weren't talking, either trying to protect him or themselves. A receptionist at Harewood Corporation, where Mrs. Montera claimed he worked, said they'd never heard of him.

Theofanis frowned as he pressed the phone harder to his ear—as if that was going to help him interpret Isadora Montera's broken English. "The truck showed up but no Mr. Alvarez?" he repeated back to her.

"*Sí*, his truck here, but no him."

"Someone must have given him a ride then. Probably a girlfriend, like I said before."

"No, no girlfriend."

"You can't know that."

"I know. No girlfriend. Paulo work for bad people. He say they up to no good. You talk to them."

Burns tapped him on the shoulder and grunted.

Like it wasn't hard enough to understand the old woman without pig noises in his other ear. "Not now," Theofanis said.

"You might want to hear what came in on the scanner."

Theofanis muted the phone. "What?"

"Anonymous tip to the sheriff's office. Body found at Goose Pasture. Hispanic. Not like we get many bodies around here. Might be Granny's missing guy. Seems to match her description."

Great. No dinner with jurisdiction squabbles for dessert—the perfect Saturday night. "Who's responding for them?"

"Ash and Kendricks."

Ash. The first bit of good news of the evening. He and DeAndre Ash met frequently for drinks at the Tall Timbers bar. That nice wife of his had invited him to share dinner at their house several times. Ash was the only guy in the Sheriff's Office that wasn't a total dick. Theofanis told Mrs. Montera he'd call her back. She was insulting him when he broke the connection.

"Let's go."

3

SUMMER GLARED AT THE DEPUTY, the one with the penguin body. "I told you exactly eight times, I don't know the guy. I've never seen him before."

"And yet there's only one vehicle—yours." The deputy waddled over closer to her and stopped, his head tilting to one side. "Kind of odd, don't you think?"

"Easy, Kendricks," the cherub-faced police officer said. Theofanis. George Theofanis, he'd told her his name was. "Give Miss Cassidy a break. She's trying to be a good citizen."

"You know what I think?" Kendricks didn't wait for a response. "She's out here on a date and the guy makes a stupid blunder—the kind guys are always making—like telling her about this other chick he's been seeing—and this nice young lady whops him on the head with that kayak paddle. And who can blame her?"

Summer scrunched her face. "A bright guy like you can figure out that man has been dead for days."

"It's true, Kendricks." The cherub shook his head. "That guy smells worse than you after you hit the gym."

Deputy Kendricks sniffed and pointedly turned his head toward the other deputy, who looked like the Green Hulk, only he was black. "Let me finish. She never dreams it's going to do permanent damage—let alone kill him. So she drives off. She figures, let the jackass walk home. See how he likes that. She drives off and comes back after he doesn't show up for work or for class or whatever. When she sees he's dead, she calls us. It's not like she doesn't have feelings. She doesn't want to see her boyfriend eaten by buzzards. She's a nice girl who wants his mother to be able to bury him."

Was this guy a moron, or what? "Looks like he was shot in the chest, not whacked in the head. I doubt if whoever did it expected him to go to work. Anyway, you're welcome to check my kayak paddle for blood."

An officer identified by Theofanis as Burns crow-walked over to them, his chest thrust out. "Found his wallet. Name's Paulo Alvarez. There's one of those electronic gate keys that says Harewood Energy Corporation on it."

For a few beats Summer couldn't breathe. Burns described the rest of the wallet's contents, but his words became background buzz, an accompaniment to the night insects' scritching and wing-singing. Summer's head felt weightless.

"Anything else, Burns?" Theofanis asked.

Burns held out a plastic bag containing a beer bottle like he expected a gold medal. "Found this near the body. Probably tossed out by a fisherman long time ago, but we'll check it for prints."

The bottle had a distinctive script and eagle on the label. Yuengling. Summer's brand. She swayed from one foot to the other. This couldn't be happening. Justin's face surfaced in her mind. She could see him pushing his bangs out of his eyes. Heard him insisting on the Wacissa trip. The deputy would find her fingerprints on that bottle—she knew it.

She closed her eyes and took three deep yoga breaths, blanking out Justin and Harewood, erasing the bloated body, expelling the fetid odor. Her heart rate slowed. Enough of this shit. She turned toward her truck. "You guys have any more questions, call me. I'm going home."

The nice cop accompanied her to her vehicle. "Don't let their questions upset you." He opened for her and closed it once she was settled inside. He stood watching her, his hands cupped over the open window.

She gripped the wheel and closed her eyes. "Did he suffer?"

"No, I don't think so."

She nodded and as soon as he took a step away, she raised the window. She drove back to the highway, her eyes flicking to the rear view mirror every few seconds to be sure no one was tailing her. A few miles down the road, she pulled over to the shoulder, set the brake, and rested her head on the steering wheel. Her stomach heaved. The body hadn't been there when she arrived at Goose Pasture that morning. She would have noticed the odor. Would have seen the crushed grass.

Her eyes closed. Somewhere in Loblolly Lake at least one innocent-looking person pushed a grocery store cart and pumped gas from a rubber hose like everyone else. Drank beer at the Foos and Booze. Someone who looked like ordinary folks but had hidden fangs.

Who the hell was Justin? What had she gotten herself into?

Six

Sunday

I

DRAGON'S BREATH—HER OWN—WOKE SUMMER UP Sunday morning. Her eyes cracked halfway open. Oh man, not good. She shuttered them against the light. She tried to swallow, but her tongue had the texture of thick felt. Ironic how last night's drinking led to this morning's dry mouth. She'd had four or five glasses of wine.

Pressure right behind her forehead—painful, but she'd done worse damage to herself on other occasions. Now that she was conscious, she remembered the blowflies executing their thin-legged dance steps across the dead man's mouth. The bagged bottle of Yuengling.

Her eyes flew open again, replacing the images with the safety of her bedroom. She stumbled to the bathroom. With a toothbrush she slew the dragon in her mouth and anointed her face with that most precious of all resources. Water.

If she were going to do battle in the world today, she needed food. Desperately. Eyes half closed, she shambled barefoot to the kitchen.

"Yiii—" She stifled the yelp of surprise.

Dayita Patel sat at the kitchen table with a cup of coffee. "Good morning."

The end of the evening came back to Summer. As soon as she got home, she had called her friend. Dayita had insisted on spending the night on Summer's couch. "Not necessary," Summer remembered saying. Dayita's response: "I think of you as my sister."

That disturbed Summer almost as much as finding the dead body. Summer only had one sister, and she was gone. Dayita was a good friend—her only real friend—but you couldn't replace a sister.

For someone in yesterday's clothes, Dayita looked disgustingly well put-together. Her freshly braided black hair trailed down the back of one of Summer's armless swivel chairs all the way to her waist. She even had applied fresh make-up, evidence of the miniature beauty shop packed inside that hobo-style purse.

"Yogurt a week past its use-by date is all I could find in your fridge for breakfast," Dayita said, a trace of accusation in her voice, "but I made you coffee."

"Thanks. We'll go out to eat soon as I shower."

Half an hour later at their favorite Mexican restaurant, Dayita sat opposite her, sipping black coffee and eating a scrambled egg—one measly egg—all she would order because she was dieting again.

"You okay?" Dayita asked.

Summer shrugged. "Yeah, last night's wine helped." She didn't even like wine, but she couldn't even look at a bottle of Yuengling yet. It would only remind her of the mess she was in. She struggled to swallow another mouthful of sausage and egg burrito. "I have to figure out what it all means. Justin doesn't show up, so I go out on the water alone. When I come back, I find the body of a guy who has a gate key in his wallet from Harewood. A Yuengling bottle is found nearby. It can't be coincidence."

Dayita set down her coffee so hard it sloshed onto the table. "How many times have I told you that you are too trusting of guys?"

Had to get in another I-told-you-so, didn't she? Sometimes Dayita sounded more like a mother than a friend.

Dayita held out her hand. "Give me your cell."

"What for?"

Dayita wiggled her fingers impatiently until Summer complied. Dayita tapped the screens on Summer's phone and her own for a few minutes. "As long as you have your phone with you, I'll know where you are."

One side of Summer's mouth lifted in disgust before she realized how obvious her disapproval must be. She neutralized her expression, but surely Dayita realized Summer was not the kind of person who needed to tweet her location and mundane activities to "friends" every few minutes and she had no tolerance for those who did.

Dayita rotated the satellite map on her screen toward Summer. "Chill. I linked our phones on Google Latitude, so if you get in trouble, I'll be able to find you. A safety precaution. Promise I'll never use it unless I have to. Let me show you how it works."

"No need. I'll figure it out." Creeped her out to think someone could spy on her that way. Tech toys, as well as friends, needed boundaries. First chance Summer got, she'd remove whatever linked their phones. "I need to find out if Justin is connected to Harewood."

"What did you say his last name was?"

"Freese, or something like that."

Dayita searched the university student and social networking sites. She tried Friese, Frieze, Fry and other variations, but no men in the right age group turned up.

Because he'd mentioned Cincinnati, Summer googled his name and Ohio, but that search didn't uncover any possibilities. They were making too much of this. Guys ditched girls all the time, especially girls they barely knew. Especially when the invitation was issued after a few drinks. She'd studied probability theory in a physics class. Coincidences happened way more often than people realized.

Yet the other side of that theory prickled Summer's skin. Humans are extremely good at noticing data that could have an underlying common cause. That, she remembered, was from a journal article by MIT cognitive scientist Josh Tennebaum. We learn nearly all language through the brain's ability to make connections from coincidence. By the third or fourth time a woman appears in front us and says the word "Mama," we associate the word with her.

More than one scientific discovery had come about because of the brain's ability to link seemingly disparate events. Her brain was connecting these events for a reason, but she couldn't prove a connection. At least not yet.

She pocketed her phone. "Better shove off or we'll be late."

They were the last of nine young women to arrive at the Recreational Sports Complex. They comprised the intramural Ultimate Frisbee team.

Summer and Dayita had met at an Ultimate Frisbee camp the summer between sixth and seventh grade. A camp both attended on needs-based scholarships. For reasons Summer couldn't totally explain, she let Dayita past the barrier she maintained with other girls. She knew it was partly because Dayita hadn't withered like others when they realized Summer could quote from books verbatim.

For half an hour they practiced throws, with Summer and Dayita guiding the newbies.

Summer grasped one of the newcomers by the elbow. "Hold your forearm still. The only movement you should make is with your wrist. Keep the disc level."

They worked on aiming the elbow at the target and executing a wrist snap. When Summer demonstrated her skill at hitting a disc golf basket and zipping the disc through slim horizontal targets, a newbie accused her of being a sharpshooter.

"You haven't seen anything yet." Dayita handed Summer a pen. "You're looking at the Annie Oakley of the Frisbee world. Never misses. Come on, Summer; show them how it's done."

Heat rose to Summer's face.

"Come on," Dayita said. The others chimed in until Summer relented and whipped the pen at the target.

"Awesome!" one said. The girls took out whatever they could find in their backpacks. A ruler. A penlight. A flash drive. She nailed the target every time. Big deal. Not exactly a skill in hot demand, though it did come in handy when she played darts. Surfer Dude had taken his loss gracefully, but maybe Justin had been turned off. Or was he connected to Harewood? If only she knew for sure.

Then came the part of practice Summer liked best. Scrimmage. She ran the length of the field, wind lifting her hair, her legs and heart pumping. She leapt in the air to catch tosses sailing her way, her vertebrae stretched to full length. She ran and ran—no time for anything but the exhilaration of exertion, of a body maxed out. Blood filled every cell with bliss—okay, only endorphins kicking in—but better than doing drugs. She ran and she ran and she ran, and a river of blood coursed through every part of her body and she felt so alive. She would miss this when she graduated and moved on.

For two hours Summer didn't see the dead man's face or wonder if he had an anxious family waiting for his return. For two hours she didn't think about her sister Chrissie. For two whole hours she forgot about how much trouble she might be in.

SEVEN

Monday

I

THE SMELL OF EXPENSIVE LEATHER and high quality furniture wax in Isaac Harewood's waiting room made John Hu's skin itch with desire. Harewood's receptionist sat at a mahogany desk with string inlay. The top was covered in tooled red leather. Certainly the university didn't buy furnishings this expensive. Artistic black and white close-ups of unusual plants and animals lined the walls. The way the photographer captured light and shadow reminded him of Ansel Adams. Quality oriental rugs lay on the floor, not the tawdry commercial-grade wall-to-wall installed in his office. Hu dreamed of working someplace like this.

Fat chance, with that stubborn witch Claire Dunham refusing to reword her findings. He wished he was permitted to pass along what Howard Grice had told him in confidence. Two tenured positions axed from science and two more from the art side of the college. Adjuncts let go. Teaching loads likely to double. This meant less time for research and even fewer dollars for the university, since research brought in money. Hu came out of the meeting with Grice worried about his own job. His Porsche still had three years of payments, and he had talked his wife into a bigger house financed with a mortgage worth more than the house would sell for in today's market. He felt as if he were treading water and his calves were cramping.

Dunham was a notorious grind. She worked late into the evening and on weekends and expected the same of her students. Unbending when a student pled for a better grade. She wasn't going to bend on this report either. Grice insisted on talking to her himself, but the president didn't understand what she was like. Authority figures didn't intimidate her at all.

The grad assistant who'd run the tests played handball with Claire Dunham every week—were they having an affair? If so, he could use the scandal against them. Hu had to cement this connection with Harewood. This was his chance for a lucrative private sector job.

By the time Harewood granted entrance to his inner chamber, Hu was ready to lick dirt from the CEO's Italian dress shoes if that's what it took. Instead, for the first time in years, he found it difficult to think in English. He stumbled over the simplest words as he explained Dunham's report.

Harewood flicked a speck of lint from the sleeve of his hand-tailored suit. "You're her boss?"

"Yes . . . no . . . in a way." He sounded so lame. "Universities don't function quite like business. Academic freedom is highly valued."

"Freedom is over-rated. Most people like to be told what to do. Choice only confuses them. Perhaps you need to tell this woman how to word the report."

"That would not be possible." The idea of anyone telling Dunham what to do was laughable. Harewood didn't have a clue what working in a university was like. Secretaries, salesmen, and junior executives tolerated being ordered around because they had little choice. But every professor Hu had ever met possessed supreme confidence in their views because of their advanced degrees. And Dunham knew what she was doing. A damn fine scientist, one hampered by a stubborn refusal to acknowledge the reality of university operations today. Sometimes you had to compromise to get funding. Why couldn't Dunham grasp that? The grant report would disclose the possible conflict of interest. Readers could draw their own conclusions.

Harewood stood and strode over to his ceiling-to-floor window wall. It looked down upon a fountain in a lushly landscaped courtyard. He ran his fingers over a mosaic-topped table that stood by the window as if he cherished the stones. They glistened in the sunlight—almost as much as the man's slick head.

It took tremendous effort of will for John Hu not to touch his own smooth chin as Harewood stroked his facial hair. Playing with that beard before speaking appeared to be one of the man's eccentricities.

"You'd be surprised what is possible, Dr. Hu. I was hoping to do business together in the future, but perhaps you don't share my vision for Florida."

Harewood's money was dripping through his fingers like drops of water. Hu's hands formed fists as if to grasp this opportunity. "Oh, but I do. You're a genius. Public-private partnerships are the wave of the future, and your plan for the Everglades is brilliant. It is an honor, sir, to work with you."

What Hu was going to do was unscrupulous. Regrettable, but he had no choice. "I can't force Dr. Dunham to change her report, but I want to help you achieve your remarkable vision to solve Florida's water problems. There might be a way to persuade her to see these wells from a businessman's perspective."

For the first time during the meeting Harewood smiled. He pivoted away from the window.

"Do tell."

2

ISAAC HAREWOOD PRACTICALLY SHOVED JOHN HU out of his office. What a potentially lethal piece of ammunition Hu had delivered! Perhaps HEC should hire a bigshot like the dean. The prestige and university connections would benefit the corporation in ways he was only beginning to appreciate—even if he didn't really like academics. They rarely understood the real world.

Isaac ran his fingertips over the mosaic-topped table for luck before flipping open his mobile. Wouldn't do for Julia Lambert to listen in on this conversation.

One quality Isaac Harewood admired about Bailey Douglass, besides her tits, was her ability to get things done.

"Bailey, we have a problem."

"Honey, you might have a problem. I don't. I make problems go away."

The woman's throaty voice reeked of sugar, but Isaac had witnessed the ruthless nature that lay beneath that Southern drawl. "Cut the crap."

"Aren't we in a pissy mood today."

He imagined how those auburn eyebrows raised while she said

the words—a statement, not a question— but he didn't have time for pointless banter. "Dunham won't bend, but Dr. Hu might have provided me with the leverage we need to change her mind. Get your investigators to check out Summer Cassidy. She's one of Dunham's students. See if there's anything embarrassing about their relationship."

In the pause that followed, Harewood heard her breathing.

"These days it's difficult to embarrass anyone."

"Find something. Anything you can use against Dunham. Everyone has dirt under their nails. Mishandled funds. Cheating scandals. Illegal drugs. I want this problem to go away."

"How far do you want me to go to remove this problem?"

"Do whatever it takes."

3

"WHAT'S UP?" SUMMER ASKED. Her mother rarely phoned, only when her pill-induced fog receded enough for her to remember she had a daughter who inhabited the world of the living.

"What's up? I've called your number all day. You discovered a dead body, that's what's up. How can you even ask me that?"

Summer flopped onto her flowered bedspread, one her mother had chosen. It looked like something for a grade-schooler. "How'd you find out?"

"Not from you, that's for sure."

Her mother sounded peeved. Like she needed to take one of her pills.

"Mrs. Patel called and I had to pretend as if I knew what she was talking about and of course I didn't because you confided in your friend's mother instead of your own."

Dayita had a big mouth. Told her mother everything. "You get hysterical over the least little things."

"I'm not hysterical. I'm concerned about you."

Right. Concerned. As if her mother was ever concerned about anything besides her charitable foundation.

"What were you doing on the river alone, anyway, Summer? You've always been too reckless, too wild. I just don't understand the things you do." She paused, and Summer wondered if her mother had remembered she was supposed to be acting concerned, not critical.

"Mrs. Patel thinks the discovery might have upset you. Of course it would upset anyone, but she seemed to think it might have upset you more—more than most people."

Upset more than most people. Those words danced awfully close to her mother's forbidden topic of Chrissie. "I'm fine."

"What about MIT? Have you heard anything yet?"

"No." Her acceptances still were only from the University of California-Santa Barbara; Penn State; Cornell; the University of Oregon, near her father; and right here at Florida Sci-Tech. She wasn't used to failing at anything academically. Why didn't MIT want her?

"I have to leave for Denver in the morning. Are you going to be all right?"

"I'm fine."

"I'll cancel if you need me. You aren't going to be arrested, are you?"

Summer grabbed a pillow and positioned it under her head, her legs bent at the knee and dangling off the side of the bed.

"Why would I be arrested? I found a body and reported it. End of story. Nothing to tell. Have a nice trip."

She closed the phone. Her mother was always tripping—to Denver, to Miami, to Kansas City. Any place that would let her raise money for the Chrissie Cassidy Bicycle Safety Foundation. And if she wasn't tripping to a big city, she was tripping on Elavil or Paxil or Xanax. Sometimes she tripped both ways at the same time. Everyone understood. Everyone felt sorry for her.

So Summer had found a body and reported it. End of story. Nothing to tell.

Except when she closed her eyes and tried to sleep, the dead man's face imprinted itself on the inside of her eyelids. She saw the flies, and then the face would morph into Chrissie, then the man, then Chrissie.

Nothing to tell, except that deputy had called her again, asking questions he thought clever. Only they weren't. *How long had she known Alvarez? Was Alvarez going to go public with information that would undercut her thesis and prevent her from graduating? Would she mind coming in and being fingerprinted?*

And the cops had visited the Foos and Booze and quizzed Tom, her bartender buddy. Kendricks—the one who looked like a penguin—had shown Tom a photo of the dead guy. Tom assured the deputy

Paulo Alvarez had never set foot in the place. But he'd also told them Yuengling was Summer's brand.

4

GEORGE THEOFANIS PROPPED HIS FEET ON HIS DESK AS HE PROMISED ALVAREZ'S LANDLADY the police were looking into Harewood Energy Corporation, the bad men who employed Alvarez. Her words, not his. The detective's promise didn't satisfy the insistent woman, but he managed to end the phone call when a stack of papers dropped near his mousepad. Theofanis didn't have to turn around to figure out his liaison from the sheriff's office, DeAndre Ash, stood behind him. The big guy's rasping breath gave him away. If Ash didn't stop smoking, he was going to die early. Ex-football player. You'd think he'd know better. Theofanis raised his brows, asking an unspoken question.

Ash's smile was earnest and proud. "Harewood's quarterly filings with the IRS. Guess what?"

"Out with it, Ash, before you drop dead from those cancer sticks."

The smile widened to expose even more of Ash's slightly yellowed teeth. "Isaac Harewood is damn near bankrupt. The bank is ready to put his yacht in foreclosure—"

"Aw, you're breaking my heart."

"Months in arrears on house payments—"

"That's no house, it's a museum. You seen that place?"

"—lost a fortune—two fortunes—in the market, way behind on taxes."

"Follow the money—that usually provides answers," Theofanis said. "Alvarez's body was dumped out there. The girl didn't do it." Pain had wracked the girl's face when she asked if Alvarez had suffered. Her mother, Jordan Cassidy, had asked the same question when her daughter died in that hit and run. He had no idea if victims suffered or not, but he told the survivors what they needed to hear.

Ash rested his big haunch right on top of the papers he'd laid on Theofanis's desk. "Yeah, I know."

"Your partner was ready to arrest her." Working with Burns was bad enough, but Ash had it much worse. Jameson Kendricks made Officer Burns look like Albert Frigging Einstein.

"Kendricks got a burr up his butt about her, no doubt about it.

No way that skinny little girl killed Alvarez. If she had, why would she call us and stick around?"

"She was out kayaking all day. And how would she have moved Alvarez's truck back to his apartment and why would she remove all the fingerprints except the ones on the beer bottles?" Alvarez's truck had been wiped clean.

"The first phone call that came in about the body—the caller who wouldn't give his name—that's who I'd like to talk to."

That anonymous report about the body had been logged by the dispatcher ten minutes before Summer Cassidy's call. Placed on a throw-away cell. Find the man who placed that call and they'd solve Alvarez's murder. Harewood Energy Corporation was involved in this somehow—Theofanis would bet on it.

"Kendricks is way off base about the girl."

"Yeah, but it hasn't stopped him from harassing her about coming in for fingerprints. He's still going on and on about the Yuengling bottle recovered at the site. Anyway, he's been pulled off Alvarez as of today. Department can't spare both of us—there's a big drug investigation going on, so they need him to handle general dispatches. It's just you and me on this one."

"Hang tight, Ash. I'm going to call Phil Snyder. See what else we can learn about Harewood."

Phil Snyder was a three-hundred pound gorilla—who had to be pretty damn good at his job as a broker since he'd managed to keep Theofanis's small IRA from losing money so far in this recession. Guy was a magician who drew on insider information and acted on hunches about a company's true worth that slipped by other folks.

Theofanis bypassed the social niceties that began most phone calls. "Got a favor to ask of you."

"What's new?" Snyder said.

"Aw, come on, I don't bug you that much."

"Yeah you do."

"You like it. Makes you feel important. Need all the info you got on Harewood Energy Corporation."

"You can get that online."

"I need what I can't get online easily. The buzz."

"May I ask why?"

"You can ask."

"Tit for tat, Georgie boy. That's the way it works. I make a living by collecting information. Information is power. Information is money."

Theofanis didn't answer.

"It's that homicide, isn't it?"

The man was astonishing—really. "Why would you say that?"

"Because that's what you'd be working on. Read about it in the paper. Hold on a sec."

Over the phone line came the sound of fingers tapping, and then silence, more tapping. "Here's a bit of buzz. Those wells Harewood's been drilling might have problems. There've been public hearings on them. You could have learned that yourself."

"Did. Don't see how a few little water wells have much impact on a big corporation like HEC. Guy's gotta be mega-wealthy."

"Those little wells cost about three mil a piece.

Theofanis whistled softly. "Corporate statements—can you access them?"

"Quarterly statements are easy. They're posted on the company website, but that's not what you need. You want the bank statements and tax returns regulators see."

"Can you get them?"

"Not legal."

"Not what I asked."

"Call you back later."

Theofanis drummed on his desk with both hands. "Yowza, Ash, now we're getting somewhere."

He opened brainstorming software on his computer and typed in "Alvarez" in the first cartoon-like bubble that materialized. Next he spidered out a line to a new bubble and typed in "HEC." From there he added "Harewood financial trouble" and "public hearings on wells."

Ash watched over his shoulder. "That's some crazy stuff. I hate computers personally."

"Can't live without them these days."

"I can. I get Kendricks to type all our reports. It's about all he's good for. Unless annoying the hell out of Joe Public counts."

When the phone rang, Theofanis saved the file. It was Phil Snyder.

"Here's a piece of news for you: a couple of sell orders have gone out on a large block of HEC stock options. It's broken into several small sales units, but all from the same source."

Theofanis asked a question, though the answer seemed obvious. "Whose options?"

"Seller not disclosed." A significant pause. "Only one person owns that much stock in the company, Georgie boy, and you know his name."

Theofanis slapped the desk in front of him. Oh, yeah. He added another piece to his web drawing: "stock sales."

"And you aren't going to believe what else I found, dude. This is monumental. This is outrageous. You're going to lose your lunch. No, you are going to owe me lunch at The Diamond." Then Phil clammed up.

"Do I have to come over there and beat it out of you?"

"I pulled this month's bank statement and the three before it. Guess what? There's a different address, a P.O. Box, on this month's statement. Last month there was a street address."

What did Phil make of that? "So?"

"So the bank didn't suddenly move from their building. Someone wants anyone interested in HEC's finances to communicate with the owner of the P.O. Box. Ask yourself why."

The hair on Theofanis's arms stood at attention. Holy shit. This was big. Potential fraud on a monumental scale. "Can you keep this to yourself a while?"

"Not long. Feds need to know jut as soon as I move money out for my clients."

"Wouldn't that be illegal?"

"My business lives and breathes on who has information first, Mister Detective. Information separates the haves and the have nots."

Phil Snyder was smart enough to realize having information like this might also separate the living from the dead, but Theofanis added a warning anyway. "Be careful, buddy. As you said, this is big."

And dangerous.

5

Isaac Harewood sipped an aperitif of Drambuie and closed his eyes as he fully absorbed Thelonious Monk's "'Round Midnight" playing through Bang & Olufsen speakers in his den. It had been a rotten day. When the phone trilled, he thought about letting it go to voicemail.

His caller I.D. announced "Mata Hari." A joke. Harewood would humor him.

"What's the world's greatest corporate spy in the sky have for me this time?"

"Trouble. A local broker is digging into your business."

"Name?"

"Phil Snyder."

Harewood listened closely to the details of Snyder's inquiries and actions, then said, "Thank you. I'll take it from here."

Isaac retrieved a legal pad from the roll top desk on the far side of the den and drafted a plan. Every contingency had to be considered. Then reconsidered. Seven drafts and six cups of coffee later, he deemed his plan solid.

He debated whether the super spy knew too much to keep around, but decided he was too useful to remove. For now.

Harewood glanced at the antique clock on his entertainment center. Four in the morning. He pulled a throw-away cell from his bottom desk drawer. If anyone ever subpoenaed his phone records, he wanted no trace of his next calls.

EIGHT

Tuesday

I

CLAIRE DUNHAM HAD NO DESIRE TO SUPPRESS the irrational surge of happiness as she drank the world in. Sun filtered through the live oaks and painted lacy shadows along the path that cut through campus. Azaleas spilled color all over Loblolly Lake in a riot of rose, pink, and white. A lightly bearded young man passed by in flip flops, his elbow bent, phone pressed to his ear. A gaggle of girls cut across the grass in front of Claire, one a former student who called out a cheery "Good morning, Dr. Dunham." She answered with "How's it going?" Her standard greeting.

Although the morning was cool, sweat tickled her neck by the time she hiked from her office to the university's administrative building. It was an unplanned trip, but when Howard Grice called personally and said he wanted to talk to her immediately, she put aside the student's thesis proposal for the fall term she'd been reading. Luckily, Claire always wore walking shoes and comfortable slacks to work. She hadn't worn a dress since her sister's wedding years ago, and then only at her mother's insistence. As she passed by the fountain near the main entrance, she tilted her head back to watch a cardinal zip by against a clear blue sky streaked with wisps of cirrus clouds. They foretold another gorgeous March day. This meeting with Howard Grice was not going to upset her. She would float through this as if she were tubing down the Ichetucknee with a cooler of beer floating beside her.

She would behave like the professional she was.

She would suppress her fury over the email that landed in her inbox that morning. Her friend Alice Leymon had been placed on leave pending the result of a bogus investigation into her travel expenses.

The governor had appointed Hugh Palmer—that self-serving, world-class ass-kisser—as interim agency head. Palmer would take the lead in the Harewood hearings. Claire hoped Senator Vargas, who had been friendly to environmental causes in the past, would not go forward with the legislation Harewood wanted.

Though the university president kept Claire waiting twenty minutes, he welcomed her as if they were long lost friends and grasped her forearm with one hand while he shook with the other. All pretense. She slid into the leather chair in front of his desk.

"First, let me compliment you on the superior job you've done consistently securing grants for your department. Your diligence is appreciated, Claire, let me assure you of that."

"That's not why you called me in here." Well, shit. That wasn't exactly cool.

"No." Howard Grice took off his wire-rimmed glasses and rubbed the bridge of his narrow nose before sliding them back on. "John Hu warned me you don't care much for social niceties, so I'll move on. I realize you are consumed by your heavy workload and may not be fully cognizant of the ramifications of your report on these wells. I wonder if you are aware of the importance of Isaac Harewood's efforts to save the Everglades. The land is such a treasure, home to thousands of species, many endangered—the Florida panther, several palms, the American crocodile, loggerheads—you probably can name more of them than I can. Finally someone has been able to push Congress into funding habitat restoration. That someone is Isaac Harewood."

"And you're lecturing me because?"

Grice's lips pinched. "I see you're every bit as difficult as John suggested, and proud of it."

"I'm proud of being a good scientist. If you expect me to change my report so Harewood will continue to toss money—"

"Now wait a minute! It's not about—"

"—in the university coffers, forget it." Her fists were clenched so tight in her lap her nails bit into her palms. She forced herself to relax. Take a chill pill, as the kids said. Not let his hypocrisy get to her. She liked her job. Wanted to keep it.

"—money. It's about what's good for Florida, for the environment, a strike against global warming."

"I'll tell you exactly what I told John. I can't change the amount of arsenic or uranium in the water. It's there. I won't lie about it. Scientific research means nothing if people can't rely on it. Look at the damage done when scientists even consider withholding facts. Those hacked emails at the University of East Anglia set back public opinion on global warming by years. Those scientists tried to suppress critics. They manipulated data to mask years when temperatures fell, instead of honestly explaining that climate refers to long-term changes, not short-term weather patterns. Transparency and honesty matter."

"No one's asking you to—"

She leaned away from him until her spine touched the back of the chair, her tone factual, devoid of emotion. "Then what are you asking?"

"You're not facing the reality of universities today. Professors like you only have jobs because—"

The threat brought her to her feet. So much for cool.

She finished his sentence for him. "—because of men like Isaac Harewood making big donations. I know. But when somebody in Sarasota or Little Havana turns on their tap, they put their trust in people like me to make sure their water's potable. That's a trust I won't betray. Not for you. Not for Isaac Harewood. I don't care how many turtles he saves."

"I guess we're done here. Have a good day, Dr. Dunham."

She offered him an anemic smile. "You too."

On the way down the steps of the Prescott Building, one of her graduate students called out a hello. Claire was ten steps beyond the girl before she processed the greeting. Rather than yell over her shoulder, she pretended she hadn't heard. Two squirrels skittered across the path and up a dogwood in full bloom, showering bits of bark below as they played their games. A piece fell into her hair. She dug it out of her kinky curls and tossed it back at them. Screw the squirrels. Screw John Hu and Howard Grice. And screw the endowed chair that was never going to be hers. Instead she was probably going to be fired. She should have been more diplomatic.

When she got back to her office, she woke up her computer and typed a letter to Howard Grice expounding all the points she wished she'd made in his office. She wanted the conflict of interest that had developed between the university and Harewood Corporation on record. She would send the letter by certified mail and demand a sig-nature verifying receipt. She proofed her efforts and printed the letter out. Read it over one more time.

In a hurry to append her signature before she changed her mind, she dropped Hu's pen. It rolled deep into the knee-hole area under her desk.

She crawled after it and as she backed out, she banged her head on the open center drawer. Immediately she dropped cross-legged to the floor, eyes closed, one hand pressed against the bump to reduce the throbbing, the other slamming the offending drawer shut. An ex-tensive catalog of curse words spewed from her mouth, many of them twice and employed in creative combinations.

When the neurons slacked off sending those urgent pain messages, she withdrew her hand from the wound and wasn't surprised to find blood. She was no sissy. It really hurt.

Carefully, she scooted backwards and slid her heels under her butt, ready to rise from the squat when she spotted a thumbnail-size black metal case attached underneath her desk. She touched it gingerly, and then explored it with her fingers. From her desk drawer she withdrew a penlight and crawled back into the knee hole to inspect the case.

She couldn't accept what her brain was telling her. It made no sense.

Someone had bugged her office.

A wild yelp of laughter escaped. What a joke. Nothing dramatic ever went on in her office. She racked her brain to think what it might have recorded the past few days. Ming-Mei Liu arguing for an A rather than an A minus on her midterm. Aidan Johnson, flirting with silly compliments, as if charm would convince Claire not to dock his grade for habitual tardiness. She had been a tad smartass in her replies, but everyone expected wit and sarcasm from her. It wouldn't get her fired. A few colleagues stopped by to chat, one who complained bitterly about John Hu's favoritism toward coastal projects over ground and surface water issues.

She recalled a bunch of one-sided phone calls, too, some of them private matters. One was to MIT, when she learned that Summer Cas-sidy's own mother had written to the university claiming her daughter was too immature, and possibly too unstable to be so far away from home. Such bullshit, she assured the admissions counselor. It was inconceivable how a mother could betray her own daughter like that. Claire couldn't tell the girl. Some hurts were too much to bear.

Another was Joe Barrineau, calling from Boston, describing the house he'd bought, one he thought she'd love. When was she coming to visit him?

Suddenly it wasn't a joke at all. It was as if someone had crept into her bedroom and watched her sleep. She felt violated. Who had placed the bugging device—and why?

A student? But why?

Had a colleague hoped to gain something? John Hu had asked persistent questions about the Harewood grant and obviously sicced the university president on her. Didn't seem like his style, though, to spy.

The most likely candidate, she decided, was Harewood Corporation itself. Those people had the kind of money to pay for information, and they had been upset enough by her report they had talked to Hu and Grice. Still, what would they gain by bugging her office?

James Bond intrigue didn't happen to academics. She touched the device again, as if to assure herself of its existence. Accumulated aggravation with Hu and Grice, the bug—it all bubbled its way to her throat. She yanked the black device from the wood with every intention of stomping it under her foot until only teensy atoms of plastic and metal were left. At the last minute she reconsidered. She was going to find whoever did this. Gingerly Claire searched under her desk until her fingers located the tacky circle where the device had been. She pushed it back into place, hoping the residual glue would hold.

This much she knew: whoever had violated her privacy would be sorry.

She took her cell outside under the cluster of live oaks that lined the path to the Earth Sciences building and speed-dialed Barrineau. Damn. No answer. She left a "call me" message. Damn Barrineau, anyway. Why had he moved away?

2

MARY GLOTFELTY'S VOICE SOUNDED RAGGED, and George Theofanis heard the tears in her voice. Phil Snyder was dead at forty-two. Theofanis felt as if he'd been force-fed a plate of maggoty meat. He wasn't that important as a client—not on his salary—but Mary notified him right away because all three of them had gone to high school together.

"He collapsed right onto his desk in front of a client. Must have been his heart."

"You're kidding. I was just talking to him." Phil's death so soon after that talk didn't feel right. It didn't feel right at all. "Mary, I need a list of the clients he saw this morning."

The silence on the other end of the phone told him the request shocked her.

"I wouldn't ask if it wasn't important," he said. "It's police business."

"Clients' financial information is strictly confidential."

"Of course it is, but all I want are the names of people who entered his office this morning."

She promised to fax it to him.

As soon as Mary ended the conversation, Theofanis made certain the coroner would treat Snyder's death as suspicious. He didn't believe the heart attack scenario for a minute. Yeah, the guy was built like a full grown male seal, thick all through the middle, but Theofanis was to blame for his death. If only he hadn't pried information from him.

Who else knew about that phone call? He glanced at Burns. No, Theofanis had been alone with Ash in his office. Surely Ash was not involved in any sinister plot. After all, he'd delivered the financial information that started the line of inquiry that ended in Phil's death. Someone Ash told at the sheriff's office? Or someone Phil had contacted? He mentioned he would warn several clients to sell their HEC stock.

Somehow Harewood was at the crux of everything rotten happening in Loblolly Lake. All Theofanis had to do now was prove it.

He dialed the company's main number and asked to speak with Isaac Harewood.

"Mr. Harewood isn't in this morning," an anonymous female voice told him.

"When do you expect him back?"

"Whom am I speaking with?"

"Detective George Theofanis. It's imperative that I speak with him."

"I'm afraid Mr. Harewood headed for Tampa in his Gulfstream at five this morning. We don't expect him back until late this afternoon.

Would you like to leave a message?"

Definitely not. "Please don't bother him. I'll catch up to Mr. Harewood later."

3

THE INTERCOM BUZZED. ISAAC HAREWOOD PUT THE HEADHUNTER on hold—though the search for an engineer was of paramount importance, now that he was back from Tampa. Kee-rist Almighty, didn't Julia understand how critical it was to find someone to fix his wells? She was a steady sort, gray-haired and stout-waisted, a real looker when she was younger and still decent enough for her age, but her job was to protect him from interruptions. This afternoon she had failed.

"Yes, Julia?" He spat out the words.

"Sir, there's a Detective Theofanis to see you."

"Did he have an appointment?"

"He's a detective. With the police department."

What in the world did the police want now? Another donation to their benevolent fund? How did they ever manage to solve a crime when they were always begging for money? Cops, government inspectors, environmental regulators, county commissioners—they were all a bunch of parasites living off hard-working businessmen.

"Give me a minute to finish this call." Harewood depressed the button to switch back to the headhunter. Before he properly ended the conversation, the door to his office opened and a young man in khakis and a polo marched in like he owned the place.

Harewood frowned. "Let me call you back in a bit, Sylvia." He hung up and stared at the round face of the detective as he approached. Geez. Loblolly Lake was in trouble if this guy represented their finest. His skin possessed a porcelain finish. Eyes electric blue. He looked like an aging altar boy, someone who'd pull a squirt gun on you. As the detective moved closer, Harewood realized he'd misjudged the age. The skin and the roundness of the face lent the illusion of youth.

Harewood made an effort to sound solicitous. "What can I do to help you this afternoon?"

"Know this man?" The detective tossed a photo onto Harewood's desk.

For a second Harewood was afraid to examine the photo, afraid somehow a mistake had connected him to that nosy broker. But no, his former engineer's face lay before him, barely recognizable. His skin was pasty, the mouth gaped open, and a fly rested on an eyeball with impunity. Harewood jerked away, fighting back the gag reflex that threatened to heave the Eggs Benedict he'd eaten as a late brunch on the plane. His eyes lost focus. He swiveled his chair to face out the tall windows. He sucked in air. Why was the detective here, questioning him about Alvarez?

"That's an extraordinarily gruesome photo," he said. "Sorry, I don't recognize him."

"The groundskeeper outside cutting the grass—he recognized him. Said the fellow worked for you."

Harewood picked up the photograph again and pretended to study it. He'd miscalculated—of course the detective knew Alvarez worked here or he wouldn't be standing in this office. Knew even before he'd talked to the groundskeeper.

"You'll have to . . . this is such . . . such a shock. I have so many employees I can't possibly meet them all. What in . . . what happened to him?" Harewood slipped his hand inside his pocket and stroked the piece of jasper on his key chain.

The detective reinserted the photograph into a manila envelope. Not waiting for an invitation, he occupied the chair opposite Isaac and took out an electronic device, his fingers poised to take down Harewood's words. "When's the last time you saw the victim?"

Harewood ran his hand over his scalp, a light sheen of oil transferring to his fingertips. "Hard to say. I don't interact with employees on work sites often. What happened to him?"

The detective's fingers tapped the screen. "How often?"

"How often what?"

"Do you interact with your employees on site?"

"I have dozens of work sites all over the country. I visit them all at least once a year."

"When did you last visit the site where this man worked?"

Harewood remembered the last visit well—two weeks ago when that slimeball wetback tried to blackmail him. "I can check my schedule and records and let you know."

The detective raised that cherubic face from the phone and gazed steadily at Harewood. Didn't say a word. Harewood had no choice but to buzz Julia. "Find out when I last visited Pine County Site Four, would you?"

The detective's fingers tapped away and Harewood winced as he realized he'd made another error—an admission he knew the location of Alvarez's field office. An uncomfortable silence festered in the room. Harewood's blood pumped so furiously the vibrations drummed in his ears. Finally Julia buzzed and announced a date two weeks prior as his last scheduled trip to site four.

The detective tapped the information into his device. "Your office manager identified the victim as Paulo Alvarez. She has a better memory than you, Mr. Harewood."

"I'm more aware of the global picture than the details, detective." Geez—Julia should have alerted him to the focus of the detective's visit. Warned him that she'd identified the Border Rat.

"What exactly did Mr. Alvarez do for you?"

"I believe he is an engineer."

"Doing what?"

"He is—was—one of several men who oversaw operations at my wells. ASR wells. They store water deep in the earth."

"Location of these sites?"

Harewood buzzed Julia and requested maps of the relevant well sites.

"But why are you . . . surely you don't think . . . what do you think happened to the man? You never said."

The detective pocketed his electronic toy and stood. He tossed what looked like an email print-out onto Isaac's desk. "Mr. Harewood, the IRS has no record of Mr. Alvarez's employment with you. I doubt if you made them aware of the fellow cutting your grass either. But I bet they have already discovered your company's having a bit of financial trouble. I imagine they'll be in touch soon."

As soon as the office door closed, Harewood skimmed the email from the IRS again. He crumpled it in his fist. Bunch of bloodsuckers! As if he needed more harassment from them. He tossed the email in the trash and buzzed Julia for a cup of his special green tea.

She entered and set it down before him. "Is there anything else I—"

"Please close the door. behind you."

Elbows propped in front of his laptop, Isaac Harewood logged on to the pitiful newspaper Loblolly Lake put out. He searched for clues about what the police actually knew about Alvarez.

"Holy shit!" He jerked away from the computer and knocked over the nearly full cup of tea.

He buzzed Julia again. "Get in here."

She opened the office door. "Yes, sir?"

"Don't just stand there. Clean this mess up."

He reread the story. Only merited four sentences. Police and sheriff's department were cooperating in the investigation of the homicide. Cooperating? That would be unusual, to say the least—the two departments generally pissed all over each other. They were questioning persons of interest—so, was he one of them, a person of interest? He had a contact in the sheriff's office. He would find out. He printed out the story.

Julia returned with a wad of paper towels in each fist.

"Forget it," he said. His papers were ruined already anyway. "Tell Morrell to get his ass in here. And ring Bailey Douglass. Don't let her secretary put you off with any crap about taking a message. Tell her I'm canceling our contract if she doesn't speak to me immediately."

Julia turned toward the door.

"Don't be a fool. Leave the towels here."

His molars ground together as he dabbed the spilled tea. Papers might be ruined, but no sense in marring the finish of his desk.

Morrell's eyebrows were raised as he came in, and Isaac wanted to slap him. Or Julia. She must have warned him Isaac was angry. He shoved the newspaper story print-out under Morrell's nose.

"A detective came to question me about Alvarez's homicide. Now, why would he do that?"

Morrell blanched. "No idea. You, me, Bailey, Julia—no one else is aware of what Alvarez tried to pull."

"Julia? Why the fuck does Julia know?"

Morrell tried a weak smile. "She knows where all the bodies are buried, so to speak. Sometimes she's the one who buried them."

"That's not funny."

"It wasn't meant to be."

Julia let him know Bailey Douglass was on the line.

"Get out of here."

Morrell stood there, mouth opening as if to protest.

"Now."

The office door whispered shut behind the CFO.

Isaac almost spit into the phone. "Kee-rist almighty, Bailey, you're supposed to handle—"

"Let's be careful what we say on the phone, Isaac."

Right. Douglass and Associates had that automated message about calls being monitored for quality control that played before Bailey's secretary came on. He had dialed her number himself a couple of times. Was that what she meant about being careful? Or did she think someone else might be listening in?

"I'm at my Tallahassee office this afternoon," she said. "Shall we meet over here, say in an hour and a half, at the Mockingbird Café?"

"Just tell me—"

"Not now. See you in ninety minutes."

"Make it an hour."

"Ninety minutes. Don't speed."

He slammed down the phone. Plenty of people had reason to kill Alvarez. He was a sleazy little wetback. That detective had no reason to suspect Isaac at all. Still, his blood raced so forcefully the veins on the top of his hands had plumped like electrical wires.

He couldn't sit still another second. He intended to get out on the highway and push the Jaguar into the red zone. Burn off steam. He threw open the door to his office and plunged into the corridor.

"I'm going out," he announced to his secretary.

"But you have an appointment at four-thirty."

"Cancel it, Julia."

"I already rescheduled it when you canceled it for that last minute trip to Tampa."

"Handle it. I pay you handsomely to handle details like this yourself."

As he entered the elevator, he heard a noise like a hiss and turned his head. For an instant, he thought it was Julia, but that was absurd. Must have been the teapot releasing steam or the air conditioner whisking on.

4

As Harewood stood over Bailey Douglass on the outdoor patio of the Mockingbird, he had an excellent, though brief, view of her cleavage. Nice, but not enough to relieve his worries.

"No strings tie me to this Alvarez business, right? Please assure me your investigations can't be traced." he asked.

Bailey raised her right eyebrow and the corresponding side of her mouth. "Good evening to you, too." Her throaty laughter washed over him and relaxed the knots in his neck. "I run a well-respected lobbying firm, not Dial-A-Hitman."

He laughed with her and touched her shoulder briefly by way of an apology. It was just that in over twenty years of business he'd never come so close to the brink before. The IRS would demand fines from HEC, but Morrell would negotiate the amount and delay the payment. Everyone hired illegals. BFD. Theofanis had nothing else on him.

He set his Drambuie on the cast iron table. The sun was angled low enough that the umbrella didn't block it. Isaac hated sun that slanted directly into his eyes. He touched the oily sheen of sunscreen on his scalp. Did it really block UV rays all day the way the bottle claimed? This Florida sun was causing a melanoma epidemic.

"So what's the plan?" he asked. "We only have a week to make sure this goes my way."

She set her sancerre down. From experience, he knew she would only nurse one glass. She was the kind of woman who had to monitor her weight or she'd shift from Sex Goddess to Sloppy Fatso overnight. Bailey was way too serious about control to ever let that happen.

"My staff has assembled an impressive video showing all the jobs created through ASR projects like yours," she said. "Well-casing manufacturers. Engineers. Construction workers. Lab technicians hired to test and monitor the wells. We show the faces of all these workers. Plus we have a Chamber of Commerce president testifying that access to water brings other jobs to an area. It supports a growing population, which creates more jobs, construction, and agriculture. It's a remarkable video, Isaac. You're going to love it. The audience at the first hearing loved it. Almost brings tears to my eyes with all the flag-waving music."

Was she being a smartass? He searched her face but no hint of sarcasm showed in her expression. She touched a few icons on her computer tablet and turned the device to let him watch the production for himself. The spiel was good. Really good. But good wasn't good enough. He needed a promise of immediate return on this investment. His BP stock wasn't worth even half of what he'd paid for it. The Panhandle lakefront development properties were being offered for sale at one-third their original asking price—and still weren't selling. His broker called yesterday and said GE had sliced their dividend. Advised him to cut and run, take his losses. Easy for his broker to say. She wasn't behind on her mortgage payment.

Harewood had to admit this presentation was professional. "I hope it works its magic on Senator Vargas and those parasites at the Department of Environmental Protection. What's the back-up plan?"

"That's proving more difficult than I first thought. My people haven't uncovered what you seek on Dr. Dunham, and though I've turned all my charm on the senator, he has steadfastly resisted."

Bailey's charms were legendary. Senator Vargas must be quite the Boy Scout.

"We're pursuing other avenues," she said, "but you don't need to be bothered with the details yet."

That sounded like the same line of bull Julia always fed him. "The hearing is next Thursday, Bailey. I'd like assurances before then that the senator and DEP are going to agree to exemptions for my wells."

The lobbyist smiled. "Have I ever let you down?"

"Not yet." That smile reminded him of all the reasons he didn't trust her. He stood. "About Alvarez. You're sure no documents in your office connect me to him?"

Her lower lip protruded a bit. "I'm hurt that you keep asking."

He didn't believe for one second that she was hurt. He only hoped she was telling the truth.

5

THAT RED-HEADED SLUT DIDN'T FOOL JULIA LAMBERT, not for one second. The lobbyist's assets spilled out of her vee-neck silk blouse like a couple of blanched cabbages. Isaac drooled like a testosterone-charged fourteen year old in their presence. He hadn't even touched his drink. No, he was too busy trying to touch Bailey Douglass.

Julia's ribs squeezed together as Isaac and Bailey shared a private joke. That woman manipulated Isaac into ridiculous positions. Why, he paid her three times Julia's salary! What had he gotten for his money? An empty wallet. It was Julia who came through for him, time and again. Hadn't she left her children with her ex-husband to follow Isaac to Florida? She had only seen her grandchildren once when her son and his wife stopped by on the way to Disney World. Not that she was exactly pining away for the presence of kiddies—the mothering genes had bypassed her. Or she'd squandered what she had of those instincts on Isaac.

Sun streaming through the windshield spurred yet another hot flash. Julia touched a button to lower the window on the passenger side of her white Ford Taurus, a car as invisible as a middle-aged woman. As invisible as Julia. She might as well lower the window on the side facing her boss. It wasn't as if he was going to notice his office manager sitting in her car across the parking lot from the outdoor café. He never noticed the Monday morning muffins and Friday afternoon cookies she baked for him and the office staff. Often he seemed oblivious to the burdens she shouldered to make his life easier.

By now she had hoped he'd see who really appreciated him. Thought he would have married her by now. She understood all too well the company's true financial state. Before she shuffled mail into the ap- propriate boxes, she always studied the bank records and retirement account statements. As clearly as if it were happening again right that moment, she pictured Isaac standing in front of his employees, claim- ing his own portfolio was largely invested in HEC.

I'd advise you to double your own investment—remember we put in matching funds, he'd told them. She understood why he had to lie to others, but it hurt that he continued to lie to her.

Her molars ground against each other. Minutes later she'd over- heard him telling Niles to sell his company stock options while there was still money to withdraw. Julia wanted to shift her money out, but Niles insisted they had to unload Isaac's options first or they might be out of jobs if he found out. He promised she would be next in line, right along with his own investments. Dangerous to put too much out there at once, he said.

Dangerous to wait, she'd told him. She understood as much—more—about the company than Isaac or Niles did. Isaac had pushed Alvarez too hard to produce results with the wells. After Alvarez had rushed the cycling and chemicals leached out of the rocks, she overheard him trying to blackmail Isaac about falsified financial statements.

Julia even knew how Alvarez had found out. He thought the company figures were too good to be true. This Mexican lady in his apartment complex worked at the bank and he persuaded her to show him the original document. When it didn't match the one the company distributed, that conniver thought he'd discovered gold—or at least a one-way ticket back to Mexico. He should have listened to Julia and dropped the matter. Instead, he'd gotten the one-way ticket he deserved.

Alvarez had come to her with the documents before he went to Isaac because, like everyone else, he trusted her. Long ago Julia made it a priority to serve as company mother to secretaries, surveyors, custodians, and draftsmen. Isaac was an exceptional man, a great man, but HEC had expanded until he lost touch with some aspects of the business. Like the hundreds of employees who would find their so-called golden years destroyed because company stock became worthless. Including Julia.

Well, she wasn't the kind of gal to go down without a fight. Isaac Harewood was going to learn there was nothing—nothing—she wouldn't do for him. Bailey Douglass would disappear as soon as Isaac's troubles become public, insulating her firm from any hint of scandal. It was Julia, not the big-breasted Ms. Douglass, who would stand by him until he took his last breath.

6

CLAIRE SMACKED THE HARD LITTLE BALL INTO THE WALL near the front corner. It took a lucky bank off the adjoining wall. Summer shouldn't have been able to return it, but the girl whirled and hooked it with her right hand. She lobbed it over her head high against the front wall. Summer was impossibly long-limbed and coordinated.

The move caught Claire off guard, and though she raced to her left, the ball bounced off the floor twice before she caught up to it. That made eleven points for Summer, end of the match. The girl never deferred to Claire because of her age or position. Never threw a match. If she had, Claire would have stopped their Tuesday games immediately.

Summer competed ferociously. Reminded Claire of herself. She shoved her kinky hair out of the way with a towel and mopped the sweat from her forehead.

Summer sucked on her stainless steel water bottle. "You were off your game today."

Without removing the towel from her face, Claire nodded. Should she confide in her young lab assistant? Not a good idea. A certain professional distance was important.

Yet Claire longed to explain to someone—anyone who'd understand—why she had lost her temper with Hu and President Grice and put her job in jeopardy. She wanted to confess she thought she was being followed by a black Honda, but she wasn't sure. The surveillance device had made her paranoid.

She took her phone out and speed-dialed Joe again, and then turned the phone off before it rang. He hadn't responded to her last message. Hell, no, I'm not quitting my job, she'd told him when he'd proposed. She replayed the pleading in his voice: But I want you to come with me. She had answered in cold, clipped syllables: Do what you have to do, and I'll do what I have to do. After that display of Arctic Woman, what right did she have to reach out for support now?

Claire and Summer headed for the showers. In the locker room, they weren't alone so Claire couldn't have confided in Summer even if she wanted to. A middle-aged brown-skinned woman in gym shorts was yakking on her mobile. "Sure, Shug, I'll stop at Publix. I need to pick up broccoli for dinner."

You couldn't get away from those phones. Everyone had one glued to their ears.

Summer finished her shower first. Claire lingered under the hot water. As they finished dressing, Claire noticed the same pudgy woman on the bench with her phone.

"Yeah, Marvin, I'll pick up your beer on my way home."

The hairs on Claire's neck stood on end. It took a few seconds before she understood why. The woman had been talking about groceries when Claire headed into the showers. That was one long conversation about dinner. Too long. She had never seen the woman at the club before.

This was crazy. She was a damned geologist, not a secret agent. She retrieved her briefcase from the locker.

As she was ready to leave the club, a black Honda was parked along the curb down the street. She froze. Was it the same one? Though the dark tinted windows prevented her from seeing in, Claire instinctively sensed the driver slouched inside, with the opposite window lowered to prevent cooking in the late afternoon sun.

Summer had her hand on the bar to push open the glass door.

"Wait," Claire called out. She opened her briefcase and removed a flash drive containing the final grant report with her digital signature. The pudgy woman on the cell phone emerged from the locker room.

Claire pressed the flash drive into Summer's palm. Claire's lips barely moved, her voice little more than a whisper. "Keep this someplace safe."

Her lab assistant, though wide-eyed with unasked questions, was smart enough to pocket the device in her shorts. No wonder she loved this kid. If Claire had a daughter, she would have wanted her to be quick-witted and confident, like Summer.

As Claire pulled her car into traffic, the black sedan stayed two cars behind. Enough of this B.S. Time to involve the police.

7

SUMMER TOOK THE STEPS TO HER SECOND-FLOOR APARTMENT two at a time. Not that she was in that big of a hurry, but it made for a great workout. Like boot-camp without the drill sergeant.

She burst through the fire door, ready to charge down the hall, but halted as she spotted Dayita leaning against the cheap drywall in the corridor. Her appearance here at this time of day was so unprecedented, so unexpected, Summer's steps slowed to a crawl.

"What's wrong?" Summer unlocked the door and they went inside. She dropped her backpack on the floor by the bookshelf where it fell with a thud that was startling.

"I've been trying to call you, but your phone went straight to voicemail," Dayita said.

Summer thought back. On the way to the club, she had talked

to an admissions official at MIT and gotten the run-around again. While she and Claire were playing, the phone would have been in the locker room. She wouldn't have heard it ring. Twice on the way home Summer had called Claire on her cell, but the professor hadn't answered. Summer was dying to discover what all the drama with the flash drive was about.

"What's wrong, Dayita?"

"This afternoon I was walking over to the Earth Science building to see you. On the way, the strap on my sandal broke—"

Oh lordy, a headline-worthy event. Fashion faux pas never happened to Miss Perfect.

"—so I was just a minute too late. I wanted to tell you about this new app I developed in the computer lab this morning. It's really cool. Not only cool. A money-maker."

This story was going somewhere. Summer just had to be patient.

"Anyway, someone was watching you. That guy you played foosball with—Justin? I'm pretty sure it was him."

Summer's throat slammed shut. Justin! The scene at Goose Pasture flashed through her mind. No, stop. Why assume evil intent?

"I bet he wanted to apologize." But how had he located her? She hadn't told him she was a student, let alone a science major. Maybe he'd gone back to ask the bartender, or he could have found her bio on the Internet, where everyone's lives were displayed in bits and bytes for all to see. Except for Justin's.

"He hopped in his car and followed you out of the parking lot," Dayita said.

Creepy. Why didn't he talk to her on the way into the club?

"You made it to the club all right, so I didn't call the police."

Good thing—that would have been a major over-reaction. "Wait—how'd you know I was at the club?"

"Remember the software I installed on your phone?"

Right. That was creepy too. Summer had to get rid of that app.

"But guess what? I got a partial license plate number. He was driving a dark green Volvo. With a little more time, we might be able to find out who Justin really is."

"What we need is a photo," Summer said. Or a police sketch artist. No, not police—she had seen enough of them lately—but thinking of sketch artists jiggled a memory of Ty saying he drew people's faces lickety-split. "Let's make a visit to Walmart tonight."

"I don't like to shop there."

"Relax. With any luck, I'm going to make a deal in the parking lot."

She hoped to trade a safe, warm bed for Grace Franceschi for a sketch of Justin Freese-Freeze-Fries—whatever his name was.

8

CLAIRE DROVE STRAIGHT TO THE POLICE STATION after her handball match with Summer. She'd never been in a police station before. It was like entering an alien world, an over-air-conditioned realm that smelled of baby powder scented air freshener with undertones of body odor that refused to be subdued. Sounds assumed a hollow quality in the cavernous lobby. People strode or stomped across the linoleum in all directions without making more than cursory eye contact, each one pursuing his own agenda.

After registering her complaint at the front desk, she was told to wait. She chose a metal chair with two empty seats on each side. Five minutes later, a detective marched toward her and shook her hand. A short, trim man, George Theofanis stood nose-to-nose with Claire.

He must have found Claire's story odd because he drove her to her office in an unmarked car to inspect the bug. His hand resting on the doorknob, he turned and cautioned her to be quiet once inside. She tried not to be insulted, but couldn't help thinking she *was* a Ph.D.

Theofanis eased the legs of his creased khakis slightly as he squatted to peer under her desk. If he had any opinion about what he was seeing, his face didn't give it away. He took several digital photos of the device but left it in place. Theofanis attempted to lift fingerprints, though he'd warned her at the police station they were unlikely to find any but hers. Before leaving the office, he hid a tiny video camera between two heavy tomes in her bookcase. He aimed to capture anyone who came to retrieve the bug.

When they stepped back into the hall, the detective admitted he didn't have much hope the camera would catch anyone. "It was a professional-grade surveillance device. A real pro won't come back for it."

Especially true, she realized, if the black Honda had followed her to the police station and then to her office. She hadn't seen it outside the station, but the world had thousands of black cars. They didn't exactly stand out.

By the time Theofanis finished, and she pulled into her carport, it was after nine. Self conscious and edgy, she forced herself to walk normally along the concrete path to her modest brick ranch-style house. It was in an older neighborhood near campus, one with a reputation for safety. Solid. Thoroughly middle class. In her bedroom she wriggled into a cotton tee-shirt. She grabbed pre-washed greens from the fridge, tossed in a handful of dried cranberries and pecans, and splashed the salad with balsamic vinaigrette. With good French bread, real butter, and a glass of Sauvignon Blanc, that would have to suffice for dinner. Not that she wanted food anyway. She sat at the Shaker-style dining table. Was the Honda out front? She couldn't resist peeking out the window, making sure her body remained hidden by the curtain. No Honda. She was acting foolish. She wouldn't look again.

Ten minutes later she did. And fifteen minutes after that.

Every nerve in her body jangled when the phone rang. It was only Alex, in demando-voice mode. Frigging man had some kind of gall to contact her again after she'd thrown him out of her office.

"Where have you been?"

"Alex, do you have any idea how much you sound like my mother back when I was fourteen and an hour past curfew? Let me clue you in—I didn't like it even then."

"Sorry. I was worried when you didn't answer the phone earlier."

"Why would you worry? I go places. I have a life, and I thought I made clear you aren't a part of it."

"I picked up an order of that fabulous cookies and cream bread pudding you love from the Redbud Café. I wanted to share."

She closed her eyes, remembering the sumptuous dessert in her mouth. She swallowed the temptation. "Very thoughtful, but not tonight. Not any night." He was unbelievably obtuse.

"Not even with a scoop of vanilla ice cream?"

It had been a mistake to bring him home from that art gallery. She admired his pottery. Less so his stories, which seemed trite. Even less his performance in the sack. Though he was five years her junior, it required a major effort to pump him to tumescence. She had brought him home because she was a little bit tipsy, because she was a lot lonely without Joe, and because she was trying to convince herself she'd made the right decision in not moving to Massachusetts. None of which were good reasons to sleep with someone.

"Good night, Alex. I'm going to bed."

"Alone?"

She laughed without humor and disconnected. A street light barely illuminated the cars parked along the road in front of her house, the last residence on a dead-end street, a fact that had always made her home a little more private than the others, a little more desirable. Now, as she peered out the front window, the house only seemed more isolated. For the first time in her life, she drew the living room curtains closed.

She spent the next hour running her fingers under tables and around the frames of paintings and upending lamps in a search for another listening device. That detective should have thought of inspecting her house. She found nothing, but that didn't mean it wasn't there. For a long time, she lay in the dark on the couch, fully dressed except for shoes and bra, a chef's knife on the coffee table beside her. Just in case. Twice she peeped through the curtains at the empty street. Ridiculous. What did she expect to see—a bogeyman?

9

ONLY A DOZEN OR SO CARS DOTTED the Walmart parking lot, making it easy to spot Ty's van along the perimeter. Light, dimmed by the van's tinted windows, glowed within. Exactly what were the etiquette rules for approaching an occupied van after dark? Summer didn't want to startle Ty but knocking on a window seemed the only way to make contact.

She raised her fist but the rear lift gate rose before she had a chance to knock. He dropped to the edge and dangled his shoes over the left tail light. "I'd offer you a chair but I don't have any."

What was Summer supposed to say to that?

One corner of his mouth lifted. "Joke. Obviously a bad one."

Curled inside a Dora the Explorer sleeping bag, Grace blinked and coughed as if she might awaken. Instead, she grasped the edge of one of those ratty-looking blankets kids love and settled back to sleep.

"Summer has a favor to ask of you," Dayita said.

"Shoot."

"You said you drew people's faces. I wondered if you could sketch someone from a description."

Ty's eyes grew darker with each part of her story. The planned kayak trip. The way Justin stood her up. The body at Goose Pasture. The bottle of Yuengling that probably had Summer's fingerprints on it.

Dayita laid her hand on Summer's arm. "I saw this same guy following Summer from class today. Got a partial license plate number. With a sketch—"

Ty cut in. "I've never attempted to sketch from a description before, but let's give it a shot. Let me get paper."

Dayita shook her head. "It would be a lot easier to draw at Summer's kitchen table. Then we all can see what you're doing."

Ty glanced at Grace.

"She can sleep in my bed while you work," Summer said.

He leaned away from her.

Boy, was he touchy! He didn't need to worry—she wasn't about to offer them a home again. "Just for one night."

In the end, he agreed to accompany them. Summer drove slowly, keeping the van in her rearview mirror. When they parked at her apartment, Dayita climbed in the back of the van, scooped up Grace, sleeping bag and all, and handed her out to Ty. She woke briefly and asked where they were, promptly falling back asleep when she heard Ty's voice: "It's okay, Sugarpop."

After settling Grace into bed, the trio clustered around the kitchen table. Dayita located a website with basic face shapes.

"The one with the square chin," Summer suggested.

Feature by feature, Ty added eyes, nose, mouth, brows, and hair.

"His hair parted on the left," she said, approving as Ty made the change. "And longer bangs. He kept pushing them away from his eyes."

Summer tilted the paper so the pendant light over the table illuminated the sketch to its best advantage. "Pretty close."

Dayita scanned the sketch and emailed it to herself and Summer. "I'll try to match it to a name tomorrow."

"Send me a copy too," Ty said.

Summer hadn't expected that. Did he plan to play detective, or perhaps start a new career as an artist?

Ty drifted over to the bedroom door, Dayita and Summer tiptoeing behind him, and, for a quiet moment, they listened to his sister breathing, a slight rattle marking each inhalation.

"Getting late," Ty said. "We'd best head out."

He took a step into the room, his progress halted when Dayita touched his shoulder. "Sounds like Grace might be getting a cold. You should let her sleep here the rest of the night."

Summer agreed. "It'd be a shame to disturb her again."

"It's settled then." Dayita opened Summer's hall closet and took out the only spare sheet and blanket inside and handed them to Ty. Summer heard her whisper to Ty: "I'd feel better if you kept an eye on Summer tonight. In case that Justin guy . . ."

In case he what? Summer pretended she didn't hear. Pretended she wasn't relieved when Ty accepted the linens.

Almost funny, wasn't it—Miss Morality persuading a guy to sleepover on Summer's couch?

After Dayita left, Summer told Ty to make himself at home. He sacked out on the couch, reading *Crime and Punishment,* rather than the thriller or crime fiction she'd expected. Intriguing. He positioned himself, she realized, so he could watch her apartment door, his backpack on the floor within reach. What items would an essentially homeless man carry in his backpack? While she was thinking this, his eyes lifted from the page and met hers. An odd current, pleasant and yet alarming, traveled from her chin up both sides of her jaws, stopping short of her ears.

She hurried into her bedroom and closed the door. This was no time to indulge in a goofy attraction. On the other side of the room, Grace slept fitfully, her breathing still raspy. Summer checked her email, both relieved and chagrined that the Greek detective at Goose Pasture hadn't sent her a message. He said he would contact her if they had any developments about the body she'd found. Maybe he'd forgotten. He hadn't summoned her for fingerprints either, thank heavens.

For five hours, she worked on her thesis, wading through two new related research projects completed by others, creating separate folders for each on her computer, and cutting and pasting notes into them. She proofed her pages for the umpteenth time. A little after one in the morning, she saved her work on the hard drive and on a flash drive.

Summer also sent a copy of her thesis to her online storage account before closing her laptop.

When she undressed, she found Claire's flash drive in her shorts pocket. She had forgotten to call Claire. Now it was too late.

Summer stowed the flash drive in her desk drawer and climbed into bed. She turned off the table lamp, and as her eyes adjusted to the dark, she spent a full minute, chin propped on her fist, watching the little girl. Fawn-colored hair splayed across the cream pillowcase. In sleep, Grace's thumb, damp with slobber, found its way into her mouth. Periodically she suckled three or four times; then her mouth would gape open, thumb resting on the bottom lip. One hand clutched the edge of a shabby pink and white fuzzy blanket to her neck as if it were her greatest treasure.

The rise and fall of the girl's chest seemed magical and mysterious. How could it be that one minute a living person inhaled and exhaled, and the next that breath stilled forever? Had that Hispanic guy she'd found known he was experiencing his last breath? Had Chrissie known—at the last second did you think to yourself, This is it, there isn't going to be any more?

Did that knowledge bring you peace or a final overwhelming sorrow?

Summer let her head sink into her own pillow. She was tired. Exhausted, really. Yet as she tried to sleep, her mind flitted over the day. Her morning class. A slightly embarrassing moment when she'd passed that boy—Adam, Alan, whatever—on the way to the lab and he'd asked for her cell number. She'd scribbled a string of numbers, two deliberately illegible, and folded it into his hand. She thought about Claire. The sketch of Justin. The flash drive. Ty's brown eyes. Sugarpop—she smiled, remembering Ty's nickname for Grace.

The flash drive. What was on it? She rose and without turning on the light, lifted the lid of her laptop. The screen illuminated. She retrieved the drive and plugged it into a USB port. Summer opened the only folder on the device. She spent the next half hour clicking through documents. The final grant report contained no surprises. It was essentially her own report. Not a word changed. Several financial spreadsheets related to the grant were exactly what you'd expect, hardly mysterious. To honor Claire's request fully, Summer sent a copy of the flash drive contents to her online storage. Now it was safe.

What was up with Claire? If only Summer had made that phone call. Her professor didn't have texting service. Claire had to deliver a lecture series in Tampa and it was unlikely Summer would be able to connect with her until she returned Monday.

Summer tucked the flash drive back in the drawer and wandered out to the kitchen to get a drink of water. On the way back, she bumped a toe on an object leaning against the wall. "Sshhiii—" She let the soft curse trail off, so she wouldn't wake everyone. She bent over and steadied the hard plastic. It was plugged in via a charging cable that snaked under her end table to the electrical outlet. Despite the dark, she discerned black and silver curves, a shape foreign yet somehow familiar. Tentatively, she stroked a small piece of cold metal that protruded from it, and jerked away, as if she'd violated someone's body without permission. It was one of those new prosthetic legs. She'd heard about their incredible capabilities. Her eyes flew to the couch where Ty lay immobile, his eyes wide open. If only he'd say something.

The silence stretched out, long and hollow.

NINE

Thursday

I

THE BLENDER WHIRRED THE YOGURT around and the scent of fresh mango and strawberries reached Summer's nose. She reached for her wallet, but the waitress in the yogurt shop stopped her.

"The gentleman outside paid for your orders," she said.

Dayita looked as surprised as Summer felt.

"What gentleman?" No one had been seated at the tables outside when they passed by. Yet abracadabra! Ty and Grace had appeared, as fast as they'd disappeared from her apartment before she'd gotten up the other morning.

Looking at him now, she remembered the hard, smooth curves of the prosthetic leg, remembered the moment their eyes had locked in the dark. Was that why he'd taken Grace and left without saying goodbye or thank you? Kind of freaky to think he'd come in her bedroom to retrieve his sister and Summer hadn't woke up.

Grace was scarfing down her fruit and yogurt as if she were starved. Probably was. Summer remembered reading one in four children in the U.S. was currently raised in poverty with uncertain access to adequate food. No question Grace was one of them. And Summer held a smoothie that should have gone to the child. She would find a way to make it up to her.

Bells tinkled as Summer and Dayita exited the store.

Summer's chair scraped across the cement as she positioned herself across from Ty. It was a perfect day to eat outside, sunny with a light breeze. "Thanks, but you shouldn't have."

Dayita somehow managed to pull her chair into position without making a sound. "Yes, thank you for the yogurt."

In the bright sunlight Summer noticed for the first time that Ty's closely trimmed beard disguised a smattering of tiny red scars. Shrapnel wounds? She had been wrong to dismiss him as "too Hollywood" when they first met.

A manila envelope lay on the cast iron table in front of him. He pushed it toward her.

She undid the metal clasp and extracted three sheets of paper. The top two were from a military dossier on Jake Fowler, but the photograph was the guy she knew as Justin Friese. The details painted an ugly picture. Dishonorably discharged from the U.S. Army in 2009 for theft. A civilian arrest record. Even though the mugshot was far too contrasty, Summer identified the mustached man as Friese. Facial hair made him look older. She read over the arrest form. Internet fraud charges. Plea bargained and served ten months.

"How did you get this?" Dayita asked.

Yeah—good question.

"Friends with access." His expression remained inscrutable as he lifted another piece of paper from his backpack. "I wasn't sure I should let you see this, but you better know exactly what you're dealing with."

The emails' "to" and "from" lines had been redacted. Summer skimmed the rest of the memo and exhaled noisily through her mouth.

"They discharged Jake Fowler for theft, but that's only because they couldn't prove the more serious crime," Ty said. "If you have any sense, you'll stay away from him."

No lie. Jake Fowler had likely murdered two of his comrades on an army base and made the bodies disappear.

Dayita's ankle bracelet jingled. "I told you to quit talking to strange guys."

Summer stifled an impulse to kick that dainty little foot. "Everyone is a stranger until you meet them."

They were sitting at a table with a strange guy, one they had only met a few days ago. She didn't know much about Ty, yet she trusted him instinctively.

2

ALL THE CORONER HAD BEEN ABLE TO TELL THEOFANIS after her initial examination was that a tiny red dot on Phil Snyder's neck could have been caused by a poison dart. "Could have, but highly unlikely," La-Wanda Johnson said. "That's international spy stuff. Not the kind of thing that happens in Loblolly Lake." Furthermore, she asserted the kind of poison that simulated a heart attack would be difficult—or impossible—to detect.

"You'll just have to wait until the tox report comes back from Tallahassee," she said.

So he had waited for her call. It finally came but she refused to talk over the phone. "You need to see this for yourself," she said.

She wouldn't have insisted on his making a trip to the morgue if the tox screen hadn't delivered a surprise. He was so preoccupied in speculating what was in that report he nearly hit a pedestrian on the drive across town.

He barreled through the swinging doors that led into the morgue.

LaWanda didn't wait for him to ask. She handed over the preliminary toxicology report. "Succinylcholine."

Theofanis had never heard of it.

"It's a powerful muscle relaxant," LaWanda said. "A high dose quickly paralyzes its recipient and mimics the effects of a heart attack within fifteen minutes. It denatures quickly. I thought you were crazy when you asked me to treat this like a homicide, but you were right. The drug isn't part of a normal tox screen. Phil's death would have been written off as natural if not for your hunch. Guess the world of international spies has arrived at Loblolly Lake after all."

More like international corporations.

"Hospitals use the drug to allow the insertion of a breathing tube into the throat of an unconscious patient, so it would be readily available to medical personnel—or someone stealing from a hospital pharmacy," she said. LaWanda had done some research and found you could buy handheld devices easily concealed in purses or briefcases or pockets. "Heart attack guns are probably for sale on the Internet, if you trawl through the right sites," she said. "The victim might not be aware of anything at all or might feel like a mosquito had bitten him. A full autopsy report is months away, but this should give you enough to get started."

Indeed. First on his agenda was finding out if any hospitals in the region had reported thefts of the drug. Also if any of Harewood's leadership team had spouses or relatives that worked in hospitals. But this heart attack gun stuff—that sounded like a weapon a military or intelligence officer would know about. When he got back to the office, he would see if any Harewood people had military backgrounds.

Succinylcholine and heart attack guns—Ash wasn't going to believe this shit.

TEN

Friday

I

SUMMER CARRIED A STACK OF PLATES and used silverware into the Patels' kitchen. The room smelled of the yummy cumin and curry that spiced the lentil and rice dish Mrs. Patel had served for dinner. Dayita's mother was as short and round as Dayita was tall and slim, but their faces bore such similarity anyone would peg them instantly as mother and daughter.

Mrs. Patel refused Summer's offer to wash the dishes and shooed them out of the kitchen. "Dayita has news she is dying to share with you. I made her wait until after dinner, but now, go sit on the sofa."

Summer lowered herself onto a teak futon, one Mrs. Patel had culled from the used furniture discarded by college students when they moved out at semester's end. All the Patels' furniture had been acquired that way. As a real estate manager, Mrs. Patel had tipped Summer off when to raid the parking lot behind popular student housing units so she could furnish her own apartment.

Dayita tossed a stack of computer printouts onto the tile-topped teak coffee table.

Summer picked up a color photograph of a younger Ty Franceschi without the Hollywood beard. "You dug into Ty's background?"

Easing down beside Summer, Dayita crossed her legs at the ankle. "The dossier he gave us on your foosball partner? Not ordinarily accessible. It made me wonder about him."

True. Dayita's computer skills were legendary on campus. She was a crack programmer, trained in Internet security—and capable of hacking almost any system. Not that they'd spent that much time and effort to track Justin because they'd finally dismissed him as a coincidence. It just seemed so bizarre that someone might actually have tried to entangle her in a murder investigation.

Dayita handed her more pages. "Turns out Ty did a stint as a Navy SEAL."

Ahhh, one of those primo guys in the U.S. military arsenal. The studs who took out Osama bin Laden. She flipped to the next page, a military discharge, followed by an employment record with a private security contractor. "He became a mercenary?"

"Exactly. He was injured extracting a low-level diplomat kidnapped by terrorists. To uncover that gem, I had to hack into—never mind."

Dayita was frowning. Guess that info wasn't the kind of stuff that got posted on Facebook or indexed on Google.

"Lost part of his leg and two guys in his unit in that gig, but the diplomat survived," Dayita said. "Ty spent months in a rehab hospital."

Dayita sifted through the papers and located copies of birth and marriage certificates. "The little girl is his half sister."

Summer skimmed the sheets. Twenty-nine—he was a little older than she'd thought. His mother was single when she had Ty at seventeen. Married nine years later to a man who adopted Ty. So it wasn't his birth father that had died in the car accident.

"Very thorough," Summer said.

"You haven't seen anything yet." With a little cat smile, Dayita presented Summer with copies of online news articles.

The first covered a protest against mountaintop removal in southern West Virginia. The name Harewood Energy Corporation jumped out. Then Summer spotted another name. Norman Franceschi. Grace's father—Ty's stepfather—had been the leader of the protest group, Water Warriors. So the protest movement that started in West Virginia relocated to Florida with the founder's stepson carrying on his work.

The next article detailed higher than average incidence of cancer in residents and developmental delays and birth defects in children of this small West Virginia community. Harewood Energy Corporation denied any connection between their mining operation and the illnesses.

Ty had said his mother had cancer. He blamed Harewood Energy Corporation for her death—and for whatever was wrong with Grace.

Summer skimmed the last two articles. One detailed Ty's arrest for blocking the entrance to a Sunburst Corporation drilling operation in Pennsylvania. The other listed his name as a co-plaintiff filing suit against Fairhope Energy for destruction of privately owned water wells in West Virginia.

"Looks as if he is going after all sorts of polluters," Summer said.

With partially hooded eyes, Dayita pressed the final piece of paper into Summer's hands. "Took digging, but I found out Sunburst and Fairhope are subsidiaries of a company HEC owns. I wasn't trying to butt into your business, but I wanted to be sure Ty wasn't on Harewood's payroll. With the police questioning you about that body, you need to know who your friends are."

Until this semester, Summer would have counted HEC as her ally, but somehow she and Harewood were now aligned on opposing sides. Dayita's research must have taken hours. Summer wanted to find the right words, ones that would recognize the solidity of their long friendship, but everything that came to mind sounded sappy.

She swallowed. "Thanks."

Dayita nodded. "Ty has an unusual intensity that makes me wonder what he's capable of. Don't his eyes scare you a little?" She slipped the end of her braid between her lips.

Yes, his eyes scared her. Not the way Dayita meant.

Dayita flung her braid over her shoulder. "Some vets come back so damaged they can't live normal lives anymore. Ty might be one of them, but not even Isaac Harewood has enough money to buy him off."

Mrs. Patel came in, dish towel in one hand. "And with Summer's determination to get her doctorate, we don't have to worry about her letting this man get too close. He's too old and too complicated for you. No sense inviting trouble into your life." She laughed a little, and then turned serious. "Dayita told me about the little girl. It sounds as if she might be autistic. That child needs to be in preschool. Early intervention is important for children with disabilities. You tell him that if you see him again."

The last of Dayita's printouts had an address for Paulo Alvarez, the man at Goose Pasture.

"I thought we should talk to his family or neighbors," she said. "They might shed light on who might have murdered him."

Good idea, and not only to find leads. If Summer learned what Alvarez was like in life, she could replace the haunting picture of what he looked like in death. No one should die without others noticing the passage. "I'd like to express condolences to someone who cared about him."

Fifteen minutes later the girls arrived at 121 Washington Street, Number Two, the address listed for Alvarez. Outside, the apartment building looked like dozens of others in town. Neatly trimmed hedges abutted the façade, grayed by mildew near the base of the board and batten siding. One of the downsides of a warm, humid climate: ubiquitous mold.

No lights on at Number Two. They knocked, and when no one answered, knocked again.

"Guess he didn't have a family," Summer said. "Or they have already moved out. Let's try the other apartments."

A woman with the longest chandelier earrings Summer had ever seen and her two preschool-age daughters lived in unit one. The woman spoke only Spanish. From high school classes, Summer was fluent enough to converse—barely—and learned that Alvarez had rented for about two years and kept pretty much to himself. They also learned the landlady, Mrs. Montera, lived in unit three.

Dayita knocked on the landlady's door. Lights were on, but no one answered. Just as they had decided to leave, an elderly woman threw open the door. She held a handful of hairpins, attempting to arrange her hair into a bun. The pin in her mouth didn't keep her from talking. "No like people see me with hair down. You come in."

A large painting of the Virgin Mary in traditional blue robes dominated one wall of the tidy apartment. A silver crucifix hung over the modest television set, which was broadcasting a soap opera.

"You want cookies? Milk?"

Summer perched on the end of the couch. "No thank you, Mrs. Montera. We came to offer condolences to Mr. Alvarez's family."

Sorrow gave her already crackled skin the appearance of stained glass. "You know Paulo? He like my son. A good boy."

"I was kayaking, Mrs. Montera. I found . . . him." Summer avoided calling her discovery "a body." He was a person. People loved him. She struggled for the right words. Mrs. Montera offered Summer a tissue from a box stashed on an end table.

"No, thank you."

Mrs. Montera pressed the tissue into her hands. "You take."

What was she supposed to do with it? She never cried.

Mrs. Montera's eyes watered, and she whipped another tissue from the box. "Poor Paulo. I write his wife. She write back." Mrs. Montera went into her bedroom and came back with a letter that she read aloud, translating. The words told of love, of separation, of loss that was now final.

Mrs. Alvarez had sent a photograph of her son, Paulito, a dark-eyed child who would never know his father. Summer quickly passed the photo off to Dayita.

Mrs. Montera bustled across the room and shuffled through a stack of magazines. From *Nueva*, she shook out two folded sheets of paper. "I not trust police. I trust you. Paulo give me these. Keep safe, he say. Don't know for what, but I hid them. You read."

They were financial statements to Harewood investors. Exactly alike. Summer skimmed over them. No—not exactly. The dates were alike. The numbers were different.

"Holy shh—" Summer glanced up at the portrait of the Virgin Mary and broke off. These documents were probably what got Alvarez killed! "Mrs. Montera, would you mind if we took these? I can make copies if—"

"No, no, you take. No use for me. I phone him on night he gone. Last thing he say, 'You was last person I expect to see.' Like he know this person. Someone he work with, yes?"

"Didn't you tell the police this?"

The tiny woman shook her head. "No trust for them. You good girls. I know this here." She tapped her chest. "You smart college girls. You know what to do with papers."

Back in the truck, Summer's hands trembled with excitement. "Someone altered the original documents to hide the company's true financial state. Someone at HEC."

"The little boy has such beautiful eyes."

Summer's excitement drained away. Yeah, the monsters had torn apart another kid's life.

"We shouldn't tell anyone about these papers yet," Dayita said. "Mrs. Montera is right. We don't know who to trust."

"Not even Ty?"

"His hatred of Harewood Energy might make him careless. He might get himself killed. Or he might kill someone else if he thinks they were responsible for what happened to his family. Let's watch him for a while and see if he's stable."

Summer understood Dayita's reservations, but she didn't share them. If Ty wanted to kill Harewood or someone else at HEC, he would just do it. He wouldn't waste time making speeches or organizing protests or blogging about clean water. And his love for Grace— *I'm all she's got*—that would keep him anchored.

After dropping Dayita off, Summer drove past her apartment building and swung wide to enter the parking lot. She braked. Ty's van was parked down the street. She pulled in behind it. He got out and leaned against his back bumper, arms crossed. Her truck door creaked as she opened it and stood in front of him, matching his stance.

An unspoken question hung between them.

He finally answered. "I have to park somewhere for the night. Might as well be where I can keep an eye on you. Make sure Jake or Justin or whatever he's calling himself today doesn't show up here."

A spasm of coughing came from the van. Summer took her spare apartment key out of a zippered coin compartment of her wallet and held it over his hand, which was still tucked under his elbow. He made no move to accept her offer.

"Grace's cold sounds worse." She dangled the key as if she were going to drop it. "Let her sleep inside again tonight. You can keep a close eye on me from my couch."

He didn't move. A stubborn one. Well, she was stubborn too. He could retrieve the key from the ground if he refused to uncross those arms. She let go. Like a magician pulling a fast one, he flipped a palm up to catch it. Whoa! He might be the first guy she ever met with the reflexes to match her in Ultimate Frisbee or foosball.

Yes, he could keep a close eye on her. But not too close.

ELEVEN

Saturday

I

SUMMER HOPPED OUT OF BED and into a one piece black bathing suit that had seen better days. She tugged the fuzzy, snagged spandex down over her tushie. She pulled purple gym shorts and a U-Be-Wild Frisbeefest tee-shirt over the suit and was fastening the Velcro on a pair of water sandals when Grace tugged on the hem her tee-shirt.

The girl's features were swollen from sleep, her hair tangled, her pj shorts sliding down her hip on one side. "Where you going?" she asked.

"Saturday morning. Going kayaking." Summer yanked the pj's back up to Grace's waist and centered the seam line. "Want some breakfast?" Luckily, she had restocked her cupboard and fridge after Dayita had complained.

The child followed Summer to the kitchen. "Marshmallow Sugar Crispies." *Mawshmallow. Cwispies.*

"I don't have that kind of cereal. You can have oat circles or granola or fruit."

"I want Marshmallow Sugar Crispies."

"They're junk food."

"Marshmallow Sugar Crispies."

"You are what you eat, kiddo." Summer poured oat circles into a bowl for Grace. "Want blueberries or strawberries on top?"

Grace wrinkled her nose. "They're yucky."

Summer fixed herself a bowl of vanilla yogurt and strawberries topped with organic honey and oats granola.

"What's ki-ack-ing?" Milk drooled down Grace's chin.

"Don't talk with your mouth full." Geesh, how quickly she'd fallen into sounding like her mother—back in the days when her mother still sounded like one herself. "My kayak is a little boat for one person. I paddle it down the river."

"I want to come."

"Not a good idea."

"Why?"

Many reasons. The kayak only held one person, Grace had a cold, and Summer couldn't imagine dealing with a four year old on the water. Did kids that age know how to swim? Before Summer responded, Ty joined them, emerging from the bathroom fully dressed in jeans and faded tee-shirt, C-leg attached and functional.

"Why what?" he asked.

"I want to go too!" Grace screamed, a horrifying shriek that seemed as if it might stretch into eternity, yet Summer found it reassuring. The tantrum made Grace seem more normal, less closed off in her crayon-colored world.

Ty raised his eyebrows: an unspoken question.

"Kayaking," Summer said.

"How about going with me instead?" Ty said. "We can rent our own canoe."

Amazing how fast she calmed down.

He asked Summer if he might have a cup of coffee.

"Help yourself to any food you want. My kitchen is yours." She found a cup for him and inspected the rim. Looked a little cruddy. She wiped it with a dish cloth and rinsed it before she handed it to him. "Taking a kid out on the water isn't a good idea unless she can swim."

"My dad used to take me out when I was little. It'll be fun. Good for Grace."

Summer swallowed a growl. Good for Grace. Not so good for Summer. If they were coming along, the Slave Canal was out. She was in a hurry to erase the memory of the last outing and replace it with a good one. But the canal was no place for a kid.

"Guess we can put in on the Wakulla," she said. "There's a place that rents canoes. They'll have life vests, too."

"I've been down the Wakulla before. Easy float."

Really? So, Mr. Mountaineer had visited Florida before. "Okay, then. Might be fun." Fun as long as Grace was safe. Fun if Grace could be happy for several hours without her crayons. And how was Ty going to manage that fancy prosthetic leg? It had computer chips in it. Surely you couldn't get it wet. She was burning to ask, but it wasn't the kind of question you could blurt out.

They made arrangements for Ty to follow Summer to the planned end of their river journey, where he would leave his van. If Grace tired quickly, Summer could drive them back to his van. If not, they could paddle back to the starting point.

Ty took all three of their bowls to the sink, rinsed them out, and loaded them into the dishwasher.

By the time Summer finished packing her gear, around 6:30 a.m., Claire would be awake. She tried her professor's number, letting it ring a long time. No answer. She left a voicemail. What was the big deal about that flash drive?

As the trio headed north on the highway, pale pink streaks crept upward behind the loblolly and slash pines lining the road, their edges painting patterns of black lace against the sky.

2

BEFORE CLAIRE HAD FINISHED HER FIRST CUP of coffee at 6 a.m., the doorbell rang. What now? Her nerves were frazzled. Because she'd found the bug, she'd decided to come back from Tampa early. The trip had about done her in. A semi had drifted across the center line. If she hadn't reacted quickly and driven with two tires on the rumble strips along the shoulder while she laid on the horn, she'd be dead right now.

She glanced at the arm of the sofa, where the slacks she'd had on yesterday, lay discarded. If it was someone she didn't want to see her in just panties and a tee-shirt, she wouldn't answer the door. Too early for strangers to come knocking. She peeped through the fisheye viewer and an instant surge like a mega-dose of caffeine walloped her.

She threw open the door and leaped up, letting her calves encircle Joe Barrineau's waist. "Honey Bear! What the hell are you doing here?" She kissed his cheeks, his nose, and then pushed her tongue down his throat. Her hands travelled through his hair, all over his face and neck.

She jumped down and led him toward the kitchen while she peppered him with questions. "Why didn't you call and tell me you were coming? Tell me you hate the history department at BU. Are you moving back?"

Joe laughed and lifted her into his arms. He carried her to the bedroom, kissing her softly this time.

"You have coffee breath," he said.

"You come all the way from Boston to tell me that?"

"No, I drove all night from Boston to tell you this." He lowered her to the bed and slid his hands under her tee-shirt to her small breasts. He was stone-hard and let his body do all the talking. Claire had no arguments with that. He came fast—they both did—and she was glad. It meant he hadn't been getting any in Boston. Guiltily, she thought of Alex. Bah! Alex never meant anything to her, and she'd never led him to think differently. She would never have let him pick her up at that art gallery if she hadn't had one glass too many of their free wine.

Later, after coffee and scrambled eggs—and brushed teeth—they made love again, this time more slowly, Claire on top, fingering every hair on his chest with exquisite tenderness. She should have married Barrineau.

"I missed you," he whispered into the hollow of her neck.

To her surprise, moisture formed at the corners of her eyes.

3

SUMMER PULLED HER TRUCK INTO THE GRAVEL LOT by the river, Ty and Grace beside her. A red two-seater kayak holding a middle-aged couple glided atop the deep green water under the bridge on US Route 98. Grace tugged on Ty's tee-shirt and pointed at it. It was the most interest Summer had seen Grace show in the world outside herself. Little kids usually wore their bliss in front of the whole world. Not this kid.

Ty held Grace's hand as they crunched across the gravel to the small wooden rental stand. Ty paid a man with a sun-weathered face thirty dollars for four hours in a canoe.

Summer retrieved her kayak from the truck and positioned her rig at water's edge, her ponytail swinging to one side as she stowed a tote with drinking water, sunscreen, and other necessary gear inside the hatch of her little orange kayak. She caught Ty watching her, but he quickly looked away.

He buckled Grace into a life vest and settled her into the bow seat of their canoe. "What's the first rule?"

"Don't stand or the boat will tip over," Grace said.

"Second rule?"

"If it tips, not to woe-ee because the vest will make me float."

Ty positioned his hands as if to squeeze her shoulders from behind, then stopped short of touching her. "Good job, Sugarpop."

Bent over, ready to launch, Summer heard the man from the rental stand addressing Ty. "Noticed your limp."

She knew without looking exactly how Ty had grown stiff and tight-lipped.

The man continued. "Got a son lost a leg in a car accident. He likes to get out on the water, too. You've found the secret—keep doing what you love to do."

"Plan to," Ty said.

Summer pushed her kayak into the water as if she hadn't heard. After a few strokes, she looked back. Ty pushed off with his paddle, handling the canoe easily. Its design had a very slight lift in the bow and stern, not enough to make it weave, the right amount to navigate easily around obstacles like the stump in front of him. He pointed out the pair of turtles stacked atop each other on the gnarled wood.

Summer witnessed the next few minutes as if in slow motion. Grace's behind lifted off the seat. Her body twisted to the left and one pink tennis shoe inched off the bottom of the canoe. She leaned over the side of the boat to see the turtles. Summer tried to call out. Wanted to warn Grace she was on the verge of falling overboard. Wanted to save her. But the words lodged in her throat and refused to rise. All the years of athletic training, of honing her reflexes, failed her.

Ty's baritone boomed and he stopped rowing. "Grace! Rule number one! Sit!"

The girl dropped back quickly onto the seat and Summer swallowed the bile that had risen in her throat. The child was safe. No thanks to Summer. She should never be allowed near a child. Never.

At least Grace showed interest in something besides a coloring book. That thought lasted only a few seconds—because Grace slipped a crayon and paper from her backpack and began sketching.

Summer back-paddled once, so Ty could pull alongside again.

Light sifted through the leafy canopy and cast shadows along the shoreline, darkening the shallower water until it appeared almost black. Their paddles slurped rhythmically as they cut through the green water in the middle of the river. Summer inhaled air scented with rotting vegetation, fresh greenery and a hint of fish.

Ty rested his paddle across the gunwales. "I missed stuff like this while I was overseas."

"I'll bet. I can't stand to be away from the water for long. Did you enjoy a lot of outdoor adventures with your family?"

He started to paddle again, and Summer matched his pace. "My folks took me on terrific whitewater trips before my mother got sick. She fought the cancer into remission for years, but when she was pregnant with Grace it came back and slowly consumed her body. She had a feeding tube the last few months."

"That must have been tough." Summer glanced at Grace, who dropped one piece of paper onto the canoe's bottom, reflexively taking out another sheet. That child was obsessed.

"I was home on leave and heard a nurse ask my mom what she missed most about her previous life. 'E-ing,' she mouthed. She had to repeat it four times before I translated for the nurse: Eating. Food. After that, I couldn't eat in front of her."

She couldn't read his expression, could only imagine what he must have gone through.

As they glided slowly down river, they disturbed a blue heron wading along the bank. It took flight with a noisy flap of wings.

"My physical therapist told me the secret to leaving the war zone behind is to be, right now, in the moment," he said. "I try."

"Good advice." Let the day and the river take you away.

Grace was still drawing. She never seemed to be in the moment. Another piece of paper hit the bottom of the canoe. "See what she's drawing," Summer said. "What's so important that she isn't even looking at the river?"

Ty selected the last sheet, examined it, and then turned it around for Summer to view. On the paper, turtles lay stacked across a stump, their exterior shapes perfectly captured. The shapes became uniquely Grace's, though, their shells divided into boisterously colored diamonds, triangles, and pentagons.

Grace found her own way of being in the moment. That was all anyone could do.

4

JOE WHISTLED AS HE LEFT Claire's house. He slid into his Prius, trying to remember the words to the tune—what was it? "What a rare mood I'm in; Why, it's almost like being in love." Ah, Nat King Cole. He laughed aloud at himself for slipping into such an old-fashioned song. Yet no wonder. It was an old-fashioned moment. Claire had said yes! Yes, yes, yes! He hoped she wouldn't change her mind. No, she wouldn't. She meant it. She was ready to marry him and move to Boston at the end of the semester. Only six weeks from now. She was smart and resourceful—she'd find another teaching position, if not for the fall semester, surely in the spring. He promised her the next move they made would be for her career advancement, and he meant it.

The sun was out full force, the vast blue sky marred only by a jet streak. He loved Claire's neighborhood, the retro pastiche of the old brick homes. He had deliberately chosen an older home in Boston with her in mind. Not that he thought at the time she would ever consent to join him. Still, as he searched properties with a real estate agent, he had found himself thinking, Claire would love this staircase, Claire would appreciate the light in this breakfast room, Claire's pottery would look great on the mantel.

Joe turned the ignition and backed up a bit, away from the black Honda parked so close in front of him. Almost touching his bumper. Oh well, he wouldn't let a dumb jackass spoil his mood. Yes, yes, yes!

He whistled while he waited his turn at The Breadline, scanning the chalkboard specials, smiling back at the lady in front of him who was openly chuckling over him, but he didn't care. The special of the day was the Humdinger—diced chicken breast, mango chutney, and cashews on a croissant. He ordered two.

When the chef/waiter/cashier (and probably chief bottle washer and bookkeeper) served them, he laughed at Joe. "Mister, she must be quite a woman to have you in such a fine mood today."

Joe accepted the sack of sandwiches. "You wouldn't believe what a great woman."

"Know how you feel. Got one of them myself."

An endorsement for the sandwiches. A happy chef prepared food with pleasure and a desire to deliver pleasure to others. A grouchy chef, on the other hand, inflicted his misery on the world with a heavy hand on the salt or salad dressing. At their age, both Claire and Joe watched how many calories they consumed, but the lemon curd/coconut and red velvet cakes displayed under glass by the counter looked so delectable—and so obviously homemade with love—Joe asked for a slice of each. While the chef boxed the goodies, Joe imagined dividing them with Claire. They would feed each other forkfuls of cake and icing. And he would suck crumbs off her lips afterward. Yes, yes, yes!

When he pulled in front of her little house, the black Honda was gone. Good. He might have been tempted to tap its bumper. Dumb jackass. The bags clutched in his hand, he sprinted to the front door. It was locked. A little odd. Was she taking another shower? He rang the bell and waited, but Claire didn't come.

The metal latch of the gate in the privacy fence clicked as he opened it. The gate shuddered as he slammed it back in place so the latch would catch. It could be stubborn. Joe tried the French doors leading to the dining room. Also locked. He'd only been gone half an hour. Where was Claire? He cupped his hand over his right eye to block the glare of the sun against the bedroom window and peeked in.

5

AFTER AN ENERGETIC START, by noon an unenthusiastic sun flirted in and out of hazy clouds—which was okay with Summer. Meant the rest of the afternoon wouldn't be Hades hot. They disembarked at the St. Marks City Park to picnic. The first leg of the trip had taken a little more than an hour and a half. They lollygagged so Grace could watch coots and herons and even a tiny snake writhing in the tannin-stained water. Grace's serious observation of each creature was fascinating. You could almost see the synapses clicking in her brain, making mental photographs of each new species. Grace didn't get excited, didn't squeal or smile like most kids.

In between bites of peanut butter and jelly sandwiches, Summer examined Grace's drawings. The child had captured the form of an alligator perfectly. She'd drawn the snake, too. Every single drawing had

Grace's signature touch: the jewel-colored geometric internal designs.

Summer held up a drawing of manatees—a cow and her calf with friendly, homely faces. "This one's my favorite."

Grace didn't respond. She had finished eating and was drawing again. Summer leaned over to see what had attracted her attention this time. Ahhh—the spaniel leashed to a nearby picnic table. Mrs. Patel was right. Ty needed to have her tested.

Summer re-focused on Ty, who was telling her about his work in the navy. It sounded as if he did more work on land than at sea. She studied his face while he talked about his training as a SEAL. Geesh—keeping the altered documents they'd received from Mrs. Montera secret was stupid. She filled him in on their trip to Alvarez's apartment.

His eyes sparked. "I'd like to see those papers when we get back. Sounds like exactly the ammunition we need to knock down Harewood's house of cards."

"Also information that could get us killed. Don't forget that."

"Have you shown the cops?"

She shook her head.

"Don't." His face was grim. "Harewood always has locals on his payroll."

"We know to be careful. Dayita didn't even want to tell you." She bit into an apple. A loud crash of metal against metal sounded nearby. Before Summer could turn her head to see what it was, Ty slammed into her. Her apple arced out of her hand. Her neck whipped backward. As his body covered hers, her head clunked into the concrete. What the hell had just happened? What the?—there was a gun in his hand. Who brought a gun to a picnic?

She shoved Ty off her. His muscles twisted like thick cables. Blood surged visibly through his neck, his forearms, his hands.

Of course—post traumatic stress disorder, triggered by loud noise. She slid to the farthest end of the bench and jumped to her feet. Until now, she had only read about PTSD. But it was more than a label. It was real. And scary.

Summer glanced at Grace, wondering if Ty's over-reaction would upset her. Obviously not. The child colored away, oblivious.

Ty lowered the gun to his lap.

Summer sat back down, keeping the length of the bench between them. "It was only the lid to the trash can."

Ty's Adam's apple heaved as if he were trying to swallow gravel. "Sorry."

"It's okay." Summer could smell the sweat that soaked his tee-shirt, a pungent odor like vinegar. The smell of fear. She adjusted her own tee-shirt and gingerly explored the back of her arms, scraped raw from the slide along the concrete. She touched the knot rising on her head beneath her ponytail scrunchie. Loosening the elastic dialed back the pain a notch.

"The noise—did it remind you of something that happened in Iraq?" she asked.

He steadied his arms on the concrete table top. His answer came in little bursts between deep breaths. Probably trying to expel adrenaline. "On my last mission, an extraction, our Little Bird got hit by a missile."

"Little bird?"

"Helicopter."

So that's what happened to his leg. "Must have been terrifying."

"Two guys were sitting right beside me one minute and the next they were gone. I was alive. They weren't."

"That would be tough to accept." She bit her lip. Not any harder than losing a twin. "Did you have to kill people when you were in the service?"

He didn't answer.

"I don't blame you if you don't want to talk about it."

"Talk's cheap." A muscle in his neck twitched. "I still have a shit-load of garbage to work through, but don't tell me I need to see a psychiatrist."

Summer grunted assent. "Most psychiatrists are trying to learn what's wrong with you so they can figure out what's wrong with themselves."

He tried to smile, but it didn't come off. "Sounds as if you have experience."

She shrugged. Didn't want to go there. The more her mother ig-nored her, the more risks Summer took. Like escaping from this lame church camp her mother had send her to when she was twelve. Coun-selors expected her to make mosaic ashtrays and pipe cleaner crosses. Instead, she spend two adventurous days fishing and camping primitive style in the woods nearby before sheriff's deputies tracked her down. Or like hitchhiking to the river and kayaking the Slave Canal all by herself when she was fourteen.

Twice during her senior year of high school, she twirled her hair up into a bun and tucked a pillow under a loose shirt, pretending to be pregnant. She waddled into a convenience store, fake wedding ring on her finger, to buy beer. Even got the clerk to load the cases into her truck so the "baby" wouldn't be stressed. The kids at the parties laughed their asses off. The third time she tried this stunt, she got caught.

She knew these escapades would get her in trouble, yet she couldn't restrain herself.

Her mother paid her own psychotherapist, Dr. Therese Neymeyer, to talk to Summer. Together they unraveled reasons for Summer's behavior. A need to get her mother's attention. (Wasn't going to happen. Summer couldn't compete with whichever of Dr. Neymeyer's drugs du jour cajoled Summer's mother into facing another sunrise. She couldn't compete with a dead twin.) Her father's taking off two years after Chrissie's death. (All kinds of kids got along without fathers. No need to get her panties in a wad over that.) Attempts to plug the hole in Summer's life left by the death of her twin. (Did it really take an expensive education to figure that one out?) A desire to die herself, to join her twin, to quiet the survivor's guilt and the pain. Summer couldn't think of a smart comeback for that one. She stopped seeing the therapist.

Finally, her mother resorted to a New Age crystal healer and then a psychic who claimed she could channel Chrissie. When Madame Gia darkened the lights and faked Chrissie's voice, Summer rocketed to her feet. "This is pure horseshit," she said. Her mother left the red imprint of her palm on Summer's face and a far deeper injury with her words: "Why did you make her go away?" Her mother sobbed and sobbed. Summer never knew for sure if her mother meant that Summer had silenced Chrissie's voice at the séance, or if her mother had finally said aloud what Summer felt her mother believed: it was Summer's fault Chrissie died.

They never went back to Madame Gia.

Sometimes the memory of Chrissie throbbed like a stoved thumb; sometimes it stabbed like an elbow banged into a doorway; other times it ached like an infected tooth. The pain never lessened. No therapist could sprinkle magic dust to undo the loss.

Summer looked over at Ty. He was breathing normally now, but no magic dust was going to fix him either. She gathered their gear from the picnic table. Grace put her crayons in her backpack but left the drawings sitting on the table. Ty gathered them and started to stow them in his bag, but when he saw the top drawing his mouth tightened. He blinked twice, then wadded up the paper and tossed it in the trash without losing his cool over the clanking lid. Grace, oc-cupied with loading her backpack into the bottom of the canoe, didn't notice that he'd thrown out her picture.

Ty joined Grace without offering a word or sign to Summer. A crust from Grace's sandwich was lying on the table. Summer had planned to leave it for the birds, but instead she walked it to the trashcan. She lifted the lid and pulled the drawing out. It took a moment to pro-cess the curves and the protrusion. Then she understood. A prosthetic leg. More precisely, a foot and calf. Decorated with red hexagons and purple triangles and blue diamonds. It had a funny curly line coming out of it that took Summer another few seconds to interpret. Ahhh. An electric wire for charging the device.

Ty was missing a leg from the knee down. A tough break, but she wasn't going to pity him. He had survived his deployment. Which was more than the guys sitting beside him had done.

To distract Ty from dark thoughts, on the paddle back to their put-in point, Summer told him all about her master's project.

"ASR wells are an important source of drinking water for over-stressed areas like South Florida," she said as she paddled upstream. "They can benefit communities during droughts, but these particular wells aren't behaving the way they should." She thought again about the flash drive. "A lot of money for the university rides on the findings. Dr. Dunham is getting pressure to soften our conclusions."

Ty rested the paddle against the side of the canoe. "That would undermine trust in the university."

"If she's half the person I think she is, she'd resign first."

They paddled for a while in silence, listening to the call of birds, the sound of the paddles as they stroked the water, and the occasional intrusion of a car rumbling down the nearby highway. Ty's jaw line had been rigid when they'd started back, but it was relaxed now.

The water: best therapy of all.

After they drove back to the apartment, Ty slipped a yellow plastic bottle from his backpack, threw back his head, and swallowed another one of those pills. Dry. Hesitated and took another.

She touched her head where he'd slammed her down on the concrete bench. Dayita had reminded her about all the trouble vets were having readjusting to civilian life. Suicides. Even a couple of murders. Yet Ty had turned over every penny of his signing bonus with the private security force to pay for his mother's health care—that had been one of the nuggets Dayita had unearthed.

That didn't seem like the kind of guy who would hurt someone, but what were those pills? And what had he seen when he'd looked across that concrete bench with his gun? He didn't seem very stable. She had been wrong to tell him about the documents Mrs. Montera had given her.

And why were birds always cropping up in her life? Another Little Bird.

Chrissie wanted to be a bird. A dozen or more lined the power wire bordering Mason Street, sharp-beaked sentinels paying homage to her sister's broken body sprawled on the pavement. Starlings, Summer had decided years later when she browsed through a field guide, but whether it was true or not, she couldn't say for sure.

6

AT THREE-THIRTY, JOE WAS STILL SITTING in Claire's kitchen answering Detective George Theofanis's questions. During the pauses, Joe replayed the way Claire had screamed "Honey Bear" when she opened the door and saw him. Just that morning. It seemed so long ago now.

"Please, I need to be at the hospital with Claire," Joe said.

"You want us to catch whoever did this, don't you? Every passing hour makes the trail that much colder. Tell me again. Why did you come to the back of the house?" Theofanis asked.

"I've explained at least four times. I came to the back of the house because the front door was locked. Claire had no reason to lock the door because I was only making a sandwich run."

"The sandwiches in the bag." The detective jerked his head toward the counter.

"Yes, the sandwiches in the bag." Joe had tried to be understanding the first few times he answered the same questions. Now he had grown tired. He wanted to be with Claire. Needed to be by her side.

"Then what?"

"I opened the privacy gate and looked through the French doors into the dining room. I looked through the bedroom window and saw Claire lying on the floor. She was bleeding. So I grabbed the patio chair and swung it against the window." The sounds of shattering glass and snapping vinyl grids remained fresh in his mind.

He rubbed his right shoulder and elbow, which ached like a son-of-a-bitch from the impact. He should ice them down, but he felt guilty for even thinking about himself. What must Claire be going through? Though he didn't attend church now, he had been raised Catholic. He closed his eyes and prayed with all his being, sending love toward the hospital across town. *Live, Claire, live. Live for me. For us.* Theofanis's voice pulled him back into the room.

"Why didn't you telephone for an ambulance?"

"I did."

"But not right away."

No, you moron, she would have bled to death. "As soon as I had applied pressure bandages to the most serious wounds, I called."

"She was still bleeding when the ambulance arrived."

"She had many wounds requiring extensive surgery."

"Who do you think did this to Miss Dunham?"

"Dr. Dunham. I have no idea."

"You say she agreed to marry you."

"Yes, we got engaged this morning."

"You know what I think? She turned you down and you couldn't handle it. You went psycho. No one would blame you. Women make us all crazy."

"She didn't turn me down, and I'm not the kind of guy who attacks women. She turned me down three months ago and I certainly didn't attack her." Joe disliked this Theofanis, though he understood the detective was only doing his job. This whole stinking mess sucked.

Why did this have to happen today of all days?

"Why did you bug her office?"

"What!" Joe put his hands on the table to steady himself, as his whole world view was losing its underpinnings. "Her office was bugged? That doesn't make any sense."

A crime scene technician found Claire's mobile, which had apparently been knocked under the bed during the struggle. He dusted the phone for prints, turned it on, and held it out for Theofanis to see.

Theofanis read it aloud. "Last number she called was 852-566-2929."

"That's my number," Joe said. "My cell."

"Seems she called you at 1:15," Theofanis said.

Joe shook his head a little to clear it. He had left for The Breadline a little after one. "Must have been right after I drove off. A black Honda was parked outside when I left. I remember being angry because it was actually touching my bumper."

"You were angry?"

"At the driver of the Honda." Geez, this guy twisted every word Joe said until he sounded like a maniac.

"But you were angry. What did Claire want when she called?"

"I didn't get the call." Joe pulled his cell out of his pocket. The screen alerted him to Claire's voicemail. He retrieved it.

Her voice was barely recognizable. Besides the recording being scratchy, Claire was whispering. "Joe, pick up, please! Please come back. Someone's in the house." The message recorded thuds and the sound of splintering. Must have been the bedroom door. A scream. Fierce cursing. A man's roar of rage. Screams. Moans. Followed by silence more dreadful than any noise Joe had ever heard.

Theofanis took the phone from him. "This is evidence." He replayed the message.

What if Joe never heard Claire's voice again? She'd lost a lot of blood. He should be with her. If—when—she came to, she needed to see him there. Joe's molars ground together in the back of his mouth. He wasn't a violent guy—like he'd been trying to tell this detective— but if he had to pick one person in the world to beat to a pulp right now, it would be Theofanis.

"I'd like to have the phone back as soon as possible."

Theofanis looked at him but didn't respond. The detective's mobile rang. He listened for a minute. "Thanks," he said.

The detective eyed Joe. "The voicemail corroborates your story."

"It wasn't me!" He didn't give a damn if the rage showed in his voice. He let out all his repressed frustration. "That's what I've been telling you bastards all along. Can I leave for the hospital now?"

The detective was still studying him. "Got a call from the hospital. She's still in surgery. I'm posting a guard on her door until we figure out who did this to her."

"Can I go now?"

Theofanis nodded. "You could always go. You weren't under arrest."

Now he tells me. Joe tore out of the front door.

7

GRACE WAS DRAPED AROUND TY'S NECK, mostly asleep, when he carried her into the apartment. Cute, the way he tickled her nose with her own pigtail to wake her up.

The three of them ate a simple dinner—a cassoulet of beans, rice and tomatoes Summer had thrown into the crock pot before leaving for the river that morning.

"Great dish," Ty said. He avoided looking at Summer, and she wondered if he felt the attraction as strongly as she did. If she closed her eyes and brushed her fingers through the air, she thought she might actually touch the bonds forming between them, as if they possessed physical properties.

"Yucky," Grace said, but after the first bite, she attacked her food with gusto. Soon her head was drooping, done in by the water adventure.

Summer should have realized the child needed a nap. More evidence she sucked as a caretaker.

"Let her stay here again tonight," Summer said. Ty's eyes darted toward her, and then back at his plate. "I mean, she's worn out." He kept eating in silence. Geez, she was making the situation worse. This didn't have to be complicated—she didn't want commitments from him. "Look, you're welcome to the couch again if you want it, or you can sleep in the van—whichever. It's just for one more night."

"Fine."

She tucked Grace into bed, a bit grimy. The child deserved a thorough scrubbing in the morning before she returned to sponge baths in Walmart bathrooms.

In the kitchen Ty was washing dishes. Beside him, she dried. Even though their arms didn't touch, the fine hairs on her skin stood on end, responding to his skin's signals. His arm brushed against hers and she made the mistake of glancing up. He looked at her as if he divined her secrets. Like the way she'd always wanted a guy to massage the underneath of her toes. She didn't dare breathe.

Summer let the dish towel drop to the counter and escaped to the shower. She locked the bathroom door. Quickly lathered up and rinsed. Scooped her wet hair into a ponytail. Pulled on jeans and a tank top. Grabbed her truck keys.

"I have to meet Dayita," she said as she bounced over to the front door. "It may be late when I get back, so go ahead and sack out on the couch whenever you want."

Only when she reached her truck did her heart rate slow down.

8

DAYITA SLID INTO A BOOTH, DIMLY LIT by a Tiffany-style lamp sporting a beer advertisement. The bartender was already popping the top of a Yuengling and setting it in front of Summer. Yeah—she was that well-known here. As usual, Tom didn't ask for payment. Before long, he would steer some patsy to bet against her friend in foosball or darts. If the wrong guy ever caught on to the hustle, Dayita didn't like to think about what would happen to her friend—or to the bartender.

After ordering a mojito, Dayita noticed Summer's still-wet hair. She'd obviously left her apartment in a hurry. "You sounded flustered on the phone. What's wrong?"

"Nothing. Just didn't want to sit home on Saturday night." Summer's eyes cut to the gray metal napkin dispenser.

Uh huh. Lying. Summer rarely shared feelings, despite the many years of their friendship.

Dayita was eleven when her mother thrust a registration form for Frisbee camp into her hands and told her she was going.

Dayita tossed the form onto the kitchen table. "I hate sports."

"This isn't a sport. It's fun."

"No way I'm wasting a week playing a stupid game like Frisbee."

Her mother laid a page from the Loblolly Lake newspaper in front of her. In the photo above the center fold, Summer stood near her mother, arms crossed, scowling slightly, obviously irritated by having to pose for the photo accompanying the safe bicycling story.

Mrs. Patel laid a finger on Summer's chin. "You have to be this girl's friend. She isn't happy."

"How can you tell from one lousy picture?"

"I know."

"How?"

"I just do. We have to help this family." Her mother hid her face in her hands. "If we don't, I am going to be born into the next life as a deformed beggar or a leper."

The tears worked and Dayita went to camp.

At first, Summer mostly ignored Dayita, her clumsy efforts to learn the fundamentals of Frisbee almost as pathetic as her attempts to befriend the haughty girl who was clearly the best athlete at the camp. Yet by week's end, they were friends. Real friends by the time school started up again. Summer didn't have the slightest bias against foreigners. She didn't ask dumb questions like why Dayita's mom had a statue of Lakshmi on a credenza as well as a painting of Jesus on the wall. She didn't act like Dayita smelled bad because she ate food seasoned with spices Americans had never heard of. At first, Summer's forehead wrinkled as she struggled to understand Dayita's mom, but over the years both her mother's accented English and Summer's ability to parse it improved.

Summer was the best friend Dayita had ever had. They shared a desire to learn and tacit recognition of their status as outsiders. They shared everything but their feelings. And the reason her mother had pushed the girls together in the first place.

Friends or not, aspects of Summer's personality annoyed the hell out of Dayita. None more so than the stunts she pulled at the Foos and Booze. The gambling hustles were bad enough, but the sexual encounters with guys were downright stupid. They had gradually increased over the past two years. Dayita blamed Dr. Dunham for Summer's attitude. Dunham believed that men inhibited women from reaching their potential. Other female professors managed to balance careers with children, but Summer was too blinded by admiration of her mentor to consider alternatives to noncommitment.

Around nine thirty, Dayita tracked Summer's eyes to the bar. Tom, the bartender, inclined his head toward Dayita's and Summer's table, and the guy Tom was chatting up swiveled on his bar stool and looked in their direction. Short and stocky, the soon-to-be victim was not particularly good looking, but he had a thick crop of curly nutmeg-colored hair. He seemed personable in his interactions with the bartender. The mark went back to chatting with Tom.

"Don't do this," Dayita said.

"What?"

"That guy with the brown hair—you're scoping him for a hustle and hook-up. Remember Justin-Jake?"

"Oh, come on. How likely is it that another creep will come along any time soon? Besides, I never saw Justin again outside the bar."

"I'm afraid some guy's going to hurt you."

"The only way a guy's going to hurt me is if I let myself get so in-volved with one it distracts me from my career goals. We've had this discussion before, so drop it, okay?"

The fellow with the nutmeg hair slid off his bar stool and sauntered toward them. Dayita became aware of the tinkle of her ankle bracelet, the way her leg pumped back and forth. Why couldn't she sit still?

Because she wanted to smack some sense into Summer—that's why. She uncrossed her legs and planted her feet on the floor.

Challenged to play darts, Summer sprung from the booth. She shifted her weight to one leg and rotated the other on the ball of her foot, a stance meant to be both flirty and innocent. Huh! Nothing innocent about it. These seductions were almost the only times Sum-mer smiled, but no real joy fueled the expression. Dayita's mother had been right: Summer was unhappy, but picking up strangers would never fill the hole in her heart.

Dayita lacked the power to stop Summer's self-destructive behavior, but she would at least make sure her friend got home safely afterward. She pulled out her cell and tested the app. Still worked. Might as well check her email while Summer played this guy for a fool.

9

SENATOR FELIPE VARGAS'S KNEES WEAKENED as he watched his son Manny cross the bedroom in his Spiderman jammies. The boy was so innocent. So unbearably precious.

Manny picked up a model F-16 from his nightstand and sent it into a nose dive toward his bedspread, which was printed with dozens of different kinds of planes.

The boy plopped onto the bed. "Mom's mad at me for getting in that fight at the game, isn't she?"

The senator smiled a little. "I understand why you jumped in to defend your teammates. It was a natural thing to do. But there are better ways to solve problems. Fists and guns and bombs never really solve anything."

Manny flew his plane past his father's face with a rrr-rrr-rrrrrrr. "But you were a fighter pilot."

"Yes, I served my country. But even if you win a war with planes and bombs, the real work comes afterward." The senator stroked his son's dark hair. "The real work is negotiating peace. Do you understand?"

Manny stood on the bed and spun around with the F-16. The boy exposed his new permanent teeth and imitated gunfire. "Eh-eh-eh-eh-eh-eh."

The senator sighed. Perhaps when the boy was older they'd have this talk again. He took the plane from him and laid it on top of the chest of drawers that held the boy's clothing.

"Good night, Manny." He ruffled the boy's dark hair and dropped a kiss on his forehead before turning off the lamp.

Downstairs, Ana was curled up on their tan suede sectional couch, already absorbed in an episode of *Law and Order*. He jingled his car keys and leaned over to kiss her cheek.

She looked up. "Going to the office?"

"Mmm-hmm."

"You work too hard." She popped a chocolate-covered pretzel in her mouth and turned back to the fifty-two-inch plasma screen.

An hour later, he entered his downtown Tallahassee condo and poured himself a glass of Rioja. The senator unwrapped a Hershey's kiss, popped it into his mouth and walked out onto the balcony. He found the evening air cool and damp against his skin, pleasantly so.

The stunning view of the capital city from the top floor was one of the main reasons he'd chosen this unit. The expense was well worth it. Unless you saw the city from an airplane or from up here, you didn't fully appreciate the thick canopy of trees. Of course they cut way too many down and laid down way too much asphalt, but Tallahassee was blessed with more green space than most Florida cities.

He wrapped his fingers around the wrought iron railing. "Do you ever wonder if someday a developer will hold a chainsaw beside the last live oak standing and insist it is blocking growth and progress?"

Ned rose from his chair and clasped a firm hand on the senator's shoulder. "We won't let that happen, will we?"

"Sometimes I wonder if people will wake up in time."

"They will."

Felipe Vargas looped his arm around his aide's back and leaned his head closer until the familiar texture of Ned's cheek brushed against his nose. Somehow, Ned always managed to smell as if he'd just stepped from the shower.

TWELVE

Monday

I

THE LAB WAS DARK WHEN SUMMER ARRIVED Monday morning. She jiggled the door handle even though she figured it would be locked since the lights were out. But Claire's absence was so unexpected, she rattled the handle a second time. This morning the professor was supposed to review her thesis one last time before Summer defended it to the committee.

Summer found a custodian to unlock the lab and she went ahead with routine tasks. At nine o'clock another lab assistant, a chubby West African named Robert, came in. Summer had known him for several months but his English was so halting and thickly accented they struggled to communicate. Usually she settled for "good morning" and avoided conversation. She hated herself for it, but the self-loathing would only increase if she pretended to understand him when she didn't.

This morning Robert wanted to talk as he pulled books from his backpack. "Too much bad about Dock-er Dun-Em."

Too much bad? What was he talking about? She'd called Claire again Sunday morning and it had gone straight to voicemail.

"I'm sorry?" She hoped her inflection showed she didn't understand him.

Robert shook his head. "Very bad. Very bad what happen."

"What happened?"

"Doan you read newspaper?"

Rarely. Her mother's picture and news about the Chrissie Foundation might be in there. Who needed constant reminders? Besides, she'd spent her entire Sunday hiking alone through the Leon County

Sinks. April was mating season for gopher tortoises, and she'd seen several moving about. She had tramped around the Big Dismal Sink, awed, as always, by the hundred foot drop to the water which drops another hundred feet underwater. There was a cave entrance at eighty feet down, but Summer had never learned to scuba dive.

Anyway, her mobile had been turned off all day, and hell, no she hadn't read the newspaper.

"What happened to Dr. Dunham?"

"She tack and in hopsitle. Very bad. She nice lady."

Hospital, she translated. Tack? Robert was saying something else about Claire, about how smart she had been, how hard she had worked. His words sounded so past tense her head filled with a low buzz. It increased in volume until the sound overwhelmed her. Death happened so fast. You were breathing one minute and not the next. She swallowed. The noise in her head abated.

Her fingers ached from gripping the edge of the lab table so hard. She let go and collapsed onto a high stool. "When? When did this happen?"

A deep vertical line creased Robert's forehead. "Like I tole. Satidee. She been in hopsitle Satidee. Still sleep. Very bad."

Sleep? Did he mean a coma? Summer grabbed her backpack and shoved her shoulder into the lab door. It swung open and she sprinted down the corridor, which seemed darker, narrower than normal. Before she reached the end, Dr. Hu exited his office and strode purposefully toward her. Because she was running—or because he knew what had happened to Claire? Summer halted.

"Dr. Hu, Robert seems to think Dr. Dunham is in the hospital."

"I was coming to see you. She was attacked in her home. I just came from the hospital myself. Dr. Dunham is in ICU. She needs her rest, so I don't advise going to see her yet. She asked me to retrieve any files you have on the grant." Hu blinked and touched his slicked-back hair. It didn't move. Gel held it in place like concrete. "She is concerned about meeting the deadline. I am going to handle all the paperwork for her. The least I can do."

She had never warmed to Dr. Hu when she'd taken one of his courses, but part of that involved her difficulty understanding accents. She was a much better visual than auditory learner. Difficult situations often brought out the best in people. She remembered neighbors and friends bringing food to the house when Chrissie died.

"Of course," Summer told him. "How kind of you to help Dr. Dunham. When do you need my files?"

"I was hoping you'd get them now. She said the report was finished and I'd like to proof it one more time, sign it and send it off."

But Summer remembered the strange urgency when Claire pressed the flash drive into her palm. Keep this somewhere safe, she'd said. Was Hu lying? The blink, the way he touched his hair—were they "tells" like in poker?

Summer had always sensed a strain between Claire and Dr. Hu when they occupied the same room. They remained overtly polite, but never showed signs of the camaraderie Claire shared with other professors on Summer's committee. She didn't think Claire was prejudiced toward Hu because he was Chinese . . . but Claire was not an easy person. She scorned the weaker students. Summer intuited her mentor would have little tolerance toward people like Chrissie or Grace.

Robert had said Claire wasn't conscious yet. Tough circumstances often brought out the worst in people too. She had seen that in the way her parents turned away from each other. Summer wasn't relinquishing any files until she understood why Claire asked her to protect the flash drive.

"They're at home, Dr. Hu. I'll get them right now."

He smiled. "I'd appreciate that very much."

It didn't make sense, his wanting Summer's files. The grant would be on Claire's computer in her office. Why wouldn't Hu access the report there? She turned to leave.

Hu's voice stopped her. "I look forward to hearing you defend your thesis, Miss Cassidy."

He was on her committee. Someone she should keep on her side—at least until after her defense. Who knew when that would be, with Claire in the hospital.

Despite Hu's warning, Summer headed for Loblolly Lake Hospital. A Pink Lady directed her to the ICU waiting room. Summer stood inside where a TV on the wall was set to CNN at a low volume like an insect's buzz. It reinforced Summer's disorientation. She dropped into a seat and stared at the TV, her thoughts roaming in all directions. Though she didn't believe prayer changed physical events in the world, not really, she closed her eyes and tried to send positive thoughts and energy outward toward Claire. It was impossible to conceive of a vital force like Claire Dunham hooked to monitors.

After a few minutes, Detective Theofanis entered and motioned her to follow him to the hallway.

"You have a falling out with Dr. Dunham?" he asked.

He had to be kidding—he wasn't really asking her this. "No. We were close. She's my lead professor."

"Where were you Saturday morning?"

For a few seconds her mind blanked. Then she remembered. "On the Wakulla River with Ty Franceschi and his sister Grace. We were on the water From dawn until late in the afternoon."

To think her professor had been lying in the hospital Saturday while she and Ty floated down the river. She felt guilty, even though it was irrational. When tragedies happened, rivers should flow backward, lava should bubble forth, people should stop in their tracks and take notice. So weird, the way life churned on. People kept shopping for new jeans, eating ice cream, playing meaningless games like Frisbee.

Theofanis nodded. "Okay. Don't let the questions upset you. I had to ask."

They walked back into the waiting room.

Theofanis whispered, "How's she doing today? You talk to her fiancé?" He flicked his chin toward the other side of the room.

Claire engaged? She tried not to appear surprised as she looked in the direction of the detective's chin. The Prius guy. Claire's boyfriend. Or former boyfriend. He looked like shit. Hadn't shaved. Wrinkled shirt and slacks. Mussed hair.

"I haven't met him," she said. "Only seen him."

Until now, she hadn't crossed the line between Claire's professional and personal life. She remembered how Claire had reacted when the one boyfriend dared to show his face in her office. But this was different. Her mind made up, she marched over and cleared her throat to get his attention. "Hi, I'm Summer Cassidy, one of Claire's—I mean—Dr. Dunham's students."

The man stood and offered her his hand. His smile, though tired, creased the skin by his eyes. "Claire's told me about you."

Looked as if that line between personal and professional wasn't firm. His smile faded abruptly when he looked at Theofanis. He inclined his head slightly in acknowledgment and then ignored him.

"I'm glad you came," he continued, speaking only to her. "I'm Joe Barrineau."

"How is she?"

Summer learned Robert was right. The professor was still unconscious. So exactly what was Dr. Hu's game? With every detail Summer learned, her muscles tightened. Claire—stabbed dozens of times—who would act with such violence? A boyfriend? Unconsciously, she took one step back from Joe Barrineau. Then dismissed the idea. His demeanor and appearance practically shouted his love and genuine concern. Who then? She would have asked Theofanis but he'd disappeared.

Joe gave Summer his cell number and encouraged her to call to check on Claire's progress. Summer made her way out of the Intensive Care Unit. Claire had to be all right. Summer couldn't imagine a world in which a strong presence like Claire Dunham could be silenced.

This was a serous setback for Summer's thesis defense. Claire was the only committee member who had command of the ASR research. Summer's graduation might be delayed.

She pushed those thoughts away. They were unpleasantly selfish when Claire lay unconscious a few steps away.

2

ISAAC HAREWOOD PARKED HIS JAG in the handicapped spot in front of Bailey Douglass's firm. He kept the motor running and silently thanked Willis Carrier for inventing air conditioning. He loosened his necktie. Maybe he was on the verge of a heart attack. He rubbed his left shoulder and found it somewhat sore.

As Bailey slid into the passenger's seat, those magnificent boobs, encased in a purple blouse, brushed against the dash. Not for the first time, Harewood wondered how she managed not to topple over when she walked.

She lightly touched the sleeve of his shirt with her lacquered nails and gave him no chance to get in the first word. "You can relax, Isaac. I swear we had nothing to do with what happened to Dr. Dunham."

Gee-zuss H. Kee-rist, like he wasn't going to worry after reading about the attack in the paper. Julia Lambert and Niles Morrell swore they were not behind the assault on Claire Dunham either.

But the police knew about the succinylcholine that took out Phil Snyder—how they figured that out was a complete mystery. Too much bad shit was coming down at once. The attack on Dunham would keep those clowns in the police department agitated.

"Do you know who attacked her?" he asked.

"No. My professionals installed and monitored electronic surveillance in Dunham's office and we had an operative present when she played handball with the girl. My people followed Dunham, but they didn't interact with her in any way. We didn't find a trace of inappropriate behavior between Dunham and the girl. Now, the girl's quite the little bed-hop. Not always a bed. One guy bragged to my detective that he porked—his word, not mine—Miss Cassidy standing up in an alley outside a popular bar. So tawdry, the college girls these days, not an ounce of shame, so there's no blackmail leverage there. Anyway, the newspaper interviewed Dunham's fiancé, so I'm afraid that was a bad lead you were given. The professor's not gay."

"I don't give a flying leap about their sex lives right now, Bailey. Should I expect that detective to knock on my office door and lead me away in handcuffs?"

She turned tiger eyes on him, which usually sent a thrill straight to his groin. Especially when he was in proximity of those watermelons. This morning they nauseated him.

"No policeman's coming. Promise. No one associated with my firm attacked the professor. The woman we engaged to follow Dr. Dunham did take down a tag number of a car parked outside both the gym and her house. That information may prove useful. We aren't sure yet."

Even if Bailey was telling the truth, his contact in the sheriff's office said they were trying to connect the murder of Isaac's employee and the attack on a professor studying his wells. "Can they trace the surveillance device back to you? To me?"

"Of course not."

"Get it out of her office immediately."

The redhead eyed him as if he were an unreasonable child. "Only an amateur would do that."

"I want the damn bug out of her office."

"It stays."

Isaac heard—or only imagined—veiled threats in her words. Any further argument and he thought he was likely to find out exactly what was in her files on him. No doubt she knew about the art hidden in an overseas vault. She probably knew about his net losses, knew how the whole pyramid scheme propping up his corporations teetered on the edge of collapse. He needed time. A few more months and he thought he'd be dug out of this hole.

"I want this nightmare to be over." He rubbed his left arm and flexed his elbow, on the alert for any twinge of pain that might indicate a heart attack. None yet. He was inexplicably disappointed.

3

SUMMER, AS USUAL, ESCHEWED THE IMPOSSIBLY SLOW ELEVATOR in her apartment building lobby and pushed open the fire door that led to the stairwell. The air inside the closed space chilled her skin. As she bounded up the concrete steps to the second floor, she analyzed recent events. Harewood had a hissy over the grant's conclusions. Did HEC believe getting Claire out of the way would delay release of the final report? Hu had lied about Claire—but why? The final report was already written, and Summer didn't understand why that report would matter to Hu one way or the other. Unless he really was trying to help. But that didn't explain the lie.

She shoved open the fire door on the second floor, retrieving her key as she traversed the carpeted corridor. She pocketed it when she saw the door to her apartment was slightly ajar. She had two more steps to reach it when a loud crash stopped her cold. Summer stood still for twenty seconds, debating the best course of action. Should she go in? Or find the apartment superintendent or one of the guys who lived in the building to go inside with her? Then, with relief, she remembered giving Ty the key. If Grace's cold had gotten worse, he would want her out of that van.

Scooting sounds came from her bedroom. She peeked in, expecting to see Ty and Grace. Instead a man built like Arnold Schwarzenegger whirled away from her desk and bulled his way toward her. She back-stepped quickly into the living room and shoved an end table between her and the giant. Her lamp fell and splintered against the wall. In two steps she would be out the open front door. She turned to see how close he was and that's when she spotted her laptop tucked into his armpit.

"Hey! You can't take my computer!" That laptop was an extension of herself. Like an extra arm. Or a part of her brain. Her thesis was on there. The grant report. Email contacts. Her only possession worth fighting for.

Without thinking, Summer grabbed her Frisbee from the bookshelf and hurled it full force at the bridge of his bulbous nose. He growled. His free hand shot to his nose. When he pulled it away, blood covered his palm. She grabbed a book and hurled it. The pages flared open and it fell harmlessly at the giant's feet.

He charged across the distance remaining between them, his face distorted in a snarl, elbow cocked. She backed toward the door just as his right fist connected with her jaw. On the way down, she saw a deep keloid scar snaking its way along the side of the giant's thick neck. It disappeared beneath the back edge of his muscle shirt. Her head rammed into the door frame. She registered a flash of surprise at how hard it was, before blacking out.

Her face was cold. Damp. She opened her eyes and blinked twice to focus. The world was white and bumpy and so far from her face. Oh, the sprayed finish on the ceiling. Synthetic carpet loops itched her forearms as she attempted to move. Ty's face loomed over her. She pushed away the damp dish towel he was using to wipe her face. She blinked a few times and turned her head. A wave of pain rolled over her. When it passed, she turned her head again and saw the broken end table and shattered lamp. Her Frisbee lay by the bathroom door.

The whole insane episode flooded back. The giant with the keloid scar! Her laptop!

Ty helped her sit up. She fought against the dizziness that threatened to send her back to the carpet.

As she stood, a new wave of disorientation washed over her. She let her knees fold and eased into the nearest kitchen chair. "Have you called the police?"

"They're on the way."

She tried to talk without moving her jaw. "What are you doing here anyway?" Not that she wasn't glad.

"I parked the van down the street to keep an eye out for Jake Fowler—the guy you knew as Justin—in case he followed you home."

Her head hurt. How had he known what time she would—she guessed anyone who uncovered Justin's various aliases could find her class schedule. "Wasn't Justin."

"I saw the body builder run from the building, so—"

"—you checked on me," she finished.

Surely the theft of her computer was related to the attack on Claire and to the body Summer had found at Goose Pasture. Was the giant tied to all three? She looked around the apartment. Grace? Where was Grace? Her voice cracked as she managed to voice the question.

"In the van. I locked the door."

"You can't keep leaving that child alone." Ooww. She'd moved her jaw and it made her head throb even worse.

"I was supposed to run while carrying Grace? Take the steps two at a time with her slung over my shoulder? Not knowing if I was going to find you alive or a bloody—"

"All right," she whispered through nearly motionless lips, "go get her now."

He crossed his arms. "Some girls might actually be grateful to have a knight run to their rescue."

Technically, he hadn't rescued her. She would have revived on her own. Still. She cradled her jaw in her hands before speaking. "Thank you."

"You're welcome. I'll be back as soon as I retrieve Grace." He grabbed the key off the kitchen counter where he'd left it that morning. He twisted the lock and pulled the door shut behind him.

She stood. Her right leg screamed at her. Must have twisted it when she fell. Her pelvic bone ached too.

She hobbled to the kitchen, her fingers trembling as she took two pain relievers with a glass of water. She filled a zippered plastic bag with ice and cradled it against her jaw. By the time Ty returned with Grace and her crayons, the ice had numbed her pain somewhat. She practiced flexing her jaw. Far from perfect, but bearable.

There was a knock on the door. Ty opened it.

With disbelief, she saw the cherub-faced cop standing in her entrance. No way. It hadn't even occurred to her that he might respond to the call for help. He wore khakis and a green polo shirt. "They drag you off the golf course to handle a computer theft?"

Ty answered. "I asked for Detective Theofanis. There's a chance this robbery is connected to the body you found and the attack on Dr. Dunham."

Detective Theofanis surveyed the damaged furniture. "It's been an exciting week in Loblolly Lake, that's for sure, and Miss Cassidy seems to be in the thick of it."

He'd already accused her of murder. How long would it take for him to decide she'd brought this theft on herself through drug dealing, prostitution, or an angry boyfriend? Ty sat on the couch with Grace and let Summer handle the detective on her own.

Theofanis photographed the smashed coffee table and lamp. The gaping hole in the drywall. Summer's injuries.

"He take anything besides the computer?" Theofanis asked.

"No."

"I'd appreciate your taking a close look around and seeing if other items are missing."

Fine. He wouldn't take her word for it. She felt like five tons of concrete had fallen on her head, but she hobbled from one room to the other, skirting the broken furniture, flinging open drawers and cupboards. "Nothing else gone—see?"

She marched into her bedroom, the ice pack still pressed to her jaw, and she opened the desk drawer. Her checkbook was still there. This was the first she'd thought to look for it. She slammed the drawer shut, turned away, and then realized something was wrong. She opened the drawer again and fished through it, shoving a ball of rubber bands, a box of paper clips, an assortment of pens and markers out of the way. The flash drives! All of them—gone. Claire had told her to keep her flash drive safe. Now it was gone.

The detective hovered in the bedroom door. "What'd he take?"

"My flash drives."

Theofanis's expression was unreadable as he made a note on his phone. "Your major professor is in the hospital and your laptop and data have been stolen," he summarized.

"Yes." She sank onto the edge of her bed, letting out a long breath. Absently she picked at a tiny pink flower printed on her bedspread.

Theofanis stood over the lone chair at Summer's desk. He photographed the dust that outlined the shape of her missing laptop. Along the back of her desk on two by four's separated by bricks, Summer displayed rocks she'd collected on hiking trips.

The detective touched an unusual piece of limestone she'd found near O'Leno State Park. "Nice collection."

"Have you found who attacked Claire?" she asked.

"What was on your computer and flash drives?"

"Anyone ever tell you it's annoying when you don't answer their questions?"

She waited for a response but none was forthcoming. She relented and answered his question. "Stuff that would bore the daylights out of most people. My thesis on ASR wells and Claire's final report on Harewood Energy Corporation's wells." He didn't ask what ASR stood for. Odd. Everyone else did. She told him about Claire's strange request. Her scalp tingled and she grasped the edge of the bed as that House of Mirrors sensation wobbled her again.

Theofanis rested his phone on his knee. "What can you tell me about Dr. Dunham?"

The question made her squirmy, as if she were about to violate Claire's privacy. Summer tried to relax as she enumerated the many courses she'd taken from Claire and their collaborative research on ASR wells. She mentioned they also played handball.

"She have male friends?"

"Some."

He looked up expectantly.

"I didn't actually meet any of them—except her fiancé this morning at the hospital. I'd seen him before when he came to pick her up after handball, but it's been a while. I think he moved away or they broke up and she was pissed about it. She hasn't dated much since that I'm aware of—but I don't really know much about her personal life."

Summer flashed on an angry face. "I did see another man leaving her office in a snit; I think it was last week."

Theofanis waited, his fingers poised to take notes.

"Claire was blunt. Didn't want him hanging around."

"You only see him the one time?"

"She was more than blunt. She was brutal."

Theofanis looked up from his device, expressionless. Waiting.

"Only the one time."

"She call him by name?"

"Not that I remember."

"You get a good look at him?"

Summer shook her head, which gave her a sensation similar to a boat rocking in a choppy sea. She laid the ice pack down. Using both hands for support, she wiggled her backside around on the edge of the mattress so her feet were planted more solidly on the floor. "Dark hair."

"His clothes?"

"Grungy. Jeans. Big white shirt. It was dirty."

"Age?"

She wasn't good at guessing ages. "Thirties? Younger than Dr. Dunham."

"Do you know of any reason someone would want to hurt her?"

"No."

"It wasn't the same man who attacked you today?"

"No."

"Is there anything about your research project that might offend people or might make them angry?"

She figured he meant angry enough to attack Claire. The headache was slowing her thought processes. "Harewood is less than happy with the report. Their wells are contaminated." When Theofanis raised an eyebrow, she added, "The water's not potable. The arsenic and uranium will prevent him from selling it."

Theofanis looked as if he had a bad taste in his mouth. "Arsenic?"

"There's a little arsenic in all water, and there can be a lot in ASR well water at first. It usually attenuates." She noticed his blank look. Hard to tell if he understood. She shrugged. "It's complicated."

"Do you have copies of the stolen data?"

Should she trust him? So many strange things were happening. "Dr. Dunham's computer in her office would have a copy of the final grant report. And I have copies of my thesis and her report."

"Where are they?"

"Safe." Everyone on her committee had a preliminary copy of her thesis. Not the final revision yet, but it wasn't that different. Just a few additional test results that verified what they already knew.

Again the raised eyebrows, the fingers waiting to enter data.

"Not where anyone else can get to them." It was as much of an answer as she was willing to give, and it seemed to satisfy him. The information was sitting in her inbox on a massive server somewhere in cyberspace. That habit of redundant back-ups proved invaluable once again.

"I would like a copy of the grant report."

"I'll email it to you as soon as I can access a computer."

"Anything else you can think of?"

"No."

He took fingerprints from the desk and then approached the bedroom door. She stopped him.

"Wait." She remembered the way Hu lied to her. Probably had no connection, but it didn't make sense. Right now, nothing made sense. She told him about Hu's claim that Claire wanted Summer to turn her files over to him. "He never talked to her. I confirmed that with her fiancé."

Theofanis entered the data into his device.

Retreating to the living room, he quizzed Ty about the interrupted burglary. His description tallied with hers. Dark hair, shaved close. Scarred neck. Body builder.

"You ex-military?" he asked Ty.

"Yes, sir. How'd you know?"

"Wondered when I saw the tattoo."

Ahhh. Summer hadn't asked Ty about the eagle tatt, the edges of which peeked out of the sleeve of his tee-shirt sometimes.

Theofanis made more notes, then pocketed his device and addressed Summer. "You need to go to the hospital and get checked out."

"I'll be fine," Summer said. "A little sore, nothing's broken."

"I insist."

"No, really. I've been worse off after a handball match." Not quite. Anyway, no emergency room. If you weren't half dead, you'd sit there all night in a rigid plastic chair waiting for someone to see you. By the time you received attention, the person sitting beside you would have coughed flu germs all over you. "I hate hospitals. Only way I'd go is strapped to a gurney."

Theofanis didn't argue. "It would be a good idea if you went home for a few days. Be with family. Or stay with friends."

Right—as if Summer was going to run across town to her mother, who would be hysterical and treat Summer as if she were still nine years old. Besides, her mother was in Denver. "I'll be fine . . . really," she added when Theofanis didn't move toward the door.

"At least let me notify your mother."

The long silence in the room battered Summer's ears. Finally she answered. "I'm well over eighteen. I can take care of myself."

The detective opened his mouth as if to protest, but closed it again and nodded. "Call if you remember anything else—or if you need anything."

He surprised Summer with that last. An intensity in his cerulean eyes made her think he meant it.

Soon after Theofanis left, Ty hauled the lamp and coffee table to the apartment complex's dumpster. When he returned, his eyebrows bunched together. "You think it's safe in this apartment?"

Summer lowered the ice pack from her jaw. "You mean he might come back?" She hadn't considered that possibility.

"If someone wants to get rid of the data, there's one place it still exists for sure."

In her brain, but it wasn't the only place. There was Dr. Dunham's computer at work and the files Summer had sent to cloud storage.

"You should stay somewhere else for a few days," Ty said. "Play it safe."

For how long? She couldn't hide out for weeks until Claire was well enough to oversee Summer's thesis defense. Ahhh—they wouldn't have to. She and Claire were supposed to give a presentation to Senator Vargas, the Chair of Communications, Energy, and Public Utilities Committee at the final hearing staged by the Department of Environmental Protection. Once all the evidence was disseminated to the public and the government, Harewood would have no further interest in them. Trouble was—the invitation to present was in Claire's name—and she was out of commission. Summer was supposed to tag along for the experience, though Claire had promised Summer the opportunity to deliver a large portion of the report's conclusions herself. No one else knew that, though. She had to find a work-around. Claire wouldn't want her to give up.

The answer was obvious. Dayita's access to the university computer system. Piece of cake. She'd studied the latest security systems.

Half an hour later, Dayita plunked her laptop on the kitchen table. "I really don't want to do this. I'm supposed to stop hackers, not become one."

"I know," Summer said.

"I could get into big trouble."

"Claire would back us up one hundred percent if she were able to." Summer pulled up a chair on Dayita's right. Her tailbone ached as if an iron spike had been driven into it. Ty stood behind Summer, his fingers curved over the top of the padded chair. The heat of his hands reached her shoulder blades, a warmth that spread all the way to her nether-regions.

Dayita's fingers flew over the keyboard. She pouted when she hit a firewall, but it only stopped her momentarily. Over the next half hour Dayita tapped her way through the university system and onto Claire's desktop. She slid the laptop over to Summer. Quickly Summer located correspondence with Senator Vargas and with the Department of Environmental Protection. She scrolled through the list.

"Bingo! The invitation to present Thursday—two days from now. The letter asks the university for input on HEC's request for an exemption on arsenic levels."

"Dr. Dunham's not going to make that meeting," Dayita said.

"Right. I'm going in her place to represent the university." Summer smiled. If Hu could lie, so could she—and she'd do it better. She fired off an email to DEP officials on Claire's letterhead with the university logo. It established that grad student Summer Cassidy would take the lead in the presentation. Dr. Dunham would also attend if she was able to make it.

"What if they ask for identification?" Dayita asked.

Good point. Summer typed out a letter of introduction and backdated it to the middle of last week. She transferred the file to Dayita's hard drive and hit print. "Voila! I'm all legit, and I already have the final grant report from Claire."

Dayita tried to reclaim her laptop. "Let me close down this connection now before someone over there realizes they've been hacked."

"First, let's pull a copy of the grant report Claire prepared for Harewood. It won't hurt to make a hard copy on your computer." Always back up multiple ways—that was her mantra, and now that so many copies had disappeared, she deemed it more important than ever.

Summer pulled up the file. Her head injury must be worse than she thought. No way this was right. She checked the date on the calendar on Dayita's computer to be sure she wasn't confused. "Too weird," she said.

"What?" Dayita asked.

"Someone accessed this file already today. About an hour ago."

"Who?" Dayita said.

"No idea." One of Harewood's people? Dr. Hu? Summer printed the file and returned the laptop to Dayita to close the connection. "Girlfriend, you're the best. I'm glad you're on my side."

Summer scanned the print-out, flipping through the pages. A quick glance told her Claire's report contained many of the wording changes Harewood had suggested to her in that bogus scholarship interview. "Someone has changed the wording, particularly the conclusions."

"Whoever accessed the file today?" Dayita asked.

"Gotta be. Claire wouldn't have done this without telling me. If we can figure out who did this . . ." she trailed off.

Ty was the only one not gloating over what they'd uncovered. "We still have a big problem. Staying in this apartment isn't safe until after you've met with that senator and his decision is disseminated to all the media."

Summer glanced at Grace, whose brown ponytails swung so far forward they nearly grazed her coloring book. Ty was right. You shouldn't take chances with kids. "I guess I can schlep across town to my mother's, or stay in a cheap hotel room for a few days if I live off peanut butter sandwiches the rest of the month."

"My mother would let you sleep on our couch," Dayita said. "We have plenty of blankets."

"If someone wanted to find you, the first places they'd look are your mother's and your best friend's place," Ty said. "And a skilled hacker can break into credit card databases. A good con artist can talk a hotel desk clerk out of information. I have a better idea."

His eyes were so dark looking into them was like being sucked into a well. She shook off the feeling. Such nonsense, but her voice emerged raspy all the same. "Let's hear it."

4

"RELATIONSHIP WITH CLAIRE DUNHAM?" SWEAT BEADED on John Hu's forehead. He hoped the detective couldn't see it. What did the man mean by *relationship?* Hu rolled his Waterford pen between his fingers. He'd found it in Claire's office a few hours ago and repossessed it. He couldn't believe the witch had stolen it.

The detective waited. Apparently he wasn't going to clarify the question.

"Our relationship was very professional. I have the greatest respect for Dr. Dunham's work."

"How would you describe the level of professional jealousy?"

What was the detective implying? That Hu might have stabbed his colleague? The nerve! Hu touched the hair over his right ear. "None at all. We worked quite well together, in what little interaction we had. You see, Dr. Dunham is a hydrogeologist, which means she works primarily with underground water movement, while my specialty is coastal water. We don't have the need to collaborate often."

"So it didn't bother you that she published far more often?"

Hu's mouth twitched and his eyes flared briefly before he regained control. "I wrote the seminal work on the effect of fish farming on coastal habitats, detective."

"You refer to the book published in 1995."

If only Hu could throw this uneducated, pathetic little man out of his office. A detective was never going to achieve anything of significance. The man would be laughable if he wasn't so damned annoying.

"It has never been out of print," Hu said. "My book is widely used as a resource in the scientific community. It's a standard acquisition in every university library both here and abroad. The text has been translated into fourteen languages."

The detective's fingers tapped on the tiny keyboard. "You are familiar with Summer Cassidy?"

Sweat tickled Hu's neck. He ran a finger around the back of his collar. "Of course. Ms. Cassidy is one of our finest students."

"Why did you ask her for a copy of the Harewood grant application?"

Hu's stomach knotted up. He was powerless to stop Theofanis's pushing. He raised his chin in defiance. "I thought only to help Dr. Dunham meet the grant deadline. It would be a tragedy after all her work if the university had to return funds because of a missed deadline."

The silence snaked its way past the batik painting on the wall. Hu sensed its effect on the sailfin tang, which suddenly darted about in the saltwater tank, aggressively invading the clown fish's territory. The very absence of sound insinuated itself into Hu's ear like a worm that caused exquisite pain.

Yet the detective said nothing. Nothing. Nothing. His fingers tapped and tapped on the tiny screen. The detective was toying with him.

Finally Hu smoothed his hair back and heard himself saying, "I may have misled Ms. Cassidy slightly this morning when I asked if she had a copy of the grant."

Detective Theofanis looked up from the phone and waited.

"I might have suggested Dr. Dunham asked me to obtain it, though I only intended to request it on her behalf."

The detective's wordless eyes held Hu's, and then those fingers tapped, tapped, silently.

The clown fish hid behind a large chunk of coral. Hu could sense its desperation.

"It was my duty as dean to submit the final report and secure the grant payments as soon as possible. I am sure it is what Dr. Dunham would have wanted."

The detective stood and pocketed the phone. "Thank you, Dr. Hu. I would like to see Dr. Dunham's office now, and I'm going to need a copy of her appointments and all the data on her hard drive."

Hu held onto the edge of his desk as he rose. "I couldn't possibly invade her privacy that way. I'm sure you understand."

The detective opened a piece of paper and gave it to Hu. "This is a warrant. We're conducting a murder investigation."

Hu thought his knees were going to collapse. "Murder? You mean Dr. Dun—you mean she died?"

"No, not Dr. Dunham. One of Harewood Corporation's employees."

Now that the detective was actually talking, Hu could barely concentrate, his mind hooked on "murder" and "Harewood Corporation" in the same sentence. He expelled a long breath and tried to grasp what the detective was telling him.

"Whoever attacked Dr. Dunham will only be charged with attempted murder. I spoke with the hospital an hour ago and they believe she will survive though she lost a lot of blood and suffered internal damage. I doubt if she'll be back on her feet this semester."

"Are these—events—" Hu couldn't bring himself to say *murder*—"connected? Connected to the university?"

"The key to Dr. Dunham's office?"

Two officers joined them in the hallway. Hu forced one leg to move and then the other until he made it to Claire's office. He left the detective alone. He couldn't bear to watch him examining every little detail. Hu realized now that Theofanis's sappy face disguised a formidable opponent. Before long, the detective would figure out someone had accessed Claire's computer this morning and made changes to the grant narrative. If they suspected he'd breached Claire's security, would they also think he had attacked her?

That led him to ponder who might be guilty. Howard Grice? Hu would tell the detective about the way the university president leaned on him to pressure Claire. Of course, Howard couldn't have anything to do with these—events—but why let the trail lead only in his own direction? After all, he only followed orders and fulfilled his duties for the university. In America the buck stopped with the president.

5

GEORGE THEOFANIS LOVED PUZZLES AND THIS CASE provided plenty of pieces. As he had suspected, the interview with the university president hadn't delivered any new suspects. Hu was simply trying to divert attention. Theofanis hadn't trusted Dr. Hu from the get-go though he was uncertain exactly what formed his opinion. The man's overuse of aftershave? Hu's nervousness and reluctance to cooperate?

After Hu had left Claire Dunham's office, Theofanis had retrieved the video camera he'd placed across from her desk on his first visit to the geology department. The tech guy who had accompanied him quickly determined Dr. Dunham's computer had been accessed—twice—since her hospitalization. The first violation had occurred only a half hour before the second, and it had happened right there in Dunham's office. Since access to a professor's office and computer passwords was strictly limited, according to the university president, Theofanis suspected Dr. Hu himself. Especially since the only file accessed was Harewood's grant. Not only accessed but modified. The tech staffer had quickly pinpointed cases of altered wording and data on arsenic levels that had been changed.

The detective downloaded the retrieved video to his computer. He couldn't help smiling as the footage confirmed his theory. Hu had changed the report. As the video wound into the final moments, Theofanis laughed out loud. Hu was fuming over a pen he found on Claire Dunham's desk. After a storm of cursing in what Theofanis guessed was Mandarin, Hu wiped the pen off with his handkerchief and pocketed it.

The second violation of Dunham's computer was a hack job from an off-campus site. Could have been anybody, but he suspected a student or someone hired by Isaac Harewood. The PD's techie said the Harewood file had been downloaded, as well as the professor's customized version of university letterhead.

Theofanis launched his mapping software. Ovals with off-shooting spokes that connected to more ovals peppered the screen in front of him. He entered several new ovals spidering away from Hu's name. He created another bubble with an over-sized question mark and typed in the words *second hacker.*

He had the tech department trying to recover what had been typed into that letterhead template, but the document hadn't been saved on Dunham's computer, so it was hard to say if they could retrieve it. Depended on whether it had been downloaded before alterations were made and whether a temporary file might have been created. In any case, he had sent a squad car to the Cassidy girl's apartment with orders to pick her up for questioning. She was brainy and might have the skill to hack her professor's computer. Somehow, she was at the center of everything happening in Loblolly Lake. Of course, Harewood Corporation had access to tech wizards, too. Not a chance they would voluntarily cooperate, though.

On a whim, Theofanis picked up the phone and dialed President Grice again. "You said you would help with the investigation any way you could. Could you get a list for me of students with extreme computer skills, the kind necessary to trace who accessed Dr. Dunham's computer?"

"A few students in our computer security department have those skills. We certainly want to press charges if the culprit is identified," Grice said. "I'll have to get back to you with the students' names."

Theofanis clicked off. At some point, he would tell Grice that Hu had changed the Harewood report. First, he had to be sure Grice wasn't involved more than he was letting on.

Theofanis studied his ovals again. All the spokes led back to one oval, which he dragged to the center of the screen and enlarged. Harewood Energy Corporation. He drummed his fingers on top of the mouse. Who killed Alvarez and why? Who had attacked Dr. Dunham? And who stole the Cassidy girl's computer and flash drives?

His mobile rang. Grice again.

"Our computer security chair highly recommends one girl. Says she's a whiz and if anyone can trace the hackers for you, she can. Says she's better at this stuff than he is. Name's Dayita Patel." Dr. Grice rattled off her contact information.

"I appreciate your cooperation."

"Happy to help, detective."

Theofanis tried the Patel girl's number but a computerized voice said the phone wasn't in service at this time. He left a voicemail requesting her assistance and a call back number. He called the department chair, thinking she might be in class or a lab and he could get in contact with her there. Instead, he learned she hadn't attended classes today. "Uncharacteristic," the department chair said. "She practically lives here."

Without really seeing the words, Theofanis picked up Harewood's financial records and riffled through them again. It was always about money. And the power and influence money could buy. Still, the professor had been stabbed twenty-one times. That spoke of anger, of passion. He was groping through the dark, trying to find the edges of the pieces. All of Phil's clients the morning of his collapse had checked out clean—except one man Theofanis hadn't been able to track down. Jacob Fry. The information form Fry had filled out for Mary Glotfelty had a bogus address, and no trace of Fry existed online. Obviously an alias. Theofanis had Mary working with a sketch artist he'd brought in from Tallahassee, but he didn't have much hope that it would lead anywhere.

That Theofanis would solve the puzzle he had no doubt. He only hoped it would happen before someone else got hurt.

Ash barged into the cubicle that served as Theofanis's office. "Just talked to Niles Morrell on the phone. Threatened to look into financial misdeeds at HEC. Rattled his cage. Morrell implied Harewood micro-managed HEC financial matters."

Theofanis glanced at his watch. "I think we should go chat with Harewood in person before HEC closes for the day." He swung his chair away from the computer and stood up. "You oughta stop smoking. You might live long enough to get as good at this as me."

Ash laughed. "Better'n you already. Who broke this case open while you were drawing little clouds on your computer?"

"Only thing you ever broke was wind, Ash. Let's go visit Harewood's pretty little museum." He wouldn't be at all surprised to find the office manager there at the mansion. Ms. Lambert intoned her boss's name with the same reverence other folks reserved for the Lord Jesus Christ.

As the pair stepped into the parking lot, Theofanis's mobile rang. "Yeah?" he said. He listened for a minute, and then turned to Ash.

"Harewood's on hold for now. That was the team I sent to pick up the Cassidy girl. Apartment's empty. They checked with the instructor of her morning class. She didn't show up today—and she never misses."

Theofanis phoned Loblolly Lake General Hospital and spoke with a woman in the records department he'd dated a few times. Summer Cassidy wasn't sitting in the emergency room—that's what he'd hoped, that the girl had gotten that jaw checked out. Summer Cassidy was probably fine. Gone shopping. At the movies. Still, he wished he'd put her in protective custody. Especially after what happened to Phil.

His stomach lurched. He'd been present once before when her mother received the news every parent dreads. He never wanted to go through that again.

6

THE SUN WAS LOW ENOUGH IN THE SKY TO STRIKE DIRECTLY IN THE EYES as Summer drove Dayita into Ichetucknee Springs Campground. Thankfully, she'd remembered sunglasses. She'd taken a pain killer to numb her headache, but the bright light didn't help matters. She could see Ty and Grace following in the van.

They drove up to their campsite. As light filtered through the trees, it softened and bathed the forest with a spiritual glow. They planned to stay away from civilization until Thursday's meeting in Tallahassee with the senator and DEP officials.

Ty got out of the van and pocketed his sunglasses. "Shouldn't you let your mothers know you are here?"

Dayita's laugh sounded edgy. "I called her when while we were driving here. Mom thought it was cool that we were going camping."

Tickled, Summer failed to hold in her laughter. "Your mom would have conniptions if she discovered a maaannn—" she dragged the word out until it was a mile long—"was accompanying her Little Red Riding Hood on an overnight trip." Unlike Summer's mother who never knew what was going on.

Ty frowned. "You had to lie to Dayita's mother?"

"I can take care of myself," Dayita said. "It'll be okay."

Summer repressed another laugh. If there was anyone who couldn't take care of herself in the woods, it was Dayita. But she'd be fine with Summer there to look after her. And this wasn't exactly wilderness camping. Ty and Grace would sleep in the van.

By the time Summer pitched her tent, the light was already dimming under the pines. Crepuscular creatures like raccoons and owls would soon appear.

Ty swung his backpack out of the van. "Let's take Grace on a quick hike before it gets dark."

"Hike?" Dayita said, the fear in her voice almost palpable.

"The trail is quite tame." Summer pointed ahead. "See? It's even marked by a sign like a street."

"I've always loved camping," Ty said. "Before you were born, Grace, Dad and I used to go fishing and we'd pan-fry bream or trout and make s'mores."

The four of them padded along, their footsteps muffled by pine-straw carpeting the forest floor.

"Aaaaaaa!" Dayita flicked a spider off her arm and stomped it with her pink flip flop. "I hate camping."

"Our mom was like Dayita," Ty told Grace. "Every snake or spider, no matter how small, warranted a screech. She hated the outdoors."

Too weird. How could anyone tolerate being indoors all the time? Summer got antsy if she had to go more than a week without a good outing. Even though circumstances forced them on this particular journey, no reason they couldn't enjoy themselves.

As they went deeper into the woods, the ground became uneven. Ty, who was in the lead, stopped and slipped a small electronic device into his cupped palm.

"What's that?" Dayita asked.

Ty held the device up. "Wireless remote. It controls my c-leg."

Dayita glanced at Ty's legs. Summer watched his face. He knew Summer had seen and touched the leg. Guess he'd decided there was no way to hide it out here. He'd have to plug it in to recharge it some-where in the campsite, wouldn't he?

Ty sounded like he was reciting from a textbook. "This prosthetic's computer chip senses the pressure and demands on a knee fifty times a second and makes adjustments."

Dayita reached for the remote and studied the buttons. "Very cool."

Geesh. Someone says he's missing a leg and all that computer-crazed girl has to say is 'cool.'

Dayita asked what each button controlled. Ty explained, but when she wanted to see the leg, the muscles in his neck and arms tensed. He grabbed Grace's hand. "We'd better push on before we lose the light."

As they moved along, Dayita worried about snakes and bugs. Sum-mer alternately reassured her and made fun of her. Summer stopped to finger the glossy leaves of an eight-foot shrub. "Wow—a native *Calycanthus floridus.*"

Dayita tilted her head. "It's kind of scrubby looking."

"Watch your mouth. Sweet shrub is an endangered species. This is early in the season for it to bloom. " Summer rubbed her fingers again over one of the leathery leaves. "Smell that!" She held her fingers under Dayita's straight nose. Before Summer was willing to move on, she sniffed one of the blooms and insisted Dayita and Grace do the same. Grace sniffed bloom after bloom, a rare smile spreading across her face.

"Nice," Dayita said, shifting past Summer.

"Nice? It's fantastic. You might never get to smell wild sweet shrub again in your life."

"I'll try to survive."

Humph. The girl just didn't get it.

7

THEOFANIS TRIED TO MAKE HIS VOICE on the phone as soft and soothing as baby lotion. "We're trying to locate Summer and she seems to be missing. Your daughter didn't show up for classes today. With a college student that really wouldn't cause the slightest concern—"

"Missing?" Jordan Cassidy panicked, as Theofanis had expected. "What do you mean Summer's missing? She never misses a class. Never. Not even when her grandmother died. She attended the funeral and went right back to school."

"We're concerned because someone broke into her apartment this morning and—"

"What?" Mrs. Cassidy shrieked. "Why didn't you call me right away?"

He winced. "Please try to stay calm. It took us a little time to track you down in Denver. We have no reason to think she is in any danger."

"Have you called her best friend? If anyone knows where Summer is, it would be Dayita. I've got her phone number. Let me get it."

"Wait—did you say Dayita? Let me put you on hold."

"Detective? Don't you—" Jordan Cassidy's voice ranged somewhere between irate and hysterical, but Theofanis cut her off anyway. He shuffled through the papers scattered on his desk until he found the notes he'd taken when he'd talked with President Grice. Oh yeah! He'd found the missing hacker. What were Miss Dayita and Miss Summer up to? He reconnected the line. "Sorry about that. Dayita Patel, right? I have her contact information already. She didn't show up for her classes today either."

An agonized wail came over the line. "My God! How long have they been gone?"

"Your daughter was home this morning, so not long. The girls may be shopping. Gone to a movie. We have no reason to believe they are in any danger, but we need to locate them. When's the last time you talked to Summer?"

More snuffles. "Monday, after I found out she discovered the dead body. You didn't inform me about that either. I'm her mother. I have a right to know what's happening to my daughter."

Theofanis could imagine how huge the whites of Jordan Cassidy's eyes were, how she was pushing her fingers through her pageboy as she spun around. She wouldn't remember him, but he remembered her only too well from the accident involving the other twin. During his first week with the department, he had been part of the team dispatched to the scene. It was his first experience with that kind of grief and he'd never forgotten it. He'd kept up with Jordan Cassidy ever since. Her picture popped up regularly in the paper to promote fundraisers for that bicycle safety organization. She even had a cartoon character designed to promote it named MacBike.

"I suggested she call you," he said. "She refused. Said she was fine."

"My daughter only acts tough, detective. Hard as a rock outside, I'll give you that, but that child is full of tears inside. I'm flying home immediately. If you only knew, if you only knew what we've been through."

"Yes, ma'am. One of my buddies was the lead on the hit and run. He was pretty shook up by the accident."

So shook up he took early retirement six months later. It wasn't just the accident, which was bad enough. The aftermath dragged on and on and finally dragged him down. The mother had a nervous breakdown, and nine-year-old Summer had been catatonic for days after finding her sister's body. The family disintegrated.

Theofanis's buddy caved from the failure to find the person who ran that child down and left her to die in the street.

8

SUMMER DIDN'T BELIEVE IN GOD. Hadn't since she was nine years old. She'd knelt and pleaded with God to bring Chrissie back, but nothing changed. Gone was gone. There was no resurrection, no answer to prayer. Ever since, Summer refused to believe in anything she couldn't prove through her senses, through science.

But sometimes, like right now as she stood under a gibbous moon in the forest, the wall between this world and Chrissie's world shimmered as if it might dissolve. With the insects singing their night songs and the logs crackling as they settled closer to the ground, Summer heard Chrissie whispering to her. If she stretched out her hand and separated the curtain of fog, she might reach right through into another dimension, one where the light of her sister burned as brightly as the fire that warmed Summer's feet and cast a lambent glow on the faces of Grace and Dayita as they huddled on a split log bench with a coloring book.

Seeing them brought this world back into focus for a moment. Ty seemed to be doodling on a blank piece of paper.

Summer wandered over to another log and sat down, facing away from them, cradling her knees into her chest, listening to the insects chatter. Listening for Chrissie's voice. Did her sister understand Summer would give anything to undo the events of the last day of Chrissie's life? For the thousandth time, she whispered, "Dunmee," sorry in the secret language they had shared as toddlers. Summer only remembered a few of their special words, ones her parents had perpetuated after the twins had shed their first language for one they could use with others.

A short while later, Ty lowered himself on the log beside Summer, smoke wafting off his shirt. She surely smelled the same way. Okay with her. She'd always liked the scent of wood burning. She detected a hint of just-mown grass, too, perhaps the combination of his deodorant and his sweat. Her body responded with a warming of the skin.

He handed her a partial pencil sketch of the giant who had attacked her.

"You got close enough to see all this?" she asked.

"His nose or mouth aren't filled in, but I remember the basic shape of his face, the hair, and the scar."

"Make his nose fat and bulgy like Gérard Depardieu or Walter Matthau. And he had a gold-capped front tooth. Left side, top front."

Ty roughed in her description and showed her the additions.

"The bridge of the nose was narrower, a little longer before it widened. The lips were fuller," she suggested. Soon the sketch looked remarkably like the giant. She hoped Ty could turn up the thug's identity, as he had with Justin/Jake.

"Those financial statements—the chief financial officer would have been responsible for them," Ty said.

"He spoke at the hearing. Glasses, gray hair." She couldn't remember his name.

"Niles Morrell. Harewood's right hand man."

"You think he killed Alvarez?"

Ty shook his head. "I've interacted with him several times. Strictly a white-collar crime kind of guy. He's no angel, but he's not the type to do his own wet work."

Wet? Oh, blood. Summer grimaced.

Ty sat quietly beside her. She liked this about him, that he didn't need to fill every moment with senseless sound.

Grace giggled over whatever Dayita was telling her. Dayita worked well with kids—something Summer had never realized before. Grace was coming out of that shell Ty believed she'd thrown up after her parents died, though he admitted he barely knew his half sister. He'd been deployed on missions nearly all of her short life. "Grace is an adorable child," she said, and meant it. Her face was absolutely round and sweet, especially when she smiled. Though that was rare.

"How did someone else's kid come to mean so much to you that you'd offer to take her into your home?" Ty asked.

Summer shrugged and looked away. Her reaction stemmed from what happened to Chrissie. Didn't everything? Her mother had speculated endlessly on what might have happened that day when the twins were nine. Waiting by the ice cream truck, Chrissie may have given up; decided Summer wasn't coming back with the money for ice cream. Or the ice cream man had driven away, his siren song fading in the distance, and Chrissie headed to her grandmother's house. Or Chrissie had to pee and didn't want to use the public bathroom because Mama said not to.

But Summer didn't believe any of these stories. The truth was so dark she would never share it with anyone.

She had never even mentioned her twin to Dayita. But Summer's voice rose softly into the fog. "My sister died, my twin. She was only nine years old."

She told him about disobeying her mother and going swimming. About leaving her sister alone at the ice cream truck while she biked home for money. "I can't stop thinking if I had been there, I would have seen the car coming down the street and hollered, "Look out!" in time for Chrissie to move out of the way." She had called out the warning endlessly in her mind ever since.

"I keep thinking if I'd been there, the car would have killed me instead." Sometimes she wished it had. Anything would have been better than seeing her twin, a mirror of herself, lying on the pavement. Her sister looked intact. But just like that—her breath was gone and would never come back. Just like that.

That was only part of the story. The part not locked away.

Summer had only seen the woman's back as she drove off, leaving both girls, one living, one dead, in the middle of the street.

Ty leaned in closer, so close she thought he was going to touch her but he stopped short. They were so close the heat from his arms distracted her from the disturbing memories. For some minutes—she had no idea how many—they listened in silence to frogs croaking, insects scratching their wings, logs burning and collapsing onto themselves before Ty began talking.

"After the missile exploded, I used to wonder why I'd survived. If I'd have been seated anywhere else, I would have been one of the dead ones. I couldn't figure out why my buddies died and I didn't. When the medics pulled me out of the wreckage, I was holding a leg. They evaced it with me to the hospital, but turned out the leg wasn't mine. Belonged to Sprague. Don't know why I was holding it."

They sat together without talking. She wished she could comfort him, but any words she could muster would be too weak to heal the damage she sensed. Though they weren't touching, Summer became aware of the heat from his thigh where it rested near hers on the log bench. It was more than energy transference. More like warm maple syrup making a slow, sensuous journey through her veins.

Her reaction was nothing more than a natural hormonal response to a male suitable for mating. The likely stimuli were pheromones released by the apocrine glands along with touch and warmth. They switched on a chemical reaction. Sure, her breathing and heart rate increased. Yes, her muscles tensed and her skin flushed. Big deal. It was science. Thinking this response to Ty was somehow unique was totally ridiculous.

He took her hand in his, and the warm syrup flowed again. He breathed words next to her ear, and tendrils of her hair tickled her cheek. "When life slaps you down, you have to get up and move on. Be in the moment. Now."

Summer liked Ty. But there was more graduate school to come, and even in the now there was so much sorrow. The body she had found covered in flies. And Claire in the hospital—Summer wondered if she'd regained consciousness yet. The only way Summer had found to forget the past was when she threw her whole self into physical activity. Chasing a Frisbee. Kayaking a river. Foosball. Sex. Activities that demanded concentration from her whole body. That wasn't the kind of now Ty was talking about. His was more peaceful. She wanted to get there. Didn't know how.

In this bittersweet moment, she longed for things she couldn't name. She was glad to be alive, with the night air cool against her face, her fingers entwined with Ty's. She tilted her head back. Through the clearing in the tree canopy, a few stars and a three-quarters moon silvered the sky as they peeped through the fog. The night was a pearly gray, a pearl to treasure.

Thirteen

Tuesday

I

John Hu drummed his Waterford pen against the portfolio ten or twenty times before he became aware of Dr. Grice's pretty receptionist scowling at him. He stopped, but wondered if the other office noises bothered her as much or if she'd grown used to them. The copy machine's soft scritch of paper against paper. The low whine of a laser printer. A young woman's flirtatious laugh, muffled as it traveled down the corridor. Hu re-crossed his legs, positioning the left one on top. For the hundredth time, he glanced at his new Movado watch, an extravagance he now wished he'd bypassed. The bills were mounting up. His wife had ordered custom-made drapes for the living room. Then the washer died, so they replaced both the washer and dryer with top-of-the-line models, all on credit because the car and house payments were sucking him dry.

He'd brought the portfolio along, not because he needed the papers inside for this meeting, but because he disliked empty hands, disliked deciding what should be done with them. Folding or clasping them in the lap was too effeminate. Gripping chair arms too defensive. Resting one on a crossed knee and the other on the thigh seemed the best choice but left him exposed. Better to hold onto paper and pens, the weapons of academics.

He glanced at his watch again. Grice was treating him with such disrespect on purpose, of that Hu had no doubt. Thirty-five minutes of waiting like a delinquent schoolboy outside the principal's office. He touched the hair over one ear to reassure himself that his mousse was holding. It released a hint of sandalwood. He loved the exotic fragrance because it reminded him of his grandfather.

Finally the assistant said he could go in. As Hu entered, he held the portfolio in one hand, the pen in the other. Grice didn't stand or offer to shake his hand. Instead he continued to read the document. His rudeness extended so far as to turn the stapled page, his eyes skimming it from top to bottom before aiming a blistering glaze directly between Hu's eyes.

"I thought we had an understanding," the president said, "that you were going to handle the Harewood grant."

Hu clasped the portfolio tightly and raised his chin. "I have handled it, sir, as you requested. The final report was submitted yesterday."

"That's not how I see it. Not when a detective walks into my office and practically accuses me of altering a report. This report." Grice raised the document in his fist and shook it. "I made clear to him I hadn't touched this report until he gave it to me. Hadn't seen the report. Hadn't read one word of it. I made clear it was your responsibility. I also let him know you had access to Dr. Dunham's computer password."

Hu smoothed his hair back over his ear. "I don't keep a list of our faculty members' passwords, though I'm sure my secretary does."

"Nice try, like your weak attempt to deflect blame onto me, but your secretary wouldn't have reason or the required knowledge to alter the grant's wording."

"You told me to!"

"You're mistaken, Dr. Hu. I told you to make sure Isaac Harewood could live with the report Dr. Dunham submitted. I certainly never suggested going behind her back to alter it. I expected you to show leadership within your college. Now it seems the university is being questioned in a murder investigation. How did you let these matters get so out of hand?"

"I had nothing to do with that murder. I never even heard of this Alvarez."

Grice's voice sagged. "I know you had nothing to do with the murder, but our name is connected now to this investigation. I don't like it. We're in the middle of a major fundraising drive. We don't need bad publicity."

Hu's mouth went dry. Publicity? It wouldn't come to that. His reputation would be ruined. "The university's very limited involvement won't make it to the papers, will it?"

Grice tossed the morning paper across the desk toward him and Hu skimmed while the president talked.

"We're already linked to the Alvarez story. Only one sentence. So far."

Hu skimmed until he found it. The article said the Harewood Corporation funded a Sci-Tech grant to study the wells Alvarez worked on.

Dr. Grice rubbed the bridge of his nose. "I don't like to see any mention of the university in a story about a murder. It's a full-time job keeping football players out of the police reports."

Grice was over-reacting to one little sentence that didn't even suggest the university was aware of wrongdoing. No one read the local paper anyway.

Grice laid the report down. "Your judgment throughout this whole incident calls into question whether you are the best person to lead the College of Arts and Science."

The blood surging through Hu's ears nearly drowned out the rest of the speech.

"Let's do some deep soul-searching over the next few days. Consider whether you might wish to devote more time to research. Maybe it's time to write another book. Take a sabbatical. Of course, with the university facing a financial crunch, it would have to be unpaid. But I'm sure your new book would meet with the same success as the last."

Hu almost laughed. He had no significant new research for a book. He certainly didn't have savings for an unpaid sabbatical. Academic books only earned a pittance for the author, as Grice well understood. All this worry about the university's reputation was only an excuse. Grice wanted to replace the highest paid member of the College of Arts and Science with someone younger who would grasp the prestige of the position at any salary.

If the university was really having such a difficult time, the president should have refrained from redecorating his office with real leather chairs and original artwork. Unpleasant visions presented themselves in rapid succession. A foreclosure sign on the expansive lawn of Hu's home. His wife peeking out from her custom-made curtains to watch the neighbors slowing their cars to stare at their disgrace. Repo men showing up at the front door for the Porsche. He would give up his

Sunday golf foursome before he would arrive in a rust bucket, so the others could gossip about his fall behind his back.

It must not happen. He drove the point of his Waterford pen deep into the seat of the president's leather chair.

2

THEOFANIS'S ENTIRE DUPLEX WOULD FIT INSIDE Harewood's foyer. How much was enough for guys like Harewood? Theofanis followed Ash into the more intimate den, which was only half as big as Theofanis's duplex. The entertainment system alone must have cost hundreds of Benjamins.

"As I was saying, gentlemen, I was out of the area during the time frame of Mr.—Snipes, did you say it was?—collapse." Harewood reached into his center desk drawer and pulled out a piece of paper.

"Snyder," Theofanis said. "Phil Snyder."

"Right, Snyder. Why you would think I know this man? My investment counselor lives in New York. Here's my itinerary and a copy of the flight plan my pilot filed at the airport. We flew into Tampa that day. We left early in the morning and didn't return until afternoon." Harewood handed the papers to Ash.

They were on the right track. Harewood had expected them and had the paperwork where he could put his hands on it easily. Theofanis didn't yet grasp how Harewood had engineered Phil's death, but he aimed to find out.

Ash scowled as he examined the papers. "We'll want to talk to your pilot."

"Of course, you must." Harewood jotted down a phone number on a notepad and tore off the top page. "Loblolly Lake is fortunate to have such effective law enforcement agencies. I appreciate all you do to keep our citizens safe."

"Thank you, Mr. Harewood. We do our best." Theofanis smiled. It would be a pleasure to bring this arrogant, condescending asshole down.

3

SUMMER'S EYES WERE FROZEN OPEN but she couldn't see. She struggled, flung her head left, then right, back again, then straight forward and her eyes, which had been closed all along, opened for real into darkness. She gulped in air that smelled of damp earth and her musty sleeping bag. She lay still, concentrating on deep breaths to quiet the panic that drew her out of sleep.

That dream again. The one where she stood over Chrissie's body. Her sister lay on the pavement, right leg cocked to one side, her eyes and mouth open as if she'd seen the bogeyman that hid in the closet until their mother turned the lights out.

Many nights Chrissie had whispered that something evil lived inside the closet, the same space that, during the daylight hours, overflowed with jeans and flip flops, Barbies and benevolence. Summer squelched her own fear to reassure her sister. Right now, lying in the tent beside Dayita, Summer knew her sister had been right.

Something evil *did* live in the dark. The back of her throat closed with the same thrust of terror that always stole her breath at the end of the dream. That moment when Chrissie's face turned toward her and whispered *Don't leave me alone.* In a seamless moment her sister's body shifted into her own. Lifeless on the pavement.

When Summer woke from the dream, she was always gasping for air and she realized she'd been holding her breath in her sleep. Was she subconsciously trying to join her sister? For a measureless space of time, Summer lay in the dark wondering how close she had come to death.

This night, more than others, Summer sensed the presence of evil. Claire lay unconscious in the hospital. Harewood's engineer had become an incubator for fly larvae. A giant had stolen her computer. She unzipped her sleeping bag and leaned forward to open the tent flap so she could watch the sky lighten from black to dark purple to gray. By then, she could get up without anyone thinking she was crazy.

She crawled out of the tent and stretched. The irrational fears of the night sloughed off like dead skin. Mist rose continuously. Some people hated fog, but Summer found it beautiful. It magnified and isolated the morning calls of cardinals and jays.

The hammer of a lone woodpecker engendered in her chest a spiritual joy as her eyes sought the source of the sound. Unfortunately she was unable to pierce more than a dozen yards through the rolling cloud that enveloped the forest.

Almost immediately Ty joined her and banked up the fire to make coffee. His face wore an odd cross between the sluggishness of sleep and the tension of pain.

"You're up early," she said.

"I never sleep much." He turned his back on her, but she recognized the rattle of pills shaking from plastic containers. He swallowed them with water from a thermos.

"Yeah, me—" She broke off. Last night's dream seemed as foolish now as the way she and Ty had sat linked together sharing the log seat. No sense in making confessions that might encourage an impossible connection to grow. In a few weeks, she'd graduate and move on to earn her doctorate. Ty wasn't a college boy grateful for a little slap and tickle after an evening at the Foos and Booze, where both parties separated afterward to chase their own goals and pursue their own lives.

After granola bars and coffee, Summer slipped into the tent, where Dayita still lay sleeping, curled on one side. Summer backed out of the opening, dragging her buddy's pack with her. She deposited herself cross-legged in front of the now-glowing fire and pulled Dayita's laptop from the bag.

Ty groaned. "Can't you go off the grid for even one day?"

She avoided his eyes. "Thursday I have to convince Senator Vargas to block any dilution of clean water standards. Then he will advocate against Harewood's ASR wells." She couldn't resist looking up at him as she laid out her mission. "This is my first chance to use my training. I want their eyes to light up. I want to knock their socks off. I want to blow them off the frigging planet."

Ty ran a hand over his crewcut. "Since we share mission goals, how can I help?"

"Keep the fire going and the coffee warm."

While she prepared PowerPoint slides, Ty prepared for a walk into the woods.

"Don't get lost in the fog."

"No worries. You're talking to the Ultimate Soldier." He showed her a pair of night vision goggles in his pack and then checked to make sure the remote for his leg was working.

He swung the backpack on his shoulders and set off. Summer watched his back until he disappeared into the fog-shrouded trees, thinking again, with amazement, how well he had adapted to his prosthesis, how independent and efficient he was. She resumed work on the slides.

In less than an hour, she had developed what she thought was a convincing presentation of statistics. She started with facts about the human body, that up to sixty percent of the body was water; the brain, even more—seventy percent. Blood—ninety percent. For newborns, the percentages ran even higher so babies were even more susceptible to poisoned water. At any one time, half the hospital beds in the world were occupied by those suffering from water-borne disease.

Ty returned, and finally Dayita crawled out of the tent in a hot pink flirt shirt, a ruffly affair hardly suitable for camping. She folded a blanket into a neat square—to protect her equally inappropriate light pink jersey slacks—and sat down by the fire, which had collapsed into orange embers. Summer choked back a laugh and turned away, pretending to cough. Clearly, the girl was as much a virgin at camping as she was at other fun parts of college life. After Dayita sipped juice from a thermos, she re-braided her dark hair in one long plait down the back. She wiggled her French-tipped nails toward Summer.

"Let's see what you have."

Those nails with their rhinestone paste-ons almost made Summer start laughing again. They looked so out of place. Ty peered over Dayita's shoulder to watch the presentation.

As the slides progressed, Dayita's lips pursed more and more. When the last slide faded, she shook her head. "It's about as exciting as reading Deuteronomy." Dayita mouthed the name as if she were rolling spoiled food around in her mouth.

Summer hadn't read that book of the Bible, but she gathered it was less than engaging.

"I thought it looked pretty good," Ty said.

"Don't read all those numbers out loud—statistics bore most people," Dayita advised. "You need video and strong photographs."

"Great," Summer said.

Dayita held up her phone. "You can get video footage of Harewood's wells with our phones. If we leave for Tampa soon, we can get back before dark. Summer, can you find a few national experts on ASR wells to testify over videophone about the danger of these arsenic levels? People who will verify the health risks?"

Summer knew of several scientists and engineers who would gladly participate, but she didn't have their contact information. Their emails had disappeared with her stolen computer. Anyway, she wasn't sure these men would have phones with built-in video applications. Several experts' phone numbers, she recalled, would be on business cards stashed in her desk drawer.

Ty nixed the idea of Summer going back to her apartment to get them. "We're out here so you can't be found. If someone is watching your place . . ." He let his voice trail away.

"No one would recognize me," Dayita said. "I can sneak back to your apartment and look for the numbers."

Doubts about Dayita's scheme swirled in Summer's mind. The plan had been to stay in the woods until Thursday morning. Dayita was to check in with her mother every day. Otherwise, they were supposed to be in hiding. It wasn't worth putting her best friend at risk.

Then Summer almost slapped herself in the head. She could retrieve their phone numbers from their company and university websites. And if she couldn't get good video or audio with a phone interview, she would type in their testimony. It wouldn't be as effective as a recording, but it would be safer for them all.

4

WHEN A FINGERPRINT FROM ALVAREZ'S ROOM came back as belonging to a middle-aged black woman, a private investigator named Treela Timms, Theofanis pounded his desk with his fist. They were finally getting a break in the Harewood case. Immediately, he called Ash. Wasn't like he could hide this development for long anyway.

Before Ash could drive across town, a Suit hired by Douglass and Associates showed up to protect Ms. Treela's rights during questioning. No surprise when Treela Timms pled the fifth. Nor when the Suit appeared like magic after Theofanis contacted a judge to obtain a warrant for Timms's client records. Her lawyer claimed work-product doctrine protected the documents the police sought from Timms's small company.

The judge ruled in favor of the police department. Timms's attorney had expected no other outcome in a murder investigation. That kind of delaying tactic pissed off judges because it wasted their time.

Theofanis was studying his computer ovals again when DeAndre Ash sauntered up wearing his trademark smile.

Ash laid a sheaf of documents on Theofanis's desk. "Guess who regularly uses Timms to do investigative work?"

Theofanis's cherubic face glowed. "Douglass and Associates."

"Bingo. Harewood Corporation's financial records indicate large checks written to retain the fine Miz Bailey and her Associates. What do you suppose Bailey Douglass wanted her investigator to find in that apartment?"

The entire male population of Loblolly Lake lusted after the lobbyist, one of the most eligible and desirable women in all of Florida. As far as Theofanis knew, none of them had ever gotten to first base with her. "I believe I'll pay the fine Miz Bailey a visit."

Ash chuckled as he pushed open the door to the parking lot. "The sheriff's department would be remiss if we didn't send along a representative. Some days this job is such a pleasure."

"For once, you speak the truth. Try to keep that little wiener from saluting in the lady's presence."

"At least if my flag flies, the lady will notice. Yours limps along half-mast in comparison."

"Shoot, Ash, the black guys in your department have been complaining you got the tiniest instrument of any man they've ever seen. They're worried you're gonna ruin your race's reputation." Theofanis yanked the cruiser door closed and started the engine, momentarily drowning out the continuing repartee.

Theofanis winced inwardly at the thought of how he would sound to an outsider. Throughout the irreverent back and forth, he pondered how the social fabric had changed. And how it hadn't. He wasn't really a racist, sexist bastard. Theofanis supposed men told the first penis jokes back when they lived in caves. They'd still be telling them when humans lived in a galaxy far, far away. And just as he respected Ash's abilities, Theofanis respected Bailey Douglass for her intelligence, ambition, and success. But it didn't stop him from admiring her additional assets.

Another observation troubled him as they drove past the mall, past the entrance to the university campus, past the chain of car dealerships lined the left side of the road. Traffic always slowed when drivers spotted the cruiser even if they weren't guilty of speeding. Everyone carried around a truckload of guilt. Sinners, one and all. Some more than others. No matter how educated or how civilized men became, they would always find reasons to murder.

5

BAILEY FLUNG HER OFFICE DOOR OPEN and greeted the policeman and deputy as she would good friends, lightly touching each man on the shoulder as he entered. She was glad she had worn a purple blouse with her charcoal suit today, a combination most men found irresistibly striking, one that made the most of her fiery hair.

The two men asked preliminary questions, skirting the real issues, pressing to see where Bailey was going to invoke privilege. She studied the men during their opening moves. Ash looked like the typical cop. Big man. Tad overweight, not too much. Cigarette odor clung to his clothes.

Theofanis looked like he sang in the church choir. On the short side with skin that glowed. Baby blue eyes. Bailey immediately assessed him as the biggest threat. Not because he was necessarily smarter than Ash. Certainly not because he was white. No, the threat came because people would always underestimate him and let their guard down eventually, as they did with her.

Ash was inquiring about the nature of the work Treela Timms did on the Harewood case. Bailey interrupted with "the gift." When you quickly offered useful information, your adversaries assumed you were cooperating. And she had a plum.

"Douglass and Associates wants to fully cooperate with your investigation in every way we legally can. We aren't sure what this information means, but I'm sure you'll make use of it. While Ms. Timms performed surveillance work for us, she noticed a black Honda parked for long periods of time on Cherokee Drive."

Theofanis blinked, his eyes widening slightly. Bailey figured he was processing that he'd heard the address recently.

Ash spoke first, his eyes narrowing. "Why was Timms watching Dr. Dunham?"

Bailey tilted her head slightly to one side to show she regretted withholding information. Attorney-client privilege. "I can't reveal the nature of the work they were hired to do. I'm one of Mr. Harewood's personal attorneys as well as a lobbyist for HEC. But I can share the license tag number of that Honda if you would find it useful."

Theofanis input the number into his smart phone as she read it out. She suspected he was already searching the database for a match.

Ash scowled. "Your investigator is tied to one murder and now quite possibly an attempted murder as well. I think you should—"

Blue eyes glowing, the Pretty Boy's hand shot out to stop Ash. "We'll be back."

Of course he would. Days from now after he tracked down Dr. Dunham's attacker. "I hope the license number proves helpful," Bailey said.

Theofanis stopped at the door, turned, his expression hardly a smile, but hinting at appreciation nonetheless. "I think you already know exactly how much help it will be. Have a nice day, Ms. Douglass."

Yes, he was the dangerous one. He measured her better than most men. And she wasn't talking about her boobs. She would do a little investigating of her own into the affairs of George Theofanis. Everyone had weaknesses.

6

TY KEPT RAISING OBJECTIONS to leaving Dayita and Grace alone. The drive to the nearest ASR well and back would take Ty and Summer six hours—a long time to be alone with an unpredictable child,.

"I'm an experienced babysitter," Dayita said. "She can color while I jazz up the presentation."

He had to admit Dayita got along well with Grace. But what if one of them sprained an ankle? Or a snake bit them? Dayita seemed so inexperienced with outdoor life.

She dismissed his concerns. "I'm so over my fear of camping now that I found the bathhouse and hot showers. I can even use my hairdryer. Besides, there are dozens of people nestled into tents and RVs nearby. We'll be fine."

Before they left, Summer gave her truck keys to Dayita, and she had a fully charged cell, so Ty supposed in an emergency, she would be able to get help. Still, he worried during most of the drive toward Tampa. Even though he left Grace sitting by herself sometimes, he stayed near enough to respond if she swung into one of her rare but disconcerting fits of crying or rage. He shook off his misgivings as he parked on the road outside the ASR well site in his van. No sense in dwelling on events unlikely to happen.

Through binoculars, Ty watched Summer working the site manager, a pudgy middle-aged man in a baseball cap. For her cover story, she pretended to be a student reporter doing a story on the importance of the wells as future water supplies. She was twisting one leg around, a schoolgirl kind of sexy. All that practice she got seducing guys in bars and hustling foosball was coming in handy—yeah, he knew about that. Within minutes, she led the manager off toward a trailer that probably served as an office.

Ty used his remote to set his leg to perform at high speeds on a smooth surface. He opened the car door and slipped inside the chain link fence while the administrator was distracted. Ty shot video with Summer's phone. The horizontal metal tanks—Ty had no idea what was in them or what their purpose was—would make boring video. Too stationary. The best he could do was create motion by walking past the equipment. He zoomed in on knobs and gauges, holding each shot steady for a few seconds. Summer would be able to add a voiceover that explained what all these pipes and dials did. Ty kept looking over his shoulder at the trailer. He wanted a final shot of these orange flags from the right angle. He knelt on his good knee and steadied the camera above his artificial joint.

He glanced at the trailer just as the manager looked out the window and spotted him. The manager whipped his baseball cap onto his head and bolted out the door. "Hey, what do you think you're doing?" he shouted across the compound.

Ty took off running for the gate, his feet pounding on the concrete pad. He made it to the van. If he waited for Summer now, her cover would be blown. Ty peeled out, tires screaming on the asphalt. He slapped the steering wheel with his palms and whooped. He was back, baby! It was the first time he'd put his leg to the test outside therapy or a gym and it had performed flawlessly. Better than his real leg.

He sped around a curve and executed a U-turn that bounced the van onto the grassy shoulder before he pulled back onto asphalt. He eased more slowly down the road toward the ASR site. Pulling onto the shoulder again, he idled where he could watch the gate without being seen.

A few minutes later, Summer strolled through the gate and headed down the road toward him. She turned and waved, presumably to the old guy. Ty drove to meet her.

She climbed in. "He asked where my car was."

"What did you tell him?"

"That my girlfriend dropped me off and went back to that roadside stand we passed where the couple was selling strawberries? I said she'd be right back."

Ty blew out air. "He bought that?"

"Why not? Could have been true."

Pretty clever of her, actually. Summer reacted quickly on her feet. She looked over the footage while he drove. He hoped Grace and Dayita had experienced an uneventful day, one without alligator or bear encounters. And, with luck, he and Summer would get back to the campground before the evening showers in the forecast arrived.

7

HAREWOOD PACED IN FRONT OF THE WALL OF WINDOWS in his office that overlooked the courtyard. It was late afternoon yet the sprinkler system was still watering the row of perennial hibiscus shrubs, which had leafed out but wouldn't bloom for another month. He made a mental note to complain to his landscape staff. He'd told them a hundred times to water only in the wee hours of the morning. It was more efficient. If he wanted to sell water to the municipalities, he also had to promote conservation of resources.

When Julia buzzed him that Bailey was on the line, he had his secretary connect them immediately. He touched the Bluetooth device clipped to his ear. Before Bailey could say hello, he began to quiz her about Senator Vargas.

The lobbyist dropped hints that she had a back-up plan concerning the senator. "You don't need details."

If she had been in the room with him, he'd have been tempted to grab her by the shoulders and shake her.

"Easy for you to say. I'm the one who's going to lose money if Vargas doesn't fall in line."

Her sugary voice took on a sharper tone. "Listen, I only called because one of my investigators, Ms. Timms, has been arrested."

"Never heard of her."

"Of course you haven't, but I didn't want you to be surprised if that detective asks you about her."

Would have been nice if he had appeared genuinely surprised. Now, it couldn't happen. He had heard the name Timms.

Bailey continued. "I don't want you to respond when the detective asks about Ms. Timms. You haven't heard of her. You had no idea she worked for me, and you are unaware what assignments she might have. She has no connection to Harewood Energy. Clear?"

Isaac tugged downward on the close-cropped hairs where they met at the cleft in his goatee. "What was Ms. Timms doing for you? Did it have a connection to my company?"

"You don't need to know." She paused. "Isaac, are you responsible for a break-in at a certain graduate student's apartment?"

The skin tightened across Isaac's cheekbones. "Graduate student?"

"Don't play dumb. It doesn't become you. No one else had a reason to want that girl's computer." She paused to speak to someone in her office. He heard her ask the person to close the door before she continued. "The police are exploring a connection to your ASR wells. My sources in the sheriff's department tell me copies of that original grant report are floating around. In fact, from a letter that arrived at DEP, it looks as if the girl plans to take Dunham's place Thursday and make a case to Senator Vargas. Don't worry about it. I'm taking care of the senator. You have a corporation to run. Stay out of the way. Your actions need to be more circumspect."

"What are you going to do?"

The phone clicked in Isaac's ear. He swore softly. If he couldn't sell the water, the bank would call in the loans on the land for the ASR sites. During good times, it wouldn't matter. At this point, it would cause a chain reaction. The elaborate pyramid of loans—of one subsidiary leveraged as collateral to buy another—would all tumble down. Hell, someone was going to end up in jail for bank fraud. Wasn't going to be him. The paper trail led safely away.

He hadn't made his fortune by relying on anyone else, and he wasn't going to start now. He wasn't one of these CEO's who turned operations over to others. He maintained oversight. Control.

The sprinklers had come on under the lemon trees. The ill-timed watering needled him until he couldn't stand it any longer. Competent help didn't exist in this state. He buzzed Julia.

Her sycophantic, disembodied voice floated into the air. "Yes, Mr. Harewood?"

"Please inform the landscape staff the sprinkler timer needs to be reset. Again. Emphasize that the timer needs to be reset every time we lose electricity. Every time. How hard is that to understand?"

Why couldn't the incompetents running this town keep the electricity on? The power was always going down. Every time it stormed. Every time a tree limb touched a power line. Every time he and his secretary fired up their computers simultaneously. Every time a dog peed on a pole. Sure, he had generators for longer outages like those caused by hurricanes or tropical storms, but those brief bouts of power loss caused a multitude of annoyances.

"Yes, Mr. Harewood. I'll take care of it."

"See that you do." She should already be taking care of it. That's what he paid her to do.

Isaac strode into his executive bathroom and relieved himself. Third time since lunch. What was wrong with him? Prostate? He zipped up, washed his hands thoroughly, and paced through his office again.

He stopped by the black and white photo of ASR Site Number Two that hung on his back wall, then at the photo beside it. The one of him shaking the hand of the governor. He, Isaac Harewood, was Somebody. Somebody on speed dial with mayors and governors and executives across the country. Somebody who took charge.

Dr. Dunham was out of the way. However it had happened, he wasn't going to let himself worry if Bailey had engineered it. If she had, she'd done it on her own.

The way he saw it, the primary remaining obstacle to getting exclusion for the wells was that snip of a girl, Summer Cassidy. All he had to do was make sure she was out of the way until after Thursday. By then, the exemption would be a done deal.

Isaac fumbled through his stash of throw-away phones and dialed a number he had memorized. He would make sure that little girl didn't attend the final public hearing with the senator and DEP officials.

8

ASH PERCHED ON THE EDGE of Theofanis's desk, ignoring the fact that his butt was wrinkling the papers scattered haphazardly across the surface.

"Still no trace of the Cassidy kid?" Theofanis asked.

"None. Talked to the girlfriend's mother. Mrs. Patel. Claims she has no idea where the girls are. She didn't seem concerned, so I think she's lying. You gonna put her under surveillance?"

Theofanis coughed as if he were choking.

Ash shifted his weight from one cheek to the other, causing the opposite leg to dangle and bang against Theofanis's desk periodically. "Guess we're already stretching your department's resources watching the Cassidy girl's apartment. At least I had luck tracking down the dude with the black Honda."

"Alex Welch?"

"Yeah. Bought a one-way ticket to Costa Rica the afternoon Claire Dunham was attacked. Flew out of the Orlando airport. He could be anywhere by now, but his rental Honda is parked in Orlando's long-term storage lot. His photo could match the description the Cassidy girl gave you of the boyfriend who got dumped."

"You send FDLE after the car?"

Ash poked a toothpick into the slight gap between his front incisors. "Yep, the state boys are on it. We should know within the hour if Welch stabbed her. Whoever did it had to be seriously splattered. This guy has been in trouble before. He has two other aliases we are aware of, one stalking charge, one assault."

"You digging for potatoes with that toothpick? Guess you can take the boy out of the country, but you can't take the country out of the boy."

For a second, Ash's expression was priceless as he jerked out the toothpick. Theofanis only half tried to hide his smile. Too casually, Ash slid the wooden sliver between his lips and rocked the toothpick up and down.

"Think a pube's stuck in there," he said. "See, me and my wife met up and I got laid for lunch. When's the last time you got laid?"

"You were gone about ten minutes, including drive time. Gives a whole new meaning to fast food."

"Ten minutes? An hour at least, and you ain't never gonna hear

Taneese complaining like your last female—when was that? A year or two ago?"

When his phone rang, Theofanis was spared having to respond. It had been all too long since he'd been in a relationship. Not a year. Not that long. This job didn't leave a lot of time to scout for a good woman—though his definition of good might not square up with everyone else's.

He listened intently to the voice on the line. "Thanks. I'd appreciate a call when we can talk to her."

He looked up at Ash, who was still banging his size fourteen loafer against the desk. "Dr. Dunham is out of the coma. Not coherent, but they don't think it will be long until we can talk to her."

They had solved the attempted murder. The violence of the stabbing had to stem from anger or passion. The number of times Timms claimed to see the black Honda shadowing the professor indicated stalking. At first, Theofanis thought the Honda might be another group of private dicks following Dunham. But coupled with Welch's flight from the country, the pieces fit too snugly to be coincidence.

He double-clicked an icon to activate the brainstorming software on his computer. To the bubble-box under Dunham's name, he changed the wording from "mysterious rejected boyfriend" the Cassidy girl had seen leaving the professor's office to "Alex Welch." Under Welch, he added another bubble: "Costa Rica."

The phone rang again. FDLE. They found blood in the Honda. The state boys hadn't had time to do lab work, but the blood had to match Dunham's.

Ash bounced his toothpick around a few times, took it out, and laid it on top of Theofanis's papers. Deliberate retaliation, Theofanis knew, for the country boy remark. Ash was sensitive about growing up on an Alabama farm.

"Better take this news to the chief ASAP," Ash said. "She's itching to get credit for solving at least one of the crimes around here. Betcha she'll have a swarm of reporters and TV cameras here faster than you can say 'Dr. Claire Dunham.'"

"What about the sheriff?"

Ash grinned. "Nah, let's hold off letting him in on it. Between you and me, I get pure pleasure out of watching his face shine like a red light when he gets pissed."

Theofanis picked up the stack of papers and tilted them strategically. The toothpick fell onto Ash's thick thigh and rolled off onto his loafer. "Let's go give my boss a reason to smile."

Fourteen

Wednesday

I

EVEN THE SIMPLEST TASKS became difficult out in the woods. Dayita popped the dead battery out of her laptop and inserted her spare. She only hoped it would last while she needed it. Summer had emailed her the ASR video footage, and she and Ty were on their way back.

The obvious choice to begin the PowerPoint was the photo Dayita had taken of shallow water coursing over rocks a few yards from their campsite. The shot was beautifully framed by a branch of lacy leaves overhanging the bank. Perfect for a title slide—at least in Dayita's opinion. Yesterday Summer had shot the head spring of the Ichetucknee with its eerily glowing aquamarine water, but the scene was too exotic for the opening slide. The people viewing this presentation needed to think of ordinary water sources. The next shot Dayita selected depicted a doe drinking from the river. That one subtly reminded viewers that water was more than beautiful. Creatures drank it. How fortunate that Summer happened upon the deer last night. Dayita suggested it was a lucky break, but Summer, with her typical arrogance, said it happened because she knew where to look.

The next shot Dayita wanted—and didn't have yet—was water flowing from a tap. She could easily snap that shot at home or in the park's lodge.

On the slides of statistics, Dayita inserted video of the ASR wells. Dayita watched the whole presentation again. They had uploaded a telephone interview Summer had done with an ASR expert, but she had been unable to contact another expert vital to the presentation. His university website listed no contact information for individuals, only departments. "What a pisser," Summer had said. "Dr. Hearn's business card is in my desk drawer. He'd give me a good quote."

Maybe they couldn't go back to Summer's apartment, but Dayita was going home to collect her family photos before that presentation. As soon as Summer had shown her the presentation, Dayita had seen that Kriyamana Karma was offering her this singular opportunity. A chance help her distant family members, release the negative consequences of her mother's actions, and perhaps set herself free from karmic obligations.

Dayita's mobile alerted her to an incoming call. Her mother's voice sang with excitement. "Honey, I've been trying to reach you. Did you see the morning paper?"

And how would she have read the paper out here in the middle of nowhere? "No."

"They found out who attacked Dr. Dunham and it isn't related to her work at all. It was a boyfriend. A stalker. Dr. Dunham is conscious now. They expect her to make a complete recovery. So you and Summer can come home. Whoever stole her computer had no connection to Dr. Dunham's attack. It was just an ordinary burglar."

Tension fell away from Dayita's shoulders. Wow—all that worry for nothing. Conjuring up nonexistent connections between disparate events.

"How's Grace doing?" Mrs. Patel asked.

"Fine. Coloring as usual. We're coming on home."

"I'm on the way to meet a potential client, so I won't be home when you arrive."

"You shouldn't drive and talk on the phone." Of all people, her mother should know it wasn't safe, not even the hands-free Bluetooth she used now. Yakking was a distraction, yet all real estate agents drove, ate, and even used the bathroom while talking on their phones. Communicating with clients was essential.

All right—back to civilization. Frisbee camp took place on a university campus and you stayed in dorms. That was Dayita's idea of camping. Last night, she'd had trouble going to sleep thinking about all those creatures out there in the dark, only a flimsy piece of nylon between her and them. What if a snake crawled out of a hole in the ground under the tent floor? Could it bite through the nylon? What if a bear found them? Summer had hung their food up high over a tree limb with a rope, but what if a bear decided to try a taste of people? The tent was no match for sharp claws.

She would leave the tent for Summer to pack up. She was outta here. She strapped Grace into the passenger seat of Summer's truck. Now all she had to do was drive a stick shift. Couldn't be too hard. She'd watched Summer countless times. How different could it be from an automatic?

The truck lurched as she let off the clutch and they headed back toward the entrance. The Family Tavern came into view. It was a large wooden structure with a big second story screen porch that jutted out into the air. A huge pine—Summer would have rattled off the exact name for it—sheltered one end of the tavern, and a small American flag greeted guests at the door.

She parked the truck and took Grace inside. She thought about calling Summer and telling her they were leaving, but she was afraid they'd try to talk her out of it. She'd leave a note instead. And text them, too, about the time she thought they would get back.

Inside the game room were pool tables and the obligatory Budweiser overhead light fixture. Every bar had one. The best feature of the room was a stone fireplace with a hand-crafted wooden mantel. Somewhere inside the building a male voice, Southern as all get-out, was singing: "My kids are all stupid, The wife's ugly as sin, I should have known, Not to marry my kin." She snickered, then stopped. It wasn't funny. Especially to her. Sometimes people had to marry their kin.

Dayita located the owner of the singing voice. His name was Don Young, the owner of the campground. She left a note for Summer explaining they had gone back to the Patel household. She couldn't wait to get back to the world of paved streets and the familiarity of her own bedroom.

More important, her mother's photographs from her village in Bangladesh that would put a human face on the damage bad water inflicted. Terrible pictures that made Dayita shudder. She took Summer's truck keys from her back pack and asked Don Young for one more favor: could he explain what the clutch was for? He rolled his eyes and accompanied her for a quick lesson in driving a standard shift.

She smiled as she pulled out onto the highway. She would be half-way to Loblolly Lake before Summer and Ty returned and realized she and Grace were gone. The truck made a strange grinding noise as she pulled out onto the highway.

2

BAILEY FANNED THE PHOTOGRAPHS across her mahogany desk like a deck of cards. She sighed. She liked Senator Vargas—she really did. He was a genuinely nice guy, devoted to kids and the environment. The thought of the senator's humiliation sickened her. She imagined the pain of yet another wife thrust into the public eye.

She would tell Treela Timms to make abundantly clear they did not intend to expose the senator or ask for money. All they required was for him to introduce the legislation she'd prepared to acquire an exemption on Harewood's wells. She might even offer to destroy all the photos once the bill was introduced. Usually she held such weapons in reserve for the next time she needed a favor. Most politicians and movers and shakers deserved to be manipulated. Over the years she'd watched the snakes embrace each other one day and hurl knives at each other the next. One day they were proclaiming the children are our future and the next they slashed spending on education. Such a vicious art, politics. Vargas seemed less hypocritical than the others.

The photos, all of decent quality, clearly depicted the senator romantically kissing and embracing his aide on a penthouse balcony.

Bailey sighed. "How'd you manage to get these?"

Treela's eyes were the color of weak tea, framed by glasses, her face one you'd forget right after you saw it. Her cheeks bulged as she talked about her craft. "Camera with a telephoto lens attached to a remote controlled airplane. Bought a new lens for this assignment. Usually I require a wide angle. I earn a little extra cash taking overhead shots of homes for real estate agents. The view from up in the sky—a whole new perspective to offer buyers."

Scary what technology could accomplish these days. Bailey bundled the photos and shoved them into the manila folder.

She frowned at Treela. "Let's hope this effort of yours doesn't wind up as disastrously as the Alvarez affair."

Her nose wrinkled. "Not likely. Wish I knew where Alvarez stashed the evidence he claimed to have on Harewood. I bet the copies of our photos are in the same place."

Bailey closed her eyes, recalling the shots of Alvarez transferring a large quantity of weed to his truck. She supposed Niles Morrell had pressured Alvarez to participate in his operation. As an undocumented worker he had complied, maybe even willingly, to supplement the pittance Isaac Harewood was paying him.

If only they'd held off mailing those photos and note offering Alvarez an airline ticket in exchange for the incriminating evidence he had on HEC. Bailey had known Treela for years, trusted her, but the evidence was going to look incriminating to Theofanis and Ash. Especially if they ever found out that Treela had purchased the one-way ticket to Mexico in Alvarez's name.

"You haven't recovered the note."

"No, but the cops haven't either. I hope Alvarez torched it along with the photos."

Bailey wasn't counting on it. That Theofanis was a sly one. Wouldn't surprise her if he built a solid case before he hauled Treela in again for questioning.

The investigator took out a tiny digital recorder. "Gathered another bit of information this morning that will interest you."

Treela touched the "play" arrow. Bailey's eyebrows rose as she recognized Harewood's voice. Her lips pressed together as she listened. At one point she swore softly. She slid the time lapsed bar to the beginning and listened again.

She got up, walked over to her window, and looked at the overcast sky. "What a fool."

"What are you going to do?"

She glanced over her shoulder at Treela Timms, exhaled, and resumed staring at the shifting clouds without really seeing them. "It's his problem. I told him to stay out of this, that I would handle it."

"You're not going to warn him the police are watching the Cassidy girl's apartment?"

"Why should I? He doesn't listen to me anyway." Empty words spoken in a snit. She would call Isaac. He might be acting like an idiot, but he was her idiot. He had infused Douglass and Associates with considerable sums of cash over the years. Legal ethics required her to do her best by him. Though she could almost laugh at herself—the irony of considering ethics at all—since she'd learned of Harewood's plans through illegal wiretapping. She would call. Those shady operators Isaac hired to occupy the Cassidy girl until after Thursday's ruling would be walking into a mine field. Out of the way—what would that mean to the men Isaac hired? He was so careless with words. She thought about that recording she had of him telling her to do "whatever it takes." He didn't mean murder, but it would certainly sound that way to the police. She was going to confront Harewood with that recording. It was for his own good. Maybe he'd figure out she was bluffing—she couldn't really turn the tape over to cops. But perhaps it would scare him into letting her handle what needed to be done with real professionals.

3

DAYITA FANNED THE PHOTOGRAPHS across the chipped coffee table, one her mother had retrieved from a dumpster after a college student abandoned it at the end of the term. Her breath grew ragged as she held the pictures, giving attention to each one. Her aunt struggling to carry water back from the village well—the same well that was killing her and poisoning her family and neighbors. Amazing how much this aunt looked like her mother.

The next shot was her uncle, a man wasted by cancer until merely a transparent sheath of skin laid over bone remained. Then her cousin Nakeesh, one photo of a healthy little boy, another of a teen with repulsive skin eruptions. A tear fell on a black and white shot of her aunt posing on the stoop of their small house. Dayita brushed it away. She didn't even remember these relatives, but she'd heard stories about them all her life. Their world was so different from hers and needlessly miserable. Despite knowing about the poisoned water for decades, the international community had done little to resolve the problem. No one cared about poor peons who lived on the other side of the world.

Gradually she became aware of pain in her hands. She opened her fists and discovered she had clenched them so fiercely a row of red dents like just-born moons etched each palm. She rubbed her thumbs over the marks, easing the discomfort. If only it were as simple to erase the agony of the villagers in her mother's country.

She might not be able to do much for them, but she could help Summer make sure it didn't happen here. Sweeping her hand across the table, she scooped the photographs into a single stack again and took them into her bedroom. She turned on her computer and her printer/scanner so it would warm up. Over the next half hour, she scanned photos and added them to the presentation. Summer included too much statistical, scientific stuff. People's eyes would glaze over. They needed to see human faces affected by contaminated water. Delivered in conjunction with statistics, the presentation would pack a real punch—right in the guts of those government regulators.

This would earn her mother a few more karma points. She was guilty of working too hard to sell houses. She wanted to feed and clothe her daughter—was that so hard to forgive?

Dayita's improvements to the presentation would be atonement for an accident that never should have happened. Her mother spent hours on her cell phone. She called clients while she made Dayita's breakfast. Pushed a couple to close the deal by calling on her way to her second job as a waitress. Phoned the newspaper classified editor to tweak ads on the way home at night. Always on the phone.

Of course she had panicked after she hit the little girl on the bicycle. Of course she drove away and traded the car to an out-of-state relative who would ask no questions. Of course she was tortured by what she had done. Who wouldn't be?

Her mother punished herself by eating until she was morbidly obese. Feeling bad? Stuff another bag of chocolate chunk cookies down the throat. Prayers for forgiveness not helping? Eat five servings of lentils and rice.

Dayita didn't learn of her mother's sin until two years after the accident when she had forced her daughter to enroll in Frisbee camp. Her mother had followed the Cassidys' life, mostly through newspaper clippings, like the one announcing the couple's divorce. Her mother gave monthly donations to Jordan Cassidy's bike safety foundation and sometimes she even spied on Summer.

"If you ever tell," Mrs. Patel had told Dayita the day she registered for Frisbee camp, "you will become an orphan. I will kill myself before I go to jail."

Summer would be surprised to discover Alvarez's murder, Dunham's attack, and the computer theft were simply random events.

No hidden conspiracy wove its way through the streets of Loblolly Lake. Nothing nearly as sneaky as befriending the twin of the girl your mother had killed.

4

IN THE PRIVATE MEETING ROOM of the Ramada Inn, Isaac Harewood's voice and heart rocketed upwards as he sang the words "God Bless America." The final chords of the song—*my home sweet home*—banged from the piano and swelled from the throats of his fellow Rotarians. Isaac blinked away tiny beads of moisture that formed in the corners of his eyes. Silly, but he couldn't help the way that song and the shared patriotism moved him. This country and its bounteous resources had enabled him to build an empire, and if its foundations had crumbled somewhat recently, he'd rebuild. It was the American way. The poor were either lazy or stupid or both, and didn't deserve the same rewards as those who worked hard. The pastor from St. John's Methodist Church spoke the blessing in a voice ridiculously soft for a minister. Isaac could barely make out every other word.

As if on signal, Rotarians rose and shuffled to the buffet table, chatting with friends and business contacts. Other than deals cemented at the Pete Dye golf course, more business took place at these meetings than anywhere else. Isaac moved in bigger circles, usually, but local connections still mattered. He chatted with a county commissioner about a possible zoning change near his corporate offices as he surveyed the lunch offerings. The fried chicken and collards looked especially inviting today, but with the advent of his shoulder pain, he opted for the baked fish and rice pilaf. No sense courting a heart attack. Further reflection nearly changed his mind. The fish the hotel procured was probably mercury laden. He much preferred eating at home where Noni, the chef he stole away from the last governor, prepared ethereal dishes fit for a king.

The hotel fish was dry and over-cooked, the rice bland and flavorless. And the commissioner didn't seem all that interested in Isaac's opinion that the zoning changes would cause undesirable traffic congestion on the street that fronted Harewood Corporation headquarters. In fact, she had briefly closed her eyes after she crunched into the fried chicken, her attention focused on her taste buds. Why did she come to these luncheons if not to listen to citizens, especially important ones?

Isaac was pleased when his cell vibrated in his jacket pocket. His table companion needed reminding that Isaac was a vital link in the local economy—the provider of a hundred local jobs and considerable tax revenue. Not to mention a frequent donor to charities and political campaigns.

Bailey didn't bother to say hello, and no sugar softened her voice today. "You'd better listen to this tape and listen good."

Isaac heard a scratchy recording of his own voice: "I want this problem to go away." Then Bailey's: "How far"—several words were inaudible to him—"to go to remove"—another inaudible word—"problem?" Then his own: "Whatever it takes."

Isaac pushed back his chair and stalked to the hallway outside the banquet room. He nodded at a waitress bustling by to refill the fried chicken and kept his voice low. He vaguely remembered the conversation, but couldn't place the context. "What is this crap?"

"This is a tape of you ordering a hit on Dunham."

"Are you out of your frigging mind? That's not what I was saying."

"I'll turn the tape into the police and let them draw their own conclusions."

She was bluffing. Had to be. "No, you won't."

"I will—unless you call off those thugs you hired to keep the Cassidy kid out of the way. I told you not to"—another inaudible jumble of words—"watching her apartment."

It was a bad connection, full of hisses. Isaac only caught bits of the rest, but pieced together the gist: if Theofanis caught Isaac's men-for-hire, they would turn on him and never look back. He dug his fingers into his smooth skull. "The police are watching? How do you—" He broke off. How did she find out about the men he hired? She had to have a source in his top management staff. The Methodist minister passed by on the way to the restroom. Isaac turned his back on him.

"Okay, okay. I'll call the whole plan off."

"See that you do."

Saliva pooled in his mouth as he flipped the phone closed. The same competent waitress exited the banquet room and looked at him quizzically. He attempted to rearrange his face into a semblance of normalcy. He pushed past the hotel receptionists, an elderly couple arriving with a bellhop in their wake, and a woman with a clipboard pressed to her chest. A glaring sun beat down on the asphalt and reflected off the hood of his Jaguar. The usual flush of pleasure he took in owning the machine was repressed by the chill that penetrated his bones. He would not fare well in prison. Without all the fine objects he'd accumulated, without the power and respect his wealth commanded, who would he be?

From his private perch behind the steering wheel, he loosened his handmade Belisi Palm tie and dialed Fowler. After ten rings, Isaac quit counting. He wiped the sweat from under his collar. Because he didn't know what else to do, he dialed again. The ringing stretched on and on. Interminably. Crap—in his obsessive caution, Fowler had probably tossed out another phone.

He called Julia and asked her to try to contact Fowler. "If you reach him, have him call my mobile immediately."

He also asked her to arrange for Patrick—his pilot—and Gulfstream to be on standby until further notice.

5

Her truck! It was gone. Summer pulled out her cell and texted Dayita: *Where R U?*

Her eyes scanned the LCD screen of her phone; then she expelled a long breath. "Thank God. They are at Mrs. Patel's and Grace is coloring. Dayita says not to worry about her. They found out who attacked Dr. Dunham. One of her old boyfriends. Not about the ASR wells at all. The strange events aren't related, Dayita says."

"That's a relief," Ty said.

As she read on, she whooped. "Claire's regained consciousness and she's gonna recover completely."

"Wonderful news," Ty said. "I'm sure you're relieved."

The battery meter on her phone was down to two bars. She turned it off to conserve what remained. They grabbed her tent, hopped back into the van and headed toward Loblolly Lake.

Summer rolled down the window, remembering what Mrs. Patel had told her. It seemed much longer than a few days ago. "Mrs. Patel thinks you need to enroll Grace in school. She said early interventions were really important for children with autism. Is that what's wrong with Grace?"

Ty's face darkened. As he reacted to her suggestion, the van eased up and then lurched forward. "She lost her parents in the last year. She needs time to heal."

Seemed like more than that to Summer. Some special needs children had unusual gifts. Grace's was art. Ty's denial might be a normal reaction of a family member when confronted with an unpleasant truth. Or perhaps he didn't want an additional distraction from his work with Water Warriors.

But he did have a point. Grace had sustained enormous loss and experienced so many changes. She needed time to heal. Maybe they all did. Years had passed since Chrissie's accident, and Summer was still coming to terms with the loss. She thought she'd made a lot of progress lately. Progress she attributed to being surrounded by people she cared about. Dayita. Claire. Grace. Ty.

Claire's imminent recovery lifted a huge cloud from Summer's thoughts, one that had hung in the back of her mind since learning of the attack.

Which boyfriend, she wondered, had attacked Claire? Summer had seen several come and go over the years. If she had to guess, it was the guy who dared to visit Claire in her office. That guy with dark, messy hair she'd told to get lost. He'd been angry. Still, Summer didn't get it. How could a lover get angry enough to try to kill someone else? It wasn't logical. There were billions of people in the world. Someone rejects you, go find another lover.

Obviously not everyone agreed with Summer's outlook. You're too trusting—Dayita's accusation. Justin turned out to be Jake Fowler, a guy with a rap sheet. What happened to Claire could have easily happened to Summer.

The wind coming through the passenger window lifted her hair and should have lifted her spirits, but worries niggled at her. Strange events not related? The logic seemed flawed. Even if the angry boyfriend wasn't linked to the other events, someone had stolen Summer's computer and her flash drives and Alvarez was dead. Someone doctored those financial statements. No one had solved those crimes yet.

Summer was a scientist. She hated unanswered questions.

"They shouldn't have gone back," she said.

Ty stared at the road ahead. "I know."

Summer turned her phone on.

6

THE WRINKLES ON THE RAIL-THIN APARTMENT SUPER'S FOREHEAD deepened and he set the telephone back in its charging station on his desk. "Company policy—no one but the renter is allowed to get a key."

Dayita pulled her thick braid over her shoulder and twisted the end between her fingers, tilting her head to one side. "But you've seen me with Summer, Mr. Rodrigo—I practically live here."

He shook his head. "I seen you before but I can't do it. I could get fired."

"Come with me and watch the whole time. I have to find a list of phone numbers in Summer's desk drawer. She needs them. It's an emergency."

"I don't have time to watch you messing around. Second floor unit has a backed up disposal. Students are always putting stupid stuff down the sink. Bacon grease. Paper. Rubber bands. One girl gave herself a haircut over the sink and washed the trimmings down the drain. You wouldn't believe the gunk I pull out of disposals. You'd think college students would be smart, but no."

Dayita put on her most understanding smile. "There's book smart and then there's life smart. Someone like you has lots of life smarts."

"You got it. These kids can spout off Latin names for every fish in the ocean. They come up with weird ideas like the whole world's getting hot and we're all gonna die. Don't know shit about—"

Dayita let her expression show she wasn't the kind of girl you used that kind of language around, especially not with Grace standing beside her.

"Sorry," he said. "What're your names?"

"Dayita." She nudged Grace. "Honey, he asked your name."

"Gwace. Can I color?"

"As soon as we get into the apartment."

He reached up to unlock a metal wall cabinet. Dayita was glad he had on a belt. Even with one, he was so skinny his navy work pants nearly fell off his butt.

He extracted the key to 221 from the cabinet. "Take good care of this, Miz Dayita. Bring it back in five minutes or I'll come after you. I'll be in 203 fixing the disposal."

In the elevator she replayed the whole scene in her mind and laughed out loud. She was pretty good at deception. She let herself and Grace into the apartment and went straight to Summer's bedroom. She started rummaging through the center desk drawer's mélange of junk. Paper clips. Tape. Rubber bands. A birthday card from Summer's dad with a movie theater gift card inside. Seemed like hundreds of papers. She texted Summer: In your apartment. Where is contact info for interviews? She didn't suppose Summer would answer within the allotted five minutes, so Dayita started going through all the scraps. She found several business cards, but they contained appointments for haircuts and teeth cleaning. One neatly banded pack of letters appeared to be bills. She checked her phone. No response from Summer. At last she found a printout of phone numbers and emails. The first was family and friends. The one under it was probably the contact information Summer needed. Looked like professionals in Summer's field. Dayita grabbed it and straightened up. As she did, she heard a click. "Grace?" The kid wouldn't leave, would she? She was used to sitting still and coloring.

Dayita stepped out of the bedroom and into the hall. Grace was no longer on the couch. Too late, Dayita sensed motion coming toward her from the bathroom. A man's hand pressed a smelly cloth tight against her face and she involuntarily dropped the paper with Summer's contact information. Her hands flew to her face to remove the cloth. She couldn't see, couldn't breathe. She tried to scream but the sound was swallowed by the cloth. Someone grabbed her arms and pinned them. Though dizzy, she twisted away, but her captor bent her arms backward until she thought they would wrench out of the sockets. Shock waves of pain rocketed between her shoulder blades. Though her eyes were still covered, she saw a black-and-white whirligig spinning round and round. Pungent odor overwhelmed her senses. The world grew dark and she started to float.

7

THEOFANIS WAS SLOUCHED IN THE FRONT SEAT of the unmarked cruiser alone, listening to a book on tape, one of Randy Wayne White's Doc Ford novels. The reader's voice was cresting during a tense scene when the ambulance arrived outside the Cassidy kid's apartment building. No siren, but its emergency signal light swirled a red warning to the world. The apartments occupied a corner lot, so Theofanis had parked on the side street where he could watch both front and rear entrances.

Ash was out sick with a cold. Theofanis had told him to stay in bed because he didn't want to sit beside Ash all day and get sprayed with germs.

Theofanis took out a handkerchief and blew his nose. Already he was coming down with the same bug. Nonetheless, he had taken two cold tablets and reported for duty.

Right now Theofanis wished his partner were here to share his misery. He should get out and see what was going on, but it would blow his cover if anyone else was interested in the Cassidy kid. He decided to stay put for the time being.

Two EMTs scurried in with a stretcher. Exactly eight and a half minutes later, they emerged through the same door carrying someone on the stretcher. No IVs. A mask over the face. That much Theofanis could see from the car. He swore to himself. He supposed he'd better make sure it wasn't Summer Cassidy on that stretcher. He slammed the car door and trotted over to where the EMTs prepared to hoist the stretcher into the ambulance.

"Hold up," he said, hoping the busybody neighbors who had gathered to watch wouldn't see the discreet flash of his gold badge. "I need to see who you're transporting."

The biggest of the EMTs was much larger than Theofanis in both height and build, someone Ash might have met on a football field in earlier days. Though the big guy's body partially blocked the view, Theofanis could see the other EMT—a ferret-face with wire rimmed specs—lean over the patient with a penlight to check the woman's pupils.

"Old lady having a stroke." The big guy talking moved aside and immediately Theofanis saw it wasn't Summer Cassidy. The lump under the sheet was far too large to be the girl and the skin on the one hand that stuck out was too dark. Yet in the rush to make the right decision, an impression formed that he was missing an important detail. It lurked in a corner of his brain, but he couldn't shake it loose and pull it into conscious thought. He wished his partner was here to bounce the details around.

"Gotta go now or we're going to lose her," the Ferret said.

The big guy moved quickly for one his size to hoist one side of the stretcher into the ambulance. Theofanis stepped out of the way.

"All right then," the detective said. "You fellows need an escort?"

"We'll be fine on our own," the Linebacker hopped into the driver's seat and slammed the door. Within seconds, the vehicle had carried its precious cargo away, siren blaring.

By the time Theofanis reached his car, the high-pitched sound had already faded into a thin thread. He wondered if it was worth continuing the surveillance or if his cover was blown. He could get someone else to come out a few hours early. He was still making up his mind when one of the skinniest guys he'd ever seen approached his car. The stick figure knocked on his window. Theofanis rolled it down.

"Yeah?" he said.

"You a cop?" the Stick asked. "Miz Jennifer says you showed a badge."

Guess that answered the question whether his cover was still in place. "Yes, sir. What can I do for you?"

"I'm the super." He jerked his finger toward the Cassidy girl's apartment building. "You better come inside—take a look around."

What now?

"You got any of them CSI tools you should bring 'em along."

CSI tools. Right. TV had convinced the world that every cop performed all those scientific tests. They thought the results would magically pop out in an hour and an arrest would result. What a joke. Theofanis put in a call for assistance. At the very least, someone else had to take over surveillance.

Fighting a wave of nausea—nothing good awaited him inside that building—Theofanis followed the superintendent. They took the stairs rather than the elevator. It would be faster, according to the Stick Man. The door to 221 stood open. No furniture overturned, no sign of a struggle. Not like the last time Theofanis had been in the apartment. Place looked neat, clean. Especially for a college kid. Only thing out of place was a single sheet of rumpled paper on the carpet in a small hallway visible from the entrance.

"See here—" the super swept his bony hand toward the back of the apartment as he led the way in—"this is exactly how I found it. The door wide open. That girl was only supposed to be in here for five minutes, see, and when she didn't come back I went looking for her. When I heard the siren, I ran downstairs."

Theofanis walked toward the rumpled paper, a little dazed. He was still missing the super's point. Why was Summer only *supposed* to be in her apartment for five minutes? And how had she walked into the building without Theofanis seeing her?

The skinny man rambled on. The detective listened while he bent down, bracing his forearm on one knee, to read the paper. Someone had stepped on it. Multiple times. Appeared to be a list of email addresses and phone numbers.

"It wasn't my fault. I can't afford to lose my job. I got asthma and need my insurance."

Theofanis hoisted himself up. "What wasn't your fault?"

"Ain't you listening? I gave that girl a key but she was only supposed to be in here five minutes and she's a good friend of Miz Summer's. A really good friend. I seen her here lots of times. All she was supposed to do was grab that piece of paper. She said Miz Summer needed it. It was an emergency."

"What girl? Who'd you give the key to?"

"I've been trying to tell you. Miz Dayita, Miz Summer's friend. And she had that little girl with her. The kid's been around a lot recently too."

The skin, Theofanis thought. That's what had been bothering him. He visualized the scene in his mind: an oxygen mask covered the face, a shower cap hid the hair, and most of the body lay beneath a sheet. One hand was visible, the skin smooth and unblemished. No age spots or visible veins. Damn—those goons had snatched the Patel girl right in front of him. Now he had to report his blunder to the chief and call Ash in from his sick bed. The department would need every available resource on this one.

Overriding any concern for his reputation was worry about the girl. Did someone want the little computer whiz for her hacking skills? Had she hacked into the wrong place and been discovered? Or had the kidnappers simply gotten the wrong person? Whatever the Linebacker and Ferret had planned for Dayita Patel it wouldn't be any kind of picnic. The child must belong to the army vet. Where was he?

Theofanis closed his eyes and shuddered. Someone would have to notify the families.

8

"YOU SNATCHED THE WRONG GIRL, YOU BLOODY MORONS!" Jake Fowler screamed into his mobile, right into Roman Jeglinski's ear.

"I'm not going to listen to any more of your mouth, Jake. You treat me with respect, see."

Respect. The guy was thick, like trying to reason with a three-hundred-pound hamburger. Shuffling sounds suggested the phone being fumbled or passed around.

Sure enough, Kevin's voice greeted him next. Jake imagined his little brother shoving his glasses up the bridge of his nose. He never managed to keep them in place.

"She had a key," Kevin said. "I watched her unlock the door, like you said, and Roman waited down the hall."

"But Gee-Suzz, Jeglinski had to know it wasn't her. I mean, he got a mighty long look at her when she busted his nose with the Frisbee."

Kevin half-snorted a laugh, before answering. "Yeah, but once we got a good look, it was too late to back out."

Jake had planned so carefully. The stretcher and ambulance had been nothing short of genius. They must have hidden the child under the same blanket. "You should've left the kid there."

"This may work even better. Think about it: the Cassidy girl will do whatever you say to get her best friend and this kid back."

"What makes you think they're friends?'

"Why else would she have a key?" Kevin said. "Trust me, this will work out even better than if we had the Cassidy girl. She will bring us whatever we tell her to."

Harewood had gone crazy when he found out they had the wrong girl. Jake still didn't know how he'd found out. This whole affair had gone wrong from the get-go, but damned if it was Jake's fault. He needed to get the right girl fast and neutralize Harewood's anger. Snaring Summer Cassidy would guarantee HEC couldn't back out of their deal. No way around it. Jake was going to have to return to Loblolly Lake himself. When he got his hands on that Cassidy girl, he would get even for the way Harewood had screamed at him. He didn't take kindly to looking like an idiot.

9

THEY WERE HALFWAY TO LOBLOLLY LAKE when Summer's phone jingled the special tune that signaled a call from Dayita. Only one battery bar showed.

Dayita's voice shook as she said Summer's name. "Some men took us."

Blood drained from Summer's head. "What do you mean, took you? Took you where? Who took you?"

"What happened?" Ty asked.

Summer held up her hand to silence him and put the call on speaker.

Dayita choked out the next words. "They said you have to bring all copies of the report, your thesis, the presentation. They won't hurt us as long as we give them every scrap about those wells. They'll let us go after the DEP makes its decision. They said they'd cut my face if you don't hurry."

Summer started to reassure Dayita, but soft pops on the other end scared her. "Dayita? You there?"

Summer was trying to imagine what was happening when a man's voice came on and issued directions to a warehouse. "You screw with us in any way and we're going to mess up your friend and the kid real bad. You come alone with every fucking thing you have concerning that grant. Got it?"

An adrenaline surge made her voice steely. "Got it." She depressed the end-call on hard to turn off the phone and conserve what was left of the battery, her anger vibrating through her fingers.

"Those bastards aren't going to get away with this. Mission planning is my specialty," Ty said.

That ridiculous app Dayita had installed—they could figure out where Dayita and Grace were. "Pull over."

"Every second counts," Ty snapped.

"Do it. We can figure out where the kidnappers are holding them."

He yanked the steering wheel and the van bounced onto the grassy shoulder. "How's that?"

"Dayita set up a link so she could always locate me in case . . ." She didn't need to tell him why.

"Through the GPS chips, right?"

"Dayita set up a friend network on Google called Latitude. I've never used it, and I'm not sure how it works." Summer had never used it because, unlike most college students, she had no interest in where other people were and what they were doing. She couldn't care less if they were eating tacos or playing poker or watching a movie. She didn't tweet every few minutes. Much of what she did wasn't all that interesting, and if it was, she didn't have time to tweet.

Ty extended his hand for the phone. "Let me handle it."

In minutes he had a Google map identifying the location of Dayita's phone. "Not what I expected." He showed her the map.

Summer's eyes widened. She expected Dayita to be at one of the ASR well sites—they tended to be out in the boonies. Or in a warehouse Harewood owned since they were supposed to meet up in one. But the Google map placed them at the main compound of Harewood Corporation itself. Why go there? The phone's screen went black.

"Battery died, and my charging cable's in my truck. We gotta stop and buy a new one on the way."

Ty nodded. "I need supplies, too."

Summer leaned her face out the window. To the west, cumulonimbus clouds were rolling in, darkening the sky. A peal of distant thunder sounded. She glanced at Ty, concerned that the sound would spook him, but he didn't flinch or body-slam her. He didn't pull the gun he kept in his backpack.

10

THEOFANIS BLEW HIS NOSE AGAIN, leaning against the side of the ambulance. It had been ditched in an alley behind a string of abandoned shops with back doors left open. An elderly man who lived in an apartment over one of the shops had been looking out his window. He saw the attendants move a stretcher into the back of a dark van. He thought it odd enough to record part of the license number before it drove off. Lucky for them, he had the good sense to call it in immediately.

Thank goodness for busybodies. They performed an under-appreciated public service. A team was combing the vehicle now for fingerprints and evidence. Theofanis doubted they'd find much. Pros, obviously. Yet they'd made a mistake. They'd been seen and the busybody had given him a good description of the men. One big guy, one smaller one with glasses. Matched what Theofanis had seen, plus one interesting detail. The small guy had a tat on his right arm. U.S. Navy. When Theofanis questioned how the man could possibly have seen that, he'd taken him up to his apartment. He showed him the telescope, which he claimed to aim only at the sky. Theofanis didn't care if the fellow *was* a peeper. The additional detail was useful.

His phone jingled. Burns had a probable match on the partial license plate. The van most likely belonged to Jake Fowler. Advertised himself on the Internet as a troubleshooter. Guy had a string of priors and a reputation for accepting work that legits turned down. Fowler was a start. With any abduction, the more time that passed, the less likely a good outcome became.

Theofanis thought of the tattoo. "He ever been in the Navy?" he asked Burns.

He hadn't. Theofanis supposed that would have been too easy. But Jake Fowler had been dishonorably discharged from the military. Looked as if he had fragged comrades, though those charges were dropped. In any case, he was one dangerous son-of-a-bitch. Theofanis put out an APB on Fowler and on every vehicle registered to the so-called troubleshooter. If he showed his face anywhere near Loblolly Lake, they'd find him. Theofanis assigned one officer to track down any associates, especially any in the Navy.

The phone jingled again as soon as he ended the call. Ash. They'd found the Cassidy girl's truck parked two blocks from the apartment. "No way you could have seen it," Ash assured him. Theofanis would have recognized the truck, but not Dayita and the child. They had walked right by him.

Ash had picked up Mrs. Patel. They were headed to the Cassidy home for a hand-wringing session. Theofanis slid into his vehicle and drove as fast as he deemed safe to join Ash. In a matter of hours, this case sure had become messy again. He hated messy. He preferred information enclosed in neat little bubble-boxes on his computer.

He swore softly as a black Park Avenue slowed his progress. The car appeared driverless. Only when the road curved, did he spot a puff of snowy hair. He thought about turning on the siren and blasting by, but the chief preferred officers to save the noise for emergencies. He crept along the one-lane neighborhood roads, drumming his fingers on the steering wheel, gritting his teeth.

Ash's county-issued vehicle was already parked in front of the Cassidys' two-story red brick home by the time Theofanis arrived. As he pushed the doorbell, Theofanis wondered what Mrs. Patel would be like. Only Ash had dealt with her thus far. Theofanis spotted Mrs. Cassidy first. As he expected, she shrieked when she opened her mouth, pulling on her silvery blonde hair, pacing and whirling about. She brought to mind a tornado. Ash persuaded her to sit down on the floral-covered sofa.

What a change since Theofanis had last been inside! Before, all the furnishings had been pristine and arranged like a scene from a ladies' magazine. In the years following Chrissie's accident, a pall had descended on the house. A desktop computer and printer replaced the cushy chairs that once had been part of a conversation grouping of furniture. Only the couch remained. Stacks of papers littered its surface. Plastic crates of file folders were stacked on dingy carpet. Several overlapping condensation rings marred the coffee table.

Theofanis let Ash orchestrate the questions, preferring instead to record answers while he observed the parties involved.

Mrs. Patel was obviously grief-stricken, too, but in a quieter way. A heavy-set woman with dark braided hair, she pushed aside papers and sank into the cushions of the sofa, which faced the fireplace. Theofanis bet it had never held a fire. All for show.

Mrs. Patel twisted an embroidered cloth handkerchief with nervous fingers as she answered Ash's questions. "I wasn't supposed to tell anyone where they went. Dayita said these people with the wells are powerful and have the money to buy influence. She said not to trust anyone, including you folks. They went camping to stay out of the way until after tomorrow's hearing with the senator. But I told her you'd found the man who attacked Dr. Dunham. I thought they that they'd be safe if they came home. It's my fault. If I'd kept quiet, they would still be safe."

From his position near the fireplace, Ash reached his big paw out as if he might touch her shoulder in comfort. At the last minute, he withdrew his hand. "You couldn't have known. And we still have no proof that the abduction is connected."

Summer's mother collapsed onto her own lap, burying her face into her folded arms. "Oh Summer, my Summer. And poor little Chrissie. My babies. Please God, don't take Summer too. Not Summer too."

Mrs. Patel put her hands on Mrs. Cassidy's shoulders and lifted her into a comforting embrace, patting her back, rocking her. "She didn't come back with Dayita, so she's probably still camping. She is such an independent young woman."

Guilt caused Theofanis to lower his eyes. His harsh judgment of Mrs. Cassidy's erratic behavior seemed wrong to him now. The death of a child changed a family forever. Everyone in it, especially the mother.

He tried Summer's mobile again. He shook his head. "She must have turned it off."

He had an officer trying to locate the signals on both Dayita's and Summer's phones. If either was on, the GPS chip could pinpoint their locations. His phone jingled. He listened for a minute, a hint of satisfaction lighting his eyes. He signaled Ash to follow him outside onto the porch. He spoke to the officer on the other end. "Put out an APB on both." He ended the call and shared with Ash. "Fowler had a cell mate few years back, name of Roman Jeglinski. Big guy. And Fowler has a brother. Kevin. Guess who served in the navy, 1997-2002? We got a break."

11

THE SUV IN FRONT OF TY'S VAN RACED through the red light at Loblolly Lake's main intersection. A rapid flash whipped overhead. Ty stomped on the brake, ducked his head and pushed Summer down onto the bench seat.

Geez-louise! A lump of fear clogged Summer's throat. She should have insisted Ty not come along, or at least insisted he not drive. The muscles in his face and hands were taut. "It's okay," she said. "Only a red-light camera."

He pulled himself upright, his eyes refocusing. Summer righted herself and tugged her shirt back into place.

Ty swallowed visibly.

A horn sounded, and he put the van in gear and accelerated. "All right, all right, I'm going."

"You don't have to do this, Ty," Summer said. "I can handle it. You can be my back-up in case they don't stick to the agreement."

Ty's jaw set. "It's my sister they've got. You're not walking in there and giving yourself up to them. They'd kill all of you. You need my skill set. In the military, I specialized in search and rescue missions."

She had no choice but to trust him.

He drove past Harewood Corporation's headquarters, slow enough to study the layout but not so slow as to call attention if anyone was posted to watch outside the compound. The facility, situated about two miles outside Loblolly Lake, resembled a small college campus with its cluster of red brick buildings. A lighted fountain welcomed visitors at the entrance. The fence that fronted the entrance was an at-tractive blend of brick posts connected by black wrought iron, and at this hour the gate was closed. The parking lot lights revealed two cars.

Summer had been inside the compound when she'd interviewed for her scholarship with Harewood and that nice Miss Julia. She'd only seen a small part of the main building, but she recalled the eleva-tors to Harewood's office and the conference room were on the right as you entered the lobby. His office was down the corridor to the left as you exited the elevators on the third floor.

It was after nine in the evening, and the main building was dark except for security lights and one corner office with blazing lights on the third floor. Harewood's office. A silhouetted figure moved across the wall of windows and disappeared. A custodian? Harewood himself? Summer didn't think they would keep Dayita and Grace in the main building. She wasn't really sure why they would have risked putting her anywhere near the compound. Except it was close to the warehouse where Summer was supposed to take her thesis and the grant report. The more she considered their situation, the kidnappers didn't intend to let them go the day after the DEP made their decision. No matter what they promised. How could they risk it?

She still had Theofanis's number. Surely her phone had picked up enough charge on the drive over to make that call if she needed to. She had serious reservations about this rescue mission. Ty not only had a missing leg, his brain over-reacted to the clang of garbage can lids and red light cameras. And throughout her whole life, she had frozen in every crisis. She was weak and worthless. Chrissie's death proved that.

Since Dayita's call for help had come, Ty had seized control with a soldier's confidence and developed a rescue mission plan. They needed to move fast. They didn't know who to trust. Still, she fingered the phone, thinking of Theofanis, as they circled the Harewood compound.

As Ty turned down the highway to the right, the compound fencing became chain-link. He slid his night vision goggles on and slowed to a crawl. Ty pointed to a white wooden building bordering the fence. "That little building over there probably is the electrical power for the facility."

"How can you tell?"

"Way the building's designed gives it away," he said. "Concrete pad. Transmission lines feeding into it. The other buildings have underground utilities."

They continued to circle the compound, turning right again. Security lights were spaced far apart as they moved away from the main buildings. The back end of the compound had preserved more trees. One area was rather thickly wooded.

"There!" Ty pointed to another outbuilding.

A light was on inside, barely visible to the naked eye if you weren't looking for it. Ty could see more detail with his goggles that she could with ordinary vision. Summer craned her neck to study the building as they drove by. "Might be a custodian or a night guard."

"Don't think so. Pretty sure I saw the night watchman slouched on a golf cart near the main building. I saw a lighted screen. Probably a laptop."

Summer supposed he watched TV shows or surfed porn sites.

"I can make out a van parked along the side under that pine," Ty said. "Can you see it? That's probably how they transported Dayita and Grace here. I haven't spotted any other vehicles except those few in the front lot and the golf carts."

A sheet of lightning illuminated the sky briefly, and despite the shadows cast by the building and the pines, Summer detected the sloping front end of a vehicle. Ty was right. A van.

They passed the main entrance again, completing the circle. Near the electrical hut, Ty parked off the shoulder. It wasn't too late to change their minds. Call Theofanis. It wasn't only that Summer didn't trust Ty. She didn't trust herself. What if she let Dayita and Grace down?

Ty was on the move and she hustled to keep up with him. He hopped into the back of the van and retrieved industrial-strength wire cutters. As he made the cut, metal clinked, a noise Summer worried half the town heard. Summer tried to brace the fence so it wouldn't rattle so much as Ty worked. They had to avoid attracting the attention of any night watchman. A gust of wind flung Summer's hair across her face. She tossed her head to remove it, but another gust soon blew it back. In a surprisingly short time, Ty opened a three-foot square gap in the chain-link. He went through first and pulled the metal cutters in after him. Going through the fence might be the toughest part of the operation for Ty physically. He moved great on his leg when he was upright, but how well could he crawl through a hole?

She had worried for no reason. Ty lay on his back and crab-walked backwards through the opening. She hoped the rest of the rescue went as smoothly. Ty's next task was to cut electricity to the facility. She had faith that he was every bit as skilled as he said. Summer fingered the lumps of her backpack until she located the elongated bulge, assuring herself the package of gear ties was inside. They would need them to restrain the kidnappers once they'd disarmed and disabled them. She crawled through the opening after him. As Ty helped her to her feet, the first raindrops fell, cold against her bare arms.

12

RAIN PEPPERED ISAAC HAREWOOD as he headed toward the shed where the company stored lawn equipment. The drops felt cool and ticklish on his scalp. His hard-soled Italian leather shoes smacked against the concrete as he strode along the pathway connecting the various buildings.

He didn't see how Fowler managed to mess this up any worse than he already had, but there seemed no end to stupidity in Florida. Why had they brought those girls here, of all places? Fowler must be smoking that stuff instead of perfecting seed strains. Morrell and Fowler thought he wasn't aware of their venture, but Morrell had been right about one thing: Julia knew where all the bodies were buried. She pointed out Morrell's involvement with the grow houses made him into a perfect scapegoat.

Isaac's hand slipped into his pocket to rub the piece of jasper between his thumb and forefinger. When he became aware of what he was doing, he pulled the stone out of his pocket. It glistened in the light of the security lamp directly overhead. Suddenly all the lights blinked out. Then, of course, there was silence: the absence of equipment hum, background noise you took for granted until it disappeared. Isaac growled and flung the stone into the grassy bed that bordered the path. Any luck the stone possessed had run out. His life had turned upside down. In the morning he was calling the county commission and complaining yet again. Fat lot of good it would do. They obviously were incapable of fixing the problem.

Blindly, he stumbled on toward the shed where Fowler's thugs waited with the girls. He wanted them off his property as fast as they could tuck their tails between their legs and run. All of them. They could drop the girls' bodies off in a Walmart parking lot or a city park. He didn't care. As long as they got them away from the compound immediately if not before. Fowler could forget about getting paid. In business you got paid for services rendered, and Fowler was so incompetent Isaac was sure he couldn't properly wipe his own behind. Troubleshooter, indeed. All he'd done so far was cause trouble.

Isaac teetered slightly as his foot landed on the edge of the concrete path, halfway off onto the grassy border. Suddenly a vice-like grip engulfed his neck.

13

ISAAC HAREWOOD FELL LIMP TO THE GROUND, his fall eased by Ty.

Summer gasped. "Is he dead?"

"Unconscious," Ty whispered as he dragged Harewood off the path. He deposited the body behind a cluster of Bradford pear trees. The shadows would obscure Harewood from any night watchman who happened by.

Ty held a finger to his lips and pointed ahead. When Summer nodded, Ty assumed her eyes had grown accustomed enough to the dark so she could see, at least a little. Probably meant anyone else out on Harewood's grounds could also make out shapes in the black void. With luck, the rain would encourage others to stay inside.

Using his night-vision goggles, Ty led the way toward the rear of the compound where they had spotted the van. His ball cap kept most of the rain off his face, but his shirt was splattered with fat wet drops.

The van was parked on the right side of the shed. Ty pressed his face close to the driver's side window and his lips curled with satisfaction. Keys in the ignition. Why not? The kidnappers weren't expecting visitors.

He eased the door open to retrieve the keys and handed them to Summer. "Stay with their van."

"No way; they've got my friend."

Ty scowled. Drew his finger across his lips, signaling no argument permitted. He'd been afraid of this. Before setting out, he'd explained the importance of following orders, but he was dealing with a civilian.

He tapped his ear and then his chest, signaling "Listen to me."

She shook her head and signaled that she was going to the left side of the building. Damn, she was stubborn.

Ty moved to the right side. He froze at the sound of voices coming from the shed. Angry voices. But try as he might, he couldn't make out what they were saying. Rain splatting against the metal roof drowned the kidnappers' words with its racket. He moved as quietly as he could, cringing with every crunch of his tennis shoes on the gravel. If only they hadn't bordered this particular building with gravel—but the noisy rain would be his friend in this instance, camouflaging any sound he made.

The storage shed was about twenty feet wide by fifty long. It was designed with double doors, which would flatten against the front wall to allow passage of wide equipment. Ty passed by quickly, his knees bent to keep his body low. So far his prosthesis was working perfectly.

From the side window he could make out a golf cart plugged into the wall beneath him. Beyond were two lawn mowers, one wide-swath commercial type and a more conventional tractor for narrower spots. On the back wall hung a variety of equipment—leaf blowers, string trimmers and the like. Opposite Ty was another window, one Summer was probably looking through right now. And beneath that window sat Dayita, arms and legs tied to a webbed lawn chair, a lantern-style flashlight resting on the ground near her feet. His adrenaline pumped. Grace! Her body, partly hidden by Dayita's, was also tied, her arms secured behind her. They'd left her legs loose. They didn't begin to reach the floor. If they hurt her . . .they wouldn't. He wouldn't let them.

Ty forced himself to concentrate on what needed to be done. The giant beside Grace had to be the computer thief. A smaller guy paced toward the back of the building and then toward the front. A circle of light, a smaller flashlight, accompanied him while he spoke into a phone.

Ty tested the window, tugging gently with his fingers. Not locked. How much noise would it make if he tried to raise it? He ducked and continued to the rear of the building, which was windowless, no features worth noting.

When he met up with Summer, he motioned for her to go back the way they came to the dripping canopy of a shumard oak. His plan needed refinement before they charged in to rescue the girls. Lightning flashed in the distance again. Standing under a tree in a storm wasn't the smartest tactic, but it was a necessary risk.

"Two men," Ty whispered.

"One's the guy who stole my computer."

"Thought so. We have to assume they have weapons and that they'll use them."

"At least Dayita and Grace are okay," Summer said.

"For now, but they plan to kill them. The girls weren't blindfolded."

He was relieved when Summer didn't argue. Good soldiers didn't. He laid out his plan. "When I've had enough time to get to the window, you are going to start up their van and slowly drive a short, but safe distance away. The engine noise should pull one of the kidnappers outside. I am going to sneak through the window on the far side. I'll take out whichever man stays behind. Okay?"

Ty waited in a silence broken only by an owl complaining about the rain. Summer stared off into the distance. Ty touched her cheek, the skin soft and slick from raindrops.

He had a hunch the moisture he'd found near her eyes wasn't rain alone. Whatever was going on with her, she couldn't let them down. That was his sister in there. She was only four, for God's sake, and she'd been through enough already. Too much.

"Summer? Stay chilly. We have a mission to complete. You can't let emotions sidetrack you."

Summer swallowed and then nodded. Once again, they set off for the shed. Summer slid into the van. Ty crept into position beneath the window. If he couldn't take out the kidnappers with his hands the way he'd handled Harewood, the Bersa Thunder .38 in his backpack ensured success. He took it out and tucked it under his belt, its pressure against the small of his back reassuring.

The rumble of the van's engine disturbed the night air, his signal to go in. He teased the window upward. The pungent scent of gasoline and motor oil reached him as he maneuvered his body into a dark corner of the shed.

14

ONCE JAKE FOWLER GOT PAST THE MIAMI-LAUDERDALE BOTTLENECK, very little traffic clogged the Interstate this rainy night. He only pushed his ancient Volvo nine miles over the speed limit. No sense in inviting police attention. He'd bought the Volvo because cops would profile its drivers as stodgy suburbanites not worth their dime. Jake passed a semi hauling tomatoes to northern grocery chains. Why did anyone bother to buy them? They were tasteless as damp sponges.

In prison, he'd learned to grow his own food. Hadn't touched a store-bought tomato since. He had built four raised beds in his small backyard and planted lettuce, tomatoes, beans, squash, onions. Even had a couple of strawberry pots. And inside his old Florida-style house, the spare bedrooms were devoted to broad spectrum lights devoted to his mission to develop the finest strains of marijuana. He and Morrell would be first in line when pot went legal. They'd greased all the right palms and laid the groundwork for Morell and the governor's son to obtain a license. After Jake sold his stake in the seeds, he would ride the gravy train all the way to a mansion in the Caribbean.

A big green rectangle announced the turn-off to Loblolly Lake. He eased into the right lane, swearing softly to himself. No, he didn't want to attract attention, but that's all his involvement with Isaac

Harewood had accomplished. How had such a simple mission turned into such a major fuck-up? Harewood hadn't thought through what it might take to remove all evidence of the incriminating test results.

Now they had snatched the wrong girl, and Harewood was furious. Fowler didn't like being screamed at, by Harewood or anyone else. As a boy, he'd put up with enough of that from his father. No wonder his mother walked out the door and didn't come back. But a decent woman would have taken him and his three brothers with her.

He would never forgive her for leaving him with a man whose answer to any disturbance, no matter how small, was a swinging belt. His father didn't care where the flying leather connected. The thighs. The small of the back. His father, stinking drunk as usual, slammed his truck into a bridge abutment while Jake was still in high school. Jake attended the funeral to make sure his father was planted permanently beneath the dirt. The day after the funeral, Jake had gone back to the cemetery and urinated on the grave. He'd done it again over the hole where he'd dumped the lieutenant's and sergeant's bodies. They had screamed obscenities at him too.

They'd fucked with the wrong guy. Piss splatting on the freshly dug dirt sounded much like the rain pounding his windshield as he navigated the main drag through Loblolly Lake.

It wouldn't be long now. He pulled into the parking lot of an abandoned gas station and slipped a protective vest on under his jacket.

15

WITH A STIFF ARM CLASPED to the railing, Theofanis vaulted over the railing of the Cassidys' front porch. He landed on wet grass and skidded down onto one knee, staining his khakis. The scent of rich dirt arose from where his boat mocs had turned up a divot of grass. He righted himself quickly. "Into the car—now!" he yelled over his shoulder to his partner.

By the time Ash got his size fourteens moving down the concrete steps, Theofanis had planted himself in the driver's seat of his vehicle and fired the engine.

The car was already in motion when Ash jerked the passenger door shut. "What's going on?"

"Read the text for yourself." The phone lay on the seat.

"Tell me they didn't."

"They did."

"Stupid punks are gonna get themselves killed." Ash radioed for back-up, no sirens.

Theofanis hoped his partner was wrong, but a college kid and injured vet staging a rescue was a bad idea. A really bad idea. Amateurs shouldn't mess with animals like Jeglinski and Fowler. At least the Cassidy girl had the sense to text him that it was going down. Small consolation. They'd probably find a bloodbath in progress when they arrived. And guess who would have to tell the parents?

If he wasn't driving sixty-five miles an hour through neighborhood streets, if the road wasn't wet, if he was somebody else, almost anybody else—the thought of confronting Mrs. Cassidy and Mrs. Patel with more bad news would have made him close his eyes and weep.

If only he'd become the priest his mother had wanted him to be. Too late for that.

"Hold on." He let up on the accelerator and banked the wheel sharply to the left as they passed the First National Bank corner. Only a few miles to go, mostly a straight stretch now. That little bit of priest his mother had seen inside him sent up a prayer.

16

THE SHED DOOR BANGED OPEN. In her rear view mirror, Summer could see a circle of light bouncing up and down in the direction of the van. Perfect. She hoped Ty wouldn't get angry when he found out she had texted Theofanis. She'd heard an owl hooing in the dark; and though it was completely irrational, for a flicker she sensed Chrissie's presence.

She shook the thoughts off. She'd already lost one sister. She wasn't going to lose Dayita. And little Grace with those crayons and pink tennis shoes—Ty couldn't lose her either. If anything went wrong, Theofanis would be there to fix it. Summer drove slowly enough to make the kidnapper think he could catch up. Taking shallow breaths, her adrenaline rushing, she eased along the curves of the narrow paved road.

Her underpants clung damp against her skin, the rain soaking through to her skin. The main headquarters loomed ahead. Her pursuer had given up and headed back to the shed. Surely by now, Ty had freed Dayita and Grace. She pulled into the employee parking lot and swung the van around.

Headlights at the entrance hit her full in the face, and she had to look away. Had to be Theofanis to the rescue—what a relief!

The boxy sedan slowed to a crawl. She figured the detective intended to talk to her before charging into the shed. The sedan kept coming. She waited for it to slow down. But no, the driver accelerated. Didn't he see her? She jerked the steering wheel and pressed on the gas pedal.

Time slowed into milliseconds as headlights blotted out the rest of the world. First came the sound of glass breaking. Next the whine of metal folding in on itself. The iron smell and taste of blood. And then nothing.

No, not nothing.

The sound of plastic flip flops slapping on the linoleum and Chrissie's giggling command: "Come on, Summer!" Then oblivion.

17

CROUCHED LOW, TY SET ONE FOOT in front of the other carefully, his C-leg set to a mode that allowed flexing for long periods of time without exhaustion. He had covered half the distance to the kidnapper, using lawn tractors and golf carts as cover, when the wet sole of his tennis shoe squeaked on the concrete floor. He winced and held his breath, willing himself to stay perfectly still, to disappear, a trick he'd learned on nature walks as a kid. Most creatures, including humans, didn't notice you until you moved.

Rain pounding on the roof created enough racket that the squeaky shoe went unnoticed. The remaining kidnapper kept pushing up his glasses and flashing the lantern toward the open shed door, clearly expecting his partner's reappearance at any moment.

Ty adjusted his night-vision goggles and cat-crept closer. The small-boned man turned back toward Dayita and Grace. Again he pushed his glasses up the bridge of his nose, his gun aimed at the floor. Ty chose that moment to spring forward. He pressed his fingers into the kidnapper's jugular notch and then struck the brachial plexus nerve in his neck. The kidnapper's gun clattered to the floor. Ty kicked it under the closest tractor. When the military had taught him Dim Mak

Kung Fu, he had never imagined he'd use it in civilian life. Twice in one night, even.

"It's okay, Sugarpop," Ty said. "You're going to be okay. I'm here now." Ty cut the plastic ties on Grace's wrists and ran his thumbs over the skin beneath them twice. She jumped to her feet and clung to his leg while he worked to free Dayita's arms. As soon as Dayita's legs were freed, Ty helped her to her feet, keeping one arm around her waist for support.

"You okay? Did they hurt you?" he asked while he dragged the kidnapper's inert body by the arms, his boots rasping against the concrete. When the kidnapper's body was out of the way, Ty released his arms, allowing his narrow head to thump the floor.

"I'll be all right." Dayita's mascara had left dark trails down her cheeks and her braid had unraveled.

Ty turned off the lantern on the floor. Darkness was their friend.

The trio moved toward the door. Ty thrust out his arm in front of Dayita and pushed Grace behind him. A circle of light wavered directly in front of the door. The owner of that flashlight would see them if they tried to get out that way. Ty had to assume the other kidnapper had a gun, too. He motioned for Dayita to move behind him and the closed section of the double door. He drew the pistol from his belt and waited. The light stopped in the doorway. Ty stepped forward, his gun pointed at the giant silhouetted in the opening. The green glow of the night-vision goggles made the big guy look eerily like a comic book villain.

"Drop the gun," Ty said.

"No, you'd better put down the weapon."

The man showed no fear. Something was wrong. Ty was missing a crucial piece of information. "Why would I?"

"Because we got your little girlfriend."

A third kidnapper! They hadn't factored in another player. "Why should I believe you?"

"Figured you were going to ask that." He tugged a phone from his breast pocket and handed it to Ty.

The self-shot photo on the screen wasn't going to win any prizes, but the picture left no doubt it was Summer slumped over the van's steering wheel. Jake Fowler held an FMK .9 millimeter to her head. Ty's throat tightened, but more than ever, he needed to rely on his training. Stay chilly. Figure out how to get everyone safely out of this mess.

"Where's Kevin?" the kidnapper asked. "You better hope you ain't done nothing to him or you gonna leave here not just dead but carved into pieces and parts."

Great. More pieces and parts. The giant wanted to finish what the Taliban insurgents started.

18

WHEN SENATOR FELIPE VARGAS OPENED the manila envelope full of black and white photos, he could hardly breathe. He shoved them back inside before the intern who had handed him the envelope could glimpse the senator's shame. He asked the intern to leave him alone. Vargas collapsed into the padded chair at his desk. His first thoughts were how he would lose his senate seat if this came out. Disappointment washed over him. How selfish! His family should have been his first thought. Ana would be hurt and furious. And Manny—the kids would tease him at school. His little girl lived in her own world, closed off by her autism. Wherever it was that she lived, others couldn't harm her.

His staff—how many had guessed? He supposed most would decamp if this became public. He had never wanted anyone else to get hurt.

Hours later as he drove to the baseball park, he grew strangely calm. Almost relieved. The senator had spent most of his life imagining this day, under what circumstances the truth might emerge, and this wasn't at all how he'd expected to feel.

He strolled onto the deserted field and stood on the pitcher's mound, his neck canted upward at an eggplant-tinted sky devoid of clouds. With little pollution from ground light, a full panorama of stars invited metaphysical questions. Why was he here? What destiny thrust him to this turning point? What did God want from him?

For a few moments he lingered, contemplating the immensity of the universe and the small space he occupied within its vastness. Ever since his boyhood, whenever he faced a crisis, the senator liked to soak in the night sky. It always provided perspective. Yet small as a human was, the senator believed every single one mattered. He reminded himself of William Wordsworth's concept: you can see "the world in a grain of sand." The smallest change can have enormous consequences.

Even in Elizabethan times, though the reasoning behind the Great Chain of Being was flawed, the idea of all things being connected was something people understood intuitively. It was a concept environmentalists were always trying to push to the forefront of our minds. A whole ecosystem can shift when the smallest part is changed.

Whatever the senator did tomorrow mattered in ways he couldn't even imagine. That's what he needed to remember.

The hum of a well-tuned motor traversing the park spurred him to action. It was likely to be a long night and he had that hearing tomorrow with the head honchos at the Department of Environmental Protection. He didn't know quite enough about those privately owned ASR wells to have an opinion at this point. He hoped the hearing would clarify the issues involved.

A gust of wind ruffled the senator's hair, perhaps a forerunner of the rain forecasters predicted for Tallahassee before morning. One last time he inhaled the humid air deep into his lungs, relishing the slight scent from the stand of longleaf pines lining the sides of the chain link fence. He had argued against the city planners who wanted to mow down all those trees when they developed the park. Cheaper that way, they'd said. Keep the trees, he'd insisted. It was the right thing to do.

That's what he was always telling the little guys on his baseball team. Do the right thing. But it wasn't always easy. Sometimes no matter what you did, people got hurt. The anguish that enveloped him as he contemplated the inevitability of that sorrow, that loss, seemed as infinite as the expanse of night sky overhead.

19

THE MALE VOICE SEEMED ODDLY DISTANT and made no sense. He was talking about a gun. What gun? Where was she? Summer opened her eyes. Saw a circle of white numbers on black. A red line. A speedometer. She remembered a car ramming the van.

Someone seized her ponytail and jerked her head against the seat. Pain shot down her spine. She fought against the nausea and concentrated on the face wavering in front of her. She saw brown bangs. A square chin.

"Hi Summer, remember me?"

Unfortunately, she did. "A little late for our rendezvous at the Wacissa, aren't you?"

"Maybe we'll go there tonight and feed some gators."

"Fuck you."

The sound of his laughter lodged in her throat. She forced herself to swallow.

"Yeah, I hear you like that," he said. "But right now, we're going to join your friends for a show-and-tell party."

He yanked her out of the van by her arm. She had a severe case of jelly legs. Only his grasp on her elbow kept her from falling down.

She scanned his face. "You killed Alvarez, didn't you? Why?"

"I didn't kill him. I was just cleaning up a mess for someone else. The local cops were supposed to keep you out of the way, but nothing went down quite the way we planned. But don't get the idea I have anything against killing," he said. "I enjoy it."

He wrenched her arm behind her waist, locking it into that painful position and marching her forward. She kept moving even as shock waves blasted her neck with every step. With her free hand, she brushed a finger against the damp skin beneath her nose. Blood. She wiped the residue on her jeans.

Jake steered her through the wet grass rather than the paved paths, a more direct line to the rear of the compound. Her shoes made squooshy noises, her toes chilled by moisture seeping through to her socks.

The shed came into view. Inside, softly illuminated by a battery-operated lantern, both kidnappers and captives congregated in an open area beyond the door. That monster who'd stolen her computer had a gun trained on Ty. Behind them stood a wall with a window and a pegboard holding a large assortment of tools. Screwdrivers. Wrenches. Hammers. Power drill. Extension cords of various sizes. Bungee cords.

Jake pushed Summer inside. The air was laden with the scents of gasoline and used motor oil.

"Let's play with the bitches before we get rid of them," Jeglinski said. "You want the Indian first, Kevin?"

Technically, Dayita was Bengali-American, but it wasn't the time to quibble over ethnicity. The little guy with the glasses—obviously Kevin—reminded Summer of a rodent.

"I dig the braid." He loosened his grip on Dayita's arm to grope her. She gouged an elbow into his ribs, twisting away from him.

"Sounds like fun," Jake said, "but it ain't gonna happen. We gotta be careful no DNA traces to us. The road will be slippery tonight, and these poor schmucks are gonna have a serious accident."

He let go of Summer and shoved her toward the computer thief. She staggered and would have fallen if the giant hadn't caught her. She struggled out of his arms and stood on her own power.

"Get them into their van," Jake said, motioning toward the double door with his gun. "I found it parked outside the compound."

Kevin pushed Dayita ahead of him. She stood in the open doorway, gun at her back, silhouetted against the dark night.

Summer saw a large shadow shift slightly on the path leading from the shed—an illusion? Or could it be Theofanis? Had he received her text?

She couldn't wait for the cavalry to arrive. If they got in Ty's van, they would die. She needed a weapon. Any weapon. Her eyes cast about for a suitable missile. A wrench. It would flip fairly evenly end to end. Summer reached behind her and snatched the closest one from the pegboard. Cocked her elbow. Snapped her wrist. The shiny metal hurtled toward Jake's neck. He must have sensed her motion because he turned as it zipped through the air. With a sickening thud, it slammed into his windpipe. Jake staggered backward, clutching his throat. His legs buckled and he collapsed onto his knees. The wrench clanged against the concrete floor. His gun slid across the floor, stopping under the workbench.

The shadow outside—Theofanis, thank God!—yanked Dayita past the open door. He dove toward the ground while firing shots into Jeglinski's chest.

Ty scrambled for Jake's gun, his back turned for an instant on the action.

Jake pulled another handgun from his waistband and was raising it toward Grace.

"No!" Summer leaped toward the child and pushed her out of the line of fire. She curled her body around Grace on the floor, sheltering her, the way she hadn't sheltered Chrissie. Summer closed her eyes, not certain if it was her own body shaking or the child's.

Three gunshots exploded and footsteps thudded close by.

Theofanis's voice came from her right: "Police! Drop your weapon!"

Another voice—the small kidnapper: "Don't shoot!"

More shots followed and Summer's eyes flashed open. On the floor to her left, the glass cover of a lantern shattered with a bullet's impact, and the room plunged into total darkness.

As footsteps pounded past, she tried to curl into an even smaller space, squeezing her eyes shut again, wishing she could shut out the world. Make it all go away. Seconds stretched until they seemed like hours. The sound of her own breath roared in her ears. Who was alive? Dead?

Hands seized her shoulders, attempting to pry her off Grace.

She squeezed the child even tighter. "Leave her alone!"

"Shhuuh, it's me." Ty eased her arms away gently. "It's all right. It's over. You're okay."

A recent arrival on the police force set up a battery-powered flood-light and suddenly the shed was illuminated again.

Theofanis plunged outside and returned through the double doors. ""Where's Fowler? Where the hell's Fowler? Ash? You got him?"

The police scrambled over bodies and cursed, but Summer barely noticed. Ty pulled her to her feet and hauled Grace into his arms. "Stay beside me and keep your eyes up. Trust me—you don't need to see." He steered Summer toward the door.

Summer spun free from his grip and a scream rose in her throat. She spun in a circle, searching the floor, her stomach lurching at the blood splatter. Two bodies littered the concrete. Men. Not Dayita— where was she?

"Dayita?"

"She's okay," Ty said. "Ash has her outside. Let's get out of here."

Yes, they should remove Grace from the carnage. The child's head, thank goodness, was pressed into Ty's armpit. Summer should have listened to him. Not looked. Now another ugly memory would pop up when she closed her eyes at night.

The night air chilled Summer's face, its fresh rain fragrance welcome after the stench of gasoline, dried grass, and fresh blood in the shed.

Communication devices squawked as law enforcement set up

roadblocks and perimeter reinforcements to trap Fowler. Theofanis and Ash stomped around in a fury.

"He's long gone," Ty told Theofanis. "You won't find him."

Theofanis's round face hardened, all bone and muscle now. "I might not find him tonight, but I promise you I *will* find him."

As soon as Ty released Summer, Dayita enveloped her in a ferocious hug. "You came for me!"

Summer wriggled out of the embrace. "Of course. You didn't think I would leave you with those creeps, did you?"

"All the gun shots—I was terrified you were . . . thank God you're okay. " Mascara ran down Dayita's cheeks. "I'm sorry, Summer. This was all my fault. I shouldn't have left with Grace, I shouldn't—"

"Hush, you couldn't have known this was going to happen."

"You're crying, Summer. All the years I've known you, I've never seen you cry."

"I'm not crying."

"You are."

"I'm not."

"What's that wet stuff on your cheeks?"

"Rain." Summer swiped at her cheeks and sniffled.

"You think you are impervious to emotion, Summer, but you are like those underground rocks you study. Full of holes."

"And you're full of—"

"I hate to break up all this girly bickering," Ash said, "but have any of you seen Mr. Harewood this evening? We got a few questions for him. We called his secretary and she seemed to think he was working late this evening on the premises."

Summer exchanged a look with Ty. "Last time I saw him he was lying on the sidewalk near his office building. He must have slipped and fallen—the sidewalk was wet. We didn't have time to stop and check."

Ash stared at Ty. "He fell—is that right? Well, he isn't there now, so he must have recovered."

Other police cars and an ambulance arrived, sirens blaring.

"You're all going to be checked out by the EMT," Theofanis said.

"I'm fine," Summer said.

"You'll get checked out if I have to put you under arrest to do it. I'm not getting another lecture from your mother."

"My mother?"

Ash nodded. "You both need to call home. Your folks are worried sick."

Just what Summer needed. A hard day followed by a hard night calming her mother down.

Fifteen

Thursday

I

"Julia Lambert, office manager. May I help you?"

"Office manager! Geez, Julia, it's me," Harewood snarled into his mobile. "I know who you are."

"There's no need to be surly."

He took a deep breath. She was in love with him. He couldn't afford to lose that kind of loyalty. "Sorry. There's no excuse for the way that came out. Your voice always conveys your beautiful smile. Mine, I'm afraid, often displays my frazzled nerves. Please accept my apology."

"What's going on? The police called me at home last night trying to reach you."

"Shit. What'd you tell them?"

"The truth. You were working late on the premises."

Double shit. He had to think fast. "Not on the premises. I flew out early yesterday afternoon."

"What?"

"Yes, I had to leave suddenly. An emergency at one of the West Virginia sites." It wasn't that he didn't trust her; but she'd lie more convincingly if she believed she was telling the truth. He and his longtime pilot, Patrick, had flown out well after midnight, but there were no witnesses, and Patrick was paid to be discreet.

"But Patrick always asks me to prepare the flight plan. What if something had happened to you?"

"Please do the paperwork now. We left in a hurry."

"But what good—yes, of course. Whatever you require. Let me get one of the forms."

He could hear the metallic sound of a drawer opening and closing, the crackle of papers being ordered.

"If anyone asks later, say you forgot to file it. Got it? This is important. Really important."

"Yes, sir."

Though she sounded puzzled, she was a good soldier. She'd do as she was told.

"We're moving the headquarters back to Pennsylvania. Take care of any loose ends in Loblolly Lake. I don't want anyone left in Florida who can tell ugly tales about HEC. Unfortunate, but necessary—you understand?"

"Perfectly."

That's what he liked best about Julia Lambert. She was a woman who needed few instructions. A woman who handled details.

A woman who wasn't squeamish.

2

WHERE WAS ISAAC HAREWOOD? Last night after Theofanis had made sure all four young people were in the hands of the EMT, he had cruised by Harewood's mansion several times. No lights, other than the usual security measures, to indicate anyone inside. And Harewood didn't answer his landline.

Theofanis still couldn't understand how Jameson Kendricks showed up at the shed so fast. Nor why he had shot Kevin Fowler after he'd thrown down his gun and raised his hands. Theofanis didn't like the only answers that were coming to mind. Was the deputy on Harewood's payroll?

If only they had taken one of the kidnappers alive, they might have secured a direct link back to Harewood's administrative staff—or even Harewood himself. The best remaining hope of getting answers now lay in an investigation of Kendricks's ties to HEC.

At dawn—after only two hours of shut-eye and scarfing down a couple of leftover spanikopita his grandmother had baked him—Theofanis tried Harewood's number again. No luck.

At seven he drove back to HEC headquarters and found Mrs. Lambert already at her desk. The place still dazzled him. Unless he was mistaken, that was a one-of-a-kind art glass lamp on her desk.

Eff-ing unbelievable. No wonder they were going bankrupt.

She smiled as if she were delivering good news. "I'm sorry, Mr. Harewood isn't available right now, detective."

He frowned and waited until his displeasure registered with her— dimmed her smile a few watts—before he spoke. "Could you tell me where he is?"

She touched her fingers to her hair to ascertain her locks were still in perfect order—as if that hair-sprayed style was going anywhere. "He left for West Virginia yesterday afternoon."

"That's not what you told me last night when I called."

Her laughter was light and self-deprecating. "A senior moment. I forgot. What's going on? I saw the policemen stationed by our lawn equipment shed, but no one would tell me what's happening."

"Really? You're sure he left in the afternoon?" This didn't make sense. Who had Summer Cassidy and Ty Franceschi seen on the ground at the HEC compound last night, if not Harewood?

He drummed his fingers on the edge of her desk. "What time in the afternoon?"

"The flight plan lists two o'clock as departure time."

"You're sure? P.M., not A.M."

"Absolutely sure. I typed it myself. A copy is still here on my desk somewhere. I haven't had time to file it." She touched her hair again and fiddled with a few papers without really looking at them.

Curious and curiouser. "When will he be back?

"I'm not sure. His schedule has been somewhat erratic lately."

"I will need the number of Mr. Harewood's cell."

She shook her head without a single strand of the 'do wiggling or jiggling. "He keeps that number very private, Mr. Theofanis."

"It's important, Mrs. Lambert, or I wouldn't ask."

"What has happened, detective?"

He cocked his head, anxious to watch her reaction. "Kidnappers held a man, two women, and a four-year-old child at gunpoint in the lawn equipment shed at the back of the compound last night, ma'am."

Julia Lambert drew in a long breath and blinked. She seemed surprised. Not surprised enough. Not flabbergasted.

Her hand rose to her mouth, but it seemed an afterthought. "Good gracious—who were they?"

"That phone number now, Mrs. Lambert. And a copy of the flight plan, please."

"Certainly. Give me a moment." She fumbled through the papers again. "Why would kidnappers bring hostages here?"

A good question. "I can't discuss an on-going investigation."

"I understand. Was the gun they used the same one that killed that poor Mr. Alvarez?"

He walked around to the side of her desk and closed the space between them. He stood close, certain she would hurry to move him out of her personal space.

She handed him the flight plan.

This case was becoming curious and curiouser.

3

SUMMER'S APARTMENT WAS PACKED with waiting people. Her mother, Mrs. Patel, Dayita, Ty and Grace. It was almost noon and the sunlight streaming through the lone window in the living room seemed unusually harsh.

Dayita eyed Summer critically, a look Summer was used to and ignored. "You aren't going like that."

Summer's eyes cut to Ty, but she quickly drew them away to the small decorative mirror on her wall. Summer avoided looking at mirrors except out of the edges of her eyes. Too often, her sister stared back. A quick glance confirmed the bruise under her eye and the gash on her forehead.

She shrugged. "They're smart people. Scientists. A senator. Interested in facts, not in how I look."

"Honestly, Summer, do you think smart people don't form first impressions?" She took Summer by the shoulders and pushed her toward the bedroom.

"We'll be late."

"There's still plenty of time, sweetie, so you girls take as long as you need," Summer's mother said.

"Grrr."

"What?"

"Nothing, mother."

Ever since she and Dayita were reunited with their parents in the emergency room they had been smothered, slathered, and lathered with love. When her mother understood she couldn't talk her out of going to Tallahassee to meet with the senator, she had insisted on driving her.

Dayita pointed to the desk chair and ordered her to sit. She ignored Summer's grumbling and applied moisturizer, concealer, and foundation. Summer tried not to cringe. The contusions were even more sore now than they'd been last night when the EMT and triage nurse poked all over her. Every movement set the inside of her head to jangling like an avalanche of aluminum pans dropping onto a tile floor.

"Hey! What now?" She tried to stop Dayita from removing the scrunchie from the hair gathered at her nape. Dayita gently smacked her hand away and dragged the end of a comb across Summer's scalp. Just to be difficult, Summer wriggled around while Dayita shifted her part to one side. Dayita dug into a little bag in her purse and brought out a little rhinestone-covered barrette, which she secured next to Summer's eyebrow.

She led Summer to the mirror again. "I couldn't completely hide the damage but you look lots better."

Summer allowed herself a quick look. You could hardly see the bruised cheekbone, and Dayita had draped her hair to hide the forehead gash. She looked more mature without the ponytail.

"Now for your clothes."

"What's wrong with my clothes?" Summer looked down at her jeans and blue shirt. Well, okay, the shirt was missing a button. She'd forgotten to close the gap with a safety pin.

"Not professional." Dayita raked hanger after hanger across the metal bar in Summer's closet, examining and dismissing one item after another. Finally she flung a pair of black slacks onto Summer's bed.

"Those are for funerals! I keep them in case a relative dies suddenly."

"Today they are your big girl pants. You ought to have more than jeans in your closet. Honestly, Summer. You need to update your wardrobe."

Summer put on the black slacks and accepted the tailored blouse

Dayita had brought from her own closet.

"You planned this."

"You aren't the only one who can make plans."

Dayita looked regal in a silk brocade jacket. Ahhh. Dayita *had* planned. The ethnicity of the outfit served as staging for the slides about Dayita's relatives. After all they'd been through yesterday, Summer was amazed to find her friend so calculating.

"By the way, what did you do to my truck?" Summer asked. "I moved it to my assigned parking spot and it sounded like a moose had taken up residence under the chassis."

Dayita's cheeks already had a substantial amount of blush on them but they grew even rosier. "You probably need fresh transmission fluid. Or new brake pads."

"Brake pads don't have anything to do with—never mind." Any damage was already done.

Jordan Cassidy opened the bedroom door. "We need to get on the road, girls." Dayita complied immediately.

Before they left, Summer wanted to talk to Claire. When she'd called earlier, the nurse was bathing her. Which Summer took as a sign Claire was improving.

Summer dialed the hospital room again and this time Joe answered. "Sorry, you just missed her. They wheeled her down to x-ray to get pictures of her ribs. They don't think any bones were broken or nicked, but they want to be sure. She's recovering fast—you know Claire."

"A strong spirit if ever there was one." Great news, but Summer's stomach dropped anyway. She wished she could have spoken to Claire, gotten a few words of reassurance that she was ready for this, that she was a trained professional, not some squishy little girl.

"Please tell her my friends and I are going to the final hearing today and there won't be a dry eye in the house when we get finished." She hoped it was true.

"She told me this morning she was certain you'd go ahead without her. Said she knew you would knock those Harewood goons on their asses. Her words, not mine."

Summer smiled. Oh, yeah. That was Claire.

When Mrs. Patel entered the bedroom, Summer closed her phone.

Mrs. Patel seemed fidgety. "There is something you should know."

Conversations that began that way never ended well.

"Dayita said not to tell you, but the university's computer security division contacted her. They appear suspicious that she violated their system."

Summer's lips trembled with the apologies that would never be enough. She should never have asked Dayita to help her, to violate ethical codes, to break the law.

"If they find her guilty, it will damage her career chances greatly," Mrs. Patel said.

"Oh, God, I am so sorry! I will tell them it was all my fault, that I coerced her—"

"No, no. What you are doing means so much to her, to us, that you would take such a brave stand for the greater good. The risk to her career is worth it."

It didn't seem brave to Summer. Every path seemed wrong. How did you choose between hurting your best friend and poisoning people you didn't know?

One hand on her hip, her mother came in and mouthed, *We have to go now.*

Yes, it was time. This was what Summer had studied for all these years. Time to make a difference. Time to enter the adult world, but it was turning out to be much harder than she'd thought.

4

THEY LEFT IN A CONVOY; Summer, Ty, and Grace in her mother's ancient Volvo; Mrs. Patel and Dayita following in their Corolla.

Summer had taken one of the hydrocodone tablets the emergency room doctor had given her for pain, but only one. She needed a clear head. Despite her best efforts to remain awake, she slept for most of the drive to the state capital.

The hearing was slated for two in the afternoon in a conference room in the new Capitol Building. Her mother woke her as they entered Tallahassee. Summer sat up, her fingers prodding the hair clasp. It felt intrusive and foreign. They passed a string of eateries, small strip malls, banks, and the larger Governor's Square mall.

Summer begged her mother not to accompany them inside the

Capitol complex to watch the presentation. "I'll be nervous enough as it is."

She could tell her mother was hurt, but Mrs. Patel suggested they go shopping at the mall and that seemed to cheer her up.

Ty and the girls rode the elevator up to the tenth floor. Dayita saw a ladies' room near the conference room. She insisted on one last make-up check before going in. "Come with me, Summer."

"Not a chance."

Dayita took her hand. "Let me touch up—"

Summer pulled away. "I look as good as I'm going to. You go ahead." Dayita's gold sandals pranced past her and pattered down the hallway. Dayita always looked perfectly groomed, right down to the polished toenails. Well, almost. Last night after hours in captivity, she had looked a bit frazzled, but no sign of the stress of the day before remained. Ty went on into the conference room.

While Summer waited, she cruised the corridor slowly, examining the art on the walls. Bailey Douglass walked by with the kind of assurance you'd expect from Hillary Clinton or Condoleezza Rice. She was flanked by Niles Morrell and two other men. They made their way into the conference room where they'd be meeting the senator and officials from the Department of Environmental Protection. Not the same lady, though. The former agency head, Alice Leymon, was still on leave pending the outcome of the investigation into her travel.

When a tap came on her shoulder, her first thought: Dayita had returned, but the scent of sandalwood wafted over her. Dr. Hu!

He smiled with his mouth but his eyes said he'd backed her into a corner and couldn't wait to pounce. He rattled a piece of paper in front of Summer's nose.

"Do you know what this is?"

"I'm afraid I don't have Superman's x-ray eyes. I can't read through a moving paper."

Hu barked out a humorless laugh. "Still the same arrogant girl who enrolled in my coastal ecosystems seminar, I see. Do you remember your unprecedented request to be permitted more than the two allotted class absences without penalty?" He shook his head. "I'm sorry. Of course you remember. You have eidetic memory. You're the girl who remembers everything and doesn't need to attend class."

Summer flushed. She did remember that request, which she'd made because Hu stood in front of his students and read from the textbook—which he had written. He referenced himself in third person as "the author of your textbook states " or "the author of your textbook believes." It drove her crazy. She could quote from his text better than he could. Furthermore, because she didn't process aurally well, listening to him read aloud wasted her time.

And he was wrong about something else. She didn't remember everything—only most of what she read. "Scientific research refutes the concept of eidetic memory after the age of six. My ability to remember what I read is simply more extreme than most people's. Brain scans suggest those with hyper memories use the Method of Loci, activating regions of the brain involved in spatial awareness, such as the parietal, retrosplenial and right posterior hippocampal regions."

"Thank you so much for correcting my misperception, Miss Cassidy."

Her eyes dropped to the tassels on his shiny black shoes. Power shoes. He must polish them every day to keep them in that condition. The hem of his slacks brushed the top of his tassels and landed halfway down the heel in back, the perfect length, so Summer had read in GQ magazine in her dentist's waiting room.

If he hadn't been sneering at her, she might have added that people with extreme memories often have a deficit of social skills. She had hoped hers were improving. Apparently, they weren't.

"This paper," he said, rattling it again, "is a recommendation form from the Massachusetts Institute of Technology that must be filled out by my office." His voice nearly sang his pleasure. "*My* office alone. So it will do no good to whine to Dr. Dunham and expect her to rescue you this time."

This time, meaning he was thinking of her sophomore year, when she had made that "unprecedented" and obviously offensive request.

"Dr. Dunham explained that you don't understand oral communication well, but I hope you comprehend what I am telling you now. If I don't fill out this form, you don't attend MIT. It's that simple, Miss Cassidy."

The threat drew her eyes away from his shoes. She tried to read his expression. Surely he wouldn't carry out an act so patently unfair. Surely he was bluffing. But what if he wasn't? She had already given up the Harewood scholarship. Now, she understood ethics required her to surrender her dream of going to MIT, too. How could she, after she'd, worked toward it for so many years?

She challenged him. "I think I understand exactly what you are saying, Dr. Hu. Let me restate to be clear. You are threatening to sabotage my admission to MIT unless I change the wording in my thesis."

He stepped toward her, his smile as frosty as liquid nitrogen. "Such a smart girl, yet only a student with years of learning ahead of you. As dean, I am going to replace Dr. Dunham at the hearing today."

Yeah, the dean. A guy with power, and she didn't think he was making idle threats. She inched away, her back against the corridor wall. He had a point. Who was going to listen to a measly grad student anyway? She should just give up and go home.

But there was Dayita to consider, her personal stake in preventing arsenic poisoning, the career she had already put at risk by hacking into the university's computer at Summer's request. There was the presentation they had worked so hard on, and the past year of research, both her own and Claire Dunham's.

Summer stepped forward, landing on the toe of Hu's black dress shoe. He grimaced and shuffled out of her way.

She raised her chin. "Dr. Dunham had complete confidence in my work."

"I'm sure." A smile snaked across his face. "I do, too, which I will make clear when I lead the committee for your thesis defense tomorrow."

Tomorrow? No one had told her the meeting was still scheduled. Her legs grew limp. But as she thought about it—why not? She was ready. And she was pissed. If he refused to sign off on her thesis, he would have a battle on his hands. She would fight it all the way to the faculty senate and university president if she had to.

"I don't see how my defense can take place when the adviser I chose is still in the hospital," she said.

"I'm assuming Dr. Dunham's duties until she can return to the university. The least I can do for an ill colleague. I am fully knowledgeable about your studies since I've served on your committee from the beginning. My assistant has been trying to notify you. She said she was having difficulty."

Dayita walked toward them.

Hu moved closer to Summer again. She could smell his aftershave. His breath grazed her face as he spat our each word.

"I have to assume, Ms. Cassidy, what you have to say to the senator will not contradict Dr. Dunham's final grant report, which I have in my briefcase. Any contradictions would have to be considered in weighing the value and accuracy of your research when you defend your thesis tomorrow. I'll see you inside the conference room, then." He paused. "Or not."

Yeah, about that altered report. "I have a *signed* copy of her final report dated prior to her hospitalization. I'm sure our copies are identical."

The slap of his dress shoes on the hard floor echoed as he stalked away, tearing the paper from MIT in half lengthwise and then across before depositing it in the trash can.

"Wasn't that Dr. Hu?" Dayita asked.

"Forget Dr. Hu. Got your laptop ready?"

Dayita patted her shoulder bag. "Ready."

"Let's do this."

This hearing had attracted a larger, different crowd than the first Summer had attended. She and Dayita slid into seats beside Ty.

Hugh Palmer, a thin, nondescript man, ran the show this time, in Leymon's absence. He gave due recognition to Senator Vargas and then made a brief statement. "Florida has always led the nation in addressing the health and safety of our water. The Department of Environmental Protection strives to conserve and protect our natural resources while working with the business community for the benefit of all our citizens. It is our belief that ASR wells can play an important role in furthering this mission. We are here today to gather information and perspectives on specific ASR wells owned and operated by Harewood Energy Corporation. HEC has been an asset to Florida since moving its headquarters here. It has expanded our tax base, given generously to philanthropic causes, and provided scholarships for our youth. We'll begin today by letting HEC explain their vision for Florida."

He wasn't hiding where he stood. His introduction certainly revealed a stronger pro-business bias than Leymon's had.

Niles Morrell offered the same spiel with the same handouts he'd offered the week before. Bailey Douglass followed with her flag-waving video about American jobs and energy independence created by HEC.

Two members of the environmental community spoke next, but their presentations were lackluster compared to what a corporation could fund. When Mr. Palmer announced Ty's name, Morrell strode back to the podium. "This young man has a vicious vendetta against our company. During the past year he has been arrested for his campaign of unwarranted hostility directed at HEC. In fact, we are in the process of seeking a restraining order against Mr. Franceschi. His cyber-stalking and slander have gone too far."

The cyber-stalking charge seemed far-fetched, though Ty did have a way of unearthing information. But this was a public hearing. Key word being *public*. How could they keep him from speaking?

Palmer fiddled with the position of his glasses on his nose. "I'm not sure, Mr. Morrell, whether . . . if in light of your allegations—"

Ty broke in. "It's all right. I yield my time to the young ladies on my left."

Morrell glared. "They are obviously here with Mr. Franceschi to further his vendetta. They should not be allowed to speak for him."

At last, Palmer's glasses settled into a comfortable spot on his nose. "We can't assume they share his vendetta, as you put it. The young women have the right to present their views. Miss Cassidy is here to represent research done at the university."

Fish flopped in Summer's stomach as she stood. Dayita's laptop was out and already connected to the projection device. The opening slide appeared on the screen at the front of the room: a branch of newly sprung leaves, still yellow-green, framed water tripping over rocks. Sunlight appeared to dance on the river's surface. Water and rocks—they spelled magic to Summer. Always had. She knew Florida water as well as anyone in this room. She could do this.

She introduced herself as a hydrogeologist, and it sounded so fabulous a glow spread through her whole body.

She pointed the laser at the laptop and flipped to the next slide of the Earth as seen from space. "Water." She swept her hand across the scene. "It covers seventy percent of the earth's surface, so we have a lot of it, right?"

The next shot appeared: a doe drinking from the river. "But only one percent of the world's water is accessible for direct human uses. This is the water found in lakes, rivers, reservoirs and those underground sources shallow enough to be tapped at an affordable cost. And since animals can't drill wells, they have access to even less of the world's freshwater than humans. The vast majority of water on the Earth's surface, over ninety-six percent, is saline water in the oceans. Of the freshwater on Earth, much more is stored in the ground than is available in lakes or rivers."

A few more slides established the importance of clean water. Her years of taking nature photographs on her kayak trips paid off with an impressive collection of visuals.

Her next slide showed a diagram of an ASR well. "Remember how much water is stored underground? For centuries humans have drilled wells to access it. But today, we are using new technology." Summer explained how ASR wells worked, and the presentation was going well, she thought.

Until she started using words like *iron hydroxide, mobilization* and *attenuation* and the eyes of her audience glazed over. Dayita had warned her to tone down the vocabulary and statistics. So she shut up and let the bar chart illustrate the problem.

The Chamber of Commerce president spoke up in a tone that reeked of aggression. "Who tested the wells?"

"Good question. I ran the tests myself and—"

Before she could go on, he interrupted her again. "But aren't you just a student?"

"I graduate in a few weeks with Master's degrees in environmental science and geology. Dr. Claire Dunham, chair of the geology department at Florida Sci-Tech, and I have repeatedly tested the water over the past year. Our results replicate the data first reported to the media by the nonprofit environmental group Water Warriors."

"The one represented by Mr. Franceschi."

"Yes. In other words, everyone who has tested the water has found elevated levels of arsenic." She flipped to the next slide. "Arsenic wasn't the only chemical out of acceptable ranges. Uranium was contained in the samples at—" no numbers, she remembered—"well above EPA limits."

She clicked to Ty's video of a Harewood well site. "We don't know why these particular wells haven't responded as they should to cycling. Perhaps they were drained out too fast, too completely. But that is only conjecture based on what has happened at other wells. All I offer as a scientist is facts. And the fact is contaminant levels are too high."

The next slide was a close-up of a hand Dayita had inserted. "My friend, Dayita Patel, would like to share facts about the dangers of arsenic contamination with you."

In her silk brocade jacket with the mandarin collar, Dayita stood out as exotic. "These photos are members of my family in Bangladesh, where I was born. I was one of the lucky ones. My mother brought me to this country when I was four. This first photo shows the hand of my aunt in Chandipur. The black warts you see are from drinking arsenic-contaminated water. The World Health Organization says one in five people in Bangladesh is dying from poisoned water. The problem is fifty times worse than the Chernobyl nuclear disaster, yet no one is paying attention to it."

Summer looked around the room. Those present, especially the senator, seemed riveted by Dayita's story. No eyes glazed over by too many numbers.

Dayita clicked to new slides showing her uncle and grandmother, explaining how they'd died of cancer.

Another click. "This is my cousin when he was six." The face of a beautiful caramel-skinned boy appeared. "Here he is at twenty-four, marked by the classic skin eruptions of arsenic poisoning."

The young man's eyes were dark and haunting. How could anyone in the room not be moved by his humanity?

"Nakeesh, he—" Dayita's voice broke, and she paused until she was able to go on. "About half of the 10,000 people living in my family's village are drinking arsenic and dying from it. I keep thinking someone will stop this. Someone will help my family's village, but the world has known about the problem for over twenty years and nothing has changed."

She clicked on the next slide, the photo she'd taken of water coming from the tap at the Ichetucknee campground lodge. "But at least you have the power to stop it from happening here in the United States. The Safe Drinking Water Act is meant to protect us from the horrors experienced by my family. You must continue to enforce the provisions of this law."

Dayita turned off her laptop and sat down.

The Chamber of Commerce president approached. "I had no idea the danger these chemicals could pose. The amounts seemed so minute, a few parts per billion. Your presentation woke me up. Say, I was thinking, I belong to the Rotary Club and we have members all over the world. We often take on projects that significantly impact people's lives. I bet we could find a way to help those villagers in Bangladesh."

5

AFTER THE HEARING SENATOR VARGAS returned to his office. A bright young intern—the kind of fellow he hoped his son Manny would grow up to be—delivered a stack of mail. According to instructions, the intern had opened and sorted the letters according to urgency. The bottom manila envelope was unopened and had no postmark. The senator turned the envelope over in his hands. What now—more photos?

He held out the envelope. "Where did this come from?"

The intern shook his head. "It wasn't there when I picked up the mail, sir. Someone must have hand-delivered it."

Vargas signaled across the room to Ned, who was listening to a major campaign donor beg for a reduction of state taxes on businesses like his. Everyone wanted tax loopholes closed—unless the loophole allowed them to pay fewer taxes. Ned shook the donor's hand and turned him over to the intern.

Once they were sequestered behind his office door, Vargas opened the envelope and, frowning, shook it over his desk blotter. Hundreds of pieces of confetti fell out. Vargas recognized it as photographic paper that had been fed through a cross-cutter. One ordinary letter-size sheet of paper remained inside.

Ned extracted it and read it aloud.

"All copies have been destroyed. Do what you feel is right." Ned lowered the letter to his waist and placed a hand on the senator's shoulder. "You would have anyway."

6

BAILEY DOUGLASS APPROACHED GEORGE THEOFANIS'S DESK, and for a brief moment her whole body tensed like a big cat eyeing a potential adversary. Then she lapsed into a feline smile and Theofanis wondered if he'd imagined the aggression.

Her hair hung in soft waves feathered against her cheeks today. First time he'd seen her without a French twist—and he liked what he saw. Her expensive pumps clicked across the faded linoleum. Her office was luxuriously carpeted, he remembered with annoyance. But he'd chosen his career path, one he still enjoyed. He had no one to blame but himself for his shabby office.

He didn't stand up. It would only give her an edge in whatever game she was playing. Men always fawned over her. He would not. "How can I help you today, Ms. Douglass?"

"I believe it is I who can help you this time, detective."

She removed a folder from a beautiful mahogany-colored leather case that matched her heels and laid it atop the papers on his desk. He opened it. Slowly. He wanted to watch her eyes as he revealed its contents. He had no illusion that helping him ranked as one of Bailey Douglass's priorities.

He let his eyes fall to the folder's contents. First up: a fuzzy photograph of HEC's financial officer Niles Morrell, Deputy Kendricks, and a young man only partly visible. They clustered around a sedan in a parking garage.

"Who's the third man?"

"The governor's son."

An odd trio, but where was she going with this? He set the photo aside.

"Holy shit!" He leaned over the second photo. "Excuse my language, Ms. Douglass."

"Yes, the implications are rather shocking."

In the second shot, Niles Morrell was handing an envelope to Jake Fowler. Was Bailey Douglass trying to tell him Morrell paid Fowler to kill Alvarez? Paid him to frame the Cassidy girl? Not enough to convict her, but enough to keep her out of the way until HEC got its exemptions.

Theofanis quickly shuffled to the next shot. Jake Fowler clearly distributing money to his brother Kevin and former prison buddy Roman Jeglinski.

The next: a long shot of a suburban neighborhood street.

And the next: The governor's son going inside a house on that street.

The next: Jake Fowler exiting the same house.

"Who owns this place?" he asked.

"Jake Fowler, under an alias."

Theofanis jumped to his feet. "Where?"

"South of Miami, but he's not there now. My people already checked."

Even so, he would send a team in to look for leads on Fowler's whereabouts.

She leaned in so close he could smell her perfume, a scent more spicy than floral. She tapped a polished nail on the photo. "Look at the windows."

How had he missed it? They were too dark. One side was a grow house, the windows blacked out so the bright lights wouldn't bother the neighbors.

He still didn't get Bailey's game. What was she after?

The last item in the folder wasn't a photo. It was a copy of the doctored financial statement. Under it was the bank's original posting available to investors. He closed the folder.

"And?" he asked.

Her lips formed a moue, and Theofanis couldn't entirely swallow his smile as she caught herself and controlled her expression. "You already knew about the bank statements."

"Yep. Only a matter of time until your buddy Harewood hears from the Feds."

"Isaac Harewood tapes many conversations with employees that take place in his office. They sign a standard release at the time of employment that they are aware of this possibility."

"Tell me why I care." Unprofessional of him, but he hadn't had this much fun in recent years.

She took her phone and touched the screen a couple of times. She laid it on his desk. "I'm going to play a recording. The first voice you will hear is Niles Morrell. The second is Isaac Harewood."

She touched the right arrow icon, and Theofanis listened as Morrell confessed he had PhotoShopped in a new post office box for the bank. Harewood's voice came in clearly afterwards: "I refuse to allow anything that might damage the company. I've worked way too hard to see HEC harmed now."

Yeah, Harewood was a real saint. Awfully convenient, that recording. Theofanis leaned back in his chair and crossed his arms. "My interest in speaking with Mr. Harewood remains the same."

"Really?" Bailey leaned over and retrieved her phone from his desk, placing it back inside her briefcase. "I thought the photos made everything clear. Niles Morrell is deep into drugs and has been funneling company money into his grow operation. He couldn't afford to have anyone prying into HEC financial matters right now. He paid Fowler to get the Cassidy girl out of the way until the exemption on the water standards was approved. It was a desperate and ill-conceived scheme that spun out of control."

"Ballistic tests showed no gun in that shed killed Paulo Alvarez."

Bailey blinked. So. The pretty lady didn't know everything.

He scooted his chair back and stood. "I still need to question Mr. Harewood about his possible involvement in burglary, the murder of Paulo Alvarez and attempted murder of those young people on Harewood's property. The Feds are looking into kidnapping, income tax evasion, bank fraud—those are the issues I remember."

She shook her head and those beautiful fiery locks moved bewitchingly with her. "But surely these photos and the recording prove his innocence. Mr. Harewood is an upstanding member of the community who has always supported good causes like education and the Police Widows and Orphan Benefit Fund."

"With money that wasn't his to give away."

Ms. Douglass apparently didn't appreciate his comment. Too used to getting her own way. With a snap of her briefcase, she whirled and waltzed away on her spiked heels. The view was sublime.

The click of her heels stopped at his office door. She faced him again. Nothing wrong with that view either.

She offered the Mona Lisa smile. "I didn't mean to be rude in leaving so abruptly. I have an appointment in ten minutes with President Grice at the university and you know how parking is on campus."

He cocked his head. Why had she delayed then?

She readjusted the handle of her briefcase. "If you're free for dinner this evening, I'd be happy to address any questions you might have."

Oh, he had questions, but this woman wasn't going to answer them. He had to admire her. She wasn't like Harewood and Morrell. She might dance along the edges of what was legal and what wasn't, but she would never get caught on the wrong side of the line herself. She would hire others—like her investigators—to do the illegal stuff. The idea of dinner with her interested him. Very much.

"Maybe when this case is over."

That smile again. "I did a little looking into your affairs, detective."

"What'd you find?"

"Nothing. If you have any sins, they're well hidden."

"I've looked into your affairs, too, Ms. Douglass."

"And?"

He allowed a half smile. "Maybe when this case is over."

Later in the day, Ash brought in a sack of burgers and fries for lunch. Theofanis had already filled him in on Bailey Douglass's theories. He applied for search warrants of Morrell's home and office and asked FDLE to check out Fowler's South Florida home.

"Any luck reaching Morrell?" Ash asked.

"None. Out of the office today. Not answering his cell. Kendricks?"

"I.A. is supposed to be quietly looking into him." Ash shook his head. "Means everyone in the office will know by tomorrow. If not sooner. I knew he was incompetent, but I never pegged him as dirty. Any other leads linking this whole mess to Harewood? I can't believe he's clean."

Theofanis didn't think so either, but where was the proof? He examined the web on his computer screen. He expanded Harewood's bubble again to view every connection spidering out from it. The CFO, Julia Lambert, Phil Snyder, Jake Fowler, Kevin Fowler, Roman Jeglinski, Alvarez. People who knew the answers either wouldn't talk or ended up dead.

Jake Fowler had undoubtedly killed Phil Snyder. The hospital pharmacy up in Valdosta, Georgia, had reported a theft of the drug used to kill him. Hospital surveillance tapes didn't show enough for a positive I.D., but it certainly could have been Fowler. Right height and build. And in Fowler's rented trailer in Loblolly Lake, they'd found the heart attack gun, the kind of weapon black ops or underworld characters had access to. Fowler fit the profile. But Theofanis doubted that Morrell hired Fowler without Harewood's knowledge.

The department's tech guys said the recording of Harewood and Morrell was edited. Yet the police chief balked at issuing a warrant for Harewood. Too well known. Too connected. The wimp wanted the feds to take the lead on Harewood. Wouldn't even authorize requesting a warrant to search Harewood's office. Only Morrell's.

Theofanis looked over the bubbles on his computer screen. Some crumb had to lead to those behind the kidnapping.

Ash propped his shoes on Theofanis's desk, close enough to the remainder of his hamburger that Theofanis would not have eaten it even if he had still been hungry. He trashed the burger and wrapper and cleansed his hands with sanitizer.

Ash's mobile rang with a tune from Spiderman, "Turn Off the Dark." Theofanis eavesdropped, of course. Ash swung his feet off the desk and said they'd be right over.

"Guess who issued an invite to HEC headquarters?" Already standing, Ash didn't wait for a guess. "Miz Julia Lambert."

"Really?" On the ride over, Theofanis replayed every time he'd seen and talked to Julia Lambert. Her face seemed as plastic as a doll's. She was too perfect with the helmet hair and silvery voice. When she looked at Isaac Harewood, her eyes changed. Julia adored Isaac Harewood. She had attained status by hitching her star to a powerful man.

"Let's jiggle her tree, see what shakes out," Theofanis said.

"She's a nice Southern lady. Maybe she'll offer us a homemade cookie."

7

TOO MANY QUESTIONS REMAINED to suit Summer. They didn't know who had sent Fowler and his thugs after her. Summer knew they had come for her, not Dayita and Grace. She hoped they were all truly safe now that she'd delivered her grant report and made her presentation.

Ty didn't think so. He was camped out in his van down the street.

Who killed Alvarez? he'd asked her. She didn't know how he'd found out, but the guns in the shed weren't involved. Ty believed Harewood directed all the misdeeds from behind the scenes. Was the

CEO as evil as Ty thought? Or was Ty blind to the truth because he blamed Harewood for his mother's death and his sister's disability?

Dayita slid a stack of computer printouts across the kitchen table to Summer and scooted her chair in close. "Let's go over the records again. We have to be missing something."

"We need more information."

"I don't think there's more to find online about HEC."

Summer thought for a minute. "Let's look somewhere else."

"Where?"

"Who knows more about a company's operation than anyone else?"

"The CEO. You're going to confront Harewood."

Summer smiled. "Nope. The secretary. Julia Lambert. She seemed so friendly and kind at my scholarship interview, and I bet she knows everything that goes on in that place. She might be willing to help us."

"Make an appointment tomorrow."

Summer jumped to her feet. "Now."

"But you have to defend your thesis in the morning."

"If I sit around here, I'll only think about it and get nervous. Let's call her." Summer punched in Mrs. Lambert's number at HEC.

A voice full of sunshine came on the other end. Summer asked if she could stop by and discuss the grant again.

Dayita expressed her doubts as they went down to Summer's truck. "You should ask Ty what he thinks. I bet he'd tell you to stay as far away from that compound as possible."

It *was* the site of a horrible experience. All the more reason to face it. "I don't need his permission to go out. Besides, he's such a super-soldier, he'll probably follow us."

He did—all the way into the HEC parking lot.

"I'd invite him to come inside the lion's den with us," Summer said, "but I don't want Grace left alone."

"He should go in with you and I can stay with Grace."

Summer laughed. "You think Ty's going to allow that after the last time?"

Dayita unbuckled her seatbelt. "I'll be persuasive." She got out and approached the van, leaning down to Ty's open window. "You need to go inside with Summer. Keep her out of trouble."

Ty shook his head, the only response he bothered to give.

Dayita pouted. "Come on. Let me stay with Grace. I promise I won't leave, no matter what happens this time."

"Take the keys with you," Summer advised Ty.

Dayita stuck her tongue out.

Ty opened the van door. "Guess that would work."

"For heaven's sake," Dayita said. "I made one little mistake."

Summer coughed. "Hate to see a big one." Dayita looked hurt, so Summer added, "Just teasing."

Minutes later, Ty and Summer rode the elevator up a floor. Mrs. Lambert wore a navy suit with a silky sky blue blouse. "So nice to see you again, Miss Cassidy, and of course I remember you, Mr. Franceschi, for that impassioned speech at the community hearings. I remember seeing your picture in the papers back in West Virginia too."

Ty never had discussed his arrest with Summer. She was curious as to exactly what he had done. The newspaper account had been vague.

"Won't you come into Mr. Harewood's office? He's away and it's more comfortable in there."

His office was way larger than Summer's apartment. Mrs. Lambert directed them to leather chairs in front of a tigerwood desk. A fist-sized hunk of polished jasper in shades of amber served as a paperweight. Summer couldn't resist tracing her fingers over the flow patterns, thin curved delineations in darker brown. So gorgeous— nature's work of art!

Mrs. Lambert insisted on making them cups of tea. As she poured hot water onto the herbs, ginger and lemongrass permeated the room.

"This is Mr. Harewood's favorite blend. I special order it for him."

The reverence when Mrs. Lambert said his name—was she in love with Harewood? If so, prying useful information from her would be impossible. Summer started with her most obvious connection. "I thought if I explained why I couldn't change the report, you might put in a good word for me with the Foundation scholarship committee."

After Mrs. Lambert handed them their cups, she moved behind Harewood's desk and perched on the edge of the chair, which seemed several sizes too large for her. "I don't really have anything to do with scholarship selection, honey."

Right—that's why Summer was called into the company headquarters for that very personal interview. She hadn't really expected to get anywhere on that score with Mrs. Lambert, but it served as cover for the questions she wanted to ask. Summer lifted her cup—bone china gold-leafed and hand painted with tiny blue forget-me-nots and pink ribbons. Lordy—she hoped she didn't drop it. It was probably worth a month's rent on her apartment.

Carefully she sipped the tea, then accidentally clinked the cup against the edge of the saucer, fumbling with both hands until she had the cup safely grounded.

"You can help me with an entirely different matter," Ty said. "You might have special insight into why those thugs brought their hostages to this compound."

"Gracious, no." Mrs. Lambert's laugh tinkled as softly as her spoon against her teacup as she stirred in milk and sugar. "We don't employ anyone like that at our company. Why, those men were beastly! A crime of opportunity, I guess. They broke in, thinking the property would be empty at night. I heard all about it on the Channel Nine News. I think that's the best station, don't you?"

Ty didn't touch his tea. His thick fingers looked powerful enough to pulverize the delicate china.

Summer leaned forward, curling her fingers around the beveled rim of the desk. "Paulo Alvarez worked for HEC. Do you think he knew the kidnappers?"

Mrs. Lambert wrinkled her nose. "He didn't really work at our facility. But yes, he might have been the sort of person to know those men. He could have told them about the shed. He could have given them a key."

"Mr. Alvarez had a key to the shed?" Summer asked.

"No, but I keep the keys to all the buildings hanging up in a case in the copy room. Anyone passing through could pick one up. It's never been a worry. Mr. Harewood only hires the best people."

Mrs. Lambert stood and looked out the tall windows. "I'd forgotten you were the one who found Mr. Alvarez's body and were questioned as a suspect in his death. No wonder you're so interested in him." She turned back to face them, her eyebrows bunched as if sympathetic, but her expression struck Summer as staged.

"What a terrible thing for you, poor dear," Mrs. Lambert continued. "I'm surprised finding his body didn't upset you more. I'm sure I would have collapsed completely for weeks. But both of you should put all this behind you and move on now with your lives. I'm sure Miss Cassidy will hear from the scholarship committee soon and be off to graduate school. I would think you, Mr. Franceschi, would be concentrating on finding gainful employment."

What a nasty dig! Nonprofits performed valuable work even if they didn't deliver big paychecks. Summer was ready to quiz Mrs. Lambert about how Alvarez got paid, in cash delivered in person or by mailed check, when the intercom buzzed.

A female voice spoke. "Detective Theofanis and Deputy Ash are in the lobby, Mrs. Lambert. They said they are here at your request."

Mrs. Lambert touched her helmet of hair. "Wonderful. Send them in."

8

GEORGE THEOFANIS PAUSED IN THE DOORWAY of Julia Lambert's office. What the hell were Summer Cassidy and Ty Franceschi doing here? They just wouldn't stop meddling.

The girl still looked beat up from her experiences the evening before. Kid ought to be home in bed. After ascertaining only Ash, one step behind him, could see, Theofanis rolled his eyes to the ceiling and sighed before crossing the threshold.

Mrs. Lambert asked the officers to sit in the chairs beside Summer and Ty and insisted on making more tea. Theofanis snickered as Ash fidgeted with his deputy hat, crossing and uncrossing his legs twice,. She set the teacups and saucers on top of Harewood's gleaming wood desk. Theofanis had never seen such fancy piece of furniture outside of a museum.

When it became apparent they weren't going to drink the tea, Mrs. Lambert didn't waste any more time.

"These young people have been asking about Mr. Alvarez. I don't have any answers there, but I did discover a memo this afternoon that might interest all of you. I was filing Mr. Morrell's correspondence and was quite shocked to learn he has offered a large quantity of his own and Mr. Harewood's stock options for sale. I was certain

Mr. Harewood didn't know. I called him to be sure he hadn't autho-rized it. He was as surprised as I. At first, I thought I would ask Mr. Morrell about the stock transfer myself, but he is out of town. And I confess to being scared to confront him. So many awful things have been happening here lately."

Still standing, she presented copies of the sell orders to Ash.

Theofanis leaned over to examine them as Ash glanced through the memos. Seemed everyone was anxious to paint Morrell as the bad guy. And why on earth did Mrs. Lambert want those two kids to hear this stuff? She must be desperate to get Ty off Harewood's case.

"Do you know where we can find Mr. Morrell?" Ash asked.

Mrs. Lambert seated herself behind Harewood's desk—a fledgling swallowed up by the eagle's nest.

"He flew to Pennsylvania this morning in one of the company planes," she said. "I drove him to the airport so he wouldn't have to leave his car there."

Theofanis pulled on his ear. "Where is his car—at his home or in the parking lot out front?"

"Never out front. His Aston Martin is in our underground ga-rage. He would never leave it where it might get damaged or stolen. It's such an expensive vehicle. James Bond drove one like it in the movies, you know."

Theofanis almost laughed aloud at the eagerness in Ash's expres-sion as he asked to see it.

"You boys are all alike—wild about cars. I don't see what it would hurt. Would you care to come along?" she asked Summer and Ty.

"No," Summer said.

"Absolutely," Ty said.

"It's time for them to go home," Theofanis said.

The girl shrugged. Mrs. Lambert inserted a key, which activated access to the special elevator. It was designed to accommodate a large vehicle with ease. The elevator had rear doors, which opened to the parking lot to the left of the main entrance to the building. Theofanis remembered seeing the opening outside and had thought it might be a convenience for receiving deliveries. He'd never dreamed it was a car elevator. The rich really were different.

They whooshed smoothly below ground and the door opened.

The cave-like space before them had the same dank smell as all underground garages, but it was a cut above any one he'd ever been in before. LED lights in decorated sconces illuminated the wall, one between each of a dozen vehicles. The Aston Martin easily stood out as the most exotic car.

For a moment, Theofanis remained by the elevator to phone the department to see if the search warrant had come through. It hadn't. He asked Burns to call immediately if he heard from the judge.

Ash ran his big paw over the hood. "Wow—if this isn't something!"

"Gorgeous espresso interior finish," Ty added.

Summer shrugged again.

"Only management has the elevator key to come to this floor," Mrs. Lambert said, "so the car isn't locked. You can sit in it if you like. Everyone in management has. Mr. Morrell loves to show his car off."

Ash slid into the leather seat and made a show of inspecting the dials. "Nice."

"Be careful," Theofanis whispered. "Wait for the warrant. We don't want evidence suppressed."

Theofanis moved to the rear of the vehicle. "You know the trouble with a car like this, ladies? No trunk space—am I right? You couldn't fit a bag of groceries in there if you tried."

"My car is certainly better for groceries." Mrs. Lambert indicated a white Taurus parked near the Aston Martin.

"Any car would be better for every purpose other than showing off," Summer said.

Theofanis had seen her well-used truck. Remembering the collection in her bedroom, he suspected an unusual rock would impress her more than a fancy car.

While Theofanis directed the ladies' attention to the trunk, Ash checked the glove box, which was locked. They worked seamlessly together. A shame he was with the sheriff's department.

"You don't buy a car like this for groceries." Ash slid out of the bucket seat. "This baby has a V12 engine."

Theofanis's cell rang. He listened for a minute, grinned and snapped the phone shut. "Pop the trunk," Theofanis said. "I'll show you."

"I don't suppose Mr. Morrell would mind your opening the trunk." Mrs. Lambert's voice indicated doubt.

Ash whipped around in the driver's seat. "What about the warrant?"

"Judge just issued one," Theofanis said.

Mrs. Lambert smiled as if she welcomed the news. Then again, Theofanis had never seen her without a smile.

"Like I said, it isn't locked," Mrs. Lambert said.

A click told Theofanis that Ash had released the trunk latch. "Mr. Franceschi, you and Miss Cassidy need to stand back. Don't touch anything. You, Mrs. Lambert, have a sensible car. A Taurus has an adequate trunk."

Ash joined them by the rear bumper. "You don't get it, buddy. No one buys an Aston Martin to haul groceries."

Theofanis lifted the lid. "See what I mean?"

"Wouldn't hold groceries, but looks like it's big enough for a dirty sheet." Ash lifted the edge of a flowered flat sheet up with a pen.

"Who would put a filthy sheet in an Aston Martin—looks like dried blood. Do you think it could be blood, Ash?"

With the pen, Ash lifted the sheet one fold at a time, moving each aside slowly. "What have we here?"

"I'd say that's a handgun," Theofanis said.

Mrs. Lambert gasped. "Oh, my!"

Her reaction seemed overly dramatic, rehearsed. Management had decided to sacrifice Morrell.

"Smith and Wesson 642," Ash said. "We need to get these items down to the lab and have them checked out."

"I know Mr. Morrell shouldn't have sold that stock without telling Mr. Harewood, but surely he wouldn't have killed anyone?" Mrs. Lambert's inflection raised a notch, indicating she thought that was exactly what might have occurred. "Dear me, I've known him for years."

"We try not to prejudge anyone," Ash said. "Let the evidence speak for itself." He closed the trunk.

Theofanis escorted the group to the elevator and back to the lobby, where he arranged for a forensics team. Ty and Summer remained close on his heels listening to his phone conversation. Those two weren't going anywhere unless he physically shoved them out the door, he supposed.

Mrs. Lambert hurried to her office. Probably couldn't wait to report to her boss. With a quiet voice, Theofanis turned to Summer. "Any chance you were mistaken and it was Niles Morrell you saw sprawled on the path to the shed the other night? It was dark."

"No way."

"You said you were in a hurry and didn't stop."

She looked at Ty and their eyes met briefly and fell away. Withholding information—what?

"We stopped long enough to see his face," she said. "And his bald head."

No way to mistake Morrell's thatch of silver hair with Harewood's pate. Theofanis had thought there might have been a hat, a ballcap, something to explain how the girl could have been confused. The sheet and gun would probably tie Morrell to the Alvarez murder. Unlikely the lab would find fingerprints, but Morrell would look guilty unless Theofanis could uncover evidence clearing him. A guy who loved his fancy car wouldn't leave a bloody sheet in the trunk. Nor would a guy smart enough to be Harewood's CFO keep incriminating evidence around. If Summer and Ty were right about Harewood being on HEC grounds during the kidnapping, Mrs. Lambert had lied about the flight plan. If she lied about that, what else would she do to protect her boss?

The muscles in Ty Franceschi's neck looked tight enough to snap. "I'm not trying to tell you how to do your job, detective, but Morrell wouldn't have left the sheet and gun in his car. Especially that car."

Theofanis nodded. "You really think I haven't considered that? Go home and leave the detecting to us. You're only going to get in the way."

"But Isaac Harewood is the kind of—"

Franceschi was glowering at him. Theofanis held his palms in front of his own chest and lowered them slowly, hoping to calm the young man. He interrupted. "Take it easy. I understand why you're upset. Trust me. We're going to follow all the evidence back to its source."

Ty shook his head. "You don't understand. Harewood always walks away from the damage he causes."

Theofanis made sure the young man was looking into his eyes. "We're looking at *all* the evidence. Not only the stuff people want us to find."

Franceschi's eyes changed color slightly. He got the message. Good. "Go home. Understood?"

They nodded, but would they listen? Hell, no. Franceschi had made quite a pest of himself in West Virginia and gone to the trouble to follow Harewood to Florida. He was set on getting justice—or failing that, possibly vengeance.

Julia Lambert rejoined them in the lobby just as Kendricks hopped out of a green and white county-issue vehicle and raced through the glass doors toward them. Not good, since the deputy was linked to Fowler and Morrell. They had to keep Kendricks away from any evidence. The thought had barely registered when Ash took care of the problem. He cornered Kendricks and asked him to wait out front for the forensics team. Smart move.

Almost simultaneous with Kendricks's departure for the parking lot, Niles Morrell stalked into the lobby and confronted Julia Lambert. She didn't back away—wouldn't a woman who thought the guy had committed murder act at least a little afraid?

"What's going on?" Morrell asked her. "You were supposed to pick me up at the airport forty minutes ago. I had to get a rental."

Forty minutes? Really? About the time she called Ash and proposed they pay her a visit. Theofanis stepped between them. "Niles Morrell?"

"Who are you?" Morrell demanded. He tossed his head of silver hair like a man used to getting his own way.

9

NO WAY SUMMER WAS LEAVING, no matter what Theofanis said. She and Ty stood near the public restroom doors, where she hoped their presence would go unremarked.

She whispered to Ty, "Tell me they aren't going to fall for this bull."

His hands tightened into fists. "I've watched Harewood wiggle out of one mess after another. This time won't be any different."

She elbowed his ribs. "Shhh. I can't hear what they're saying."

They edged closer to the men, who stood in the sun's glare streaming through the glass doors. Their footsteps grew noticeably louder as they stepped off the carpet and onto the marble tile inside the doors that led to the parking lot.

Theofanis's eyes flicked over to them, a slight frown crossing his face. Too bad. Eavesdropping wasn't a crime. They had a right to be there. In fact, they had been at HEC first. She could make out the detective's words now. He was explaining to Morrell they had a warrant and detailed what they'd found in his trunk.

The CFO's mouth gaped open. "What gun? I don't own a gun."

"See, we're trying to believe you," Ash said, "but the problem is you doctored those bank statements."

Theofanis swiped a handkerchief against his nose as surreptitiously as he could and stuffed it back in his pocket. "Unloading the stock options makes your future look a little bleak, too."

"I only followed orders. I did what Isaac asked me to do. It was his idea to—"

"Oh, Mr. Morrell, I can't believe you're trying to blame Mr. Harewood," Mrs. Lambert said. "He would never—Mr. Harewood's a saint."

Morrell looked from her to Theofanis, his eyes coming to rest on Mrs. Lambert again. "*You* did this to me. I wondered why you sent me up to Scranton on a lame pretext. *You* put that stuff in my car. You and Harewood are trying to cover up—"

Julia Lambert's expression revealed to Summer that Morrell had told the truth. Some people would call it instinct or intuition, but scientific research proved it was simply accurate reading of facial expressions. Abilities you developed without even knowing how or where you'd learned them.

Summer spoke up. "Detective, I think Mr. Morrell's telling the truth. Mrs. Lambert knows more—"

Theofanis glared at Summer, who shut up, partly because of his look and partly because her words were drowned out anyway by Julia Lambert's protest.

"Me? I have nothing to do with any—how can you think I—I'm just a secretary."

"Everyone stay calm." Theofanis motioned with his palms. "Let's go down to the police station and we can straighten all this out. Mr. Morrell, we're going to read you your rights. A formality, you understand."

Morrell opened his mouth as if he were going to argue. Instead he closed his lips. Summer thought she could see moisture at the corner of his eye as he listened to the Miranda rights. He slumped, the arrogant posture of the man who'd stormed into the lobby a few minutes before evaporated. When Theofanis finished, Morrell said, "I'll go with you, but I have never seen that gun you found."

"We appreciate your being reasonable about this," Theofanis said. "Makes it easier on everyone." He turned to Ty and Summer. "I'm going to tell you two one last time. Go home. Now."

Kind of a pain, the way he ordered them around like he was their parent, but since the action appeared to be over, Summer supposed they'd be going home anyway. Ty put his hand on the small of her back, steering her toward the parking lot, a few steps behind the law enforcement contingent.

As Morrell passed Kendricks, the deputy whispered a few words to him. Morrell whirled around. His glance jerked from Ash to Theofanis and back to Ash. His mouth moved as if he wanted to speak. Then he reached toward Kendricks and pulled the deputy's service revolver from its holster.

Ty thrust Summer behind him.

Kendricks nearly lost his balance lunging after his gun. "Hey!"

Ash drew his revolver. Theofanis was quick to follow.

Cries of "Drop it—drop it now" exploded so fast Summer wasn't sure who was shouting what. Kendricks backed away to his vehicle. He got on the radio.

Morrell pointed the gun at Ash, then Theofanis, back and forth. "I can't do jail time, I can't."

He wasn't going to shoot anyone, not intentionally—Summer could see that. He was scared.

Apparently, Ash read the situation the same way. He lowered his gun. "Hey, buddy, be sensible. A good attorney—"

Morrell's gun jerked back onto Ash, his hands shaky. Nervousness alone made him dangerous. Summer thought Ash was beginning to connect with Morrell, saw something changing in his eyes.

Just then Kendricks came running toward them from his vehicle and announced a SWAT team—Summer couldn't imagine they had much experience—was on the way. The fear returned to Morrell's eyes.

"We don't need anyone else here to resolve this," Ash said. "Let's just talk this out." We are all reasonable and intelligent people."

With the exception of Kendricks, Summer thought. She sidled around Ty and spoke up. "Mr. Morrell." He swung the gun in her direction. What she intended to say got lost in a clot of phlegm that formed in her throat. She coughed and managed to go on. "I know people have been lying, please listen to me."

Again Ty inserted himself in front of her, easing closer to Morrell with barely discernible steps. "She's right. I've been following Harewood from city to city. You know that. You remember me from West Virginia. I'm not giving up until I prove his guilt. You can help. If you turn state's evidence, you'll get a reduced sentence or maybe get off altogether."

"That's right," Theofanis said. Though the kids said the right things, better than Kendricks' announcing the imminent arrival of the cavalry, he wished they'd get out of the way. "It's done all the time. You read the papers—"

Kendricks interrupted. "The gun in your trunk looks bad, real bad, but you won't get the chair if—"

Morrell's eyes closed as he plunged the gun into his mouth.

Theofanis lunged forward. "Noooo!"

Ty buried Summer's face in his chest. She didn't see the bullet's impact. But the bang and the thud of Morrell's collapsing body reverberated through her head. She smelled the gunpowder, a scent like chalk dust or burnt paper.

Ash knelt beside Morrell and checked his carotid for pulse. "Gone."

As Ty released her, she took in the blood spray and spatter and Morrell's tortured final expression. Not again. A person talking, breathing, being, one second; not breathing, not being the next. Just like it happened to Chrissie. No, she shouldn't go there.

She thought she smelled iron—Morrell's blood, his brains. She swooned and Ty's arms supported her. She forced the picture of the bodies, Morrell's and her sister's, out of her mind. Forced herself to breathe in Ty's good scent that reminded her of freshly mown grass. Her head cleared and her legs steadied. Ty led her back into the lobby and settled her into the very same upholstered chair where she'd waited for her scholarship interview. It had only been a week and a half ago. Seemed longer.

"Okay?" Ty asked. When she nodded, he said he was going to check on Dayita and Grace. He would drive the van closer to the door to pick her up and take them home. "Don't move. I'll be right back."

But she couldn't sit still. She wandered over to the glass doors and watched Ty run, his gait steady on his artificial limb.

Officers were photographing Morrell's body. His death shouldn't have happened. What had Kendricks whispered that caused Morrell to go for his gun? The deputy's last words had certainly aggravated the situation. And his holster released too easily. Tactical holsters were supposed to have retention features. Summer remembered Ty's warning that Harewood always had locals on his payroll. Was Kendricks a dirty cop?

Morrell's death eliminated one of the best opportunities to uncover the truth about Harewood Energy Corporation.

Law enforcement vehicles arrived with flashing lights. An ambulance rolled through the front gate, siren wailing, braking hard near the body.

Julia Lambert sidled up beside Summer, her footsteps stealthy, even on the marble tile. Julia's lips curled upward. "Honey, you're so lucky to be alive. You should really be more careful. Your mother has already lost one child. I'm afraid she's going to lose another."

Instinctively, Summer drew back. This woman looked like one of the ladies who attended her mother's bike safety foundation fundraisers. Even her voice had the same affected lilt, but now Summer saw past the façade.

Julia Lambert didn't know her mother. Hadn't known Chrissie. She wasn't allowed to toss their family's loss away with pissy little words. No threat was going to stop Summer from following the facts wherever they led. She had lost her twin and survived. She was strong enough to stand up to Julia Lambert.

Summer stepped closer, forcing eye contact until the plastic smile melted away.

"You and your boss have made serious mistakes. You're the ones who need to be careful."

SIXTEEN

Friday

I

AN AQUARIUM OF FISH WERE CANNIBALIZING EACH OTHER inside Summer's stomach, the effect of NSAIDs she was taking for pain. Dr. Hu's thin-lipped smile bore down on her from the head of the table but caused her no discomfort. Though this wasn't how she'd imagined her thesis defense, she was more than ready. Hu couldn't stop her. She knew ASR wells backwards and forward and could recite the statistical analysis of chemicals in Harewood's wells without referring to the text of her thesis. Still, after years of studying under Claire's guidance, Summer missed her terribly at this moment.

Moving stiffly, Summer eased into the chair next to Dr. Thomas, a tall, thin woman she didn't know all that well. Dr. Thomas had been her freshman English professor, selected because one committee member was required to be outside the department.

"My dear girl, are you all right?" Dr. Thomas asked.

Summer nodded, though every bone and muscle in her body seemed affected by the accident. Since going off the heavier duty pain relievers, the aches had grown worse. "I was in a car accident the night before last, but I'm okay."

Dr. Thomas looked across the table to Summer's Ethics in Environmental Studies professor, Dr. Lee; to Dr. Levinson, who'd led a field study in Groundwater Modeling; to Dr. White, who'd taught her Watershed Principles and Applied Hydraulics.

"Surely we can postpone this meeting," Dr. Thomas suggested to the men. "I had no idea she'd been in an accident."

The professors all looked to the head of the table at Dr. Hu.

"Ms. Cassidy is well aware of how tight my schedule has become since assuming Dr. Dunham's duties. However, we can certainly seek a continuance and postpone her graduation until after the summer term if that's what she wants."

Wouldn't that make his day? "I'm ready. Let's get this over with."

Summer had barely started to answer Dr. Hu's first question, when the conference room door banged open. Elbows out, fists tucked below her small breasts, Claire Dunham assumed a stance in the entrance like Wonder Woman. Only, instead of a red, white, and blue bathing suit, she wore a blue-patterned hospital gown.

"Who the hell authorized this meeting?" Her voice sounded scratchier than ever. It took Summer a few seconds to realize it was the result of recent intubation.

Dr. Hu rose, his expression flickering rapidly from shock to alarm to an insincere smile. "Welcome back, Dr. Dunham."

"Don't you 'Doctor Dunham' me. Howard Grice came to see me in the hospital. He said the police told him you accessed my computer and changed my grant report. You not only changed the conclusions, you took out the statement regarding funding sources for the grant, which would reveal possible conflict of interest. Grice assured me he will take appropriate action."

Dr. Hu's spine stiffened. He moved toward the door. "I'm sure you're capable of carrying on this meeting without me. While I've been assuming your responsibilities Dr. Dunham, I've gotten behind on my other important duties."

"One more thing, Dr. Hu." Very deliberately Claire picked up the top sheet of paper from the stack in front of Summer and let it flutter to the floor. With her back to Dr. Hu, Claire bent over to retrieve it, allowing her gown to part in the rear. Only Dr. Hu had a direct view, but everyone else was imagining it. Summer hoped Claire wore granny panties under the gown, but knowing Claire, anything was possible.

Dr. Thomas gasped.

Dr. Lee cleared his throat.

Dr. White maintained a neutral facial expression though his left cheek twitched once and he kept his eyes trained on Summer's thesis.

Dr. Levinson coughed discreetly to cover up a laugh.

Summer's chest convulsed with a suppressed giggle. Claire's exit from Florida Sci-Tech to Boston was sure to become one more piece of the Dunham legend.

Well-oxygenated hemoglobin infused Hu's face. Definitely anger, Summer determined from the furrowed brow and utter disappearance of his lips.

No one spoke until the sound of Hu's dress shoes pounding down the corridor could no longer be heard.

Dr. Dunham slammed the door. "Well, let's get this young woman cleared for graduation, what do you say?"

Rumblings of assent went round the table as the committee members shuffled papers and avoided eye contact.

Summer clasped both Claire's hands, noting a bruise on her right wrist, the result of an IV needle. "Are you okay? You're supposed to be in the hospital."

"Are you okay? I heard you were in a wreck."

"Neither of us is okay, but since we're here, we might as well do this."

"That's my girl."

"How'd you know?"

"Your buddy Dayita called the hospital to see how I was. I overheard some of what she told Joe and figured out the rest. I sent Joe for coffee. The nurse tried to stop me, from leaving, so I mooned her and here I am." She paused. "I made a lousy patient."

The reference to mooning caused everyone to scrutinize their paperwork again. Dr. Levinson coughed.

Though pale, Claire seemed eager to begin the meeting, but instead she got up once again and worked her way around the table to where Hu had been sitting. Her cackle was wicked. She picked up a pen Hu had left behind and carried it back to her seat.

2

THE TEASERS FOR CHANNEL NINE NEWS promised new revelations concerning Harewood Energy Corporations chief financial officer and a look at their controversial wells. Other stories included the heroic tale of three foster children on the high school track team and a shift to dry weather in the week ahead.

The lead story was the reason Dayita and Mrs. Patel, Summer's mother, Ty, and Grace were gathered in Summer's living room. Claire Dunham had phoned earlier and alerted Summer to be sure to watch the six o'clock news. The air in the apartment was stuffy, the room clotted with bodies.

During the three commercials that followed, Summer sat down in one of the kitchen chairs she'd rolled into the living room. She poked a finger in and out of a hole in her blouse, then bounded into the bedroom and changed into a tee-shirt. What looked like ice tea stains dotted the front, but there was no time to change again.

She plopped into her seat in time to catch a close-up of Isaac Harewood. The lighting bounced off his shiny head.

Harewood was commenting about Morrell. "With great sadness I have been forced to face that one of my most trusted business associates and dearest friends issued fraudulent statements about our company to investors. I trusted my Chief Financial Officer completely. Obviously, that trust was misplaced, and as CEO, I have to accept the blame for that lack of judgment and oversight. I have taken immediate steps to rectify matters and am fully cooperating with investigators. I refuse to allow anything to damage the company I've worked so hard to build. Right now, my heart goes out to Mr. Morrell's family—his wife and children. This community stands with them, sharing their grief. One misstep cannot be allowed to overshadow all the good deeds of a man's life."

"Hypocrite!" Ty snarled.

"Shush now." Jordan Cassidy touched his arm. "I want to hear what they say."

Ty was right. No matter what Harewood said about dear friends and trust and cooperation and grief, a knot of evil dwelled at his core. People were so much harder to measure than chemicals in water. She should have taken more courses in psychology.

The male anchor introduced the next segment, which began with a close-up of Dr. Dunham seated in her office. As she described the levels of carcinogens found in Harewood's wells, her face was replaced with computer graphics. The first was a dissection of typical ASR well, the second a chart of chemical levels allowed by the EPA contrasted with those found in the Harewood wells.

Summer scooted to the edge of her chair and pointed at the television. "Hey—I made that graphic."

The next shot was taken from one of the slides Dayita added in the presentation. Before and after views of the same person, first as a healthy boy and then an adult with skin sores. "Arsenic poisoning in Bangladesh has affected thousands," the anchor intoned. "University students presented these photographs to the Department of Environmental Protection this week to dissuade them from allowing any exemption to water standards."

Mrs. Patel pushed her ponderous body from the sofa and lumbered toward the television as if compelled to touch the screen. By the time she got there, the visual was replaced by another. "Dayita, that was Nakeesh! Our Nakeesh! Wait until I write to my sister and tell her that her son—your fiancé—was on American television. She won't believe it."

The broadcast shifted to commercial again.

Fiancé? Summer stared at Dayita. Unblinking, Dayita kept eyes on the screen, but Summer knew she wasn't watching the ads. How could Dayita keep this a secret from her best friend? Dayita's refusal of dates, of invitations to dance, even to play foosball now made more sense. Suddenly it seemed as if Dayita was a stranger, someone Summer had never understood or known at all.

The female anchor returned with breaking news at the state capital. A dozen reporters and TV cameras clustered around Senator Felipe Vargas on the steps of the Old Capitol Building with its red and white striped awnings and four white columns as a backdrop. Vargas was flanked by the same aide Summer had noticed at the community hearings and they were joined by the new head of the Department of Environmental Protection. The camera panned to the small audience. The lobbyist, Bailey Douglass, was unmistakable in a black and purple dress that set off her red hair. Detective Theofanis stood slightly behind her.

The senator's expression was sober as he began. "As the news event announcement you received stated, I have two statements. They will be brief and I won't take questions afterward.

"First, I will not support legislation to exempt Harewood Energy Corporation's Aquifer Storage and Recovery wells, better known as

ASR wells, from the recommended limits of chemical contaminants. I have sent a letter recommending to the Department of Environmental Protection that current regulations be kept in place. In any case, it is questionable whether state legislation could override national policy. At this point, I consider the matter closed. The people of Florida expect and deserve clean drinking water when they turn on their taps. Further, I filed a bill this morning that would limit private ownership of our water. My aide is distributing a detailed statement regarding my rationale. I believe in free markets. However, water differs from oil. You can choose not to consume petroleum products by modifying your behavior. You can drive less or choose a smaller car. You can't choose not to drink water. The public has an overriding interest in making sure water is both clean and affordable."

The female anchor was back on screen, but there was so much commotion in the living room, Summer had no idea what she was saying.

Dayita jumped up and did a little dance, her fists pumping the air. She ran to Summer and cupped her shoulders. Summer was still seated and somewhat stunned by the news that her friend was engaged.

"We did it! " Dayita said. "We stopped them."

Mrs. Patel nodded. "What you accomplished was important, Summer. I know you will get into MIT."

"Actually, I don't think I will." It would be pointless to tell everyone about the paper Dr. Hu had thrown in the trash. "I've decided to accept the offer from Penn State. It's a free ride if I accept the teaching assistant position."

Wasn't her mother going to say anything? Anything?

Finally: "Congratulations, Summer. I'm proud of you."

She didn't look proud. She looked sad. The words did little to fill the hole in Summer's chest. She supposed her mother was thinking about Chrissie. Thinking that Chrissie would never grow up to become a mad scientist, and nothing Summer could do would ever atone for it.

"What's wrong with Florida Sci-Tech?" her mother asked. "Or at least the University of Oregon so you could be near your father?"

Summer wanted to scream and stamp her feet, but that would be childish, and she was no longer a child. "It's time for me to be on my own." Her mother sucked in her lower lip.

Summer turned away from her mother, back to the television as

the senator came on screen again. A wide shot revealed the reporters in his audience. They stopped writing and all heads knifed up to
watch the senator.

"My second announcement is more personal. I have been involved
in a long term relationship with one of my aides. " He paused, glancing at the man on his left. "I regret with all my heart the pain I have
caused my family and the loyal supporters who have stood by me all
these years. My wife is beginning divorce proceedings with my blessing. I ask that you respect her privacy and that of my children during
this very difficult time. It is my wish to continue to serve the people
of Florida in the Senate, but that will be up to voters in the next elec-
tion. I have no further comments and will take no questions."

Standing tall, the senator ignored reporters shouting his name as
he strode away from the microphones and the cameras. The broadcast
segued to commercial again.

Summer motioned Dayita into the kitchen. The conversation in
the living room drifted in, a discordant mishmash of voices.

"Well, that was a surprise, wasn't it?" Summer's mother was saying to Mrs. Patel. "A shame for his family."

In the kitchen, Summer mouthed the word, "Fiancé?"

Dayita flung her braid over her shoulder. "Don't look at me like
that, Summer. I haven't seen him since I was four." She picked up a
napkin and began to fringe the edge.

"Then why?"

"It was arranged before I came to this country. It's the way my
mother's people have always handled marriage."

"But you've lived here almost all your whole life." Dayita was all
about blue jeans, Frisbees, designer pocketbooks, glittery nail polish,
and endless diets to stay slim. How could she marry a man she hadn't
seen since they were toddlers?

Dayita's eyes darted to the living room. "Keep your voice down.
My mother is watching us. It isn't about me and what I want. If he
marries me, he can come to America and get good medical care. And
they are likely to let him bring his mother and sisters over too."

Moisture welled in Summer's eyes. She opened the refrigerator
and took out a bottle of wine, angling her body so Dayita couldn't see
her face. She poured small amounts into her cheap stemmed glasses

and let Dayita pass them around. Let everyone think the wine was a celebration, but it was more like drowning a world of sorrow. What a terrible burden Dayita carried for her family. Responsibility for all those lives. Surely she could help her relatives some other way. This engagement was forged of love, no doubt, but Summer didn't know if it was the kind of love that made for a good marriage.

Jordan Cassidy's voice rose over the din of a life insurance commercial. "The senator has two children. One is developmentally disabled like my Chrissie." Her mother glanced at Grace coloring a fish in jewel tones. She didn't add, *Like Grace.* Didn't have to. "That poor woman will have to raise that child on her own, now."

"She will manage," said Mrs. Patel. "Every child brings its own blessings to a family."

A tear slid down Jordan Cassidy's cheek. "Chrissie was such a blessing. She soldiered through all the heart surgeries, never complaining. If only she hadn't been in that accident . . ."

Summer stood stone-still in the center of the room. The air in the room seemed to vibrate and time down-shifted into a gear so slow Summer thought her breath had stopped. The familiar guilt bit into her bones again. Her mother had always blamed her anyway—why not lay it out there?

"Go ahead, say it: it was my fault," she said.

Dayita grabbed Summer's arm in a steel-like grip.

"Of course it wasn't, sweetheart," Mrs. Patel said. "It was an accident. A tragic accident we all wish hadn't happened."

Wrong. During "Marco Polo," Neecie Haynes had chanted to Chrissie, *Dumbbell, dumbbell, can't catch me, dumbbell!* Ted Clinger chimed in: *You swim so slow you couldn't catch a cold if it was standing still.* Everyone laughed. Summer, God forgive her, had laughed, too. When the ice cream truck came, Chrissie didn't want to stay behind because the kids made fun of her even worse when Summer wasn't there. Even now Summer could hear her nine-year-old self say, *No way, Jose. You're slooooow. It would take you forever.* The word *slow* held such mean meaning. Her sister was probably crying when she biked toward Nana Bowmaster's house. That's why she didn't see the car that hit her. It was the secret Summer would carry to her own grave.

With those monstrous words, Summer had destroyed her family.

Her father, who never cried, bit his lip trying but failing to hold back tears. Then one day he left. He couldn't take the never-ending grief.

A grief her mother was still dealing with. She was blathering about how mistaken Summer was. An awful accident. Words. Words. More words. "It used to make me crazy that the police couldn't find the driver of that car, but it wouldn't have made any difference."

Summer snapped out of her nightmare memories. "How can you say that? That woman should be rotting in jail. She killed Chrissie. Sometimes it's almost like I can hear her saying she's sorry, like I'm remembering it, but her face never comes into focus." Summer had arrived at the accident scene in time to see the woman get in her car and drive away.

"Punishing her wouldn't bring Chrissie back," Jordan Cassidy said, blindly fumbling through her purse for a bottle of pills. As if Paxil or any other drug could bring Chrissie back.

"She has to live with what she did." Mrs. Patel's voice sounded as if she'd swallowed glass shards. "I imagine she grieves every day." Dayita's painted fingernails dug into Summer's arm.

Summer would have to live with what she'd done, too. A physical ache crashed over her with the force of waves hurled by hurricane winds against the shore. She would never be a "we" again. She would always be a part of her identical twin, yet apart.

The darkest truth of all: she loved Chrissie fiercely. Still. Always. But Summer had hated her sister with equal ferocity. Chrissie, so ill and so special, consumed every scrap of their parents' attention. Summer had been left behind during the surgeries, during the endless visits to specialists, shunted off on neighbors or sitters.

And nothing changed after her sister's death. Summer was a part of her family, yet apart. Still. Always.

Grace put down her crayon and tiptoed into the kitchen. She canted her neck until she and Summer locked eyes. The child seemed old beyond her years.

She tugged on the pocket of Summer's jeans. "I want Marshmallow Sugar Crispies," Grace said.

Summer wanted to stroke Grace's tiny fingers. But it wasn't something you did to a kid who hated to be touched. "Let's talk your big brother into a trip to the grocery store."

3

THEOFANIS KEPT TY AND SUMMER WAITING in the station's lobby for half an hour, hoping they'd go away. They were persistent little buggers. The girl should go back to school and forget about Harewood Energy. Too many people had already gotten hurt digging into HEC affairs. He finished paperwork on Morrell's suicide and called them into his office. He had them sit while he stood, his backside propped against his desk, his arms crossed.

He cocked his head to one side, noting the girl moved gingerly, the visible bruises the least of her injuries. "Well?"

When they both started to speak at once, Summer deferred to Ty. "Morrell was framed," he said. "That deputy egged him on and he made sure his holster wasn't secured properly."

"I guess you think I'm an idiot who doesn't know how to do my job." He smothered a yawn with his hand. He'd gotten little sleep for days.

Summer jumped into the conversation. "Mrs. Montera told me—"

Theofanis cut the girl off. "What were you doing talking to her?"

"Offering condolences. Do you want to hear what she told me or not?"

He nodded. Lord, he was cranky. The lingering cold and lack of sleep were clobbering him.

"Mrs. Montera talked to Alvarez on the phone the night he died. Someone showed up while they were on the phone and Alvarez said this person was the last person he expected to see."

The "last person" in more ways than one. Could have been Morrell. Maybe Alvarez expected Jake Fowler to hand over the money, rather than someone more important. But the last person he expected to see—probably not Morrell or Fowler.

"I know you already have copies of the doctored bank statements, but did you know Paulo Alvarez had copies of them?"

Geez. There was the motive. "You realize you have withheld evidence in a murder investigation. A criminal offense."

The girl raised her chin defiantly, winced, and quickly lowered it again. "We didn't know who to trust. Neither did Mrs. Montera."

"Morrell didn't own any guns," Ty said.

Oh boy, Franceschi couldn't wait to lay that one on him. "How do you know that?" Theofanis asked.

"I talked to his wife this morning," Ty said. "Morrell—"

"You mean you pestered his grieving widow the day after her husband died? That was real sensitive of you." Theofanis had been to her house, too, to pay his respects. Sure, he'd asked subtle questions, but that was his job.

Ty continued as if he hadn't been interrupted. "He never shot a gun before in his life."

"He figured out how to do it real fast yesterday, didn't he? Besides, wives don't know everything about their husbands. Bet she didn't know about a lot of activities he had on the side."

"If you mean the campaign contributions he made to get pot legalized, she was aware of them," Ty said. "That doesn't make him a murderer."

Didn't make him a saint either. The photo Bailey Douglass had given him of Morrell handing an envelope to Fowler also made the CFO appear guilty. Of course, the envelope could have been going in the opposite direction, Fowler giving money to Morrell. And there was no way of knowing what was in the envelope for sure, and even if it was money, they couldn't prove what the payment was for. And they had no evidence if others—like Harewood—also were involved. No way of knowing—yet.

Still, if Franceschi had useful information, Theofanis wanted to hear it. "Anything else you kids think I should know?" Theofanis asked.

The skin around Franceschi's eyes and mouth tensed. Didn't like being called a kid, Theofanis guessed. Too bad.

"That night at Harewood's shed, Fowler told me he didn't kill Alvarez," Summer said. "He said he was cleaning up someone else's mess."

Interesting. "Fowler's word is hardly credible."

"He had no reason to lie to me," Summer said. "He intended to kill me before the night was over."

"And Julia Lambert threatened Summer," Ty said. "Told her to quit meddling or her mother might lose another child."

Exactly what Theofanis was afraid of. These two had no idea what kind of snake pit they were stepping into—the girl didn't anyway. Franceschi was an ex-military, could probably take care of himself. Jordan Cassidy was right about her daughter, though. Hard outside; not so tough inside. She'd nearly fainted when Morrell's gun had gone off.

Time to be a hard ass. "I'm going to tell you the same thing Mrs. Lambert did. Go back to school. Or hang out on the beach and drink beer. Play Frisbee. But this isn't a game. For God's sake, leave the investigating to professionals. The IRS and Securities and Exchange Commission are investigating Harewood. Jake Fowler is still out there, and I don't need to remind you how dangerous he is."

"Any leads on where he might be?" Ty asked.

Theofanis shook his head. "A man using one of his aliases bought an airline ticket to New York City. My guess is he's long gone. Like you said. Out of the state, or out of the country by now."

Summer threw up her hands. "So you file a few papers and forget about that poor man I found—is that it? Case closed. No one cares."

Why did the public always assume the police didn't care when they couldn't come up with an easy answer? "The Alvarez murder case is still open and we're working on it every day," Theofanis said.

Franceschi wasn't going to listen to him, but for the sake of the girl's mother, he had to try with her. "You're a smart young woman. Stay as far away from Harewood Energy Corporation as you can. Listen to me. Hell, listen to Julia Lambert. She was right. Summer, your mother doesn't need to lose another child. You have no idea how—" The girl's jaw was rigid, and Theofanis was beyond tired. "Go home. Get out of here."

After they left, he rubbed his eyes and dragged his fingers down his face. He woke up his computer. With the bodies piling up—Alvarez, Snyder, Fowler's younger brother Kevin, Jeglinski, and Morrell—he and Ash had lost the easy sources of evidence. Now they would begin the painstaking task of digging through the paper trail. Sooner or later, they would piece together clues that led to the murderer.

One person remained to interrogate: Deputy Jameson Kendricks.

4

AWARENESS OF AN UNNATURAL CHILL, OF NAKED EXPOSURE, gradually aroused Summer from sleep completely. Her shoulder throbbed as she turned over. Grace lay beside her. For one so small, she was remarkably adept at hogging sheets. Her cold lingered, reason enough to persuade Ty to use the couch one more night.

Summer yanked the sheet back over her arms. You'd think she would sleep like the dead after all she'd been through—but no, every time she moved she discovered a new ache. The red LED output on the alarm clock read 1:38 a.m.

An unfamiliar click came from the living room. Despite all the pills Ty had taken before he lay down, he must be having as much trouble sleeping as she was. Summer slid out of bed. They could watch a late movie together.

She was nearly to the bedroom door when a soft voice in the other room made her pause. "Didn't expect to find you on the couch," the man said. "The slut ought to treat you better than that."

Her heart pounded. That voice addressing Ty was familiar—who? Oh, God! Jake Fowler.

Ty's baritone sounded steady, measured. "That's such an ugly word. Says more about the person using it than the one spoken about."

One toehold at a time, she inched across the carpet until her body was sheltered behind the partially open door, her head cocked just enough to see beyond. It took a moment for her eyes to make out Fowler in the darkness. He stood beyond the coffee table. Ty was seated on the couch, his shadowy profile barely visible.

She ducked her head back behind the door and glanced at Grace. Still sleeping, pink blankie clutched in her fist.

"I've been expecting you, Fowler," Ty said. "So have the police. They're watching this place."

"Nice try. No one is out there. I did recon for over an hour."

"How'd you get in?"

"With a key. The one my brother took from that Indian bitch. You remember, my dead brother?"

The key the building superintendent had given to Dayita—Summer had forgotten all about it.

Jake was still talking. "Now, get your ass in there after your girlfriend. You're both going to pay for killing my little brother."

Ty would only be able to hop without the C-leg. The prosthetic was plugged into the wall between Fowler and the bedroom.

Fowler laughed without humor. "You're not such a tough guy without the bionics. This is almost too easy."

Summer needed a weapon. Her eyes traveled over the tissue box, alarm clock, advanced environmental problems textbook, hairbrush. No good. Her rock collection! She grabbed the nearest hunk of co-quina, wincing as a rough edge of shell sliced into the underside of her knuckles.

Steps—they were coming. Her mind raced. Ty would enter first. She would only get one chance to hit her target—and though she hadn't seen it, she knew Fowler had a gun. What if it went off when she hit him?

A chance she had to take.

Ty flung the door open all the way, other hand braced against the frame. Jake shoved him through, then fumbled for a light switch.

Summer squinted, bracing herself against the glare she knew was coming. As light flooded the room, she cocked her elbow and whipped the rock toward Jake Fowler's face. It connected beneath his eye, the ragged texture of imbedded shells instantly drawing blood. He roared.

The gun made a sound like spitting, knocking Ty backwards into the wall. A dark spot appeared on his right shoulder as he slumped to the floor.

Summer bellowed and leaped at Fowler, seizing his gun arm and dragging it toward the floor. She launched her mouth at his nose and bit down as hard as she could. A hunk of flesh came off in her mouth.

He screamed and flung her across the room as she was spitting out flesh. Her head banged against the closet door and the world grayed like fog rising over a river. She fought to remain conscious.

A madman, Fowler charged two steps closer. She couldn't get to her feet. He was going to kill her.

But Ty rolled sideways and yanked Fowler's legs out from under him. His torso slammed into the floor, the impact ejecting the gun from his hand.

Ty grappled with Fowler, rolling and grunting in a fierce tangle of arms and legs.

Summer crawled, carpet fibers scratching her knees and elbows, as she made her way toward the gun. It lay inches from where the men wrestled. Fog clouded her brain again. She couldn't see. Couldn't move. Then Chrissie's voice sang out wordlessly across the misty barrier. *Over here, Summer.*

Marco, Summer called.

Chrissie whispered, *Polo.*

She hauled herself toward the voice and located the cold metal grip of the handgun. She pulled herself up onto her knees and steadied the gun in front of her. It was heavy, unwieldy, because of the silencer on the barrel.

One man stood over the other now. She blinked to focus and saw two legs. She inserted her finger into the trigger guard, exhaled, and squeezed.

The recoil rocked her backward onto her butt, the gun now aimed at the overhead light. She righted herself. The bullet had hit Fowler in the gut. He staggered backward, then fell to his knees.

He wasn't dead yet. She aimed for his chest and pulled the trigger again.

SEVENTEEN

Saturday

I

THEOFANIS YAWNED AND ACCEPTED THE CUP OF COFFEE Ash had brought in from the nearest convenience store, cheaper than Starbucks, better than the station's brew, which always tasted slightly burned.

Ash pried the plastic lid off his take-out cup. "Hate these things. The holes on top are too small. Can't get more than a dribble out and the coffee always ends up splashing on my clothes."

Theofanis brought the crook of his arm up to catch a sneeze.

"You still sound like you belong home in bed. You didn't use that stuff I told you about, did you?"

Theofanis blew his nose. "I'm not putting a slimy stick up my nostrils. It's disgusting." He'd watched Ash do it and was grossed out by the soggy mess hanging off the end of what looked like a Q-tip. "Besides, I don't think that kind of stuff works. I'll stick with traditional cold remedies."

Ash shrugged. "Suit yourself. But look how fast I got over my cold, and you're still stick. I'm just saying."

Yeah, yeah. There was probably some other reason for Ash's miraculous recovery. Theofanis wasn't buying the idea that slime on a stick could cure anything.

"Any word from the hospital this morning?" Ash asked.

"Franceschi's condition upgraded to fair."

"The girl?"

Theofanis shrugged. "Okay, I guess. Stopped by her mother's house. Miss Cassidy was still asleep."

Ash grunted. "Won't be an easy thing to get past. Even killing an asshole like Fowler would take something out of you."

"I left some information about counseling with the mother, but she didn't think the girl would go." Jordan Cassidy had been quite adamant: her daughter had no use for psychologists.

"Well, you tried." Ash gulped down the last of his coffee and disposed of the cup. "I cried like a baby to I.A. this morning about all our leads in the murders dying off. They gave us the okay to take a crack at Kendricks. He's on leave pending the investigation of Kevin Fowler's shooting, and a look into his taking payoffs from Morrell. Knows he's on the way out. I think he'll squeal for a deal."

Theofanis finished off his coffee. "What are we waiting for? Let's haul him in here."

An hour later, Jameson Kendricks walked into the police station interrogation room with a little less stick-up-his-ass attitude than usual, a lawyer at his side, a short middle-aged woman Theofanis had seen in court before. He couldn't remember her name. Luckily, Ash did: Snodgrass. They settled into their seats, Ash opposite Kendricks and his lawyer. Theofanis sat at the far end of the table.

"Let's get one thing clear up front." Ms. Snodgrass had one of those slow Southern voices that took twice as long to get something said as it should have. "My client has nothing to say to you until we hear what you have to offer. No games. No threats. Just tell us what you can do for him and save us all some time."

Ash shook his head. "Now, Ms. Snodgrass, you know that's not how it works. Until we know what Jameson has to offer, we can't make any counter-offers. Jameson here is my partner, so you know I'm going to do my best for him."

Former partner, Theofanis thought. They would never work together again.

Kendricks gave the lawyer a look that said he'd known her tactic wasn't going to work. Slow as he was, he had been through a few of these sessions before, just not on the lawyered up side of the table.

Ms. Snodgrass tugged down her overly snug suit jacket, attempting to cover the waistband of her slacks. "Let's try this. You ask a question and my client and I will consult about whether it is in his best interests to answer. I'm here to insure his rights are protected."

"Fair enough." Ash opened a folder and slid the photograph of Niles Morrell handing an envelope to Kendricks in a parking lot across the table. "What's in the envelope?"

I.A. had to have asked the same question, but Kendricks and the lawyer whispered and she shook her head.

Kendricks apparently decided to ignore her advice. "Cash."

"What was Morrell paying you for?" Ash asked.

"He—"

Snodgrass interrupted. "My client wants to know what you can offer for this information. You can't expect to get it for free."

The state's attorney had given them considerable leeway to bargain for information concerning the murders, not so much on the corruption charges.

Theofanis lost patience with questioning that matched the pace of Ms. Snodgrass's vowels. He got up and stood just to the left of Ash. "You said you don't want to play games, Ms. Snodgrass. So don't. You know these questions are the easy ones. Your client faces possible accessory to murder charges. He might want to consider how many people involved with HEC have ended up dead." He ticked them off on his fingers. "Alvarez, Snyder, Morrell, Jeglinski, Kevin and Jake Fowler. Who's next?" Theofanis leaned forward, one palm resting on the conference table, the other pointing a trigger finger at Kendricks. The deputy's mouth twitched.

Ash clasped his large hands and laid them on the table, leaning closer to Kendricks. "Your best protection against the same end is to go on record with everything you know right now. I don't believe for a second you had anything to do with killing those men."

"I didn't." Kendricks's voice squeaked.

Theofanis dropped into the chair by Ash. "Then help us lock up the people who did."

Kendricks claimed he had accepted payments from Morrell to look the other way concerning the grow house, but that wasn't all he was paid to do. "Look, ever since Harewood Energy moved their headquarters here, they've been giving me a little under the table to keep them informed if anything happened in Loblolly Lake that they should be aware of. A retainer, Miss Julia said."

Theofanis and Ash exchanged a look.

"Julia Lambert?" Theofanis asked.

"That's right. First, I was just supposed to keep an eye on that Ty Franceschi. Miss Julia said he'd caused them a lot of grief in West Virginia and she didn't want him trespassing or stirring up trouble. Then one day Miss Julia calls me into her office and suggests if I come across Summer Cassidy in the line of duty I should do everything possible to get her off the streets."

"This before or after we found Paulo Alvarez at Goose Pasture?"

Kendricks looked up at the ceiling as if the answer were pasted there and looked somewhat taken aback when the answer came to him. "The day before."

Was he that stupid that he hadn't realized the implications until now? Theofanis didn't know how Ash had put up with Kendricks for the past year and a half.

"Do you know who killed Alvarez?" Ash asked softly.

Kendricks shook his head. "Wasn't Fowler, that's all I know. He bragged about his kills."

That jibed with what the Cassidy girl had told them. Fowler said he was cleaning up someone else's mess—whose?

Ash leaned closer. "Who did Fowler say he'd killed?"

"Two guys in the army. He didn't mention names. And he bragged about using this poison dart on someone. Said the poison mimicked a heart attack and the victim never felt a thing. I figured he was one of those guys who makes stuff up to look tough. Trying to intimidate me and Mr. Morrell."

Theofanis caught Ash's eye. "Morrell didn't know about the poison dart stuff until that conversation?" Theofanis asked.

"Didn't seem to."

Ms. Snodgrass's lips pursed. "Gentlemen, I think my client has given you enough information. What are you going to give him in return?"

Ash suggested the lawyer needed to relax. "I think we're going to be able to work something out for my old partner here. Just a few more questions. How did Miss Julia pay you the retainer?"

"Once a month I would meet her at Given's Bookstore and Coffee Shop and she would give me a pretty little handwritten thank you card with cash inside."

Handwritten notes. Theofanis found this bizarrely civil. "How much?"

"Two hundred."

Kendricks had sold out cheap. "What about Morrell?" Theofanis asked. "How much did he pay you?"

"Three."

"What do you know about the kidnappings?" Theofanis asked.

Ms. Snodgrass's face turned purple. "Don't answer that. My client—"

Kendricks was shaking his head and talking over her. "Nothing, I swear I had nothing to do with that."

Theofanis pressed on. "But you showed up on the scene. You shot Kevin Fowler when he'd already dropped his weapon and surrendered."

"No, that was a righteous shoot. The department is going to clear me on that one."

Righteous, his ass. "Who sent you to the HEC parking lot that day we were arresting Morrell?" Theofanis asked.

Kendricks's voice grew squeaky again. "I heard it on the scanner, I swear."

Theofanis slammed a palm onto the table. "What did you whisper to Niles Morrell just before he pulled your gun?"

"I don't remember."

"Just tell us the gist of it. You said something."

"I told you, I don't remember."

"Bullshit." Theofanis slammed the table again.

Ash pulled on his arm. "Easy now, buddy. Easy. Jameson, we're trying to believe everything you're telling us here, but we were there in that parking lot. We saw you with Morrell. We know you said something to him just before he grabbed your gun."

Ms. Snodgrass grabbed her client's arm and hauled him to his feet. "Enough. We're leaving. Call me when you're ready to talk about what you're going to give my client for all the assistance he's provided today."

"Don't worry," Theofanis said. "We'll be in touch."

Ash walked them out, saying he was getting some chow. He tossed an offer to bring something for Theofanis over his shoulder.

Theofanis shook his head. The cold tablets had sapped his appetite. He spent the next hour and a half searching Morrell's financial records for three cash withdrawals to match the amounts that appeared in Jake Fowler's bank account in April. One payment probably had something to do with Alvarez's murder; another with Theofanis's friend and broker, Phil Snyder. Plenty of circumstantial evidence pegged Fowler for Snyder's death. And now they had Kendricks saying Fowler had practically confessed to killing Snyder.

A third cash infusion into Fowler's bank account probably resulted from the botched kidnapping of the Cassidy girl's friend, Dayita Patel, and Franceschi's kid sister. He closed out the bank records and filled in more bubbles in his brainstorming software.

Kendricks fingered Julia Lambert as the one making his payments, and Summer Cassidy said Lambert had made veiled threats toward her.

He called Ash. "Morrell might not have been a saint, but so far his fingerprints haven't shown up in Fowler's finances outside of their attempts to produce marijuana seed strains in anticipation of legalization in Florida."

"What now?" Ash asked.

"How about subpoenaing Lambert's and Harewood's personal bank records?" Theofanis outlined his reasoning, hoping it would be enough to overcome the police chief's earlier reluctance to piss off HEC management.

"Kendricks gave us enough to go after them. Besides, there's something creepy about the way that bitch hangs on her boss."

"What I'm wondering is, could a she-lion be hiding inside that lamb's skin? Or could our hare be a bear."

Ash groaned, and Theofanis could hear him take a drag on his cigarette and blow the smoke out. "Enough already with the puns. Shakespeare you are not."

"Think the chief will go along with these subpoenas now?"

"Good chance."

Theofanis disconnected and settled in to the task of preparing a convincing argument. He had nearly finished when his phone rang. He recognized the number: the coroner's officer. "LaWanda, what's up?"

"Something's bugging me and I thought you ought to know about it."

"Yeah?"

"You know that drug Jake Fowler stole from the Valdosta hospital?"

"Yeah?"

"He stole quite a bit of the succinylcholine."

"And?" What was she driving at?

"It took a small amount to kill Snyder. You only found traces of it on the weapon in Fowler's trailer."

Theofanis held his breath during an interminable pause.

She dropped the bomb. "So, where's the rest of it?"

2

SUMMER SQUINTED AGAINST THE LIGHT streaming through the curtains at her bedroom window. Not her apartment bedroom, her childhood room. The twin beds were still decorated with the same pink and yellow gingham spreads, Chrissie's stuffed animals sprawled across hers as if Summer's mother expected Chrissie to return and play with them.

At first Summer couldn't think why she was here. When she tried to raise her head off the pillow and felt dizzy, the night tumbled back. She'd killed a man.

She remembered blood pouring from Ty's shoulder, remembered rocking Grace, who'd been exposed to yet another trauma. She supposed everyone would expect her to feel guilty, but she didn't. Fowler had left her no choice.

Her mother had insisted she come home from the hospital with her. For once, Summer yielded without argument. Her apartment still had crime scene tape around it and dark stains on the carpet.

Judging by the sun's angle, it was after noon. She'd never slept in like this before. Banging noises came from the kitchen. She rolled on her side and slid her legs off the bed, levering herself upright. She hoped her mother had news about Ty. She knew he'd come through the surgery on his shoulder, but he was still in guarded condition when she'd left near dawn with her mother.

Not trusting her footing, she hung onto the railing on the way down the stairs. For a few seconds, she stood in the hall and watched her mother open a can of soup and empty it into a pan.

Jordan Cassidy turned away from the stove. "Oh, you're up. I was just coming to wake you. How are you feeling?"

"Fine." Why had she lied? Couldn't she confess a weakness to her mother for once? "Actually, a little rough around the edges. Have you heard anything about Ty?"

"Upgraded to fair condition. Detective Theofanis stopped by to update us this morning. I told him you were still sleeping."

Thank God Ty was going to be all right. "Where's Grace?"

Her mother turned back to the stove to stir the soup. "The Patels heard about the shooting on the Channel Nine news and came over to get Grace. Mrs. Patel said I had my hands full caring for you and she wanted to take Grace to a counselor she knows who specializes in trauma in children."

Counselors had never done her or her mother much good, but Summer hoped Grace would have better luck. Out of habit, Summer took what had been "her" seat at the kitchen table. They had rarely eaten together as a family after Chrissie's death.

Her mother crossed the room and lifted a loose strand of Summer's hair away from her face. Summer flinched.

"The gash doesn't look infected," her mother said.

Summer had forgotten about the gash. She must look as pathetic as a skinned deer.

Her mother filled two bowls with soup and set them on the table. "Chicken and Stars, yours and Chrissie's favorite."

Yeah, her favorite when she was nine. Still, had to give her mother credit for trying. Much to Summer's surprise, the rich broth comforted her, the aroma exactly what she needed to revive from the harrowing night.

She opened a fresh stack of crackers. "What did Channel Nine say about the shooting?"

"They interviewed Detective Theofanis. He said you were a hero, said you took a cold-blooded killer off the streets permanently."

Summer frowned. "That makes me sound brave, like I had a choice."

"You were brave. I would have frozen as soon as I saw the gun." Her mother sighed. "I'm just glad this whole mess is over and you're safe."

It wasn't over. Whoever hired Fowler was still out there. And Summer knew where to look. If Julia Lambert hadn't hired him, she knew who had.

Alvarez told his landlady the person who'd arrived was the *last* person he expected to see. It could have been Julia Lambert.

Another piece of lost information tickled the back of her brain. If she'd read it, she'd remember it instantly. Had to be something she'd heard.

Suddenly she visualized Julia's face as plainly as if they were still in Harewood's office. *What a terrible thing for you, poor dear,* Mrs. Lambert had said about Summer's finding of Alvarez's body. No news account, Channel Nine or otherwise, had revealed that Summer had been the one to find the body. Reporters only said a boater returning from a river trip had stumbled onto the remains. Julia Lambert shouldn't have known who found the body—unless she'd arranged for it to happen. Unless she had sent Jake Fowler into Summer's life. And Julia knew Summer had briefly been treated as a suspect, mostly by that one deputy—Kendricks.

Because Kendricks was likely on the Harewood Energy payroll.

She considered calling Theofanis, but no, he had dismissed Ty and her as kids, ordered her to go back to school and play Frisbee. He didn't take their suspicions of Isaac Harewood's involvement in murder seriously.

Summer rose from her chair. "Thanks for the soup, Mom."

She showered, dressed, and grabbed her truck keys. Her footsteps pounded down the stairs.

"Where on earth do you think you're going?" her mother asked. "You're supposed to rest today. Doctor's orders."

Summer ran out the front door, shutting out her mother's pleas.

3

JULIA LAMBERT SET DOWN A PIECE OF ISAAC'S MAIL, half of the day's incoming letters yet unopened. The third floor receptionist informed her that Helen Iverson, a longtime member of Julia's bridge club, was here to see her. Since that had never happened before, Julia knew something was up. She told the receptionist to send Helen on back.

"Why Helen, what brings you here?" Julia noted her friend wore a strand of fat faux pearls, so she'd come straight from work.

Helen leaned over Julia's desk until Julia could smell her chewing gum. Juicy Fruit. Helen was always chewing gum to disguise her cigarette breath.

Helen's fingers massaged the tooled leather inlay on Julia's desk as if she were reading braille. "Say, your desk is really something."

"It's an antique I found in that little town outside Tallahassee. Havana, have you been there lately? Those shops come up with some great pieces."

Helen hadn't been there, so she got to the point of her visit. "Honey, the strangest thing just happened. The bank was already closed, but I was staying late helping Mr. Nettles with some extra paperwork."

Everyone knew what kind of extra work Helen performed for Mr. Nettles, and it didn't involve paper. "Yes?" Julia prompted her.

"Well, I'm not supposed to say anything, but we've been friends for so many years and you're going to find out soon enough anyway."

Julia gripped the pleats of her navy skirt and waited.

"Subpoenas came in for yours and Mr. Harewood's personal bank records. I know the company had some trouble because of the mischief Mr. Morrell got up to, and I'm sure they are just digging around because of that. But I said to myself, I'd want to know if someone was prying into my bank accounts. Julia will want to know too."

Smoothing out her skirt, Julia grabbed the first envelope she could lay her hands on and stood. Her laugh trilled through her office. "I'm sure it's a silly precaution to be sure the rest of the company was not part of that nasty business Niles got involved in. You are a dear friend to have come by with the advisory, bless your heart."

She walked around the desk, waving the envelope in the air. "I have to take this to one of our accountants, so I'll walk you out. It was so kind of you to come by."

Helen, every word a fruit-flavored puff, prodded Julia during the elevator ride and all the way to the HEC main lobby. Did Julia think the company was involved in money-laundering? Because once the police had issued a subpoena for bank records because they suspected that Green Gage restaurant of money laundering and it came out in the newspaper later that the owner was indeed guilty. Helen knew Julia was innocent, but what about Isaac?

The woman was so desperate for insider gossip to take back to the bridge club, Julia practically had to push her out the front door.

Julia had work to do. Months ago she had feared this day might come. She hoped Isaac would marry her and flee. If not, she could only think of less desirable alternatives.

4

"**Mrs. Lambert is busy and can't see you right now.**" The third floor receptionist tilted her head as if to ask why anyone would show up at HEC without an appointment.

Summer tilted her head to the same plane. "Well, you can announce me or not. Up to you."

The receptionist hopped to her feet. "She left clear instructions. No visitors for the rest of the day."

Summer jogged down the marble corridor, the receptionist quite a ways behind her, stumbling in pointy-toed stilettos. The management offices of HEC had a pleasant chemical smell today as if a cleaning crew had finished their work only moments before. As Summer arrived, Julia Lambert was jamming items into an oversized purse. It struck Summer as odd immediately. It wasn't Julia's usual handbag, which was quaint and modest in size, much like one Summer's grandmother had carried—which was why Summer remembered it.

The receptionist caught up. "I'm sorry. I tried to stop her."

Mrs. Lambert smiled. "It's okay, honey. I know how persistent Miss Cassidy can be."

The receptionist's face puckered as if she were unsure she should leave, her eyes darting between Summer and her boss. Then apparently deciding a girl with a ponytail wasn't going to be a problem, she tottered away on slim legs that looked even longer in those silly heels.

Summer waited until the click of heels faded in the distance. "I've figured it out."

"Figured what out, dear?"

"You murdered Mr. Alvarez and paid Jake Fowler to try to finger me for the crime."

Julia laughed. "Your imagination is working overtime."

"I think you sent Fowler and his thugs to keep me out of the way during the hearing."

"Are you on one of those mind-altering drugs college kids use to get high? Pot or acid or whatever it is these days?"

"I've already shared my suspicions with the police and they agree."

Mrs. Lambert shook her head and laughed. "Surely not."

The intercom on Mrs. Lambert's desk buzzed. Summer recognized

Mr. Harewood's voice. "Julia, I need the Fairhope Energy files right away. I'm on the phone with a potential buyer."

"Yes, sir." Mrs. Lambert strode to the line of file cabinets along the back wall of her office, pulled open a door, and flipped through the folders. She brought one back to her desk. "Mr. Harewood is very busy, but I'm going to see if he has a moment to talk with you when he gets off the phone. He can assure you these assertions of yours are simply unsupportable." She slung her purse over her shoulder, nearly stooping under its weight. "There are some nice ladies' magazines in that rack over there if you want to read while you wait." She nodded to the wall behind Summer.

It seemed odd that Mrs. Lambert would take her purse into Mr. Harewood's office. As if she didn't trust Summer. Or as if there was a back way out of his office and she planned to skedaddle. But Summer had been inside and there was only one exit.

The light for Harewood's line on Mrs. Lambert's phone went out. Almost immediately raised voices came from his office.

5

THEOFANIS MOVED HIS FINGER SLOWLY DOWN JULIA LAMBERT'S April bank statement. "Bingo! She's dirty, Ash. Here's the first withdrawal to pay Fowler."

Ash leaned over Theofanis's shoulder, releasing a flush of cigarette smoke from his clothing that went straight up Theofanis's nostrils.

The guy just didn't realize how offensive that odor was to a non-smoker. Theofanis coughed and blew his nose, which, he realized, must be red as Rudolph's after so many encounters with a handkerchief over the past few days. His finger resumed moving through the transactions and he stopped three-quarters of the way down the second page. "Here's another match to the deposit in Fowler's account." Below it was the third match. He turned the page to show Ash.

Ash picked up the statement, studied it, dropped it on a stack of folders in Theofanis's active pile. "Let's nail the bitch."

Theofanis grimaced. "It would be a pleasure, but we're going to need more. It's all circumstantial."

Burns sauntered by the glass wall of the office and saluted him with the middle finger just for the hell of it. Theofanis gave him a double salute for good measure, prompting Ash to twist his neck to see who had deserved such effort.

Ash rolled his eyes and returned to the matter under discussion. "We can perp walk her in cuffs along those fancy-ass marble floors right past her co-workers. Bring her in for questioning. She'll break."

Theofanis wasn't so sure. Julia Lambert was a strange bird. "No cuffs. But let's escort her over here and let her spend a few hours in our sumptuous digs."

Ash snorted. "I'll make sure she knows the smell of this station, unpleasant as it can get, what with your quality clientele, is a hell of a lot better than prison."

"Not to mention the food."

"Or the coffee." Ash frowned. "But what about Harewood?"

Harewood. They had nothing, unless Julia rolled on him. Theofanis didn't think she would. "We may have to leave him for the Feds. I understand they are moving in on him for tax evasion."

6

THROUGH THE GLASS PANES OF HAREWOOD'S OFFICE, Summer watched Mrs. Lambert cross to the tea cart and carry a cup to Mr. Harewood. Summer wasn't about to sit out here while they drank frigging tea together and plotted God-knows-what-else. She jogged over, rapped on the door, and stuck her head inside Harewood's inner sanctum. "I'd like to speak with Mr. Harewood now."

Mrs. Lambert's eyes seemed fevered and overly bright as she grabbed her blasted teapot and bustled toward Summer, guiding her back outside his office. The large bag still dangled from her shoulder. "Mr. Harewood is engaged in an important phone call about a merger, but he will be with us in just a minute. I hope you'll join me for some tea."

The woman just didn't get it. This wasn't a social visit. Summer resumed her seat. "No, thank you."

Mrs. Lambert poured two cups anyway and set one in front of Summer. "Please, I insist. Tea makes everything better."

Something was wrong. Summer could feel it in her gut. "What if we take our tea in and share it with Mr. Harewood? I'm eager to hear him defend you."

"As I said, he's on the phone."

Summer pointedly looked at the phone on Mrs. Lambert's desk. No lights indicated a line in use. "No, he isn't."

The secretary blinked, then shook her head as if annoyed. "He answered a call on his mobile just before you knocked so rudely."

Summer guessed it could be true.

Julia's smile seemed sad and tired. "I know quite a bit about you, Miss Cassidy. It's a shame you've never had the opportunity to share a productive relationship with a man of Mr. Harewood's quality."

"Did you share in the murder of Mr. Alvarez?"

Julia sipped her tea, her nose wrinkling "You look so wholesome, but you are really quite obnoxious." She stood. "Excuse me just a moment. Mr. Harewood just signalled that he needs me in his office."

Mrs. Lambert marched the dozen steps to the office again, her gait awkward because of the weight of the bag.

What all did Mrs. Lambert have stuffed in that bag? Summer's instincts told her again something was wrong. Should she call Theofanis? No. He'd be pissed that she was here.

But the last time her gut said to call him, his arrival had saved lives. Despite her misgivings, she texted him an SOS. If it turned out to be a false alarm, he'd be annoyed; but that was better than letting those two escape.

Summer rose and tread softly to Harewood's door for a closer look. Mrs. Lambert took hold of Mr. Harewood's executive chair and swiveled it to face the wall of windows that overlooked the fountain and front entrance. Summer could see one of his arms dangling over the side, so she knew he was in it. How ridiculous. He could have swiveled his own chair if he wanted to look out.

Mrs. Lambert set her bag down on the tigerwood desk. She was taking something out. Something small. The glare on the glass prevented Summer from seeing what it was. She cupped a hand above her eyes to reduce the reflections and peered closer.

For a brief moment, Mrs. Lambert's eyes darted toward the glass door and locked with Summer's. Mrs. Lambert returned her attention to the object in her hand, flicking her finger against it. A hypodermic! Summer flung open the door and raced toward Mrs. Lambert. Harewood's shiny head was slumped to the left. Was he asleep? Drugged?

Heavy footsteps were pounding down the marble corridor. The receptionist's voice squealed in their wake. "You can't barge in on Mrs. Lambert. Someone is with her."

Just as Summer prepared to launch herself at Mrs. Lambert's arm, her sneaker caught on the aubusson rug, turning the edge up. She stumbled on her next step. One small misstep, just enough time for Julia Lambert to plunge the needle into Isaac Harewood's neck.

With outstretched arms and all her strength, Summer thrust against Mrs. Lambert's shoulders. She staggered backwards two steps, and the needle remained dangling from Harewood's neck. Summer withdrew it and held it in the air. But she had no idea what drug was administered or what she should do next.

To her horror, the muscles in Harewood's face began to twitch.

Mrs. Lambert seemed oblivious. Her eyes were closed, and she folded her hands in front of her chest as if in prayer. When she opened her eyes, her expression grew beatific. "You're too late. Isaac is safe from your persecution now. He's on his way to the angels."

Summer turned toward the footsteps, and there stood Theofanis and Ash. Finally.

"What's going on?" Theofanis said.

Mrs. Lambert trilled out, "Oh, thank goodness you're here. That girl just attacked Mr. Harewood. I tried to stop her. I don't know why she hates him, but you've seen how she has tried to destroy him. Poor Mr. Harewood!"

Stunned, Summer stared at the needle in her hand. To someone coming to the scene late, it would look as if Mrs. Lambert were telling the truth.

From the entrance of Harewood's office, the third floor receptionist shrieked and covered her mouth with both hands. Down the long corridor, office doors flew open and other employees tentatively emerged to find the source of the commotion.

Theofanis slipped handcuffs from the back of his belt. Every step he took toward them seemed to take forever, seemed to punch another breath right out of Summer.

But then he bypassed her and locked the cuffs on Mrs. Lambert. A deep breath filled Summer's lungs and she could think clearly again.

Ash pulled Isaac Harewood onto the floor and started CPR.

Theofanis took out his mobile and called for paramedics. When he finished, he addressed Summer. "If I wasn't sort of busy right now, I'd cuff you too. I told you to stay out of this."

Summer shrugged. "My mother always said I was hard-headed. Besides, I tried to tell you these people were bad news and you wouldn't listen to me."

His look scalded her. "We were already on the way here to arrest Mrs. Lambert when you texted. How do you think we got here so fast?"

"Ash," he said, "you can stop. CPR won't help." He turned toward Mrs. Lambert. "You used the rest of the succinylcholine Fowler stole, right Mrs. Lambert?"

Summer knew succinylcholine was a powerful muscle relaxant. "She must have had it in that handbag," she said, motioning toward Harewood's desk. "If there's any left, you'll find it there."

"Gee, thanks for your help, Miss Cassidy," Theofanis said. "We never would have thought of looking there."

Okay, she was shutting up. He was more pissed than she'd expected.

"Why?" she asked Mrs. Lambert.

"It is sad that you, of all people, have to ask that. Isaac is such an exceptional man. He gave so much to you and so many others. I could never allow you to send him to prison. He simply wouldn't survive the deprivations." She shuddered. "Can you imagine a man like that being strip-searched and treated like a common criminal? He would be absolutely devastated without his art collection. And he's accustomed to a personal chef and hundred fifty dollar haircuts."

Haircut? He didn't even have hair. Summer supposed Mrs. Lambert meant the trace of beard that circled Harewood's jaw. It would be a hoot if that money couldn't have gone toward medical research, if millions of people weren't going hungry, if millions more weren't dying because they lacked access to clean water.

Julia was smiling again. These people really were crazy.

Nineteen

Tuesday

I

"You two hungry?" Jordan Cassidy called out.

Summer eased downstairs, taking the steps more slowly than usual, aware of Ty following a few steps behind. Her mother had insisted on his recuperating in her guest bedroom.

His presence here in this house felt awkward to Summer, as if he'd crossed into a more personal sphere than her apartment. What would he make of the Chrissie shrine in the living room? She hoped her mother had relocated some of the crates of file folders for her foundation to make room for a guest.

At the bottom of the stairs, she wished him a good morning, glancing only briefly his way before moving to the kitchen.

As they entered, Jordan held out a platter of plate-size blueberry pancakes. Good heavens—her mother hadn't made pancakes since— she hadn't made pancakes AC. When the twins were young, she had made them every weekend. The lives of the Cassidys were divided into Before Chrissie and After Chrissie. BC and AC.

Beside the platter, her mother set a pitcher of maple syrup and a bowl of sliced strawberries, lightly sugared.

"Looks fabulous! What are the rest of you going to eat?" Summer said.

Jordan laughed and fixed Ty a cup of coffee, which he accepted with his good arm, the one unrestricted by a sling.

"Thanks, Mrs. Cassidy. I'm not used to having people wait on me." Ty dropped into Chrissie's chair at the kitchen table.

Ty didn't know, couldn't know: for the first time in thirteen years, someone was sitting in Chrissie's chair. Summer could hardly breathe, her eyes drawn to her mother. Was her mother regretting inviting Ty to stay in this house now?

For a full four seconds, Jordan froze in place, her journey to her place at the head of the table halted as she stared at Ty's back, her eyes wide as a small animal's in danger of losing everything that matters. Her mother's favorite cup with a "Bike Safely" logo tilted. Coffee sloshed onto her bare foot, pulling her eyes downward. She swallowed visibly, turned, and fetched a paper towel to wipe up the spill.

By the time she finished and joined them at the table, the tension had evaporated and Summer could breathe freely again.

"How's the arm today?" she asked Ty.

"Just a scratch."

Yeah, right. "Show off."

He raised his coffee to his lips awkwardly, unused to using his left as the dominant hand. "You never did tell me what you threw at Fowler."

"Biosparite. That's a well-cemented coquina to those who can't tell one rock from another. Early settlers used it for walls of the Castillo de San Marcos and other forts because coquina is soft and cannon balls sink into, rather than shatter or puncture the walls. So I chose it over the other rocks because it wouldn't shatter when it connected with Fowler's face. I knew it would sink into his skin and cut the heck out of him."

"Now who's showing off?" He hesitated. "Did you really reason all that out before you threw it?"

She laughed. "Had you going, didn't I? No, I grabbed the closest thing I could find to whack him with."

Jordan pulled Ty's plate toward her and began cutting up his pancakes into bite-sized pieces. "Shame on you for teasing an injured man, Summer."

While they ate, a rubbery silence grew at the table. To cover the awkwardness, Summer studied a few photographs her mother had taken at the hearing and printed out. One of Dayita and Summer with the senator after the presentation. One of Dayita, Mrs. Patel, and Ty. In the last photo, Summer and Ty were side by side. She was struck by the similarity of their features, especially the eyes. Studies of couples showed people were attracted to those with similar features. Did her eyes really look that tortured? She hid the photo under the others.

"Theofanis called while you two were sleeping." Jordan Cassidy filled them in on the police department's latest developments.

Julia Lambert confessed to putting the sedative nitrazepam in Isaac Harewood's tea. Once he was drowsy, she injected him with the succinylcholine. The morning newspaper devoted the front page to coverage of the murder. It quoted her as saying, "I couldn't bear to see him suffer in any way. Prison would have destroyed him."

She also confessed to shooting Paulo Alvarez and paying Fowler to clean up afterward.

Summer's left hand was in her lap, as table etiquette required. Her mother reached under the table and clasped it. "The police found two additional cups of tea on Mrs. Lambert's desk. One had the same sedative in it that she gave to her boss. Summer, Theofanis thinks that cup was meant for you. Is he right?"

Summer stopped eating, her fork halfway to her mouth. No wonder Mrs. Lambert had been so insistent that Summer drink that tea. Once Summer was drugged, Mrs. Lambert would have killed her too.

Increasing pressure from her mother's fingers prompted Summer to ease her concern. "I was there to accuse her of murder and kidnapping, Mom. I wasn't about to drink her tea."

The grow-house scheme headlined the Florida News section of the paper. Revelations included Kendricks taking bribes to look the other way, the involvement of the governor's son in setting up the operation—and Morrell's campaign contributions to the governor. The article implied the money was meant to ease the way for marijuana legalization. The story even had a sidebar with the fancy names of various strains of marijuana and their purported properties.

"I'm so glad your work with Harewood is over," her mother said.

Summer agreed. "It's a relief to have my thesis defense and Harewood's wells behind me. I never thought my work would be so controversial."

Ty frowned. "Any job in your field is likely to lead to confrontations. Big Money and Big Business against the Big Planet."

She had just stuffed another forkful of pancake into her mouth, and started talking while trying to swallow and chew. "It doesn't have to be that way. Business and science can be partners and bring about responsible changes."

Summer's mother chimed in. "The secret is to find balance between the need for jobs and the regulations necessary to keep everybody safe."

Summer nodded, surprised to learn she and her mother agreed.

Ty got up and clumsily poured himself another cup of coffee. Instead of returning to the table, he leaned his back against the countertop. "Except greed always gets in the way."

Summer sighed. Surely greed didn't always win out. Everyone wanted to see things in black and white these days. No matter what Ty argued to the contrary, he drove a gas-hog van. She drove a gas-hog truck. Energy consumption was a given in their lives. Somehow, the country needed to find a middle ground. Or better energy sources.

"We won this one," he said, "but water is being screwed up all over the country. Folks in Pennsylvania and West Virginia can set their tap water on fire because of hydraulic fracking. Look, why don't you come to work for Water Warriors. I can't pay much—"

Much? He and his sister were living in a van!

"—but you'd be doing what you say you want to do. Making the world a better place. You don't need a doctorate to do that. There are so many problems we could work on together. Fertilizer run-off has created dead zones in the ocean. Millions of people don't have access to fresh water."

She pushed away from the table. "I know. The world's not a perfect place." If it were, her mother would still have two daughters, both intact.

Ty could forget it. She had no intentions of setting up housekeeping in her car. "I can't go to work with you. I'm going back to school in the fall."

Jordan Cassidy gathered the plates and began to rinse them in the sink. "Ever since she was a little girl, Summer has been determined to get her doctorate. I still have a badge she made for herself when she was about ten. It says 'Dr. Cassidy' on it."

Summer remembered making it. She had no idea her mother had saved it. Her mother had all kinds of BC mementoes displayed on what Summer had long thought of as the Chrissie shrine in the living room. What a surprise that she'd squirreled away AC stuff too! Probably in the bottom of a closet, but Summer's mood lightened, because her mother had saved bits of her life. And this morning she'd made pancakes and they'd actually agreed on something important.

Summer stowed the leftover strawberries in the refrigerator. "Thanks for the pancakes, Mom." Her mother stood only a yard away as she loaded the dishwasher, but the space between them seemed much greater.

Summer took two steps and tentatively slipped her arms around her mother's waist.

Her mother turned and swept her into a hug. "Oh, honey, thank God you're all right. When I think of all you've been through the past few weeks . . . I just cringe."

Summer stepped back.

Her mother's eyes watered and her voice trembled. "You're so much stronger than I thought. I guess you're ready to go off to school on your own, but I hate that you'll be so far away."

One phase of her life was ending. Ahead of her lay an unknown future. Summer hoped Ty would be a part of it.

Sun and fresh air drifting in from the open living room window beckoned. The house had become too small to hold her expanding spirit within its walls. She had faced down the worst that Harewood, Lambert, Hu and Fowler could throw at her—and she'd survived.

She turned to Ty. "Let's go somewhere. To celebrate."

"You sure you're up to it?" her mother asked. "I mean you're both injured."

Summer opened her arms as wide as they would reach and fought back a grimace. "I'm done with my thesis. Graduating in a few weeks. Going to Penn State. Life is great. Canoe trip—right now."

"No way," her mother said. "You are not leaving land or going on any dangerous adventures."

Summer guessed the temporarily one-armed Ty wasn't up for paddling anyway. "Okay, we'll go for a drive. O'Leno State Park. We can stroll along the river."

She and Ty went upstairs to get ready and gather gear. After she changed clothes, she started to enter the bathroom but saw that Ty was already there, attempting to shave with the arm not confined to a sling. She pictured herself crossing the floor and wrapping her arms around his waist and pressing her cheek against the hollow between his shoulder blades. Not a good idea. Before she could move away, he dropped the razor into the sink. He slid a soapy hand along her jaw line toward her ear and drew her into a kiss as gentle and light as the foam remaining on his chin. His hand, clasped to the side of her face, kept her from melting to the floor.

When he pulled back, he touched his nose to hers and closed his eyes. Her arms slid like water, shapeless, formless, to her sides.

2

THEY RAMBLED ALONG THE LEAF-LITTERED TRAIL and crossed the swinging bridge built by the Civilian Conservation Corps back in the 1930s. When Ty touched her shoulder, it was as natural as the dappled sun on her face. Most of the way along the river they walked together in a companionable silence different than that awkwardness over breakfast, and Summer, being a scientist, had to analyze why. The hush that fell over them now, she decided, grew out of the peaceful surroundings. Ty loved being outdoors, as she did.

Her bare arm brushed against his. A miserable sweetness traveled the length of her body. She took one step away, scrutinizing him, but his eyes were unfathomable.

The science of relations between the sexes aligned against them. The smells, the touches, the warmth passed between hands and bodies sustained attraction. The initial period of intense sexual heat lasted about a year and a half, at best. Long enough for the female to become pregnant and long enough to keep the male around until his offspring was born. Then the instinct to defend his helpless offspring and preserve his genes encouraged him to stick around. That was biology.

Her doctoral studies would consume the next two years of her life, too great a span for most long-distance romances. She couldn't help but think of Dayita, how great a distance across time and continents her relationship with Nakeesh had extended. You couldn't call it a romance, but it was still love of a sort Summer couldn't pretend to fully understand.

They seemed to fit together, she and Ty, his cracked pieces and hers. Two busted-up, screwed-up people who might help make each other whole. It wasn't science, but it might be true.

She canted her neck to watch two squirrels playing catch-me-if-you-can; and resumed strolling along the trail beside him. "What will you do next?" she asked.

"Grace and I will move back to West Virginia now. And I will continue to go after other men like Harewood, men who put profit ahead of people. My mother would be alive today if it weren't for Isaac Harewood. My sister would be . . . different. So I have to go after these guys."

"For how long?"

His voice was grim. "As long as it takes. Whatever it takes. Until they're gone."

Chills ran up her spine. His obsession with Water Warriors mirrored her mother's bike safety campaign. She understood their grief, but their lives teetered on the edge of a consuming darkness.

Summer would like to help put men like Isaac Harewood out of business—as long as it didn't interfere with her studies. But she wanted to use science to do it. She didn't share Ty's singular focus.

"I told Dr. Dunham I'd like to research the effects of hydrofracking on local water supplies in the Marcellus shale field for my doctorate—what do you think?"

"I think you should do what you want," Ty said. "Pursue your passion."

Passion. Her lips remembered the tingling sensation of Ty's kiss. Her body was sending all sorts of chemical signals his way.

Marcellus fracking research would take her into Ty's territory in West Virginia and Pennsylvania. So would attending Penn State. That, of course, played no part in her decision. Because she was a sensible woman. That's how she'd avoided romantic entanglements thus far.

Yet these past few weeks forced her to acknowledge her own life leaned too hard into books and too little into understanding people.

Dayita was right: there were dangerous folks in this world—in bars and in the business world. And much as she hated to admit it, somewhere inside, a raw spot still festered from Jake Fowler's dismissing her as a slut. The word coming from him shouldn't matter, but inexplicably it stung.

As they walked, Summer tired more quickly than she expected.

No wonder, considering her accumulated injuries—Ty slamming her onto the concrete picnic table and Jeglinski knocking her out when he stole her computer. Not to mention Fowler ramming her with his sedan and half dragging her across the HEC compound to the shed. And a few days later he had hurled her across her bedroom, her head slamming into the closet door. The past few weeks had been tough on her noggin. Her mother always accused her of being hard-headed. A trait that had come in handy.

Ty suggested resting on a split log that overlooked the river. They sat so close their thighs touched. Summer drew in the fragrance of pine- and oak leaf-scented air. His body was processing the same array of sensory input she was: the spectrum of electromagnetic waves of light filtering through the leaves, the vibrations of the water coursing over chunks of limestone and their shoes crunching leaves beneath their feet. Memories of other walks in the woods and of other people who shared those walks were sparking a dopamine surge in his mesolimbic pathway.

He shared this experience with her, yet his was unique and different. Subjective. No one had yet explained this mystery of human consciousness. Or why she was responding strongly to his chemical signature while other women might not. As Winston Churchill once said (about something else) it was "a riddle wrapped in a mystery inside an enigma."

For once, the science behind the mystery didn't seem all that important. She had never known the desire to merge every cell of her body and mind with anyone before. Was he feeling it too?

She nudged his thigh with her knee. "We have an unfinished trip on the Santa Fe," she said.

His eyes—maybe they smiled a little. "Guess we do."

"We have to get your arm back in shape, because we have to kayak a good ways to meet Naked Ed."

"Naked Ed?" He grinned—first real smile she'd seen out of him—and it surprised her to learn it was lopsided.

"You're going to love the wild man of Lily Springs. He lives in a thatched hut, has a beer named after him, and has all these sayings posted on signs by the river."

"You're making this up."

"No, for real. His signs are philosophical like 'I may not see tomorrow so I hope I'm happy today.'" Suddenly she remembered another of Naked Ed's sayings: *Love is a four letter word we don't say often enough.*

Then Ty's lips touched the gash on her forehead, her cheeks, the bridge of her nose, her neck, her lips, and oh yes—he was experiencing the desire to merge.

She floundered and the most amazing thing happened. The corners of her lips pulsed with a sensation that gradually spread along her jawline and encompassed the network of nerves surrounding her ears, delivering incredible pleasure. It felt curiously like an orgasm branching out from the kiss, like wings unfolding and taking flight from a place so deep inside it had no name. For at least a full second, she explored this new phenomenon, before detaching her brain and surrendering completely to the moment.

CONGRATULATIONS! YOU'VE FINISHED THE FIRST BOOK IN THE SUMMER CASSIDY SERIES.

PLEASE LEAVE A REVIEW FOR *WET WORK* ON AMAZON.COM OR ON GOODREADS.COM. AND BE SURE TO CHECK OUT THE SECOND IN THE SERIES, *FRACCIDENTAL DEATH*, WHICH WILL BE PUBLISHED IN THE FALL OF 2014.

Excerpt from the next Summer Cassidy Novel

FRACCIDENTAL DEATH

By Donna Meredith

ONE

Monday

I

CORKY ROGERS ISSUED A TWO-FINGERED MOCK SALUTE to Fairhope Energy site manager, Sean Walsh, who was yakking on his cell phone at the far end of the bulldozed job site. Walsh raised his chin in acknowledgment.

Behind Walsh, naked trees peppered the distant hills, their dark trunks rising like a farm of missiles aimed at the sky. So far, those hills had escaped clear-cutting in the mad rush to bring the vast deposits of oil and gas in the Marcellus Shale Field to market.

Corky secured the upper end of a long hose to his tanker truck, a routine task requiring little concentration, so his thoughts drifted toward Sloane. Yesterday the wedding gown had arrived via UPS. One corner of his mouth twisted up in amusement as he remembered Sloane sashaying around the living room, red sequins scattering flecks of light with every wiggle. He warned her that the local church-going women would gasp over those sequins clinging to her bouncy curves. She'd provide gossip fodder for weeks in that gown. Sloane shimmied for him, laughter bubbling from deep in her chest: "Honeypot, I aim to have me a Christmas wedding this town will never forget."

How a pudgy blue collar nobody had snagged Sloane still mystified him, but he thanked God every day for this unexpected gift. It had taken forty-two years to find her, but the discovery, at last, of the perfect woman for him made up for two miserable first marriages.

Corky's tanker held a full load of used fracking fluid—what they called flowback. It was destined for the holding pond ten yards from where he stood. The length of an Olympic-sized pool, the pond was already half full of gray, sludgy water.

A bag of fast food trash blew across the expanse of dirt and caught against the tires of one of the dozen trucks lined up on the site. Their red cabs were the only color in an otherwise drab landscape. Corky shivered and turned up the collar of his jacket. Following protocol, he tested the connection to his truck again. The hose, gray as an elephant's trunk and twice as fat, snaked its way down the slope to the plastic-lined pond. It dangled a few inches above the water's surface.

He threw the switch to blow off the tanker's load under full pressure. He watched until he saw fluid spilling into the pond, then stepped a few feet away to spit a wad of chew onto the dirt. He was wondering what time Sloane would get off work that night when an unexpected hiss made the hairs on his neck salute. He pivoted on one heel toward the tanker and everything went to hell fast.

The four-inch fitting which coupled the hose to his tanker's pipe split in half. The resulting water cannon hit him full force in the chest and slammed him to the ground. The blast knocked his hard hat off and propelled it more than forty feet across frozen ground. It came to rest against the site manager's feet.

On Corky's first attempt to stand, his feet skidded out from under him. He rolled sideways a couple of times, shielding his face as best he could, and finally bulled his way to his feet. On some level, he was aware that Sean Walsh had dropped his cell, catapulted over his pickup's hood, and sprinted to Corky's tanker. Walsh threw the switch to change the pump from push mode to off. He disappeared from Corky's view. A minute later, he reappeared, dragging a freshwater hose.

"Good God, Corky, you all right?" Walsh asked, running toward him. Bent over at the waist, Corky could only respond with wheezes and hacks, but he took stock of his condition. Murky water drenched his leather boots. The toxic brew was soaking through his jacket and jeans, icing his skin.

What exactly was in frack fluid? Only the boss and top engineers knew the proprietary formula, but Corky had heard the rumors. Toluene, benzene, sodium chloride, hydrochloric acid—and hundreds of other chemicals that dissolved natural gas out of shale. The company claimed the fluid was ninety-seven percent water and sand, and the rest nothing but ordinary ingredients you'd find in bottles under your kitchen sink. But if they could release the natural gas from rock, what would they do to him?

Walsh sprayed him off with a powerful flush of clean water.

"Gul-dern-it-all, Walsh, you're fu-freezing my nuts off! Gotta buh-be twen-twenty frigging degrees out here." His teeth chattered uncontrollably.

"Strip," Walsh said.

Cork peeled his clothes off and Walsh turned the hose on him again, until Corky decided his blood was icing. He dodged the spray. "Enough, you lou-lousy, ro-rotten sumbitch, enough!"

"You all right?" Walsh asked again.

"O-k-kay." He hoped he was.

"Let's get you dressed."

Corky followed Walsh into an equipment shed. The odor of diesel trapped inside nauseated Corky. He wheezed, unable to draw in enough air.

Walsh threw him a rough towel. Corky buffed his cold-reddened skin, but the physical exertion of even this simple act taxed his lungs.

Walsh rummaged through a box in the back of the shed, coming up with a flannel shirt and jeans. "Try these on."

Corky's shaky fingers managed to fasten enough of the buttons to keep the shirt on. It fit fine, though mildew clung to the fabric and the smell turned his stomach inside out. He pulled on the jeans. When he let go of the waistband, they slid off his butt.

Walsh cut off a piece of string trimmer line, looped it through the back belt loops. "For God's sake, hold still so I can knot this string. Can't have you mooning the nurses. They get one look at your ugly crack, they're liable to faint."

Finally, Walsh stared at Corky's feet, purpled from the cold. He rooted through the box again and offered baseball socks. Navy stripes circled the tops. "There's no spare boots. You're gonna have to put yours back on."

Corky couldn't feel his toes as he shoved his feet into his water-logged boots. His fingers had grown stiff as icicles, unable to manipulate the laces. Walsh bent down and tied them. As a final touch, the site manager found a quilted moss-colored mat, the kind a mechanic might lay on the ground for protection. Walsh tucked it around Corky's shoulders.

"Now what the hell happened out there?" Walsh asked.

Anger had replaced the manager's initial concern, and Corky thought he understood why. "Fi-fit-ting broke," he said between shivers. "S-sorry. I know—headaches—EPA." The company despised the Environmental Protection Agency for its regulations, rules, and paperwork. An accident meant filing a report. It meant regulators visiting the site, asking questions, reviewing safety procedures, pointing fingers.

The room swirled. If Corky took one more diesel-tinged breath, he was going to throw up. He staggered past the open door and lowered his head between his knees. The fresh air arrived too late. His stomach emptied its contents in a series of violent thrusts, followed by dry heaves.

Walsh had followed him outside, hovering at a discreet distance. Walsh's lips pressed together. "I'll move your tanker out of the way. Guess you'd better head over to the hospital and get yourself checked."

Corky remained in a squat, sucking in deep breaths, clutching the mat tightly against his shoulders. Minutes passed before he felt steady enough to stand. "Thanks for the clothes, Sean."

"You need me to find someone to drive you over?"

Corky shook his head.

Walsh pulled out his wallet and stuffed a handful of hundreds into Corky's shirt pocket. "No worker's comp. We'll pay for it. Whatever you need."

Corky trudged over to his pickup and started the engine. There was a knock on the window, and he rolled it down a few inches.

Walsh pushed a blank check through the opening. "Use this if you have to. Let me know how much. Don't tell them what happened, okay? No accident report."

Ten miles down the highway, Corky stopped at a red light close to the hospital and realized he should call Sloane. He relayed what had happened.

"Goddamn it all to hell, Corky, I told you Fairhope Energy was a rotten company to work for. Didn't I tell you that?"

She had, and he hadn't listened—anymore than she had when he'd hinted she shouldn't take the Lord's name in vain.

"My uncle told you they don't maintain their equipment. Bunch of damn cheapskates. They—" She broke off when his hacking grew intense enough to overtake her rant.

"I'll meet you at the hospital," she said.

"No need."

"I'm coming and that's that. And you're quitting that damn job. Today."

And that was that. Once Sloane Dumont made up her mind, no one could change it. When he started coughing again, he decided he wasn't even going to try.

2

HARRISON COUNTY COMMISSIONER P. J. WINE DIDN'T LOOK A THING LIKE SUMMER CASSIDY HAD EXPECTED after speaking with him on the phone. In a homey, pleasant baritone, he had offered to take her on a tour of the area. She had imagined a younger man, sturdy and slim, someone fond of flannel shirts and fishing. But as she shook the commissioner's hand in the library lobby, he reminded her of a turnip. Squat and thick in the middle, toothpick legs, and a frothy patch of long, thinning white hair on top. He wore khakis pulled high over his belly, with a cream polo shirt that kept inching its way upward despite his snug belt. A black wool dress coat was folded over his left arm.

The county library itself was also different from what she'd expected. Expansive windows provided plenty of natural light inside the modern brick structure. After meeting a couple of library staff members and browsing along the stacks, Summer followed the commissioner upstairs to view the computer stations. The half dozen users possessed the glazed-over eyes and slack mouth typical of deep immersion in the online world.

P. J. spoke in undertones appropriate for a library. He inclined his head toward a young man in a WVU baseball cap. "That fellow over there is learning landman technology." P. J. flicked a hand toward a plumpish woman of middle age. "So's that lady. Beginning landmen earn $70,000. With experience they will pull down $200,000 a year."

Summer knew landmen were basically door-to-door salesmen, convincing land owners to sign over their mineral rights, so despite the good money, the job didn't sound too inviting.

Talking incessantly, P. J. led the way down the staircase, eyes alternating between Summer's face and his foothold on the next step. His voice and the soles of his city-slicker shoes echoed as sound bounced off the stone floor toward the high ceiling. "I steer a lot of our unemployed citizens toward this online course. The instructors are experienced landmen, attorneys, and oil and gas professionals. They teach basic title research and pretty much everything you need to know about oil, gas, and wind leases."

Finally he paused for breath, allowing her space to ask a question. "How long does the training last?"

"Two weeks."

Summer forced herself not to sputter. The average hydrogeologist only made $49- 80,000, maybe $100,000 with an advanced degree and experience. Here she was knocking herself out to go after a doctorate in hydrogeology and environmental studies—and in a measly two weeks she could become a landman and make more money. Not that she wanted to. But still. She tuned back in to the commissioner, who was slipping on his overcoat while he walked.

"The demand for a whole range of jobs has skyrocketed in conjunction with the boom in oil and gas exploration in the Marcellus shale formation. Makes me wish I were a young man starting out again. I believe I'd choose oil and gas over real estate."

P. J. held the door to the street open and Summer slipped past his sizeable belly. She deliberately expelled a lungful of air and suppressed a laugh, certain her companion wouldn't find visible breath quite as fascinating as a girl who had lived the entire twenty-two years of her life in Florida. After picking up moisture from the lungs, the exhaled air was chilled beyond its dewpoint—and voila—condensation. You had visible breath. How cool was that?

For more of Summer Cassidy's adventures, check out *Fraccidental Death* in the fall of 2014.

ACKNOWLEDGEMENTS

BEFORE BEGINNING THIS SERIES, I knew South Florida had frequent episodes of water rationing. Even in North Florida where rain is plentiful we experienced rationing of lawn watering a few times in summer. But I didn't understand the scope of water issues facing the world today. Two nonfiction books inspired me to begin this novel, which I hope will increase awareness of water issues with a different audience. *Mirage: Florida and the Vanishing Water of the Eastern U.S.*, by Cynthia Barnett, showed me how scarce potable water is becoming. Another book that helped me understand the issues was Michael Grunwald's *The Swamp*. Since those first two books, many others deepened my concern, including Barnett's *Blue Revolution: Unmaking America's Water Crisis;* and W*ater Wars: Privatization, Pollution, Profit* by Vandana Shiva. I am also indebted to countless websites, particularly those of the U.S. and Florida Geological Surveys for their information on ASR wells.

Joe Haberfeld, Professional Geologist with the Florida Department of Environmental Protection; and Van Hoofnagle, Environmental Administrator with the Florida Department of Environmental Protection; were invaluable resources on ASR wells. Mr. Haberfeld kindly read an early draft of the novel and suggested changes that strengthened the information on ASR wells. Any errors regarding the wells are entirely my own misinterpretations of the information he provided.

Former FDLE agent and sheriff's deputy Tom Berlinger read an early draft and assured me the law enforcement portrayals were realistic, or as much as possible within the constraints imposed by a novel. Any inaccuracies are all all my own.

As always, I am indebted to my critique group members for their thoughtful reading and feedback: Marina Brown, Rhett DeVane, Jane Driber, Peggy Kassees, Hannah Mahler, Claire Matturro, and Susan Womble. Readers of my later drafts helped me find and fix what I hope were the last glitches: Doug Alderson, Linda Cole, Barbara Donaldson, and Jeanne and Bill Ryder. Thanks to all of you for making this a better book.

And I am grateful to my editor Paula Kiger, who wields her Big Green Pen and locates errors everyone else misses; and to the Tallahassee Writers Association for their continuing efforts to bring quality programs for writers to the Big Bend area.

I also owe a debt of gratitude to the anonymous judges of the Royal Palm Literary Contest sponsored by the Florida Writers Association, who awarded the manuscript a second place for unpublished thriller/suspense novels. Their feedback proved immensely helpful in final revisions. The judges receive no payment for the gift of their time and expertise. Thank you.

LOCALES IN THE BOOK

Loblolly Lake is a fictional town in North Central Florida and the Florida Institute of Science and Technology is a fictional university. In no way is this novel intended to reflect poorly on any particular law enforcement agency or university. State parks and rivers mentioned in the novel do exist, but law enforcement agencies in the novel are fictional (with the exception of the Florida Department of Law Enforcement, FDLE) and would not have jurisdiction over them.

DISCUSSION GUIDE

1. Mirroring a trend among college women, Summer Cassidy feels casual "hook-ups" will help her avoid relationships that could derail her academic dreams. Her mentor, Claire Dunham, tells Summer that "Someone's career has to come first, and it's always his while yours collapses faster than a sinkhole." Are those fears justified? Can women have it all?

2. What are Summer's weaknesses and strengths? Has she grown by the end of the novel?

3. Summer has a complicated relationship with her mother. What do you think causes the rift?

4. How do Dayita, Mrs. Patel, and Ty enrich Summer's life?

5. Which characters hold power and how do they wield it?

6. A number of characters blame themselves for Christmas (Chrissie) Cassidy's death. How does guilt motivate their actions?

7. In what ways does Isaac Harewood represent both admirable and despicable qualities found in American corporate culture?

8. How do government regulations help ensure our quality of life? Can they be harmful as well?

9. Discuss the role lobbyist Bailey Douglass plays in the novel. How important are lobbyists in American governance today?

10. What ethical issues does the novel raise regarding university research? Do you accept "studies" you read about or hear about on the news as truth?

11. Where does your drinking water come from? Are you aware of any threats to it? How safe is it? Do you use bottled water, and if so, what are your reasons?

Donna Meredith

is the author of two award-winning novels, *The Glass Madonna* and *The Color of Lies* that are popular with book clubs, as well as the nonfiction book *Magic in the Mountains: Kelsey Murphy, Robert Bomkamp, and the West Virginia Cameo Glass Revolution.*

After a long career in public high schools in West Virginia and Georgia teaching English, Journalism, and TV Production, Donna became a freelance writer. Her stories have appeared in have appeared in *Tallahassee* magazine, *Goldenseal*, the *Southern Literary Review*, the *Tallahassee Democrat*, the *Seven Hills Review* and the *Midwest Review*.

She's worn many hats for the Tallahassee Writers Association, including president, vice president, conference chair, and editor of the *Seven Hills Review*, website and newsletter.

She earned a Bachelor's in Education with a double major in English and Journalism from Fairmont State College, a Master's in Journalism from West Virginia University, and an Education Specialist's degree in English from Nova University. She also studied creative writing at Florida State University. She resides in Tallahassee, Florida, with her husband John.

For more about Donna and her writing, visit www.donnameredith.com.

CPSIA information can be obtained
at www.ICGtesting.com
Printed in the USA
LVHW111738250919
632253LV00002B/154/P